THE LAND

OF THE

PUEBLOS

THE LAND OF THE PUEBLOS

Susan E. Wallace
1888

SOUTHWEST HERITAGE SERIES

SUNSTONE PRESS

SANTA FE

Library of Congress Cataloging-in-Publication Data:

Wallace, Susan E. (Susan Elston), 1830-1907.
    The land of the Pueblos / by Susan E. Wallace.
      p. cm. -- (Southwest heritage series)
    Originally published: New York : J.B. Alden,1888. With new introd.
    ISBN 0-86534-543-0 (softcover : alk. paper)
    1. New Mexico--Description and travel--Anecdotes. 2. Southwest, New--
Description and travel--Anecdotes. 3. Pueblo Indians--History--Anecdotes.
4. New Mexico--History--Anecdotes. 5. Southwest, New--History--Anecdotes.
I. Title.

F801.W18 2006
978.9004'974--dc22

                                        2006021554

Published in

WWW.SUNSTONEPRESS.COM
SUNSTONE PRESS / POST OFFICE BOX 2321 / SANTA FE, NM 87504-2321 /USA
(505) 988-4418 / ORDERS ONLY (800) 243-5644 / FAX (505) 988-1025

The Southwest Heritage Series
is dedicated to Jody Ellis and Marcia Muth Miller,
the founders of Sunstone Press, whose original purpose and
vision continues to inspire and motivate our publications.

CONTENTS

I

THE SOUTHWEST HERITAGE SERIES

The history of the United States is written in hundreds of regional histories and literary works. Those letters, essays, memoirs, biographies and even collections of fiction are often first-hand accounts by people who wanted to memorialize an event, a person or simply record for posterity the concerns and issues of the times. Many of these accounts have been lost, destroyed or overlooked. Some are in private or public collections but deemed to be in too fragile condition to permit handling by contemporary readers and researchers.

However, now with the application of twenty-first century technology, nineteenth and twentieth century material can be reprinted and made accessible to the general public. These early writings are the DNA of our history and culture and are essential to understanding the present in terms of the past.

The Southwest Heritage Series is a form of literary preservation. Heritage by definition implies legacy and these early works are our legacy from those who have gone before us. To properly present and preserve that legacy, no changes in style or contents have been made. The material reprinted stands on its own as it first appeared. The point of view is that of the author and the era in which he or she lived. We would not expect photographs of people from the past to be re-imaged with modern clothes, hair styles and backgrounds. We should not, therefore, expect their ideas and personal philosophies to reflect our modern concepts.

Remember, reading their words and sharing their thoughts is a passport back into understanding how the past was shaped and how it influenced today's world.

Our hope is that new access to these older books will provide readers with a challenging and exciting experience.

II

FOREWORD TO THIS EDITION

Susan Arnold Elston Wallace was born in Crawfordsville, Indiana, on December 25, 1830. Her parents, Isaac C. and Maria E. Aiken Elston, were wealthy and influential members of society. Susan was educated in Crawfordsville and Poughkeepsie, New York, and was by all accounts a very well-read woman for her time. Susan married Lew Wallace on May 6, 1852. Wallace served as governor of the New Mexico Territory, 1878–1881, and as U.S. Minister to Turkey, 1881–1885. His greatest achievements may have been his own literary pursuits. His novel, *Ben-Hur: A Tale of the Christ* (1880), written in Santa Fe while he was governor has never been out of print. They had one son, Henry Lane Wallace (b. February 17, 1853).

In her lifetime, Susan published six books, some of which, including *The Land of the Pueblos*, had illustrations by Lew Wallace. She also published extensively in the literary magazines and newspapers of the day. Her first publication was "The Patter of Little Feet," an unsigned poem which appeared in the *Cincinnati Daily Gazette* on April 17, 1858.

Susan died October 1, 1907, two years after her husband. They are buried together at Oak Hill Cemetery in Crawfordsville.

Her other five books are: *Along the Bosphorus and Other Sketches; The City of the King: What the Child Jesus Saw and Heard; Ginevra, or The Old Oak Chest, A Christmas Story; The Repose in Egypt: A Medley;* and *The Storied Sea.*

III

FACSIMILE OF 1888 EDITION

A PUEBLO GIRL SELLING CLAY IMAGES.
(From a sketch by Gen. Wallace.)

THE LAND OF THE

PUEBLOS.

BY

SUSAN E. WALLACE.

Author of " The Storied Sea," " Ginevra," etc.

WITH ILLUSTRATIONS.

NEW YORK:

JOHN B. ALDEN, PUBLISHER.

1888.

THE LAND OF THE PUEBLOS.

CONTENTS.

LIST OF ILLUSTRATIONS.

INTRODUCTION.

SOME years ago these writings appeared in the *Independent, Atlantic Monthly,* and *The Tribune.* My thanks are with the respective editors by whose courtesy they assume this altered shape. Several were published in a certain magazine which died young. I send cordial greeting to its chief, and shed a few drops of ink over the nameless one, loved of the gods. Fain would I believe no action of mine had power to hasten that early and untimely end. The hurrying march in which all must join, is so rapid, my first audience is quite out of hearing ; my first inklings have faded from the memory of readers except the one, beloved of my soul, who asks why the old Pueblo papers have not been reprinted. Ah, what exquisite flattery !

And just here I kiss the fair hands unseen which send such gracious messages. Dropping flowers in my way, pansies for thoughts, rosemary for remembrance, has made them the whiter and sweeter forevermore.

The Montezuma myth is so interwoven with the past and future of the Indians that every allusion to their history and religion must of necessity contain the revered name. The repetition in the compositions now collected did not appear so glaringly when they were detached. My first impulse was to omit such passages, but second thought sends out the letters as when first offered to the public, with all their imperfections (a good many), on their head.

It would be affectation to make secret what every writer understands : (and what reader have I who . is not a writer ?) the pleasure with which

5

I gather my scattered children under a permanent cover. Family resemblance is strong enough to identify them anywhere, but that is no reason why they should not appear in shape which the world will little heed nor long remember. They were written when the ancient Palace I have tried to describe, was the residence of the Governor of New Mexico ; and, in turning the leaves after seven years, I am touched by the same feeling which then moved me to pipe my little songs. Again I feel the deep solitude of the mountains, taste the all pervading alkali dust, and hear the sand-storm beating like sleet against the window panes. The best reward they brought were friendly voices answering in the blue distance across the Sierras, and cheering me with thought that I had won the place of welcome visitor in happy homes my feet may never enter; that through the bitter winter my room was kept by warm firesides under the evening lamp—there where the treasured books lie from day to day, looking like Elia's old familiar faces. Dear to the heart, beautiful and forever young, are the unseen friends whose presence becomes an abiding consciousness to the writer.

CRAWFORDSVILLE, Indiana, March, 1888.

THE LAND OF THE PUEBLOS.

CHAPTER I.

THE JOURNEY.

I AM 6,000 feet nearer the sky than you are.
Come to the sweet and lonely valley in the West
where, free from care and toil, the weary soul
may rest; where there are neither railroads, manu-
factures, nor common schools; and, so little is
expected of us in the way of public spirit, we
almost venture to do as we please, and forget we
should vote, and see to it that the Republic does
not go to the "demnition bow-wows."

Santa Fé is precisely what the ancient Pueblos
called it—"the dancing-ground of the sun." The
white rays quiver like light on restless waters or
on mirrors, and night is only a shaded day. In
our summer camp among the foothills we need
no tents. It is glorious with stars of the first
magnitude, that hang low in a spotless sky, free
from fog, mist, or even dew; not so much as a mote
between us and the shining floor of heaven.

The star-patterns of my coverlet are older than
the figures which delighted our grandmothers.
They come out not one by one, as in our skies;
but flash suddenly through the blue. Day and
night make a brief parting. The short twilight
closes, and lo! in the chambers of the east Orion,
belted with jewels, Arcturus and his sons, and
even the dim lost Pleiad, forgetting the ruins of
old Troy, brightens again. Wrapped in soft,
furry robes, we lie on the quiet bosom of Mother
Earth in sleep, dreamless and restful as the
slumber of those who wake in Paradise. I can-

7

not say, with the enthusiastic land-speculator:
"Ladies and gentlemen, in this highly-favored region the Moon is always at its full." But her
face is so fair and bright I am her avowed adorer,
and many a thousand miles from

'a——'the steep head of old Latmos,"

she stoops above the sleeping lover, to kiss her
sweetest.

Old travelers tell you the country is like Palestine; but it is like nothing outside of the Garden eastward in Eden. New Mexico is a slice of
old Mexico; that is, a western section of Spain.
"Who knows but you may catch sight of some
of your castles there!" Such was the invitation
which came to me across the Rocky Mountains.
I hearkened to the voice of the "charmer, charming never so wisely," and, "fleeing from incessant
life," started on a journey of two thousand miles.
It was in the mild September, and the Mississipi
Valley flamed with banners crimson, golden, in
which Autumn shrouded the faded face of the
dead Summer.

We sped through Ohio, land of lovely women;
past Peoria, fair Prairie City, the smoke of whose
twenty-three distilleries obscures the spires of her
churches beautiful as uplifted hands at prayer;
through the bridge at St. Louis, where the fairies
and giants once worked together, making a crossing over the great Father of Waters; on we
went, journeying by night and by day.

Oh! the horror of the chamber of torture
known to the hapless victims as the sleeping-car.
The gay conductor, in gorgeous uniform, told us,
in an easy, off-hand manner, a man had been
found dead in one of the top berths some weeks
before. I only wondered any who ventured there
came out alive. "Each in his narrow cell forever laid" went through my mind as I lay down

to wakefulness and unrest in blankets filled with
vermin and disease. The passengers were the
same you always journey with : the young couple,
tender and warm; the old couple, tough and
cool ; laughing girls, in fluffy curls and blue ribbons, who found a world of pleasure in pockets
full of photographs ; the good baby, that never
cried, and the bad baby, that cried at nothing ;
the fussy woman. everybody hated, who counted
her bundles every half hour, wanted the window
up, and no sooner was it raised than she wanted
it down again. There, too, was the invalid in
every train on the Pacific Road. A college graduate of last year, poor, ambitious, crowded four
years' study into three, broke down, and now the
constant cough tells the rest of the old tale. He
was attended by a young sister, warm and rosy
as he was pallid and chill, who in the most appealing way took each one of us into her confidence, and told how Rob had picked up every
step of the road since they left Sandusky. When
we entered the wide, monotonous waste between
Missouri and Colorado, how the brave girl would
try to cheer the boy with riddles, stories, games,
muffle him in her furs, slap his cold hands, and
lay her red, ripe cheek to his, as if she were
hushing a baby. In the drollest way, she resist-
ed the blandishments of the vegetable ivory
man, the stem-winder, the peanut vender, and
with tragic gesture waved off the peddler of the
" Adventures of Sally MacIntire, who was Captured by the Dacotahs. A Tale of Horror and of
Blood! " When the dazzling conductor illuminated the passage of the car with his Kohinoor
sleeve-buttons and evening-star breastpin, he
would stop beside the sick boy, and in a fresh,
breezy way seemed to throw out a morning
atmosphere of bracing air, as well as hopeful
words. " Now," he would say, twirling his

thumb in a Pactolian chain which streamed across his breast and emptied into and overflowed a watch-pocket bulgy with poorly hid treasure— "now we are coming to a place fit to live in. When you get to Pike's Peak, you will be 7,000 feet above the level of the sea. It's like breathing champagne. You'll come up like a cork; keep house in a snug cottage; go home in the Spring so fat you can hardly see out of your eyes." Vain words. The poor boy knew, and we knew, he was fast nearing the awful shadow which every man born of woman must enter alone. The mighty hand was on him. He was going to Colorado Springs only to die. We parted at La Junta, crowding the windows, gayly waving good-byes. I can never forget my last sight of the sweet sister, with her outspread shawl sheltering him from the crisp wind, which blew from every direction at once, as I have seen a mother-bird flutter round her helpless nestlings. The good baby held up its sooty, chubby hand saying, "ta, ta," as long as they were in sight, and the mothers smiled tearfully to each other when a rough miner from the Black Hills said, softly, as if talking to himself: "I reckon, if that young woman's dress was unbuttoned, wings would fly out."

Five hundred miles across plains level as the sea, treeless, waterless, after leaving the Arkansas River. Part of our road lay along the old California trail, the weary, weary way the first gold-seekers trod, making but twenty miles a day. Under ceaseless sunshine, against pitiless wind, it is not strange that years afterward their march was readily tracked by graves, not always inviolate from the prairie wolf. The stiff buffalo-grass rose behind the first explorers, and even horses and cattle left no trail. They took their course by the sun, shooting an arrow before them; before reaching the first arrow they shot another; and in this manner marched the entire route up to the place where they found water and encamped.

Occasionally we saw a herdsman's hut standing in the level expanse, lonely as a lighthouse; nothing else in the blank and dreary desert but the railroad track, straight as a rule, narrow as a thread, and its attendant telegraph, precious in our sight as a string of Lothair pearls. Not a stick or stone in a hundred miles. Only the sky, and the earth, clothed with low grass -like moss, the stiff sage-brush, and a vile trailing cactus, which crawls over the ground like hairy green snakes. To be left in such a spot would be like seeing the ship sail off leaving us afloat in fathomless and unknown seas.

After a day seeming long as many a month has, the fine pure air of Colorado touched with cooling balm our tired, dusty faces; and against the loveliest sunset sky, in a heavenly radiance, all amber and carmine, the Spanish peaks majestically saluted us.

Oh! the glory of that sight! Two lone summits, remote, inaccessible; the snowy, the far-off mountains of poetry and picture. Take all the songs the immortal singers have sung in praise of Alpine heights and lay them at their feet; it yet would be an offering unworthy their surpassing loveliness. Now we lost sight of them; now they came again; then vanished in the evening dusk, dropped down from Heaven like the Babylonish curtain of purple and gold which veiled the Holy of Holies from profane eyes. Fairest of earthly shows that have blest my waking vision, they stand alone in memory, not to fade from it till all fades.

At Trinidad we left the luxury of steam, and came down to the territorial conveyance. Think,

dear reader, of two days and a night on a buckboard—an instrument of torture deadly as was
ever used in the days of Torquemada, and had
anything its equal been resorted to then there
would have been few heretics.

It is a low-wheeled affair floored with slats,
the springs under the seats so weak that at the
least jolt they smite together with a horrible
blow, which is the more emphatic when over-
loaded, as when we crossed the line which
bounds " the most desirable of all the Territories."
Our night was without a stop, except to change
horses.   Jolt, jolt ; bang, bang ; cold to the marrow, though huddled under buffalo robes and
heavy blankets.   How welcome the warmth of
the sun on our stiffened limbs ; and the early
breeze, sweet and fresh as airs across Eden when
the evening and the morning were the first day!
It has a sustaining quality which almost serves
for food and sleep.   There journeyed with us in
the white moonshine spectres, shadowy, ghost-
like.   Now the sun comes up, we see they are
kingly mountains, wrapped in robes of royal purple and wearing crowns of gold.   The atmosphere is so refined and clear, they appear close
beside us ; but the driver says they are forty
miles away.   Noon comes on, hot and still, with
a desert scorch.   We journey over a road sur-
prisingly free of stones ; across a blank and col-
orless plain, bounded by mountain-walls which
stand grim and stark like bastions of stone.
Another night and another long day.   The driver
is not on his high horse now.   He has no funny
stories of the grizzly and cinnamon bear, which he
assures us can climb trees, sticking their claws
in the bark, easily as the telegraph-mender, with
clamps on his feet, goes up the pole.   Along the
roadside stretch beautiful park-like intervales,
studded with dwarf pines, that appear planted at
regular distances.

Will the day never end? I have no voice nor spirit, and begin to think the wayside crosses mark graves of travelers, murdered, not by assassins, but by the buckboard; and feebly clutch my fellow-sufferer, and shake about in a limp, distracted way, pitying myself, as though I were somebody else. I can hold out no longer. But wake up! Wake up! This is the home-stretch. The horses know it and dash across a little brook which they tell me is the Rio Santa Fé.

Pleasant the sound of running water; tender the light of the evening on the mountains which encircle the ancient capital of the Pueblos. As we approach, it is invested with indescribable romance, the poetic glamor which hovers about all places to us foreign, new, and strange. We go through a straggling suburb of low, dark adobe houses. How comfortless they look! Two Mexicans are jabbering and gesticulating, evidently in a quarrel. Swarthy women, with dismal old black shawls over their heads, sit in the porches. I hear the "Maiden's Prayer" thumped on a poor piano. How foolish in me to think that I could escape the sound of that feeble petition! Lights stream through narrow windows, sunk in deep casements, and a childish voice, strangely at variance with the words, is singing "Silver Threads among the Gold" to the twanging of a weak guitar. Softly the convent-bells are ringing a gracious welcome to the worn-out traveler. The narrow streets are scarcely wide enough for two wagons to pass. The mud walls are high and dark. We reach the open Plaza. Long one-story adobe houses front it on every side. And this is the historic city! Older than our government, older than the Spanish Conquest, it looks older than the hills surrounding it, and worn-out besides. "*El Fonda!*" shouts the driver, as we stop before the hotel. A voice, foreign yet familiar, gayly

answers: "*Ah! Senora, a los pieds de usted.*"
At last, at last, I am not of this time nor of
this continent; but away, away across the sea,
in the land of dreams and visions, "renowned,
romantic **Spain.**"

CHAPTER II.

HISTORIC.

I USED to think Fernandina was the sleepiest
place in the world, but that was before I had seen
Santa Fé. The drowsy old town, lying in a
sandy valley inclosed on three sides by mountain
walls, is built of adobes laid in one-story houses,
and resembles an extensive brick-yard, with
scattered sunburnt kilns ready for the fire. The
approach in midwinter, when snow, deep on the
mountains, rests in ragged patches on the red soil
of New Mexico, is to the last degree dishearten-
ing to the traveler entering narrow streets which
appear mere lanes. Yet, dirty and unkept, ·
swarming with hungry dogs, it has the charm of
foreign flavor, and, like San Antonio, retains
some portion of the grace which long lingers
about, if indeed it ever forsakes, the spot where
Spain has held rule for centuries, and the soft
syllables of the Spanish tongue are yet heard.

It was a primeval stronghold before the Spanish conquest, and a town of some importance to
the white race when Pennsylvania was a wilderness, and the first Dutch governor was slowly
drilling the Knickerbocker ancestry in the difficult evolution of marching round the town pump.
Once the capital and centre of the Pueblo king-

El Palacio, Santa Fe. (From Pencil Sketch by Gen. Wallace.)

dom, it is rich in historic interest, and the archives of the Territory, kept, or rather neglected, in the leaky old Palacio del Gobernador, where I write, hold treasure well worth the seeking of student and antiquary. The building itself has a history full of pathos and stirring incident as the ancient fort of St. Augustine, and is older than that venerable pile. It had been the palace of the Pueblos immemorially before the holy name Santa Fé was given in baptism of blood by the Spanish conquerors; palace of the Mexicans after they broke away from the crown; and palace ever since its occupation by El Gringo. In the stormy scenes of the seventeenth century it withstood several sieges; was repeatedly lost and won, as the white man or the red held the victory. Who shall say how many and how dark the crimes hidden within these dreary earthen walls?

Hawthorne, in a strain of tender gayety, laments the lack of the poetic element in our dear native land, where there is no shadow, no mystery, no antiquity, no picturesque and gloomy wrong, nor anything but commonplace prosperity in broad and simple daylight. Here is every requisite of romance,—the enchantment of distance, the charm of the unknown,—and, in shadowy mists of more than three hundred years, imagination may flower out in fancies rich and strange. Many a picturesque and gloomy wrong is recorded in mouldy chronicles, of the fireside tragedies enacted when a peaceful, simple people were driven from their homes by the Spaniard, made ferocious by his greed of gold and conquest; and the cross was planted, and sweet hymns to Mary and her Son were chanted on hearths slippery with the blood of men guilty only of the sin of defending them.

Four hundred years ago the Pueblo Indians

were freeholders of the vast unmapped domain
lying between the Rio Pecos and the Gila, and
their separate communities, dense and self-supporting, were dotted over the fertile valleys of
Utah and Colorado, and stretched as far south as
Chihuahua, Mexico. Bounded by rigid conservatism as a wall, in all these ages they have undergone slight change by contact with the white
race, and are yet a peculiar people, distinct from
the other aboriginal tribes of this continent as
the Jews are from the other races in Christendom.
The story of these least known citizens of the
United States takes us back to the days of
Charles V. and the "spacious times of great
Elizabeth."

About the year 1528 an exploring expedition
set out, by order of the king of Spain, from San
Domingo to invade Florida, a name then loosely
given to the wide area between the bay of Fernandina and the Mississippi River. It was
commanded by Pamfilo de Narvaez ; the same
it will be remembered, who had been sent by the
jealous governor of Cuba to capture Cortez, and
who, after having declared him an outlaw, was
himself easily defeated. His troops deserted to
the victorious banner, and when brought before
the man he had promised to arrest, Narvaez said,
"Esteem yourself fortunate, Señor Cortez, that
you have taken me prisoner." The conqueror
replied, with proud humility and with truth, "It
is the least of the things I have done in Mexico."

This ancedote illustrates the haughty and
defiant spirit of the general who sailed for battle
gayly as to a regatta, with a fleet of five vessels
and about six hundred men, of whom eighty
were mounted. He carried blood-hounds to
track natives, chains and branding-irons for cap-
tives ; was clothed with full powers to kill, burn,
plunder, enslave; and was appointed governor

over all the country he might reduce to possession.

The leader and his command perished by ship-
wreck and disasters, all but four. Among the
survivors was one Alvar Nuñez Cabeça de Vaca,
treasurer for the king and high sheriff, who is described in the annals of that period as having the
most beautiful and noble figure of the conquerors
of the New World; and in the best days of
chivalry his valor on the battle-field, his resolution
in danger, his constancy and resignation in hardship, won for him the proud title "Illustrious
Warrior." Ten years he, with three companions,
rambled to and fro between the Atlantic and Gulf
of California. The plain statement of their privations and miseries must of necessity be filled with
marvels; that of Cabeça de Vaca, duly attested
and sworn to, is weakened by wild exaggerations,
and the *Relacion* of this Western Ulysses is
touched with high colorings and embellished with
fantastic fables equal to the moving accidents by
flood and field of the heroic king of Ithaca. He
tells of famishing with hunger till they devoured
dogs with relish; of marching "without water and
without way" among savages of giant stature,
dressed in robes, "with wrought ties of lion-skin,
making a brave show,—the women dressed in
wool that grows on trees;" * of meeting cyclopean
tribes, who had the sight of but one eye; of
being enslaved and going naked—"as we were
unaccustomed to being so, twice a year we cast
our skin, like serpents;" of his escape, and, after
living six years with friendly Indians, of being
again made captive by barbarians, who amused
themselves by pulling out his beard and beating
him cruelly; of living on the strange fruits of
mezquit and prickly-pear; of mosquitoes, whose
bite made men appear to have "the plagues of

* The hanging moss, *Tillandsia usneoides.*

2

holy Lazarus;" of herds of wonderful cows, with hair an inch thick, frizzled and resembling wool, roaming over boundless plains.

Holding his course northwest, he came to a people "with fixed habitations of great size, made of earth, along a river which runs between two ridges;" and here we have the earliest record of Pueblo or Town Indians, so named as distinguished from nomads or hunting tribes, dwelling in lodges of buffalo-skin and boughs. It is difficult to trace his course along the nameless rivers of Texas; he must have ascended the Red River and then struck across to the Canadian, which runs for miles through a deep cañon, in which are yet seen extensive ruins of ancient cities. Undoubtedly he was then among the Pueblo Indians, in the northwestern part of New Mexico. He described them as an intelligent race, with fine persons, possessing great strength, and gave them the name "Cow Nation," because of the immense number of buffaloes killed in their country and along the river for fifty leagues. The region was very populous, and throughout were signs of a better civilization. The women were better treated and better clad; "they had shawls of cotton;* their dress was a skirt of cotton that came to the knees, and skirts of dressed deer-skins to the ground, opened in front and fastened with leather straps. They washed their clothes with a certain soapy root which cleansed them well.† They also wore shoes." This is the first account of the natives of that country wearing covering on their feet—doubtless the moccasins still worn by them.

The gentle savages hailed the white men as children of the sun, and, in adoration, brought

---

* Made of the fibre of the maguey, or American aloe.
† The root of the *Yucca aloifolia*, a spongy, fibrous mass, containing gelatinous and alkaline matter. It grows in most parts of New Mexico, where it is called *amolé*, and is used instead of soap for washing.

their blind to have their eyes opened, their sick that, by the laying on of hands, they might be healed. Mothers brought little children for blessings, and many humbly sought but to touch their garments, believing virtue would pass out of them. The rude hospitality was freely accepted; the sons of the morning feasted on venison, pumpkins, maize bread, the fruit of the prickly-pear; and, refreshed by the banquet, made their worshipers understand that they too were suffering with a disease of the heart, which nothing but gold and precious stones could cure. The Pueblos were then as now a race depending on agriculture rather than the chase, and were in distress because rain had not fallen in two years, and all the corn they had planted had been eaten by moles. They were afraid to plant again until it rained, lest they should lose the little seed left, and begged the fair gods "to tell the sky to rain;" which the celestial visitants obligingly did, and, in answer to the prayers of the red men, breathed on their buffalo skins, and bestowed a farewell blessing upon them at parting.

They again pushed westward in search of riches, always further on, crossed a portion of the *Llano Estacado*, or Staked Plain, and traveled "for a hundred leagues through a thickly settled country, with towns of earth abounding in maize and beans." Hares were very numerous. When one was started the Indians would attack him with clubs, driving him from one to another till he was killed or captured.*

Everywhere they found order, thrift, friendly welcome. The Indians gave Cabeça de Vaca fine turquoises, buffalo robes, or, as he calls them,

* This is still a favorite sport among the Pueblos. They sally out from their villages, mounted on *burros*, to the prairies, where rabbits are started from their coverts, when the horsemen chase them; using clubs, which they throw with great precision, like the boomerang of the savage Australian. In this way they catch a great many. It is very exciting, and is carried on amid yells and much good-natured laughter.

" blankets of cow skins," and fine emeralds made
into arrow-heads, very precious, held sacred, and
used only in dances and celebrations. They said
these jewels had been received in exchange for
bunches of plumes and the bright feathers of par-
rots; they were brought a long distance from
lofty mountains in the north, where were crowded
cities of very large and strong houses.*

It appears from his *Relacion* that Cabeça de
Vaca passed over the entire Territory of New
Mexico, went down the Gila to a point near its
mouth, struck across to the river San Miguel,
thence to Culiacan, and so on to Mexico, where
the four wanderers, worn by hardship, gaunt and
spectral by famine, were received with distinction
by the Viceroy, Mendoza, and Cortez, Marquis of
the Valley.

The venturesome hero was summoned to Valladolid to appear before Charles V., and hastened
to lay at the feet of his imperial master the gathered spoil which cost ten years of life : the hide
of a bison, a few valueless stones resembling
emerald, and a handful of worthless turquoises.

Before he set sail for Spain, Cabeça de Vaca
told his marvelous story to sympathetic and
eager listeners; and, besides, airy rumors had
already floated down the valley of Anahuac of a
land toward the north where seven high-walled
cities, " the Seven Cities of Cibola," were defended by impregnable outworks. They were
least among the provinces, where were countless
greater cities of houses built with numerous
stories, " lighted by jewels," and containing treasure stored away in secret rooms, rich as Atahualpa's ransom. Various rovers gave accounts of
natives clad in curious raiment, richer and softer

* In the Navajo country, between the San Juan and Colorado
Chiquito, are found quantities of beautiful garnets and a green
stone resembling emerald. It abounds in ruins of pueblos capable
of holding many thousand souls; in all probability the emeralds
presented to De Vaca came from that region.

than Utrecht velvet, who wore priceless gems, whole ropes and chains of turquoises, in ignorance of their actual value. One of these stragglers, an Indian, reported that the houses " of many lofts " were made of lime and stone; he had seen them " with these eyes." The gates and smaller pillars of the principal ones were of turquoise, and their princes were served by beautiful girls, whom they enslaved; and their spearheads, drinking-cups, and ornamental vessels were of pure gold. There were wondrous tales, too, of opal mountains,* lifted high in an atmosphere of such amazing clearness that they could be seen at vast distances; of valleys glittering with garnets and beryls; of clear streams of water flowing over silver sands; of strange flora; of the shaggy buffalo; of the fearful serpent with castanets in its tail;† of a bird like the peacock;‡ and a *Llano*, broad as the great desert of Africa, over which hovered a mirage more dazzling than the Fata Morgana, more delusive than the spectre of the Brocken.

A friar named Niza, with one of the companions of Cabeça de Vaca, went out " to explore the country " three hundred leagues away, to a city they called Cibola,§ clearly identified as old Zuni, on a river of the same name, one hundred and eighty miles northwest of Santa Fé. This flighty reporter testified to Mendoza that he had been in the cities of Cibola, and had seen the turquoise columns and soft, feathery cloaks of those who dwelt in king's palaces. Their houses were made of stone, several stories high with flat roofs, arranged in good order; they possessed many emeralds and precious stones, but valued

* The name still attaches to a snowy range southwest of Santa Fé.
† Rattlesnake.
‡ Turkey.
§ Indian name for buffalo. New Mexico was known to the early Spaniards as the Buffalo Province.

turquoises above all others. They had vessels of gold and silver more abundant than in Peru.

"Following as the Holy Ghost did lead," he ascended a mountain, from which he surveyed the promised land with a speculator's eyes; then, with the help of friendly Indians, he raised a heap of stones, set up a cross, the symbol of taking possession, and under the text, "The heathen are given as an inheritance," named the province "El Nuevo Regno de San Francisco" (the New Kingdom of St. Francis); and from that day to this San Francisco has been the patron saint of New Mexico.

In our prosaic age of doubt and question it is hard to understand the faith with which sane men trusted these bold falsehoods. They were mad with the lust of gold and passion for adventure; and valiant cavaliers who had won renown in the battles of the Moor among the mountains of Andalusía, and had seen the silver cross of Ferdinand raised above the red towers of the Alhambra, now turned their brave swords against the feeble natives of the New World. Less than half a century had gone by since the discovery of America; the conquests of Pizarro and Cortez were fresh in men's minds, and an expedition containing the enchanting quality called hazard was soon organized. Illustrious noblemen sold their vineyards and mortgaged their estates to fit the adventurers out, assured they would never need more gold than they would bring back from the true El Dorado. The young men saw visions; the old men dreamed dreams; volunteers flocked to the familiar standards; and an army was soon ready "to discover and subdue to the crown of Spain the Seven Cities of Cibola."

Francisco Vasquez Coronado, who left a lovely young wife and great wealth to lead the romantic enterprise, was proclaimed captain-general;

and Castenada, historian of the campaign, writes, " I doubt whether there has ever been collected in the Indies so brilliant a troop." The whole force numbered fifteen hundred men and one thousand horses ; sheep and cows were driven along to supply the new settlements in fairyland. The army mustered in Compostella, under no shadow darker than the wavy folds of the royal banner, and one fair spring morning, the day after Easter, 1540, marched out in armor burnished high, with roll of drums, the joyful appeal of bugles, and all the pomp and circumstance the old Spaniard loved so well. The proud cavaliers, " very gallant in silk upon silk," kindled with enthusiasm, and answered with loud shouts the cheers of the people who thronged the house-tops. The viceroy led the army two days on the march, exhorted the soldiers to obedience and discipline, and returned to await reports.

When the mind is prepared for wonders the wonderful is sure to appear, and time fails to tell what prodigies the high-born gentlemen beheld : the Indians of monstrous size, so tall the tallest Spaniard could reach no higher than their breasts ; a unicorn, which escaped their chase. " His horn, found in a deep ravine, was a fathom and a half in length ; the base was thick as one's thigh ; it resembled in shape a goat's horn, and was a curious thing." They were the first white men who looked down the gloomy cañon of the Colorado to the black rushing river, walled by sheer precipices fifteen hundred feet high. Two men tried to descend its steep sides. They climbed down perhaps a quarter of the way, when they were stopped by a rock which seemed from above no greater than a man, but which in reality was higher than the top of the cathedral tower at Seville. They passed places where "the earth trembled like a drum, and ashes boiled in a manner truly infernal;" watched magnetic stones roll together of their own accord; and suffered under a storm of hail-stones, "large as porringers," which indented their helmets, wounded the men, broke their dishes, and covered the ground to the depth of a foot and a half with ice-balls; and the wind raised the horses off their feet, and dashed them against the sides of the ravine. They fought many tribes of Indians, and were relieved to meet none who were "man-eaters and none anthropophagi."*

The route of Coronado is traced with tolerable clearness up the Colorado to the Gila; up the Gila to the *Casa Grande,* called Chichiticale, or Red House, standing more than three centuries ago, as it does now, in a mezquit jungle on the edge of the desert; "and," writes his secretary, " our general was above all distressed at finding this Chichiticale, of which so much had been said, dwindled down to one mud house, in ruins and roofless, but which seemed to have been fortified." With true Spanish philosophy, he covered his disappointment, and gave the place an alluring mystery, with the idea that "this house, built of red earth, was the work of a civilized people come from a distance." And into the distance he went, through Arizona, the lower border of Colorado, and turned southeast to where Santa Fé now stands, then the central stronghold of the Pueblo empire. They fought and marched, destroyed villages, leveled the poor temples of the heathen, planted the cross, and sang thanksgiving hymns over innumerable souls

* Castenada's Narrative covered 147 MS. pages, written on paper in characters of the times, and rolled in parchment. It was preserved in the collection of D'Uguina, Paris, was translated and published in French by H. T. Campans, in 1838, and now lies before me. It is wholly free from the vice of the commonplace, being tinged with the warm glow which precedes the morning light of history. Wild as the Homeric legends, it serves like them to point the way.

to be saved,—all very well as far as it went ; but the mud-built pueblos yielded neither gold nor precious metals.

Acoma, fifty miles east of Zuni, is thus accurately described by Castenada, under the name of Acuco : " It is a very strong place, built upon a rock very high and on three sides perpendicular. The inhabitants are great brigands, and much dreaded by all the province. The only means of reaching the top is by ascending a staircase cut in solid rock : the first flight of steps numbered two hundred, which could only be ascended with difficulty ; when a second flight of one hundred more followed, narrower and more difficult than the first. When surmounted, there remained about twelve more at the top, which could only be ascended by putting the hands and feet in holes cut in the rock. There was space on this summit to store a great quantity of provisions, and to build large cisterns." *

The chiefs told Coronado that their towns were older than the memory of seven generations. They were all built on the same plan, in blocks shaped like a parallelogram, and were from two to four stories high, with terraces receding from the outside. The lower story, without openings, was entered from above by ladders, which were pulled up, and secured them against Indian warfare. There was no interior communication between the stories ; the ascent outside was made from one terrace to another. The houses were of sun-dried bricks, and for plaster they used a mixture of ashes, earth, and coal. Every village had from one to seven *estufas*, built partly underground, walled over the top with flat roofs, and

---

* It is the same to-day that it was in 1540,—a place of great strength ; and the *Mesa* can be ascended only by the artificial road. The houses on top are of adobes, one and two stories in height. Water is brought from the valley below by the woman in jars of earthenware, which they balance on their heads with wonderful ease as they ascend the high steps and ladders. The present population numbers not over four hundred souls.

used for political and religious purposes. As in
certain other mystic lodges which date back to the
days of King Solomon, women were not admitted.
All matters of importance were there discussed;
there the consecrated fires were kept burning,
and were never allowed to go out. The women
wore on their shoulders a sort of mantle, which
they fastened round the neck, passing it under
the right arm, and skirts of cotton. " They also,"
writes Castenada, " make garments of skins very
well dressed, and trick off the hair behind the
ears in the shape of a wheel, which resembles the
handle of a cup." They wore pearls on their
heads and necklaces of shells. Everywhere were
plenty of glazed pottery and vases of curious
form and workmanship, reminding the Spaniards
of the jars of Guadarrama in old Spain.

The gallant freebooters traversed deserts, swam
rivers, scaled mountains, in a three years' chase
after visionary splendors; but the opal valley
and the vanishing cities, with their sunny turquoise gates and jeweled colonnades, faded into
the common light of day. Though the adventurers failed in their mocking " quest of great and
exceeding riches," they explored and added to
the Spanish crown, by right of occupation, an
area twelve times as large as the State of Ohio.

I dwell on these earliest records because it is
the habit of travelers visting ruins, which in the
dry, dewless air of New Mexico are almost im-
perishable, to ascribe them to an extinct race and
lost civilization, superior to any now extant here.
They muse over Aztec glories faded, and temples
fallen, in the spirit of the immortal antiquary, who
saw in a ditch "slightly marked" a Roman wall,
surrounding the stately and crowded prætorium,
with its all-conquering standards bearing the
great name of Cæsar.

These edifices are not mysterious except to

revered fancies, and their tenants were not divers nations, but clans, tribes of one blood, and civilized only as compared with the savages surrounding them—the tameless Apache, the brutish Ute, the degraded Navajo, against whose attacks they devised their system of defense, so highly extolled by rambling Bohemians, and threw up "impregnable works," which are only low embankments wide enough for the posting of sentinels.

I have been through many abandoned and inhabited pueblos, examining them with the utmost care, and can discover no essential in which they differ from one another or from those of Castenada's time. In each one there is the terraced wall; the vault-like lower story, used as a granary, without openings, and entered from above by ladders; the small upper rooms, with tiny windows of selenite and mica; the same round oven; the glazed pottery; the circular estufa with its undying fire; *acequias* for irrigation, not built like Roman aqueducts, but mere ditches and canals; and from the sameness of the remains I infer that no important facts are to reward the search of dreaming pilgrim or patient student.

Each village had its peculiar dialect, and chose its own governor. The report of the Rev. John Menaul, of the Laguna Mission, March 1, 1879, gives an abstract of their laws, identical with those framed by "the council of old men," the dusky senators described by Castenada; and then, as now, the governor's orders were proclaimed from the top of the estufa, every morning, by the town-crier.

After the invasion of Coronado, New Granada, as it was then called, was crossed by padres, vagabonds of various grades, and later by armies of subjugation. The same tale is told: how the

peace-loving Pueblo was found, as his descend
ants are, cultivating fields along the rivers or
near some unfailing spring, living in community
houses wonderfully alike, and keeping alive the
sacred fire under laws which like those of the
Medes and Persians, change not. The fair
strangers were at first graciously welcomed and
feasted; but the red men soon learned that the
children of the sun, before whom they knelt,
whose march-worn feet they kissed in adoration, were come merely for robbery and spoil.
The Indian was condemned not only to give up
his scanty possessions, and leave the warm
precincts of the cheerful day to work in dismal
mines, but he must put out the holy flame, and
worship the God of his pitiless master. Conversion was ever a main object of the zealous *conquistador*, and Vargas, one of the early Spanish
governors, applying for troops to carry on the crusade, writes—and his record still stands—"You
might as well try convert Jews without the Inquisition as Indians without soldiers." The first
revolt (1640), while Arguello was governor of the
province, grew out of the whipping and hanging
of forty Pueblos, who refused to give up their
own religion and accept the holy Catholic faith.

The Pueblos constantly rebelled, and escaped
to the lair of the mountain lion, the den of the
grizzly and cinnamon bear, the hole of the fox
and coyote. They sought shelter from the avarice and bigotry of their Christian persecutors in
the steeps of distant cañons, and found where to
lay their head in the hollows of inaccessible rocks;
and this brings us to the cliff houses, latterly the
subject of confused exaggeration and absurd con-
jecture.

It is well known that the first foreign invasions
were by far the most merciless, and it appears
reasonable that hunted natives made a hiding-

place in these fastnesses; that there they allied
themselves with the Navajo, who, from a remote
period, had dwelt in the northern plains, beat
back the enemy, and, as Spanish rigor relaxed,
returned from exile to their fields and adobe houses
as before. Mud walls had been proof against arrow,
spear, and battle-axe, but could not withstand
the finer arms of the fairer race. The cave or
cliff-dwellings of Utah, Colorado, and Arizona are
exact copies of the community tenements of
Southern and Moquis pueblos, varying with situation and quality of material used. The architecture of these human nests and eyries—in some
places seven hundred and a thousand feet from
the bottom of the cañon—has been magnified out
of all bounds. Eager explorers, hurried away by
imagination, have even compared the civilization
which produced them with

"The glory that was Greece,
The grandeur that was Rome."

I found nothing in them to warrant such flights
of fancy, and, like all castles in air, they lessen
wofully at a near view. Those along the Rio
Mancos and Du Chelly are mere pigeon-holes in
the sides of cañons, roofed by projecting ledges
of rock. The walls, six or eight inches thick,
are built of flat brook-stones hacked on the edge
with stone hatchets, or rather hammers, to square
angles; in some cases they are laid in mud mortar and finished with mud plaster, troweled, Pueblo
fashion, with the bare hand. Certainly, mortal
never fled to these high perches from choice, or
failed to desert them as soon as the danger
passed. Whether we believe that the hunters
were Christian or heathen, we must admit that
this was a last refuge for the hunted, made desperate by terror. The masonry is smoothed, so
none but the sharpest eyes can notice the differ-

ence between it and the rock itself, and in no instance is there trace of chimney ɔr fire-place.* The whole idea of the work is concealment.

One might well ask, with sight-seeing Niza strolling through fabled Cibola, "if the men of that country had wings by which to reach these high lofts." Unfortunately for the romancers, "they showed him a well-made ladder, and said they ascended by this means." And well-made ladders the cliff dwellers had—steps cut in the living rock of the mountain, and scaling-ladders stout and light.

The solitary watch-towers along the McElmo, Colorado, and wide-spread relics of cities in the cañon of the Hovenwap, Utah, near the old Spanish trail through the mountains from Santa Fé to Salt Lake, are built on the same general plan, and divided into snug cells and peep-holes, averaging six by eight feet. Perpendiculars are regarded; stones dressed to uniform size are laid in mud mortar. A distinguishing feature is in the round corners, one at least appearing in near-ly every little house. " Most peculiar, however, is the dressing of the walls of the upper and lower front rooms, both being plastered with a thin layer of firm adobe cement of about the eighth of an inch in thickness, and colored a deep maroon red, with a dingy white band eight inches in breath running around floor, sides, and ceil-ing" †—ideas of improvements probably deri-ved from their enlightened conquerors. There is a story that a hatchet found there would cut cold steel, but I have not been able to learn its origin or trace it to any reliable authority.

In every room entered was the unfailing mark

* Cañon du Chelly, in Arizona, on the Navajo Reservation, is a passage through a mountain range, twenty-five miles in length, from one hundred to five hundred yards in width, and is perhaps the strongest natural citadel on the earth. There is but one narrow way by which a horse can ascend its height, where a squad of soldiers could defy the cavalry of the world.
† Hayden's Survey, 1874.

of the Pueblo—pottery glazed and streaked, as manufactured by no other tribe of Indians, and invariably reduced to fragments, either through superstition or to prevent its falling into the hands of the enemy. No entire vase or jar has appeared among the masses strewed from one end to the other of their ancient dominion. I have picked up quantities of this pottery near old towns, where it covers the ground like broken pavement, but have not seen one piece four inches square.

After their first experiments the Spaniards saw the policy of conciliating a confederation so numerous and powerful as the Pueblos, and as early as the time of Philip II. mountains, pastures, and waters were declared common to both races; ordinances were issued granting them lands for agriculture, but the title in no instance was of higher grade than possession. The fee-simple remained in the crown of Spain, then in the government of Mexico, by virtue of her independence, and under the treaty of Guadaloupe Hidalgo, February 2, 1848, passed to the United States.

When General Kearney took possession of the country the Pueblos were among the first to give allegiance to our government, and, as allies, were invaluable in chasing the barbarous tribes—their old enemies, whom they tracked with the keen scent and swiftness of blood-hounds. They now number not less than twenty thousand peaceful, contented citizens, entitled to confidence and respect, and by decree of the supreme court (1871) they became legal voters.

Without written language, or so much as the lowest form of picture-writing, they usually speak a little Spanish, enough for purposes of trade, and, less stolid and unbending than the nomads, in manner are extremely gentle and friendly.

Their quaint primitive customs, curious myths, and legends afford rich material for the poet, and their antiquities open an endless field to the delving archæologist.

Nominally Catholics, they are really only baptized heathen. A race so rigidly conservative must by very nature be true to the ancient ceremonials, and their religion is not the least attractive study offered by this interesting people. Even the dress of the women (oh, happy women!) has remained unchanged,—the same to-day as described by Coronado's secretary in 1541.

There passes my window at this moment a young Indian girl from Tesuque, a village eight miles north of Santa Fé. Like the beloved one of the Canticles, she is dark but comely, and without saddle or bridle sits astride her little *burro* in cool defiance of city prejudice. Always gayly dressed, with ready nod and a quick smile, showing the whitest teeth, we call her Bright Alfarata, in memory of the sweet singer of the blue Juniata; though the interpreter says her true name is *Poy-ye*, the Rising Moon. Neither of us understands a word of the other's language, so I beckon to her. She springs to the ground with the supple grace of an antelope, and comes to me, holding out a thin, slender hand, the tint of Florentine bronze, seats herself on the window-sill, and in the shade of the *portal* we converse in what young lovers are pleased to call eloquent silence. Her donkey will not stray, but lingers patiently about, like the lamb he resembles in face and temper, and nibbles the scant grass which fringes the acequia. I think his mistress must be a lady of high degree, perhaps the *cacique's* daughter, she wears such a holiday air, unusual with Indian women, and is so richly adorned with beads of strung periwinkles. She wears loose moccasins, " shoes of silence," which

cannot hide the delicate and shapely outline of
her feet, leggins of deer-skin, a skirt reaching
below the knee, and a cotton chemise. Her head
has no covering but glossy jet-black hair, newly
washed with *amolé*, banged in front, and " is
tricked off behind the ears in the shape of a
wheel which resembles the handle of a cup"--
the distinguishing fashion of maidenhood now as
it was more than three hundred years ago. Tied
by a scarlet cord across her forehead is a pend-
ant of opaline shell, the lining of a muscle shell,
doubtless the very ornament called precious
pearl and opal which dazzled the eyes and stirred the covetous hearts of the first *conquistadores*.
Our Pueblo belle wraps about her drapery such
as Castenada's maiden never dreamed of,—a flowing mantle which has followed the march of
progress. Thrown across the left shoulder and
drawn under her bare and beautiful right arm is
a handsome red blanket, with the letters U. S.
woven in the centre.

One secret cause of the Pueblos' ready adherence to our government is their tradition that,

> " Far away
> In the eternal yesterday."

Montezuma, the brother and equal of God,
built the sacred city Pecos, marked the lines of
its fortifications, and with his own royal hand
kindled the sacred fire in the *estufa*. Close
beside it he planted a tree upside down, with the
prophecy that, if his children kept alive the flame
till his tree fell, a pale nation, speaking an
unknown tongue, should come from the pleasant
country where the sun rises, and free them from
Spanish rule. He promised the chosen ones
that he would return in fullness of time, and then
went to the glorious rest prepared for him in his
tabernacle the sun.

I have seen the remains of that forsaken city,

3

once a mighty fortress, now desolate with the desolation of Zion. Thorns have come up in her palaces, nettles and brambles in the fortresses thereof. It is a habitation for dragons and a court for owls. The site, admirably chosen for defense, is on a promontory, somewhat in the shape of a foot, which gave a broad lookout to the sentry, In the valley below, the waters of the river Pecos flow softly, and park-like intervals fill the spaces toward foot-hills which skirt the everlasting mountain walls. The adobe houses have crumbled to the dust of which they were made, and heaped among their ruins are large blocks of stone, oblong and square, weighing a ton or more, and showing signs of being once laid in mortar.

The outline of the immense *estufa*, forty feet in diameter, is plainly visible, sunken in the earth and paved with stone ; but all trace of the upper story of the council chamber has vanished. On the *mesa* there is not a tree, not even the dwarf cedar, which strikes its roots in sand, and lives almost without water or dew ; but, strange to see, across the centre of the *estufa* lies the trunk of a large pine, several feet in circumference—an astonishing growth in that sterile soil. The Indian resting in its fragrant shade, listening to the never-ceasing west wind swaying slender leaves that answered to its touch like harp-strings to the harper's hand, clothed the stately evergreen with loving superstition, which hovers round it even in death ; for this is the Montezuma tree, planted when the world was young.

When Pecos was deserted the people went out as Israel from Egypt, leaving not a hoof behind. They destroyed everything that could be of service to an enemy, and the ground is yet covered with scraps of broken pottery marked with their peculiar tracery.

The Oriental Gheber built his temple over deep subterranean fires, and the steady light shone on after altar and shrine were abandoned and forgotten ; but the fire-worshipers on the stony *mesa* at Pecos had a very different work. The only fuel at hand was cedar from the adjacent hills; and, shut in the dark inclosure, filled with pitchy smoke and suffocating gas, it is not strange that death sometimes relieved the watch. When the chiefs, who had seen the kingly friend of the red man, grew old, and the hour came for their departure to their home in the sun, they charged the young men to guard the treasure hidden in the silent chamber. Another generation came and went; prophecy and promise were handed down from age to age, and the Pueblo sentinel, true to his unwritten creed, guarded the consecrated place beside the miracle-tree, daily climbed the lonely watch-tower, looked toward the sunrising, and listened for the coming of the beautiful feet of them that on the mountain-top bring glad tidings. Their days of persecution ended, they no longer ate their bread with tears, and a century of prosperous content went by. Then they were shorn of their strength, and their power was broken by inroads of warring nations. The cunning Navajo harried their fields and trampled the ripening maize; the thieving and tameless Comanche carried off their wives, and sold their children into slavery, and their numbers were so reduced that the warriors were too feeble to attempt a rescue. Hardly enough survived to minister in the holy place ; hope wavered, and the mighty name of Montezuma was but a dim, proud memory.

Yet the devoted watchmen dreamed of a day when he should descend with the sunlight—crowned, plumed, and anointed—to fill the dingy *estufa* with a glory like that when the Divine

Presence shook the mercy-seat between the cherubim. The eternal fire flickered, smouldered in embers, but endured through all change and chance, like a potent will; it was the visible shadow of the Invisible One, whose name it is death to utter. Sent by his servant and law-giver, his word was sure; they would rest on the promise till sun and earth should die.

At last, at last, constant faith and patient vigil had their reward. On the wings of the wind across the snowy Sierras was heard a sound like the rushing of many waters—the loud steps of the promised deliverer. East, toward Santo Domingo, southward from the Rio Grande, there entered Santa Fé an army of men with faces whiter than the conquered Mexican. Their strange, harsh language was heard in the streets; a foreign flag bearing the colors of the morning, white and red, blue and gold, was unrolled above the crumbling palace of the Pueblos. The prophecy was fulfilled, and at noon that day the magic tree at Pecos fell to the ground.

After the American occupation, the remnant of the tribe in Pecos joined that of Jemez, which speaks the same language. It is said the *caçique*, or governor, carried with him the Montezuma fire, and in a new *estufa*, sixty miles from the one hallowed by his gracious presence, the faithful are awaiting the second advent of the beloved prophet, priest, and king, who is to come in glory and establish his throne forever and ever.

CHAPTER III.

THE number of Pueblo or Town Indians of New Mexico and Arizona has been variously estimated at from sixteen to twenty-five thousand. The dumb secrecy of the red race makes it difficult for the census-taker to reach correct figures among them. They have a suspicion that the Sagamore with medicine-book, ink and pen has come to question them with wicked intent; that numbering the people means plotting for mischief; and they secrete their children and give false figures, so it is impossible to arrive at an accurate estimate of their numbers. In the cultured East there is a popular superstition that the noble aboriginal soul disdains artifice, and is open as sunlight to the sweet influences of truth and straightforward testimony :—an illusion rising from the misty enchantments of distance. Come among them, and you will soon learn to make allowance for every assertion; and as for vanity and self-love I have never seen any equal that of the children of nature debased by contact with the white men. They cannot be instructed, because they know everything, nor surprised, because their fathers had all wisdom before you were born. Show them the most curious and beautiful article you possess; they survey it with stolid composure as an object long familiar. I once saw an officer, thinking to floor a *Cacique*, unfold the wonders of a telescope to the untutored mind, and explain how, by bending his beady eyes to a certain point the child of the sun might see the spots on his father; when the blanketed philosopher coolly observed that he had

37

often looked through such machines. We then gave it up. Like the Chinese they so closely resemble, nothing can be named which they did not have ages ago; and having so long possessed all knowledge, they steadily resist your efforts to show them their ignorance. They think themselves the envy of the civilized world. Among such a people one soon learns to repress assumption of superiority or effort to impress the calm listener with your grammatical sentences. The poverty of their language is indescribable. Where there is no writing, and of course no standard of comparison, the change in the sound of words goes on rapidly, while the great principle of utterance or general grammar remains. Mere change of accent under such circumstances produces a dialect. It is not easy to catch the lawless Indian tongues; those of the wandering tribes are peculiarly unmanageable, and it is wise to have a common meeting-place in the little Spanish which they pick up. They have no preposition, article, conjunction, or relative pronoun, and to a great degree lack the mood and tense of the verb. A dual and negative form runs throughout the languages, and sentences are often composed, not of the words which the objects mentioned separately mean, but of words meaning certain things in certain connections. The disheartened student, groping in the dark for signs and rules, and finding none, is glad to turn from his bewildering labor to the interpreter who has learned by ear.

The Pueblos have nineteen different villages in New Mexico, numbering in all nearly ten thousand souls. The towns are evidently smaller than they were formerly, as is plainly proved by ruins of houses throughout their ancient dominion, and old worn foot-paths, abandoned or almost untrodden, that lead from town to town, beaten by

centuries of wayfaring in some period whereof
there is no history.

They are slowly decreasing in numbers, and,
says a gentleman resident among them ten years,
"why they should gradually disappear like the
nomadic and warlike tribes, is a question not
easily solved except by the hypothesis that their
time has come. Their great failing is lack of
self-assertion. Conquered and brought down
from freedom and peace two centuries ago, to a
condition of servitude and an enforced religion,
the power of 'The Fair God' has rested heavily
on them ever since."

There are singular characteristics among these
Pueblos. Each village is a separate domain or
clan, self-supporting, entirely independent of the
government of the other Pueblos and the great
world in the country across the Sierras where the
sun rises. There is no common bond of union
among them, and so little intercourse have they
with each other that their language, everywhere
subject to great mutations, is so altered that
they communicate when needful through the
Spanish, of which most Indian men understand
enough to make their wishes known. There are
three dialects among the tribes of New Mexico,
and three or four more among those of Arizona.
Few Indians understand more than one. In the
seven Moqui villages of Arizona, within a radius
of ten miles, three distinct tongues are spoken.
The inhabitants are identical in blood, manners,
laws and mode of life. For centuries they have
been isolated from the rest of the world, and it is
almost incomprehensible to the restless, aggressive, fairer race how these Pueblos refuse any
inter-communication. Tegua and the two adjacent towns are separated by a few miles from
Mooshahneh and another pair. Oraybe is not a
great distance from both. Each mud-walled

community-house has so little interest in the
others that there is neither trade nor visiting between them. One might think the women, at
least, would sometimes pick up their knitting
and go out for a little social enjoyment and the
friendly gossip so dear to the feminine heart, or
that crafty hunters, tracking deer and coyote,
would follow the abandoned trails of the forefathers winding among the towns, but they do
not; they are too sluggish and dead, and it is the
rarest thing for a man to marry outside of his
own little tribe. I have heard the assertion that
so far from dying out before the march of civilization the increase goes steadily on—not in all the
tribes, but in the aggregate. It is not true. The
prehistoric ruins plainly prove that in long forgotten days the Pueblos were numerous and
powerful; a nation and a company of nations.
The Rio Grande valley was then dotted with
clusters of towns, and Santa Fé was the centre of
four confederacies, and among the most populous
of cities. Down the little Rio on both banks are
remains of villages, heaps of crumbling adobes,
and the unfailing sign of fleeing tribes, scraps of
broken pottery, glazed and painted with their
peculiar markings. Thinking of the bold
theories about population, one naturally asks, Who
took the census when De Soto went wandering
up and down the everglades of Florida seeking
the alluring, ever vanishing Fountain of Youth.

Every Pueblo, or village, has its own officers
and government independent of all the others,
and exactly the same and according to the
ancient customs. First there is the *Caçique*,
chief officer of church and state, priest of Montezuma, and director of all temporal affairs of the
pueblo. It is not known how the *Caçique* was
originally installed in his office, he alone having
power to appoint his successor—which duty is

among the first he performs after succeeding to his office ; nor can the most inquiring mind of the most energetic newspaper correspondent discover the origin of their judicial system.

The *Caçique*, aided by three *Principales*, selected by himself, appoints the Governor "and all the officers." The appointments are communicated to the council of *Principales*, and then proclaimed to the people. No matter how weak and shrunken in numbers the tribe, it still has its full corps of officers, all sons of Montezuma, though evidently many generations removed from the conquering chiefs who reveled in the jeweled halls of their illustrious ancestor.

The Governor is appointed by the *Caçique* for one year, and is the executive officer of the town. He is chief in power and nothing can be done without the order of the Governor, especially in those things relating to the political government. The position is purely honorary as regards salary, and the honors do not cease with the office, for the dignified place of *Principal* is awaiting him at the close of his term, and there is no anti-third term rule to prohibit his holding the place many times during his life.

Immediately after the Governor succeeds to his office he repairs to Santa Fé and seeks the agent for the Pueblo Indians to receive confirmation. This is an empty ceremony, the agent being without the authority to object or remove, but it is followed in obedience to precedent and custom, and there is no harm in humoring the ambition of the gentle wards of the government. On such days of lofty state the happy fellow, in paint and solemn dignity, brings a silver-headed cane, and hands it to the agent, who returns it to the Governor, and the august inaugural ceremony is ended. Under the Mexican rule, it is said, the new incumbent knelt before the Governor of the Territory, and was confirmed by a process of laying on of hands, and some simple formula of Spanish sentences.

The *Principales*, or ex-Governors, compose a council of wise men, and are the constitutional advisers of the Governor, deciding important questions by their vote.

The *Alguacil*, or Sheriff, carries out the orders of the Governor, and is overseer and director of the public works.

The *Fiscal Mayor* attends to the ordinary religious ceremonies.

The *Capitan de la Guerre*, captain of war, with his under-captains and lieutenants, has very light duty to perform in these piping times of peace. He is head of the ancient customs, dances, and whatever pertains to the moral life of the people. The several priests acting under him order the dances, and enforce special obedience of those dedicated to any particular god or ancient order. Each of the officers has a number of lieutenants under him.

This is a gallant array of officials for such a tribe as Tesuque, numbering less than a hundred, or Pojouque, in all twenty-six, or Zia fifty-eight haughty aborigines. I have not been able to find if they have badges and insignia of office, but I do know they strut along the streets of Santa Fé as though they were at the head of tribes like the sands of the sea-shore, like the leaves of the forest, the stars of heaven, according to the swelling sentences of the proud speeches which our early friend J. F. Cooper gave his heroes. The uniform worn is usually buckskin pants, fringed leggins, moccasins, and, in lordly defiance of the prejudices of civilization, with untaught grace the *Caçique* wears his pink calico shirt outside his pantaloons. It breezily flutters in the eternal west wind, but the sun is his father, the earth is his mother; he heeds not that cold breath though it blow from heights of perpetual snow. The tenderness of romance invests the degraded descendant of the noble Aztecan, and wherever he turns, the shades of Cooper and Prescott attend him.

As a class the Pueblos are the most industrious, useful, and orderly people on the frontier; at peace with each other and the surrounding Mexicans. They raise large crops of grain, ploughing with a crooked stick, the oriental implement in the days of Moses, and frequently stirring the soil with a rude hoe, for where irrigation is necessary constant work is required. Threshing is done by herds of goats or flocks of sheep, the floor being a plastered mud ring enclosed in upright poles. The wheat is piled up in the centre, the animals are turned into the pen, and driven round and round until the grain is all trampled out. Then the mass is thrown into the air; the wind carries away the broken straw, leaving the grain mixed with quantities of gravel, sand, etc. It is washed before being ground, but the flour is always more or less gritty. They raise corn, beans, vegetables, and grapes, the latter rich and sweet, and own large herds of cattle and sheep. They possess in common much of the best land of the Territory which, for cultivation, is parceled out to the various families who raise their own crops and take their produce to market.

Paupers and drones are unknown among them, because all are obliged to work and make contribution to the possessions of the community to which they belong.

At Taos nearly four hundred persons live in two buildings over three hundred feet in length, and about a hundred and fifty feet wide at the base. They are on opposite sides of a little creek, said to have been connected in ancient times by a bridge, a grim and threatening fortress of savage strength, many times attacked by the Spaniards but never captured. If there are family feuds and quarrels, the outside world has no knowledge of them ; men, women, and children, mothers-in-law and all, live together in absolute harmony. On the highest story a sentinel is posted. One might think this ancient custom could be dispensed with in the generation of peace since the American occupation, but they hold the wise Napoleonic idea, if you would have peace be always ready for war.

Each Pueblo contains from one to seven *estufas*, used as a council-house and a place of worship, where they carry on their heathen rites and ceremonies, and deliberate on the public weal ; a consecrated spot to which women are not admitted ; a senate-chamber where long debates on public affairs are maintained, and the business of the tribe transacted by the council of wise men, cunning prophets, and able warriors, whose duty it is to manage the internal affairs of the town. The Governor assembles his constitutional advisers in the lodge, where matters are discussed and decided by the majority. One of their wise regulations is a secret police whose duty is to prevent vice and disorder, and report in the under-ground *estufa* the conduct of suspected persons. The dingy little "temples of sin," as the old Catholics call them, are hung round with dim and fading legends and shadowy superstitions. Their worshipers have not the slightest approach to music in the horrible noises they make there— a kind of sledge-hammer beating on rude drums and blowing of ear-splitting whistles—nor have they any idea of rhythm or poetry. No correct tradition is kept without one of these arts, and in the absence of all recorded law a perfect devo-

LIVING PUEBLO. (New Mexico).

tion to custom carries their poor civilization forward as it was in the beginning. It keeps the
Pueblos a separate and distinct people, bounded
by a dead wall of conservatism to this day.
Says the Rev. Dr. Menaul of the Taguna mission,
"Religion enters into everything they do, *i. e.*
everything is done according to ancient custom.
The new-born babe comes upon the stage of life
under its auspices, is fed and clothed, or not
clothed, according to custom. It is hushed to
sleep with a custom-song, gets custom-medicine,
and grows up in the very bosom of religious custom. The father plants and reaps his fields,
makes his moccasins, knits his stockings, carries
the baby on his back, in fact does all that he does in
strict conformity to custom. The mother grinds
the meal, makes the bread, wears her clothing,
and keeps her house, makes her water-pots, and
paints them with religious symbols, according to
custom. The whole inner and outer life of the
Indian is one of perfect devotion to religious custom, or obedience to his faith." And this adoration of the past makes them the most difficult
of all people to be reached by outside influence,
a rigid unbending adherence to old time observ-
ances sets their faces as a flint against everything
new and foreign, and our mission-work seems
dashing against a dead wall. Nothing is subject
to change among them except language; they
have the most shifting forms of human speech, so
the students tell us, and desiring no improve-
ment or alteration, how can we influence them by
religious teaching? How plant new ideas where
there is no room to receive them?

Of all the millions of native Americans who
have perished under the withering influence of
European civilization, there is not a single instance on record of a tribe or nation having been
reclaimed, ecclesiastically or otherwise, by arti-

fice and argument. Individual savages have been educated with a fair degree of success, but there is no tribe that is not savage. The Koran says, "Every child is born into the religion of nature; its parents make it a Jew, a Christian, or a Magian." These North American Indians are more alike than the children of Japhet. Our culture is a failure offered to them, unless one can be detached from his tribe; return him to his people, and he goes back to the dances and incantations, the mystic lodges and time-hallowed ceremonials of the fathers. It seems as difficult to train him as to teach the birds of the air a new note, or the beaver another mode of making his dam; we cannot re-create the head or the heart of the red man He wants his freedom, his tribe, his ancient customs; he desires no change, and his sense of spiritual things is instinctive like a child's.

This rigidity of organism makes sad waste of religious teaching. Catholic and Protestant have been alike unsuccessful. Jonathan Edwards failed as signally, as the missionaries of the Territories who have lived among them for generations. There is a scarce perceptible progress. The young men have no wish to be better or different from their fathers, and they are slightly changed (can we say for the better?) since Columbus gave to Spain the gift of the New World.

Hardest of all is it to teach the Indian how divine a woman may be made, and it is argued that women are best fitted to reach the burden-bearing sisters of the red race. The Quakers succeeded no better than the Puritans, and St. Mary of the Conception was not more discouraged than the self-sacrificing bride from New England, who comes to the land of sand and thorn to teach the dusky mothers how to sing and sew, and broken in health and spirit, returns to her native hills again.

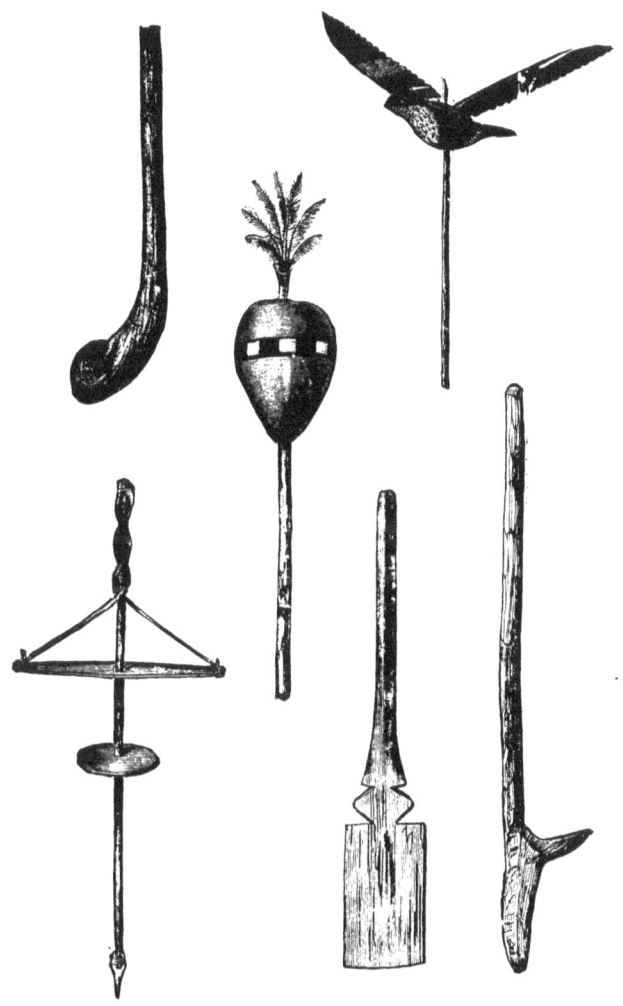

Zuñi War Club, Dance Ornaments, etc.

In winter the main industry of the Pueblos is practicing for the public dances, a training pursued with anxious care by the priesthood dedicated to the duty, as by the ambitious danseuse who fain would copy the famous winged sylphide leap attained by the lithe limbs and flying feet of Taglioni.

Their Te Deum after victories, and most sacred and beloved rite, is the *cachina* dance, which they celebrate at certain seasons of the year with great rejoicings. I have never seen it but am told it is full of contortions and fantastic leaps, ending in a jerky trot, unlike polka or mazurka, and still less resembling the gliding, sinuous action of the world-old Teutonic waltz, most delicate modulation of graceful movement vouchsafed the children of men.

When the Spaniards first conquered this country and imposed their religion on the natives, the idolatrous *cachina* was prohibited on pain of death. History records the natives held it so cruel a deprivation, that the interdict was one of the main causes of the great rebellion of 1680, when Don Antonio de Oterim was Governor and Captain General of Nueva Espagna. Many of the night dances are held in the deepest secrecy; of these the uninitiated may not speak; but other holy days commemorative of abundant harvests are high festivals to which citizens of Santa Fé are cordially invited. You-pel-lay, or the green corn dance, is a national thanksgiving involving the deepest interest and mighty preparation, besides fasting and *purification.* Some weeks before the carnival we accepted an invitation from the *Caçique* of Santo Domingo, where unusual pomp and circumstance attend the celebration of this harvest home.

It was in the mild September. Our ambulance was roomy and comfortable, the mules

were fresh, the party just such as the dear reader
loves, the breeze sweet as the unbreathed air of
Eden. I will not tire your patience with raptures
about Rocky Mountain sunlight and scenery;
the glorious peaks are always in sight, the aerial
tints from the hand of the great Master are shifting and changeable as eastern skies at sunset—
floating veils of exquisite hue hinting of a viewless glory beyond. The wagon road is always
good, and with song and story we beguiled the
way and listened with eager interest to a delightful legend, prettily told by a reporter from St.
Louis, which he said he had from one of the
medicine men of the Pueblos. All about "a
spirit yet a woman, too," who with bright green
garments and silky yellow tresses flits above the
maize fields, and in the night, robed with darkness
as a garment, draws a magic circle round them
to keep off blight and vermin.

It had rather a familiar air and flavor, and
when the story was ended, one of the audience
dryly inquired if the narrator had ever heard of
Longfellow. St. Louis then came down reluctantly and confessed to having stolen the tradition
from *Hiawatha.*

We missed our way, and in consequence had
to jolt over one bad hill, so steep and cut with
steps it reminded me of the gigantic precipitous
stairs in the flight of Israel Putnam, a blood-
curdling picture of affrighted rider and steed, the
delight and terror of my childhood. But this
was a mighty hill of adamant, on which the flood,
earthquakes and the centuries counted only in
heaven have beaten and spent their strength in
vain. We did not care for delays. Time is no
object on the frontier. We lag along with exas-
perating slowness if you want to get through;
are not expected at any place, sleep where the
night overtakes us, and loiter at will in no fear of

being behind time or caught in a shower, a hap-
hazard, good-for-nothing way of travel which
gives a mild, game flavor to the journey. If you
have a drop of gypsy blood in you it will come
to the surface, strawberry-mark and all, in New
Mexico.

As we neared the village we passed pilgrims
going up to the jubilee: men, women, children in
holiday attire, for once moved out of their stony
rigidity of face and mien, smiling back to their
last white molars in answer to the courteous salu-
tations exchanged by wayfarers everywhere in
that Territory. The natives step with an easy
swinging gait, apparently untired at the end of a
day's march as in the first hours of the morning.
Their figures in motion are n t without artistic
grace, expressing strength and fleetness; and
when interested an alert intelligence lights the
face, but ordinarily the cold, stony apathy of the
race is its ruling characteristic. One Pueblo
marching beside us that day I shall never forget.
He was a very model of sinewy strength, a perfect mountain prince, erect and stately in his
crown of green leaves, and striped Navajo blanket
draping his shoulders, held in place by one sym-
metric hand. The noblest Roman wore his imperial mantle with no better grace. The attri-
tion of civilization fails to make our aborigines at
all like "the white brother." These peace-loving
Pueblos, a pastoral people pursuing their simple
industries and trudging to market with their poor
products, are as thoroughly Indian as the wildest
Apache, with brandished knife and dripping
scalp in hand, dancing on the battle field and
whooping in triumph over the banquet of blood.

After leaving the Israel Putnam hill we crossed
a *mesa* or table-land, and, descending into the
valley of the Del Norte descried the village of the
Santo Domingo, a tribe which numbers in all

1,129 souls. A little way off the main road, on
the bank of the river, are the adobe houses, two
stories high with the usual terraces. The roofs
are supported by pine logs, are nearly flat and
covered with bark and earth. A few miles away
are the ruins of ancient Pueblos, crumbling walls
whose thickness attests their age. Like all the
prehistoric buildings, they are on a high bluff
two hundred feet above the water. All ruins
have a certain pathetic interest, but we did not
turn aside to visit these, knowing it would be
only a repitition of arrowheads, stone hatchets
and the tiresome pottery fragments. The old
arrowheads are mainly obsidian, (*iztli*) usually
black, sometimes a smoky or brown tint. They
are strewed through the earth wherever graves of
men have been found. To borrow the forcible
sentence of Holmes, "Whether the arrowheads
are a hundred or a thousand years old who
knows, who cares? There is no history to the
red race, there is scarcely an individual in it. A
few instincts on legs and holding a tomahawk;
—there is the Indian of all time."

We saw a party that day hunting rabbits with
clubs which they throw, making a whirring sound
like the boomerang of eastern savages. It is the
one sport in which women are allowed to take
part. If in whirling his missile a warrior misses
a rabbit, which is finally killed by a squaw, he is
obliged by law or custom, which is equally strong,
to change clothes with her, and they return to
the pueblo, or village, in that guise; Hercules
and Omphale. He must also keep her in fresh
meat during the next winter, serving out his
term of degradation in feminine belongings, a
target for aboriginal wit, and, for the season, the
village fool. Under such humiliating penalty for
failure, we may imagine the experts throw the
club with wondrous care and skill when women
join in the chase.

This joke is immemorially old, handed down from the ancients or fathers, and is immortally fresh and delightful, tickling the fancy of the red man.

On both sides of the river run chains of hills, those on the west side extending inland in extensive *mesas;* and not very far away to the southeast we trace, in aerial tints of supreme beauty, the serrated ridges of the Sandia mountains.

Properly speaking there are but two valleys in New Mexico; the Rio Grande and the Pecos. Should either stream go dry, starvation and famine would follow. They flow nearly parallel, from north to south, fifty and sixty miles apart, till they reach Texas. Skirting their banks are the cultivated fields, making a garden beauty with their tender verdure in contrast with the dull green of dry plains.

By the city of the saint sat a feminine mummy selling grapes. Her head was dressed by the hands of time and nature after the style of Elisha, which so diverted the bad boys of Bethel, and she looked immovable as the dead.

She and her store of fruitage, were sheltered from the sun blaze in a booth of pine boughs; a little green bower called by the orientals *succôth*, a refreshment to the eyes in the shadeless stretch of the parched valleys. The wattle of twigs and leaves is such as Israel made for himself in Canaan, and men of Galilee wove together of thick foliage on the pleasant skirts of Olivet, when they came up to Jerusalem at the feast of the Passover; such as the Sharon peasant yet builds for his family at the Jerusalem gate of Jaffa. There was much beside this shady spot to remind us of Bible pictures; the low adobe houses, the flocks with the herdsman coming to drink at the shallow stream, the clambering goats in

scanty pastures high up the rocks, shaking their
beards at the passing strangers, the kids bleating
by their mothers, the Mexican women, straight
as a rule, carrying water-jars on head or shoulder, like maidens of Palestine.   Now and then
an old black shawl, melancholy remnant of the
gay rebosa, shrouding an olive forehead, suggested the veiled face of the gentle Rebecca.
The lofty presence, the high eagle features of the
Jewish race, the lustrous eyes of the Orient are
not here, nor is the barren magnificence of New
Mexico more than a suggestion of the land once
the glory of all lands, with its verdure of plumy
palms, beauty of olive orchards, the dark foliage
of cypress trees, and white and scarlet blooms of
orange and pomegranate.

These thoughts pass through our mind as we
wait in the wagon while the driver, a Mexican
boy, bargains with Pharoah's daughter for the
day's supply of grapes. We get three fine
bunches for five cents, rich and nourishing,
grown in sandy river bottoms irrigated with alkali water.   They are sweet as the ripest Italian
vintage in terraced vineyards, warmed by the
volcanic heat throbbing in the fiery heart of Ve-
suvius.

For market, the purple clusters are laid lightly
in crates made of pine branches thick as your
thumb, bound together by green withes of bark,
lined with fresh leaves and packed on the backs
of *burros*, the scriptural ass.   The vine is not allowed to run, but is kept trimmed close to the
ground.   Every year the branches are cut near
to the parent stock, which is rarely more than
four feet high.

The forlorn little town, built round a central
plaza, was swept and garnished ready for the
holiday, and having shaken off its usual drowse
appeared quite lively. We were escorted with

much dignity to an honored seat on one of the flat roofs reached by a rickety ladder. There the ancient patriarchs of the tribe, too old to take the field, were gathered, and with them old witches without witching ways, wrinkled, withered, graceless, seated in the favorite aborginal pose on their heels. The preliminary ceremony was held a few days before, when the first ears of corn began to ripen. They were gathered by the women, and, like the Jewish first fruits, the wave-offering in the temple, were brought with solemn reverence to the high priest, who alone has the right to husk them for ascertaining if the promise of a fair harvest is assured. This done, criers were sent through the town announcing to the people that, from his bright sun-house the god of the Pueblos had smiled upon his children in bountiful crops, and they must meet at high noon on a certain day and render unto him thanksgiving and praise.

The burning sky of noon, where no cloud flings a cooling shadow, scorches the valley with tropic fervor, but these children of the wilderness love its parching heat and open the solemnities when the flooding light is at meridian.

In the centre of the open plaza four large camp-kettles of boiling corn were swung gypsy fashion over separate fires. The tops of the poles were adorned with twelve ears of corn representing the twelve months of the year. Each one was watched by four men, naked to the waist, with bodies painted white, red, green, and blue. They are the four seasons, and are elected for their skill in singing and great powers of endurance. Their duty was to dance round the kettles, keep up the fires, and sing songs to Montezuma and the unnamed god, keeping time with a cornstalk on the edge of the kettle. Did **my** reader ever hear Indian singing? He need **never**

want to. It is a long-continued strain of unearthly howls and yells of the sort to drive one
crazy, to make your flesh, aye, the very marrow
of your bones creep.

At exactly noon the grand procession moved,
led by three Sagamores, holy heralds marching
ahead, solemn and still as sphinxes. Then came
thirty-five men, the dancers proper, naked except
a small embroidered blanket, but appearing clad
by reason of a coating of white paint barred with
blue. Their legs and arms were striped with
red, white, and blue; green hemlock wreaths
mixed with red berries of the mistletoe circled
their arms above the elbow.

The same ornamentation served as bracelets,
anklets and necklaces, and resting on the thick
black locks, newly washed with amolè and glossy
as a blackbird's throat, were crowns of gray eagle
plumes. The effect of this adorning was that of
a festal robe, unique and strikingly picturesque.
Around the knees of the main actors were bands
of red cloth to which hung small shells of the
ground-turtle, eagle claws, and antelope hoofs;
and dangling from the back at the waist was a
fox tail or a fur robe, the skin of such wild animals as were killed by the wearer during the
year. They walked in Indian file, each appearing to tread in the same track, bending forward
as if weighted down with corn, which fiction is
part of the play.

The musicians were placed in a conspicuous
part of the plaza in the chief seats of the syna-
gogue such artists love. One had a drum, (*tombe*)
which he beat unmercifully, another clashed
clanging, banging things like cymbals, and a cas-
tinet player dextrously rattled deer hoofs after
the manner of the jolly end man, our friend and
brudder Bones. One ambitious artist performed
on an ornamented whistle made from the bone of

a wild turkey's wing, blowing shrilly with unlimited breath, as St. Louis observed, *sotto voce*, loud enough to split the ears of corn. There was, besides, a heathenish intrument of torture, whose name I failed to obtain, consisting of half a gourd with the convex side up ; on this was placed with the left hand a smooth stick and across it the right hand drew backward and forward a notched stick in a sawing manner, making a sound like the grinding of corn in the *metate*. Luckily this machine does not make much racket, but what there is, is of the quality calculated to turn one goose-flesh. The sound of filing saws is rich melody in comparison.

The three sphinxes, members of the council who headed the procession, made a short speech before each house, the occupants being outside and waiting. At special places they joined the choral howling of the trains, which proceeded with the dire monotony of everything Indian. Thus they went from house to house till every one was serenaded, and from each roof corn was handed and added to the common stock. My knowledge of San Domingan being rather limited, I am unable to furnish a correct report of the brief speeches. Doubtless they were like white men's public occasions ; carefully prepared impromptu. These ended, they sung and danced to the plaza, circling round the boiling kettles, in one hand rattling a sacred gourd containing grains of corn, and covered with tribal symbols and ancestral totems marked in red paint ; in the other swinging a quantity of *tortillas* (rolls of corn bread) tied together with thread, like a bunch of cigars.

The corn is a species of the very hard flint. The grains yellow or bluish black and red, sometimes all three on one cob. The stalk is perhaps four feet high, the ears growing near the ground.

Thin corn cakes, *tortillas*, are the principal iood of Mexican and Indian, and the women pride themselves on the skill and speed with which they make them. The shelled grains are boiled in water with a little lime to soften the skin so that it can be pulled off, then it is ground into meal by mashing with a long round stone, like our rolling-pin, against an oblong, slightly hollowed stone called a *metate*. A little water is added making it the consistence of gruel, and it is baked in thin cakes on hot stones or griddles of tin or copper. When done they are the color of a hornet's nest and tasteless as white paper. Once accustomed to them strangers become very fond of *tortillas*.

At an appointed signal the corn was taken from the kettle, burnt in the consecrated fire, and the ashes sprinkled over the fields to insure a good crop next year; then another fire was kindled, and kettles re-filled with corn, and when boiled freely distributed to all the people, who heartily enjoyed the banquet.

Such is the green corn dance; a yearly delight celebrated in the changeless fashion set before these people in the primeval years. New and startling figures are not in the program. Their ambition is to do all according to the traditions of the elders. As the day advanced the ecstacy increased, the dancers shuffled and hopped as if they would shuffle off this mortal coil. Convulsive stamping and leaping made with frantic gestures; the din of savage minstrelsy; the guttural, unrhythmed voices and the hideous *"tombe,"* a hollow log covered at the ends with dried hide, made a barbaric uproar that lingers long on senses attuned to harmony.

I must not close without mention of the dogs of You-pel-lay. Admitted to that equal sky, they were given the right to a voice in the mat-

ter and toward evening they embarked in a
tumultuous, unearthly fantasia. As we scaled the
Israel Putnam hill the soft night wind fell on our
hot, tired faces like the cool touch of holy water,
and floated after us the farewell symphonies of
the revelry. And they were all pow-wow and
bow-wow.

Perhaps the classic reader, if I am so fortunate
as to have one, may be reminded in this festival
of the haunted vale of Enna and its lovely fables;
mythic stories filled with hidden meaning veiled
by the splendors of the Eleusinian mysteries. It
is the instinctive spirit of gratitude to the Lord
of the harvest, the keeper of the destinies; and
the poverty of this race and their rude rites are
to the genius and varied wealth of ancient Greece
only the difference of blood and civilization
everywhere between the Old World and the New.

The squaws wear no wreaths and have no share
in these ceremonials, but adoring women are the
same the world over, and out of their own hearts
create the glory and beauty of the shrines where
they burn precious incense and kneel for worship. They looked on in secret rapture with
love-light in their eyes, an expression I have
seen in the face of a listening wife in the senate
gallery, when the man foremost of all the world
to her speaks the words which thrill the crowd to
silence. In Santo Domingo there is no noiseless
telegraphy of swimming eye or waving hand.
Little does the sullen red sachem care for the
subtle flattery of loving admiration.

CHAPTER IV.

THE CITY OF THE PUEBLOS.

TEN generations of men have come and gone since Don Antonio de Espego distilled a subtle Spanish essence in *El Palacio;* and you may break, you may shatter those walls, if you will, but the scent of Espagna will hang round it still. Under the witchery of that fast-fading charm, a troop of attendant graces hover about its *portal.* They bear musical names of sweet meaning, as the discreet damsels who welcomed pilgrims to the blessed rooms in the House Beautiful.   Perfectio (perfection), a worthless peon, in Navaho blanket, sweeps the sidewalk ; Benito (the good), a shambling Mexican boy, watching his chance for a spring at the spoons, brings the daily mail ; Mariposa (butterfly), the silliest of Slowboys, pushes the baby-wagon; while Angellus, an angel whose form has lost its original brightness, lazily watches her.   Three old witches, whom we familiarly call the Macbeths, were baptized some centuries ago Feliciana, the Happy; Rosita, little Rose; Hermosa, the Beautiful.

It is the month of July, and the cotton-wood trees of the Plaza are a mass of tender leafage in restless flutter, giving color and cool sound, most grateful in a land where sterility is the rule, fertility the rare and marked exception.   The *acequias* are open, and they moisten earth and air in the square of *alfalfa*, or Spanish clover, knee-deep.

Quite out of reach of the shady trees, in the fiercest blaze of the sun, sitting on a fragment of the Rocky Mountains, is a statuesque figure, which might represent the oldest of the Fates,

the most furious of the Furies.   It is Blandina,
the fair one, the soft one, of Santa Fè.   Her face,
like one of her own foot-hills, is worn into gutters
and seams.   Not like them so moulded by the
action of water, but by exposure to sharp sunlight and withering wind, destructive to beauty,
which make even young persons appear old.
Her skin is a parchment, which looks as though
it might date back to—I was about to say the
Flood; but that would imply that at some pre-
historic era she had felt the sanitary influence of
a shower-bath, and I would not harm an innocent fellow-creature by such an unjust suspicion.
Her draperies are a mere dissolving view.   There
sits the Mexican woman, day after day, not
begging, nor even reaching out her hand, but
following the passer-by with beseeching eyes,
haunting as the eyes of the dead.   Like all the
very poor, she keeps a dog and smokes incessantly.

The great mass of population here is very
swarthy, and there are but few who have no
Indian blood in their veins.   The traveller in New
Mexico may breakfast in a ranche where the occupants have the clear cinnamon hue; dine at
another where the faces are ashen, like the
Malay's; and pass the night at a third where
the courteous host will show the deep Vandyke
brown of the Negro.   The explanation is easy.
The different inhabitants of the several places are
sprung from various tribes.   The Ute has a dingy,
tallow complexion, the Apache is a dirty ashen
gray, while the Mohave girls have cheeks of
almost Spanish transparency.

Besides the luxuries and refinements of the
furthest East, the Moors left behind them in
Spain many descendants, the children of Spanish
marriages.   Some of these were among the
dauntless adventurers who came to *Nueva Mejico*

in the XVIth century.   They intermarried with
the Indians, mingling three strains of blood,
which mixture is called Mexican.   The conquering foreigners were not all olive-skinned.   Some
of the first who sailed the sea boasted, and evidently were, of the *sangre azul*, brought into
Spain by the wild Goths.   The lover of Prescott
will remember his description of the watchful
gray eyes of Cortez, and the clear blue eyes of
Alvarado, whose yellow locks, fair forehead, and
beard yellow as gold, gave him a peculiar expression of sunniness, from which the Aztecs called
him *Tonitiah*—"Child of the Sun."   Scattered
at long distances through New Mexico are a few
ricos, of almost Saxon fairness, remote descendants
of the people who brought the exquisite architecture of Asia to perfect flower in the shades of
the Alhambra—departing traces of the northern
tribes to which southern Europe owes some of
its best elements of strength.   Their blue eyes,
glancing from under the slouched *sombrero*, and
sunburnt hair, stringing down the *serape*, affect
one strangely.   It is like finding Albinos among
the Zuñi and Moqui Indians, and involuntarily
we ask: "What manner of men are these?"
Tawny color is seen in every grade of society and
some of the highest citizens are plainly of Indian
extraction.   The restless energy of the Spaniard,
the quick preception of the Moor, even the cunning of the roving Apache, appear to be lost in the
sluggish current which lazily beats in the pulses
of the modern Mexican.

Among the common people is one distinguishing trait, the utter lack of beauty.   I have fre-
quented every day crowds, and haunted churches,
where they are to be seen at their best, and have
found not one attractive face.   Nowhere on earth
comes age so fast or in such repulsive shape.   A
lovely baby changes to the plain young girl,

somewhat comely, at fifteen. At twenty-five not a vestige of freshness remains; not a line to remind one of beauty vanished forever. And oh! the hideous hags squatted against the walls! There is no speculation in those eyes, fixed as the eternal gaze of the Sphinx. They look old as that grim female, and I would as soon think stone lips could part into a company smile, displaying false teeth, as that these could break into laughter or song. I wonder what they are thinking about, if they think at all, or if an earthquake would make them jump. Assuredly, they are the most opaque of terrestrial bodies, and, under the old black shawl, they sit immovable, as though all the forces of the universe (rarely heard from in Santa Fé) could not start them from their secure poise.

Dr. Holmes says "the finest human fruit, and especially the finest women, we get in New England are raised under glass. *Protection* is what the transplanted Aryan requires in this New England climate." I fancy "protection" is what the women needs in the "excessive," the territorial climate analogous to that of Central Asia. On this bleak, elevated plateau, where the dryness is so intense that meat is cured without smoke or salt, the juices of the human body evaporate, leaving early wrinkles. I have seen men in high health return from a month of camping among the Rocky Mountains with crow's feet wofully deepened and the appearance of having "aged" in a very short time.

Perhaps dirt and low diet have helped to finish the completed ugliness of the Santa Fé witches; but we know extremes of every sort waste nervous force, and hasten the steps of the common enemy, who sharpens his scythe for the faces of women, and shakes the sand in the glass when he measures their years.

Moisture, when it does come, is not the gentle rain from Heaven, swelling bud and flower, as well as human hearts, to thankfulness. There is no dew ; nor is there showering mist, like that which went up from the earth and watered the garden eastward in Eden. We have, instead, high wind-storms, rain streaming in torrents, preceded by an atmosphere where men and animals are acting lightning-rods for electric currents ; keen, close lightning and the " *live* thunder " of which Byron sung. Suddenly the mighty music stops. The sun flashes out in unveiled splendor, flooding the world with blinding light, and we are tempted to tread a sun-dance in worship of the glittering God of the Pueblos, who inhabits eternity, lord of Heaven and earth, son of the morning and father of all the days.

CHAPTER V.

MEXICAN COTTAGES.

Across the way are a dozen Mexicans, wrapped in greasy old blankets, sitting like four-and-twenty blackbirds all in a row. I know their faces, and have not missed one in a month. They live in condition of body and mind hard for an American to realize. A kind of present existence, without loving reference to the past ; a passive waiting for the future, without an inquiry or a wish, a fear or a hope. Small, lank, dark-brown fellows ; eight with high cheek-bones and thick lips, betraying Indian blood ; hair long, straight, black ; eyes dark, suspicious, wavering ; habitually silent ; when speaking,

with gloomy indifference, in a voice sad as memory. Elsewhere they would go as tramps; but
tramping is a grand fatigue. They prefer to sit
round, instead.

It is said this is the bearing of every conquered race; but such is the average Mexican
wherever he is found. About the hill of royal
Chapultepec, at the base of the pyramid of
Cholula—last vestige of Aztecan grandeur—he
basks in the sun with the chameleons and lizards,
docile in temper, patient under abuse, idle as the
wind that lifts his long, black locks. Think you
such men care for advantages, natural or political—They know the joy of a splendid destiny fulfilled or the anguish of such a destiny lost?
They come of brave blood—Spaniard, Moor,
Indian—and how well they fight for their own,
the United States, France, and Austria may testify; but to us never did life appear so empty,
aimless, and joyless as the life of these sitters in
the sun.

The puzzling question of to-day is: How do
they keep soul and body together? Let us find
one in his home, if the dingy den he inhabits
may be called by that dear name. Leaving the
Plaza, where vagrants most do congregate, we
pass the cottages of " the military " (on whose
heads be the blessing of those who entertain
strangers), cross a sandy *arroya,* through which in
the rainy season a mountain torrent sweeps roar-
ing. Westward the straggling suburb stretches
toward the foothills, and, stumbling along a stony
path, we suddenly come up against a wall. It
is about six feet high, made of mud mixed with
ashes, coal, cow-horns, hoofs, mule-bones, barrel-
hoops, the wheels of a baby-wagon, cans, broken
bottles, boots, curry-combs, every refuse substance that may swell the mass in a treeless region. The top of the wall bristles with scraps of

tin, which make it hard to climb. I doubt if Romeo would try it, even to seize the white wonder of Juliet's hand. The gate is made of upright posts of dwarf cedar, thick as a man's wrist, bound together by rawhide strings, and groans and creaks in a dismal note as we push it on wooden hinges. Not a trace of iron is to be seen.

This formidable outwork encloses three puppies, of the breed called cast-iron, which look like magnified rats and act wonderfully like cats. The proprietor of the estate and his spouse, in the doorway, sit in the artistic pose called squat, at leisure profound, if not elegant. He is evidently made of the same clay as his wretched mud shanty; might have sprouted up from the ground or dropped down from the eaves.

As we enter, they rise in unembarrassed politeness. He removes his slouch of a hat with decorous gravity, and the wife entreats us to enter, saying, with the air of a princess in exile, we do her great honor. The Spanish flavor is strong here, which may be the reason she wears dragging bright calicoes all the year, and sits in the door even when the snow falls. Her raven black hair and large, full eyes hint of by-gone beauty; but it is by-gone. Premature wrinkles are worn deep by the shriveling wind, her skin is swart and sunburnt, and the roses in her cheek are only ashes of roses.

"Would she give us a drink of water?"

"With much pleasure, *Señora.*"

She diffuses an air of elegance over her pink calico toilet by throwing a dreary old black shawl round her head; and, scorning to lift her voluminous train (twelve yards for a dollar), hastens to the nearest *acequia*, or irrigating ditch, fills a mug of Indian pottery, and offers it with sweetness and grace. No new country exuberance about her, nor revelling imagination, like Dick Swiveller's; but a power of enchantment and a lofty self-poise which no surprise can startle or disturb. It is found alike in splendor or in squalor, the "grand air" of Old Spain, descended to all who have a dash of her blood.

My hostess regrets the water is not wine, and so catching is the fine charm that, ensnared and deluded, I am hardly sure it is not wine, and drink their health in the miserable ditch-water and am cheered by responsive *gracias*. I try to explain that I am under silken bonds—ribbons red, blue, white—not to look upon wine when it is red; but it is their first hearing of temperance, and they do not understand. She invites me to a seat on the *colchon*—a wool mattress folded against the wall and covered with a blanket, which serves the double purpose of bed by night and sofa by day, an Oriental custom, come down to them from the Moors. I excuse myself, being in mortal fear of old settlers in the mattress. There a lovely baby, with no dress to speak of, is tossing up its heels. I ask some questions, thinking of bright eyes far away; and she prettily says baby has no year yet, and her name is Lola Juanita Eloisa.

The earthen floor is swept with a bunch of broom, without handle, leaning against the mud fireplace in the corner of the room. There are no andirons, shovel, or tongs, and when fire is made the wood is placed on end against the back of the fireplace. A chest, a few pieces of crockery on a pine table, complete the furniture. Can you imagine love in such a cottage? Undoubtedly there is love, and in the poorest *jacal* there is no brawling man, scolding, slapping wife, or crying baby. If the walls crack, they are daubed by Magdalena Rosalia with a fresh plaster of *yeso*, or gypsum, put on with a glove of sheepskin. If

the outside flakes and cracks too badly, it is
smeared with a new coating of soft mud.   In the
spring the ground floor has another layer of clay,
the fireplace a thin coating of *tierra amarilla,* or
yellow wash, and house-cleaning is ended.   Does
the roof leak, a dab of mud is slapped on.   Is
the outer wall in holes, a lump of clay will stop
the wind away.   There is no window, and when
the door is closed the house must be dark and
stifling as a dungeon.   Above the fireplace, done
in hectic chromo and framed in tin is a copy of
the divine Madonna in the Louvre, named "Queen
of Heaven"; a band of blue stars across her
forehead, a tinsel crescent under her feet.   Hanging below it is a plaster crucifix, under glass.
When the bell chimes, Magdalena Rosalia will
seek the old cathedral, whose vaulted interior is
filled with shadows and silence—among them a
few figures, motionless as the dead asleep under
the floors—say her prayers across the rosary,
confess, and be absolved.   But Trinidad Gonzalez Ribera, in the gauzy blanket and vanishing
pantaloons, will sit dozing in the sun, deaf to the
ringing music, unmindful of bell, book, or candle.
I pass from under the hospitable mud roof with
repeated *adios* and a feeling of unreality.   I look
for a garden.   There is none.   There are no
chickens, no pig, no cow, no grass within the
gravelly enclosure.

The only sign of life is a famished donkey,
browsing on the strip of grass which borders
the *acequia* by the roadside.   He is the property
of our new friends, and occasionally the man of
many names takes him to the mountains, loads
him with limbs of dead *piñones,* and sells them for
twenty-five cents a backload.   Stopping on the
plain, he digs a few roots of *amolé,* or soap-weed;
the *yucca aloifolia,* which we cultivate for its rich
cream-white blossoms.   This is for the washing
done by Magdalena Rosalia.

Do not think she briskly knocks so early Monday morning or comes Sunday night for the clothes, as wicked Protestants have been known to do. No ; this daughter of a proud line will not shame her high ancestry by vulgar haste. She saunters along about noon, seats herself at ease, makes affectionate inquiries as to every member of the household, with a gift of continuance and native talent for rigmarole which would do honor to a legislative body. She deliberately ties the bundle of clothes, balances it on her head, and departs with sweeping courtesy and majestic flirt of pink calico train.

After walking a few blocks, she stops for a rest, adjusts her bundle into a cushion on the ground, takes from her pocket a little package of corn-husks, fills one with fine-cut tobacco from a paper box, rolls it into a *cigarrito,* and enjoys a smoke. A Monday picture in Santa Fé is the long row of wash-women, with the everlasting black shawls over their heads, sitting in the shade of mud walls, quietly gossiping and smoking. To get the clothes home is exertion enough for one day.

Tuesday she repairs to the Rio Santa Fé weakened by irrigating ditches to a shallow brook, and on its sandy bank makes a little fire for washing. Her machine is one bucket and a square tin box. She pounds the clothes between two stones. Flannels full, buttons fly, embroideries are a dream of things that were. She boils them in the box, set on granite ; rinses in the pure snow-water of the Rio ; and spreads them on the rocks to dry, as the young Roman girls do along the Tiber. Friday, in comes Magdalena Rosalia, with all beautifully white, folded in an Indian basket shaped like a deep saucer.

The proceeds of this labor buy a bag of blue corn-meal and the necessary tobacco. Twice a

week they can afford a stew of *chili con carne*
(our old friend hash, made fiery hot with red
pepper) and the living is made. As respects
worldly goods, come he soon or late, Death will
find this pair exactly as they entered life, exactly
as their fathers lived and died, in the peaceful
depths of contented poverty. Magdalena Rosalia
walks as though she was born in the purple, to
live like the lilies who toil not neither do they
spin; and Trinidad Gonzalez Ribera is free of
care as though his old Navajo blanket was a
king's coronation robe. At the grave's edge it
not unfrequently happens that his mourning
friends, too poor to spare his blanket, strip it
from his body, and lay him away in the dust from
whence he sprung, shroudless and uncoffined.

These are the happy people sighed for by weary
poets in all the ages. Simple souls who love the
sun, live close to Nature, and in the dirt house,
to which nothing is added, where nothing is
repaired except by additional dirt, are serene as
summer, filled with a measureless content. Can
we say so much for the eager, ambitious conqueror in a struggle, a battle, and a race; always
getting ready to live, looking to the future when
he may have time to rest and enjoy?

The Mexican does not wait for better times.
There is no day but this. He begins now and
the future takes care of itself.

Oh! tired woman of "the States," running on
your nerve, trying to do all the public demands
of you and all you require of yourself, leave the
place where the door bell rings every half hour.
Quit worrying over goose-parties for the Sunday-
school, Jarley's wax-works for the firemen; slip
away from strawberry parties for the Gaboon Mission; slacken the fevered rush; loosen the strings
at concert pitch and ready to snap; go to the
Mexican woman, consider her ways, and learn
how to rest.

Of course, you, my precious reader, know many things she does not. There never has been a woman's meeting in this territory of 207,000 square miles; and, in consequence, the weak-minded creature is not aware that men are great rascals, rob women of their rights, and bar the avenues to wealth and fame against them. Sing the Iliad of your woes, and it will fall on heedless ears. And, though you harp how Juliet's poetry flew up the kitchen-chimney and Portia's eloquence burnt out over the gridiron where her

> ——" red right hand grew raging hot,
> Like Cranmer's at the *steak.*"

she would quietly adjust the old black shawl (final remnant and melancholy reminder of the gay *rebosa*) and count the days till the next *fiesta*.

There are heights beyond her reach, and beyond your reach too, in spite of mighty purpose. She does not strain after them, wearing herself to skin and bone. While you, who have tasted bitter fruit from the tree of knowledge, are ready to die in a losing struggle for the unattainable, she loiters in happy valley, by good spirits tenanted, and in her easy shoe wears the four-leaved clover of perpetual content.

CHAPTER VI.

TO THE TURQUOIS MINES.

READER, are you the sort of person who rushes through life the first passenger on the earliest train; who hires the fastest coach at Niagara, to exhaust the Falls, the Whirlpool, and Lundy's Lane in half a day, and are then ready to whiz off

in the night express? If you are, then are we
no company for each other, and may as well part
at once. You are entirely unfit for frontier travel
and may go this minute. *Adios! Adios!*

But you who lingered by the Rapids; who
have a kindly glance for the smutty sentinel at
the brake; who do not threaten to die when the
gentlemanly conductor fills the car full and corks
it tight as a champagne bottle, but live on in
order to cheer a gasping fellow-martyr; who
help the mediæval lady, of convex outline, traveling with two geraniums and a canary bird, yet
keep a sympathetic eye for the young pair in the
new of the moon, murmuring, as they pass, I
too have dwelt in Arcadia.—You are the one I
love. Yours are the feet, beauteous on the
mountain-top, that go gypsying with me through
this New World, which Agassiz tell us is the
Old.

We travel in a hap-hazard way, varied with
many a digression, following no train but our
own fancies. We stop to speak with the natives
by the way, try to sketch a Gifford sunset on a
gritty scratch-book, and stray from the road for
bits of cheating mica, and for flowers which wilt
in the gathering, and change in our hands to dry
stalks and grasses.

The mountains are eternally beautiful, always
changing, forever new, and all about us is picture.
Walking for rest, the grama grass is soft and pleasant under the pilgrim's feet; the sun always
shines; the days are like the enchanted rooms in
the fairy castle, each more beautiful than every
other; the air is balm, and oil, and wine.

There is nothing pleasanter than such travel,
unless it be to float between blue and blue among
the Cyclades, and idly drift along the tideless
sea, to catch the far echo of the syren songs that
wooed the wandering Ulysses.

And now for the Turquois Mines.

To one who was an early and ardent admirer of *Lalla Rookh,* the word turquois brings up memories of old or, rather, young days among fragrant orchard trees, meadows pink and white with clover-blooms, and a certain fine-printed, sight-destroying volume of the poet whose hundredth birthday we have just celebrated. It is like a fading dream to look from the shadowy half-way house at the girl embowered among singing birds, reading, with dazzled eyes, of swords inlaid with rich marquetry, talismans, and characters of the scimitar of Solomon. Arms of

"The wild warriors of the Turquois Hills,"

who rallied to the white veil and glittering banner of the False Prophet.

The perfumed and sparkling poem which thrilled so many soft hearts at life's morning is not loved by lovers of this age. Only the setting generation—and they mainly for the sake of old times—read "The Veiled Prophet of Khorassan," and in the twilight pensively sing "Araby's Daughter," with voice not altogether fresh. In the days when that fond farewell was first sung it was taught that turquoises belonged chiefly to the Turkish and Persian Empires. Since then the ceaseless delving of the antiquary has given to the world such treasure far removed from the Shah's dominions. There are mines of high antiquity in Mount Sinai, and a bronze finger-ring, of unique pattern, set with turquoises, has been discovered in the Wady Meghara of that peninsula. It dates back to the vague, unreal period of the Fourth Dynasty; and amulets of the same material are unearthed in the ruins of ancient Egyptian towns. They are found in Arabia Petrea, in a stratum of red sandstone, of finer blue and darker shade than the Persian, and the visitor of Roman museums sees antique cameos and intaglios carved in Arabian turquois, sadly faded and tarnished by long burial. Only a few in the Vatican still retain their color.

Those of Khorassan are sold in Russia on sticks, tied in bunches like quills, and are in de-mand by jewelers of St. Petersburg, for enriching sword-hilts, handles of daggers, belts, pipes, etc. The Shah is reported to have in keeping all the finest gems, allowing only the inferior grades to leave the country.

In a curious old treatise on precious stones the turquois is described as a delicate and sen-sitive jewel, which has an affinity for its owner, changing color with his health and varying for-tunes. The fact that they do change color in a wholly unaccountable manner may explain the fanciful notion. Human hearts are the same everywhere and in all ages, and many a myth and superstition of the East is reproduced in Mexico—plain testimony that Orientalism dwells not alone in its sky and the palm trees of the valley.

It interested me greatly to find that the pretty legend of the Orient attaches to the turquois of the New World, called by the ancient Aztec *chalchuite* (pronounced chal-chew-e-te).

Like the Asiatic, the Aztecan believed it brought good fortune to the wearer, glowed in sympathy with the healthful beating of his pulse, and ominously paled in prophecy of a coming misfortune. The power of the Montezumas was absolute, as their dominion was vast; and wher-ever the green banner of the king marked the limit of his realm, the *chalchuite* was, by imperial decree, forbidden to the commonalty—the jewel sacred to the royal house. When the five am-bassadors from Totonac came to the tent of Cortez, at Vera Cruz, they defied the law (being then at war with the fierce and bloody Aztec), and wore the proscribed jewels—"gems of a bright blue stone, in their ears and nostrils."*

Readers of Prescott will remember his picturesque page describing the city of Tezcuco, where North American civilization reached its height. In the royal palace was a hall of justice, called the " Tribunal of God," where the judge decided important causes and passed sentence of death, seated on a throne of pure gold, inlaid with the consecrated turquois.

The art of cutting gems was carried to high perfection by the Aztecs, and the carved *chalchuite* is noted by every writer on the Spanish Conquest.

Father Sahagun calls it a jasper of very green color, "or a common smaragdus," so precious to the infidel that the use of them was prohibited by royal edict to any but the nobility. " It represented to them everything that was excellent in its kind; for which reason they put such a stone in the mouth of distinguished chiefs who died," like the coin poetry offered to the grim ferryman of the souls of the Greek dead.† They were valued by the heathen above all earthly possessions, and, therefore, at first held in great estimation by the Spaniards. The art of polishing them came from Heaven, the gift of the god Quetzelcoatl, a gentle deity who instructed the Aztecs in the use of metals, agriculture, and the arts of government. It was in the golden age of Anahuac, when an ear of Indian corn was as much as one man could carry, when the air was filled with the melody of birds, the earth with flowers, and cotton in the field took of its own

---

*Prescott's *History of the Conquest of Mexico*, Vol. I.

† Father Sahagun thus describes these precious stones: "*Las chalchuites son verdes y no transparentes mezcladas de blanco, usanlas, mucho las principales trayendolas las muñecas atadas en hilo, y aquello es señal de que es persona noble el que las trae.*"— *Hist. de Nueva España*, Lib. ii. chap. 8.

accord the rich dye of cochineal. Cholula was
his favorite city, where the massy ruins of the
temple dedicated to his worship form one of the
most interesting relics of ancient Mexico. By
command of the superior deities, he took leave
of his worshipers on the shores of the Mexican
Gulf, under promise to return, and, entering his
wizard skiff, made of serpents' skins, sailed away
to the blooming shores of happy Tlapallan.

The earliest mention of this historic gem is
made by the honest old soldier, Bernal Diaz.
Four *chalchuites*, counted the most precious offerings from his treasury, were among the first presents sent by Montezuma to Cortez. "A gift to
our emperor, designed as a mark of highest
respect, as each of them, they assured us, was
worth more than a wagon-load of gold." The
covetous Spaniard was enraptured with the gold-
dust and jewels, and gave in exchange—a sorry
return for the munificence of the imperial present
—a few Holland shirts, and a string of trumpery
beads, strongly perfumed with musk.

On sending the priceless Aztecan diamonds,
" worth four wagon-loads of gold," to Valladolid,
it turned out, rather awkwardly for the Spaniards,
that they were not worth so many wagon-loads of
earth.

The gossiping Herodotus of the New World
alludes to the *chalchuite* again in his narrative of
the first meeting of Montezuma and Cortez, on
the Causeway, at the entrance to Mexico, city of
enchantment. That fatal day, when the force of
his own genius brought the representative of the
strongest empire of the Old World face to face
with the mightiest monarch of the New, its pale
lustre shone dimly in the fringe of the canopy
held by the *Caciques* above the hapless monarch's head. " A canopy of exeeding great
value," says the quaint chronicler, " decorated with
green feathers, gold and silver, *chalchuis* stones

and pearls, which hung down from a bordering
altogether curious to look at."

Its delicately-traced veins, occasionally of
greenish hue, betray a near kinship to malachite.
This rich-tinted mineral is finer than the dark-
colored stone of Russia, and though by no means
costly as Shylock's turquoise, the *chalchuite* still
holds its high repute among the various tribes of
the red race.

It is valued by the Navajo beyond the garnets
and beryls of his own country, and is used as
currency among the half-civilized Pueblos of New
Mexico and Arizona. The Indian girls along the
Colorado wear it is as a love-token in their necklaces; the roving and tameless Apache covets a
blue bead as an amulet; the degraded Ute loves
its soft glimmer; and when a Mohave chief would
assume regal splendor, he sticks a three-cornered
piece of *chalchuite* in his royal nose.

Such associations fresh in mind, it was with
extreme pleasure I prepared for an excursion to
Los Cerillos, where these blue-eyed gems are
found, the only mines as yet discovered this side
the Russian seas. Twenty-six miles southwest
of Santa Fé are the long, narrow ranges of gold
and silver-bearing mountains—Placer, Sandia,
Manzana, etc.—which form an unbroken chain
on the eastern side of the Rio Grande. Among
them are three turquoise mines, which anciently
supplied the Indian market of North America.

A roomy ambulance, drawn by four mules;
various delights, liquid and solid, in a mess-chest;
a party of choice spirits, like my reader; and a
morning such as breaks nowhere but over the
hills of Paradise and New Mexico—this was our
start.

Our driver was a young Mexican, bearing a
lengthy and musical name, with which I shall not
serenade you. Juan Fresco (Cool John) is a

minute fragment of it.   He was very spruce in a
brand-new suit of kerseymere, of the sort sold
throughout the frontier by Israelites in whom
there is much guile; a handsome Navajo blanket
closely woven and brightly striped; and was
happy in possession of a limitless supply of corn
husks and powdered tobacco, which he rolled
into cigarettes and smoked, without so much as
saying, By your leave.   Had he known it was
impolite, he would have implored pardon, with
many sweet-sounding words.   Mexican women
smoke constantly, as men do, and he does not
know better.   He can live and does live on a
dollar a week; and, with *tortillas*, onions, red
pepper, and once in a great while a mutton stew,
thrives and drives the ambulance.   They say that
there is Indian blood in him; that he is cold as
death and treacherous as a tiger-cat; but I do not
believe it.

In this high, dry country, corresponding with
Western Asia, the tendency of the human body
is to Arab leanness, and Juan Fresco, who grew
to man's estate under this fierce Syrian sun, sitting against the mud wall of a Syrian hut, has a
soft Syrian face.   No positive beauty (I have
never seen out-door people except Arabs who
have), but comely features, unchanging, melancholy eyes, and a gentle, passive voice, very
winsome.

The festal day found Juan Fresco highly embellished with a yellow sash tied tightly around
his waist, securing a long knife (*navaja*) in its
folds.   Every Spaniard can use the knife with
skill, and in his hands it becomes a dreadful
weapon.   He can cast it with exact aim and unerring certainty into a post or into the heart of
an enemy at a considerable distance away; and
wherever there is Spanish blood the *navaga* is
the favorite weapon, not always concealed about

his person. Our muleteer took his pleasure sadly as any Englishmen; but his sadness is only for strangers. He is leader of the band which goes from house to house playing under the windows —the sweet Spanish invitation to the ball; gayly thrums the guitar at the light fandango; and can dance till morning as well as hold his own in any affray that may grow out of the wild license of the *baile.*

Occasionally he leaped from his seat for a pocketful of stones, gathering them as the wagon moved on, and throwing them at the heads of the mules; at the same time muttering, on the ledger lines below, sacred words mixed with names of saints. The Mexican insists a mule cannot be made to understand without such urging; and they have a proverb: " An ass's ears are made long in order to catch oaths."

[N. B.—There is reason to believe that a like superstition attaches to the Army of the United States.]

Leaving the venerable city of the Pueblos, we crossed the Santa Fé River, which in Indiana would be called a spring branch. I have often gone over it dry shod. But the poverty of the Spanish language allows only one word for running water—*Rio*, translated river. The Santa Fé Mountains round about us are a part of the great Rocky Mountain system, connecting on the north with the Spanish Peaks and Raton Mountains, including many whose summits are silvered with perpetual snow. A series of high, picturesque chains, in the morning-glow robed with a transparent purple haze, of such exquisite tint one can hardly realize those airy pyramids in a fair border-land between us and heaven are, indeed, upheavals of earth, veined with quartz and based on coarse red granite.

Words cannot picture aught so fair. The

faintest violet, the softest heliotrope are coarse
and hard beside the dreamy, poetic color, which
appeals to the eye as dim æolian soundings touch
the ear, charming the fancy with vague ideas of
a viewless beauty within the floating veil.

I cannot make you understand.   Come and
see the transfiguration which makes rock-ribbed
hills appear like tents of light, lovely enough for
angels to rest in on their upward flight.

The plain was smooth as a prairie, and our
road free of stone.   The reader must not imagine
it lay among Alpine scenery, with huge peaks
towering to the sky, forbidding our advance,
yielding at last to reveal smiling valleys and hidden hamlets, nestling close to the hillsides in
narrow glens.   Here all is on the same magnificent scale.   The plains are broad as the summits are high ; the refined atmosphere so intensely
clear the light is like a reflection from snow.   No
such extensive views are in Europe or any
country where the air holds moisture, and sometimes the landscapes seem absolutely limitless.

The Sierras are short, uneven spurs from the
main line.   They have disturbed the overlying
strata in the shape of *mesas* (tables) of solid rock,
which are a distinguishing feature of Rocky
Mountain scenery, giving it a grotesque, fantastic beauty.   The process of erosion has formed in
colossal size copies of the grandest structures of
man's art, and towering columns, temples with
sharp pinnacles, scattered pillars rise abruptly
from the centre of plains desolate and forsaken
as the wilderness of Engedi—strange and solemn
sights.   In the Painted Desert are snow-white
mesas, the *craie blanche* composition of the chalk
cliffs on the south coast of England, which dazzle
the eye, reflecting the sunlight like palaces of
alabaster or of ice.   The stone corridors of Karnak and Philae are the work of pigmies com-

pared with this noble architecture, wrought by slow processes in secret places,

"Made by Nature for herself."

Sometimes the *mesa* shapes into a rose-red wall, with fluted columns that uphold the sky. Again it is a group of gray pyramids, a thousand or twelve hundred feet high ; or an isolated, broken dome, worn smooth by the weather, picturesque in the extreme.

Nothing affords such changes of coloring as the variegated marls, lying in regular bands of red, orange, green, blue, of rainbow hue, striped and interstratified with belts of purple, bluish white, and mottled veins of exceeding richness.

Strangely enough, the traveler occasionally finds himself riding above these singular formations, and looking *down* on the " Painted Rocks."

The sheer sides of a *mesa* of gray limestone, mixed with blue clay and capped with a rim of pillared basalt, are singularly like fabrics of hewn stone. I have seen low walls of even height reaching long distances, precisely like field-walls laid by skillful masons. These, in the neighborhood of stately *façades*, with the fair finish at the top, explain how an explorer, afraid to make near approach, should go away and give accounts of vast cities, with gallant banners on the walls enclosed in heavy outworks.

CHAPTER VII.

TO THE TURQUOIS MINES.

TRAVELING westward, there came to our view
the first Placer Mountain ; behind it the melon-
shaped Sandia, 13,000 feet in air ; and far southward the detached range of the Manzana Mountains. A plateau, the highest of equal area on
the globe, varied with sterile *vegas* and dreary
sierras, which reminded the early adventurers of
their own Old Castile, and so like it one can
imagine it had once been the home of wandering
tribes, which have long since taken up their
spears, struck their tents, and sought new camps
in the furthest East.

The grama grass is low and dry, like wiry
moss, and in the distance takes a wan, ashen hue,
more ghastly than white.   The cactus is the only
shrub in sight.   A gaunt, starved thing, the leper
of the vegetable world, forbidding our approach.

The lively prairie dog (who is no dog, but a
marmot) saluted as we passed. Having early
learned the fifth beatitude, I suppress a description of him. Nor shall we ask how he exists
without water, or seek to know if there is a snake
at the bottom of his den, and a strange bird
dwelling there in peace and safety.

It was June ; but not the leafy month of June.
The only timber—dwarf cedar—which can grow
in this barren soil was cut away years ago ; and
absence of trees includes absence of birds.   The
friendly trill and flutter heard about nests in
shady places are sadly missed.   Now and then a
black wing flapped overhead, and a crow flew
down in the road. Living equally well on seed,
roots, flesh, he thrives alike in all places. And,

except this one sign of life, we may journey in some directions a whole day and see neither man nor beast, bird nor insect. We missed the woodland scents, too; the forest fragrance of mint, thyme, pennyroyal, and the beeches, whose shadows are the curtains of the morning, holding its freshness against the power of the sun till high noon. The eye soon wearies of the leaden hues, and longs for the dark leafage which is the glory of the Mississippi Valley. The blank, scorched plain, lying stark and still in the fierce, white light, brought a sense of loneliness and depression impossible to shake off. There was no rest for the sight or the soul.

But what is this apparition starting from a distant clump of greasewood—a grisly animal, apparently neither brute nor human? Rapidly coming toward us, we recognize a creature of the *genus homo.* "In the desert no one meets a friend," says the Oriental proverb; and there was a general stir for arms among the defenders, and mute shaking of the head, not intended to be seen, when nothing more serviceable than a cactus cane was found in the ambulance.

Every reader knows the border is the chosen field of the dime-novel hero; a safe refuge for cut-throats and desperadoes of the lowest grades, who live by robbery and plunder, and that it is wise for the tourist to put on his pistol with his watch, or, in the expressive slang of the frontier, he may be blighted by lead fever before sundown.

Outlaws from Mexico and Texas haunt the mountain springs and prowl about the cañons of the territories; and, in dread of them, hunters go in parties, and look well to their arms when they enter narrow defiles or a dark, lonesome gulch.

These vagabonds subsist on the fat of the land,

where the country is most sparsely settled, and
are the only buyers who have credit and are not
crowded for payment by the Israelties who con-
trol the dry goods business of the territory. The
ranchero never refuses them milk, eggs, or mutton ; and the dark-eyed Mexican girl serves them
with diligence, under promise of payment when
they come again. Given a voice in the matter,
this is not such a character as we like to encount-
er on an empty plain, even in broad daylight ;
and, as he neared us, the ladies involuntarily drew
close together and scanned him thoroughly.

A powerful fellow, of giant frame and dangerous muscle, and, though unarmed, a foe to dread
in any fight. He wore a shoddy coat, probably
bought on compulsory credit of the Wandering
Jew of Tularosa ; buckskin pants, with fringed
side-stripes of Indian work, tucked inside of heavy
cavalry boots, ponderous brass spurs jingling as
he walked ; a red cotton handkerchief knotted
around his throat. An immense slouched *sombrero*—in the style of the Mexican *caballero*—
drab, with a rosette and cord of red and tinsel,
covered his forehead and shaded eyes that were
restless and penetrating like a blackbird's. A
shaggy, unshorn mane, reddened with dust and
sunburn, fell over the buffalo neck and shoulders ;
matted beard, a very jungle, reached almost to the
cartridge-belt, and, blown aside by the wind,
revealed the outline of revolvers in his breast-
pockets. He carried a Winchester rifle easily as
a gentleman carries his cane ; a leather belt,
buckled around his waist, was filled with cart-
ridges, and bore a murderous-looking knife in its
sheath.

When this shape, of aspect threatening and
sinister, came within friendly hail, we bowed with
much suavity.

" Texas Jack ! *Buenos dias !*" said Juan Fresco,

who well became his name; and serene as summer, he shifted the reins and laid his hand on the
navaja.

The frontiersman touched his hat-brim with his
big forefinger, sunburnt to a vermillion red,
quietly passed on toward the Galisteo, and we
saw him no more. When fairly out of sight of
the outlaw, we felt brave as lions.

" A prospector," said one, mildly.

" Yes, and never without a prospect," said the
antiquarian, bringing out an old witticism.

" A black sheep without any white spots,"
added another. "They always bring up on the
frontier."

And, very hilarious under the sense of relief,
we courageously debated what we would have
done had the robber attempted robbery and
ordered us to hold up our hands. The men of
the pen would have been mere boys in the grip
of this son of the border ; and we cheered ourselves with telling tales of how "just such men "
had gone out without pistols to seek their fortunes, and had never been heard of afterward.

The weakest of weeklies is dull and insipid
compared with the daily experiences recounted
in New Mexico ; and restless souls who hate
trammels, who love danger for its own sake, and
have looked death in the face till they cease to
fear it, find a special charm in the wild " game
flavor " of the frontier.

The borderer who crossed our path was the
sort of soldier who in March, 1862, under the
rebel General Sibley, came up from Texas, forded
the Rio Grande at a point below Fort Craig,
fought the Union troops under Gen. Canby at
Valverde, and again at Cañon Glorietta, fifteen
miles from Santa Fé. In that narrow pass, where
flanking was out of the question, a severe fight
between infantry and artillery occured, in which

the rebels were victorious, and Sibley entered
the capital city without meeting further resis-
tance.

His Texan Rangers, like Texas Jack, were
half savage ; a desperate set, having no higher motive than plunder and adventure. Each one was
mounted on a mustang horse, and carried a rifle,
a tomahawk, a bowie-knife, a pair of Colt's revolvers, and a lasso for catching and throwing the
horses of a flying enemy. Not valuing their
own lives at a pin's fee, they gave no quarter and
expected none.

About eleven o'clock the breeze dropped and
the sun came up with a dry, sultry scorch, like
flame. Our spirits flagged, the stories ended,
laughter and song died away ; nor could we rouse
to the least interest in a herdsman's ranche—a
mud-built hive, swarming with Mexican drones.

"What a weary land !" said Thalia.

"All lands are weary for women," said her
elder sister ; and for a time nothing was heard
but the harsh grinding of wheels in the gravelly
sand.

In such emptiness it was a stirring event to be
overtaken by a Pueblo Indian, who passed us
with a swinging stride, rarely seen off the boards
of a country theatre. This

" Wild warrior of the Turquois Hills "

is tame enough now. Always a tiller of the soil,
he is the original, in fact, the aboriginal granger.
A picturesque figure, in a handsome striped
blanket, with red girth around his waist and a
crown of green leaves, like the classic fillet, shading his forehead. We were fortunate, too, in seeing
a half-grown boy chase jack-rabbits with a curved
stick, hurling it with whirring sound, in the style
of the boomerang, till lately thought exclusively
Australian. The stripling appeared like the

bird-hunter of the Nile, carved in *basso relievo* on the oldest tomb at Thebes. Weapon and attitude of the Egyptian are precisely the same as those of the boyish red hunter of North America.

The more we learn of Eve's family, the surer the proofs of a common parentage. Guided by the same instinct, the tools of various nations, unknown to each other, are the same and the measure of their advancement; showing how little depends on accident, and how closely they are connected with the organism, and, therefore, with the necessities of man. So striking is the parallel between aborigines in every continent that with difficulty do we divest ourselves of the idea that there must have been some direct intercommunication.

A band of tender green, restful to the sight, follows the course of a poor, tired, sluggish stream, sixteen miles from Santa Fé; and a mile or two down its soundless current we described a group of cotton-wood trees—an oasis, indeed—shading a low adobe house. The green leaves in restless flutter and the brook gave the spot an appearance of home not often found in the square of brown mud wall which makes the Mexican domicile.

Along the margin of the nameless stream is a border of alkali, sprinkled in patches like salt over the ground. Of course, we were struck with thirst at sight of running water; but prudently contented ourselves with that in our canteens, rather than risk drinking alkali, which abounds in New Mexico, so strong in some streams that fish cannot live in them. In many places the ranchero digs, to find only a mocking fluid, deadly alike to man, beast, and vegetation. And we comprehend the Arabian saying: "The water provider is always blest, being daily remembered in the prayers of the faithful."

Our road was an easy descent all the way, the Cerillos being nearly 3,000 feet lower than Santa Fé. The founder of the antique city (Don Antonio de Espego) described this country with Spanish exuberance, in a letter to Philip Second: "The earth is filled with gold, silver, and turquoises." And the gallant adventurer threw such glowing light upon it, the king at once sent a thousand men to colonize and possess the province.

As we quietly journeyed along, I pondered on the very moderate basis the heroic Cavaliers, those old Spanish filibusters, had for the brilliant reports sent back to Spain. Leaving the ambulance within a mile of the mines, we toiled wearily along the mountains, well named the Rocky. Their surface is strewn with fragments, broken as if chipped with hammers—a ragged pavement, which bruised our feet, tore our shoes, and wore out our patience; and when at last we reached the first mine, we thought it but a continuation of *Los Cerillos.* The most ancient is much the largest, and to this we directed our steps. Under the dizzy crags which overhang it is a sheltered recess, blackened with smoke and bedded with ashes made by camp-fires of Indians, who still frequent the spot, in search of the precious *chalchuite.* With difficulty we reached this cave, and, leaning over the edge, looked down and saw, not a narrow, black shaft, but half a mountain cut away. Undoubtedly, the mineral lay here which, through countless generations, furnished the Indian kings with their most valued ornaments. The yawning pit is two hundred feet deep and more than three hundred in diameter. Probably the work of aborigines before De Soto's requiem mingled with the voice of the rushing waters of his burial place; when Columbus had seen the New World only in that vision of the night, where the unknown voice whispered: "God will cause thy name to be wonderfully resounded through the earth, and will give thee the keys of the gates of the Ocean, which are closed with strong chains." On the walls of the great excavation Nature has gently, patiently done what she could to smooth the rugged crags, and has thrown out of their fissures a scant growth of shrubs, and trailed a scarlet blossom here and there on a thread-like stem. At the bottom, on stones crumbling with age, stained and weather-worn, are dwarf pines, the growth of the centuries. In this close amphitheatre there is no breeze to stir their tops, and their motionless foliage, with its somber shadows, adds to the ever-present mountain-gloom.

Thousands of tons of rock have been crushed from the solid mass, and thrown up in such a high heap it seems another mountain, overgrown with old pines and dry gray mosses. On a few fragments we noticed the turquois stain—"indication" of valuable mineral. When we consider that all this digging, hewing, and hacking were done by hand-labor alone, without knowledge of domestic animals, iron, or gunpowder, the *débris* carried away in sacks of skins, the enormity of the work is the more impressive. The tradition is that the *chalchuite* mines, through immemorial ages known to the primitive race, were possessed by the Spaniards in the sixteenth century. Indian slaves then worked them, under the lash of the conqueror, until 1680, when, by accident, a portion of the rock from which we had our first view fell, and killed thirty Pueblos. The Spaniards immediately made a requisition on the town of San Marcos for more natives to take their places; when, with a general uprising, they drove the hated oppressor from the country as far south as El Paso del Norte. I give the tale for what it is worth. Mining atmospheres are the favorite haunts of fable, and a spice of truth is enough to flavor whole volumes of stories, charming but delusive. An airy legend hovers about Santa Fé that two stones from " *La Canada de las Minas*"—" Glen of Mines"—are still among the crown jewels of Arragon. But *chalchuites* were valueless after being once submitted to the jewelers of Spain ; and the sparkling story, like many another told by the camp-fire, loses its original brightness when removed to the searching light of the student's lamp.

Careful analysis shows the constituents of the *chalchuites* are nearly the same as those of the Persian turquoises, and their formation the result of infiltration. Sometimes they are washed up by heavy rains; but usually are discovered by digging in the sandstone or are broken out from the body of the rock.

Not being disposed to dig, we retraced our path, and climbed around to the top of the shelving crag above us, and looked over the plateau. Eastwardly it stretches toward Santa Fé, beyond which the stony mountains lift their high heads. On the southwest it opens toward the Rio Grande in a measureless vista, where earth and sky appear to meet. A plain, oppressive in its vastness, lying in the midst of a stone wilderness, its sameness relieved by the solitary peaks, Sandia and Albuquerque. In every direction stand mountains grim and fixed as walls of adamant, apparently immovable as the throne of God. Low in the horizon one feathery cloud hung moveless in a sapphire sky. The world seemed stricken dead. No verdure to cool the parched grass ; no water, " the eye of the earth " glancing up toward heaven ; no waving branches, beckoning like friendly hands to cool shade and shelter : no wagon-road or foot-path to mark the

track of men; not a sound to break a stillness
which is not the hush of profound peace, but the
everlasting silence of death.

Save the one shining spot of gauzy vapor, the
blue above was without a blur. The sun was at
meridian, and in its hard glitter the scorched
summits looked like they were at white heat.
The sea is lonely; but it has shifting color,
sound, and motion. The silence of the land is
deeper. If there had been the note of a bird,
the hum of bees, even a grasshopper's chirp, it
had been a relief; but in the far-reaching desolation I alone drew breath. All else was still as
the breast when the spirit has fled.

The influence was benumbing to the senses,
and as I stood in infinite solitude, a stone among
stones, there came over me the feeling that this
melancholy waste is the skeleton of our Mother
Earth; that the dust of which all flesh is made
has been blown away, scattered to the four winds
of heaven, leaving these gray old bones forlorn
and unburied through the long, slow centuries,
till the coming of the Great Day for which all
other days were made.

The voices below were too remote for my
hearing, and (how absurd it now appears) it was
"company" to spy a speckled chameleon, sun-
ning himself on a rock; and, as he quickly slipped
between its cracks and vanished, I was left the
more alone. Listening to silence, as it were,
there swept across my memory the words of the
hymn familiar in childhood as the dear face which
bent above my cradle :

> "O'er all these wide-extended plains
> Shines one eternal day."

If the singer had ever faced the blinding glare
of high noon on the wide-extended plains of the
Rocky Mountains, he would have tuned his harp
anew, and hymned the rivers of waters in a dry

place, the shadow of a great rock in a weary
land.

I soon sought that refuge from the desert
scorch, and, snatching at shrubs to keep from slipping, scrambled down the mountain by a dizzy,
winding way, the loosened stones rolling after me
to the bottom of the mine. How pleasant the
smoke of the camp-fire ! Its leaping flame and
crackle were a welcome back to life again. And
never till then did I know how much sweeter than
harp or horn the sound of human voices can be.

Long before I joined my companions I had
heard shouts of exultation, and, wondering what
prospector had " struck it," I learned that a piece
of *chalchuite* had been brought out of the lining
of a seam where it had lain under the roots of a
stunted shrub, in appearance not unlike spice-
wood. It was near an inch in length, by half an
inch in thickness ; a large and lovely specimen,
the color sea-green, delicately shaded into blue—
the latter the result of decomposition, so the
scientist said.

The owner of this " regular bonanza " was our
driver. He made no effort to conceal his delight ;
and with reason, for it was a rare piece of mineral, and he a lucky miner to obtain it with so
little trouble, or even to get it at all. Such a
stone the gentle and gracious Montezuma might
have worn in his signet-ring or set in the clasp
of his green mantle of feather-work. Such a gift
would have made still brighter the bright eyes of
his daughter, the laughing Princess Nenetzin, the
spoiled darling, whose death was the crowning
horror of the *Noche Triste*.

I had sniffed coffee from afar, and now we
were ready to pass the cup that not inebriates,
sung by the temperate Cowper. Our cloth was
laid on a table-rock, the feast was spread, we ate,
drank, and were merry. The dumb spell of the

desert snapt, only the peace of the perpetual hills
remained. Resting in the fragrant shade of the
pines, we talked of Montezuma, the saddest,
proudest chief of Indian history, whose name is
still a majestic memory among the degraded,
broken-hearted Pueblos.

Beautiful beliefs they cherish regarding him—
the peculiar friend of the red race, shadowy above
all things, yet real above all things, who dwelt
among them as a god, yet a familiar friend. He
was the brother and equal of the Unseen One
whose name it is death to utter ; and the chiefs
still watch for him at sunrise beside the sacred
fire in the *estufa*, claiming his promise to come
again from his throne in the sun, and bring back
the faded glories of his fallen people. All their
traditions point to the second advent of their
beloved prophet, priest, and king, who disappeared from the earth when it was young, and
who will not fail, in the fullness of time, to redeem
the promise made to his red children.

The ground was strewn with fragments of
broken pottery, the unfailing sign of the ancient
Pueblo, the rightful owner of this soil. They
were colored maroon red, light clay, and dark
brown, with markings of black. At sight of them
the antiquarian fell to wandering among tombs,
discoursing on fallen kingdoms, extinct races,
wrecks of empire, and columns voiceless as the
gray stones of Pæstum. He was learned and
eloquent; but none of these things move me.
Our little scraps were but the elder and better
counterparts of the poor potteries the Pueblos
make at this day ; and merely prove, what I
believe has never been disputed, that North
America has been inhabited from a remote period.
I know there are enthusiasts who insist there was
a prehistoric race, displaced by what we call
aborigines, which had a civilization comparing

favorably with those of the Old World. What
that civilization was, let the stone hatchet, and the
dingy pottery with its graceless tracings testify,
when laid beside relics from Eturia the Beautiful.
The Western fragments are in beggarly contrast
with the exquisite vases and jewel-work which
are the model and despair of the modern artist.

Several inferior bits of *chalchuite* were dug out
of the ancient wastage ; but the color was faint,
as if they had not lain long enough for a thorough
dyeing. We added to our collection an arrow-
head of jasper and one of obsidian, nicely flaked
and pointed ; and gave a dollar for the largest
Indian hatchet I have ever seen, brought up by
the enterprising Juan Fresco from an abandoned
silver mine hard by. It was roughened and
time-worn, and had lain there how long—ah !
Quien sabe?

It may interest some believer in the perishing
theory of " Ages" to know the Stone Age is not
ended in New Mexico. Within the present generation, it is said, remote tribes have used as a
weapon, offensive   and   defensive, the   stone
hatchet, tied by a thong of deerskin to a wooden
handle. As Sir John Herschel said of something
else, this is one of those things which, according
to received theories, ought not to happen.

We lingered under the solemn pines, groping
with shadows, visible and unseen, loth to leave.
The hoary hills, so lone and untrodden, began to
be possessed of strange enchantment. The place
was ours by right of discovery. We were a band
of explorers, the first to break a silence lasting
since the morning stars sang at creation's dawn.
Perhaps the witchery was a variation of the preva-
lent miner's fever, for the day was waning when
we reluctantly gave over our search for precious
mineral.

In the shining of the loveliest afterglow this side

of Heaven, we sought the wagon, standing in the level expanse, like a ship at anchor. A freshening breeze blew cheerily, and, turning back as we drove away, we watched the swift-coming Night gather the mountains tenderly, one by one, into her bosom, and touch their scarred, stern faces with ineffable beauty.

CHAPTER VIII.

TO THE TURQUOIS MINES,
(Continued.)

NORTH of the Placer Ridges and divided from them by the intervening valley of the Galisteo, are bold bluffs of trap, the cut edges of a plateau forming a *mesa*, from which rise the volcanic cones of Los Cerillos. From these hills rushed the fiery lava-flow widespread over the country, giving it a worn-out look, desert-like and depressing to the last degree. Geologists assert that, at a very recent period in the world's changes, fire, ice, and water have, with tremendous subterranean forces, left here marks of a storm more terrible than our conceptions of the Deluge. The hot springs, now slowly dying out, are the last of the series of events once performed on a scale which almost baffles human conception. The faint departing remnants of once terrific forces point to something which must be described by a broader word than earthquake—a fiery convulsion, that altered the whole face of the country, if we may judge by the marks the storm has left.

In order to avoid a rocky unheaval, thrown out by the expiring energies of the volcanic epoch, not yet closed, we started back to Santa Fé by a circuitous route, and soon came on signs of a camp—heaps of white ashes, circled by burnt and blackened ends of piñon chips. The *vega* is sere and parched as the plains of Arabia, and in dreamy mood we could easily fancy the last tent of the Moslem had just been struck, the heavy standard folded by slim figures in sweep-ing burnous; and we glanced along the horizon for a gleam of slender spears, and the long cara-van, made spectral by distance, slowly vanishing into the mystic silence of the desert.

Involuntarily we looked for valuables dropped by Haroun and Mohammed, as they untethered the camels and packed the hampers; scattered spices; a jeweled cup of gold, with the lump of ambergris at the bottom; a white turban; a shawl of price.

No such thing.

There lay on the ground, instead, a battered sardine-box, a sliver of wagon-tongue, the broken end of a saw (pocketed by Juan Fresco), four greasy cards (also appropriated by Cool John), two used-up paper collars, and an empty black bottle. Strong testimonials to the high superior-ity of our arts, and the refinements of our boasted civilization.

A little way from the road, fastened to a scrubby piñon tree, was a fluttering white signal; and, thinking it might be a sign of distress, we stopped the willing mules, and all got out to see what was the matter. With the help of a match, we made out a rudely penciled hand on canvas of flour-bag, pointing in the direction of Los Cerillos, and below it read the bold legend,—

"SWEET HOME SALOON."

Looking ahead, we hailed Sweet Home itself. A roofless pen of pine boughs, fencing in narrow shelves of black bottles, and a camp-stool—a dark puzzle made of mule-bones and cowhide, pronounced a relic of the palæozoic age by the geologist. The establishment was guarded by a wolfish dog, which the bravest of us did not care to examine; so we hurried back to the ambulance, regardless of prickly pear, and in the valley's edge passed the white tents of the vanguard of civilization—an army of laborers, working day and night on the railroad track. They will not march till they have broken the fascinating spell, the poetic glamor which the romantic Espego threw over Nueva Espagna three hundred years ago, and which has rested on it like an alluring mystery ever since. If you would dream dreams and see visions, now is the time to come. If you would taste the wild charm, hasten to catch it before the wear of every-day travel tramples out the primitive customs. It is still to a good degree a country apart from the rest of the United States; mountain-locked and little known, severed, as it has been, from the great highways of commerce. Its history is a romance and a tragedy, and, as in every country imperfectly explored, it holds more or less of the mysterious. Here are extensive ruins; unparalleled natural phenomena; mountains, "flaunting their crowns of snow everlastingly in the face of the sun," that bear in their bosom undeveloped mines, dazzling the imagination; cañons with perpendicular sides a mile in height; savages merciless and bloodthirsty, who in undying hate still dispute the progress of foreign civilization. But the civilizer is coming; is here. The waste lands of the wandering tribes will be divided and sold by the acre, instead of the league. The dozing Mexican will be jostled on the elbow, and will wake from his long trance to find himself in the way.

A procession of phantoms is flying along "*El Camino del ferro carril*"; whispering voices are drowned in the hiss of steam; and the midnight hush of the black cañon is stirred by the whirr of beautiful wings, unheard save by ears attuned to finest harmonies. By the time this letter reaches the eyes so dear to the writer, there will be no haunted solitudes along Los Cerillos. The pick and shovels of Mike Brady and the O'Flannegans will have put to flight the finer fancies of musing antiquary and dreaming pilgrim. You know certain boundaries mark the limit of every created thing, be it real or imaginary.

Fairies never trip it on pavements. They are too delicate for such footing. Ghosts haunt only houses where men have lived and died ; and the epic of history cannot abide the screech of the locomotive nor its penetrating headlight. It requires broken, disconnected threads, doubtful testimony, dim lights—above all, the misty lines of distance   The locomotive brings the ends of the earth together, and dashes into nothingness delicate tissues woven in darkness, like certain delicate laces, whose threads break in the weaving by day.

And here is something brought by the locomotive.

In the luminous haze of the paling twilight appeared a peddler, lying beside his pack, sheltered by a rock, under which he had crept, which looked as though it might fall any moment and crush him to atoms. On nearer view, we discovered, instead of peddler and pack, the pioneer organ grinder, the first to set foot in New Mexico. His shoes were ragged and travel-worn. He wore a cast-off uniform of army blue, and a red handkerchief knotted round his throat. Sun-scorched gray hair straggled round the edge of his black skull-cap, and mingled with the dust of the ground. Overcome by heat and fatigue, he was dead asleep, one hand resting on the rusty green

curtain which draped the organ, the other holding the neck of a little brown dog, about the size
of a pinch of snuff, curled up in his bosom. In
the emptiness of the desert every peaceful thing
is welcome. We stopped, as a matter of course.

" A bad place for a tramp, unless he can eat
rock and drink mirage," said our polyglott antiquary, as he jumped from the ambulance. He
shook the sleeper gently, and addressed him in
Italian. The man slowly rose to his feet. " Ah !
excellenza," said he, in the spoken music of
Southern Italy, " your voice is like the sound of
fountains in the ear of the thirsty. Tell me, is
there no water in this land ? "

" None within six miles ; but we have a can-
teen left, which you may have," and the kindly
antiquary produced the dirty frontier flask, sewed
up in flannel, to keep its contents cool—which it
never does.

The musician unscrewed the lid, and took a
long draught.

" It is better than wine," he said, " for Victor
can drink it too," and he poured the precious
liquid in a tin cup. The little brute, who was pretty
much all tail, gave a friendly bark, and wagged
himself almost to pieces as he slaked his thirst.

" Where are you going ? " we asked.

" To Albuquerque, to Bernalillo, to Las Lunas "
—and he named the various towns and stations
on the route to Old Mexico.

" The country is overrun by Apaches—
Indians who will torture you and then kill you."

" The banditti will not hurt," said the old man,
simply, " when I give them this."

He lifted the box to its one leg, raised the curtain, turned the crank ; a warning click, and lo !
" Hear me, Norma." How strangely the familiar
air sounded across that plain, so wide, so dim, so
still ! Through a floating mist, not of the earth

7

or of the sky, I saw, not the wanderer and his
wretched instrument, but a radiant vision of glittering lights, the brilliant crowd in the horseshoe
curve, hanging breathless on the voice of the
divine singer, now leading the starry choir of
Heaven.

Surely, there is not another place in the world
where a party of sensible people would fool away
an hour on an organ-grinder. Every well-regu-
lated mind (and I address no other) will perceive
the absurdity. But it was so long since we had
heard one, he was such a delightful reminder of
bright days and brighter nights, that over and
over again we made the drowsy player drone his
dull tunes. They brought us serene and golden
Italy, the racing shadows and glancing sumbeams
of the far Campania; and, best of all, the love-
songs of home—that sweet spot, toward which I
look as the first woman, exiled forever, must
have looked toward the barred gates of lost
Paradise.

When the wheezy machine rested, we gave the
player a small (very small) fortune in loose
change and the remnants of our lunch. He had
only a cracker and two onions in his wallet, and
the wayfarer would have knelt for gratitude, had
we allowed it, while he rained blessings on our
heads, in the name of the Queen of Heaven, the
saints, and all the angels.

"Where do you camp?" asked the antiquary,
when the benediction slacked.

"Wherever the night finds me. I have a
blanket, Victor is company, and the sky is my
tent."

There was infinite pathos in the words and his
glance up to the arch overhead. The flash of
hero's armor in the changeful curtains of the
glorious tent warned us to go on ; but we were
slow to leave the stranger, and would have taken

him with us, but the ambulance was already
over-loaded.

He stood bareheaded long as we were in sight,
lazily grinding " The Last Rose of Summer," as
though he was falling asleep. Faint and clear
the music drifted after us, by distance mellowed
into sweetness. Miles away, now lost in the
valley, now low on the hills, floated

" Tufts of tune like thistle-down,"

wafted along by the soft night-breeze. When
the last wandering note died away we took up
the refrain " Oh ! who would inhabit this cold
world alone ? " and, looking at the sentinel stars,
thought pityingly of the exile, alone in his tent
—a mighty pavilion of royal purple, which deep-
ening shadows widened into a solitude vast as
eternity, mysterious as death.

The singing was very soft, for Thalia was crying, as we discovered by tiny sniffs muffled
behind her hankerchief, and you know how con-
tagious home-sickness is, and the sweeping gloom
was oppressive even with the best company.
The cheerful day, with all its trailing splendors,
was dead ; the fine gold of sunset became dross.
A pale, white shining in the east announced the
rising moon, and in its mystic glow the mountains put on spectral shapes and journeyed with
us. A solemn stillness filled the night and rested
on the party which had set out so gayly in the
morning. One by one the voices hushed, and
silence followed, so intense it was almost painful.

We will anticipate, as our friends the novelists
say, and follow the march of the minstrel—one
of the last of the gentle race of troubadours.
We heard of his safe arrival at Albuquerque and
at Bernalillo. Two days' journey southward, the
mail-boy reported having seen him, moving in a
dazed, bewildered way, mourning for the little

doggie, which was missing. "There are no sausage factories here," said our informant, with a smile of ghastly significance. "But a big Mexican dog could swallow that pup like a pill."

A lively letter from a friend in Silver City recorded his passage through the lower country. The Pueblo Indians gave him of their poor substance, and made him at home in their mud hovels, regarding him as a great medicine-man, with a magic box. In their childish curiosity, they wanted to chop open the cage and see the singing-birds inside. At a little village, whose name I do not now recall, the whole population flocked round the itinerant. He was a choice item for the local editor of the *Pharos of the Occident*, a miner living on imagination, who fancied himself a brilliant writer and financier, and in a lurid editorial he hailed the musician as the forerunner of Thomas and Mapleson, and hinted it was high time to form a stock company for the purpose of building an adobe opera-house. Everywhere the player was well received, till he reached Socorro. On the edge of the Jornado, from immemorial ages overrun by the Apache, the Western Bedouin, every trace of him was lost.

The tameless warriors of Victorio's band are deaf to "Hear me, Norma," and I greatly fear the gray scalp of the minstrel is a trophy in the belt of the red chief, and that his poor old bones lie unburied in the treeless, waterless, wind-swept desert, truly named, by the first Spaniard who dared its perils, *Jornada del Muerto*—Journey of Death.

CHAPTER IX.

At evening the gentle shepherd of New Mexico leads his flock from high pastures, where the precipitation of moisture is greatest and, therefore, grass is freshest, to the fold, or corral, in the valley. It is precisely the pattern of fold abounding in Palestine and still to be seen on the outskirts of Alexandria—an enclosure made by crooked stakes driven in the ground, poorly held together by strips of rawhide. No two are of the same length. All were twisted and gnarled in the growing, and lean out of the perpendicular. A shabby fence, uglier than everything except a mud fence, which the reader knows is the superlative ugliness. By the light of the moon we noted the fashion of the shepherd's Cain-and-Abel suit of goatskin; and, instead of the classic crook, wreathed with garlands gathered in flowery meadows, the Rocky Mountain Endymion guarded his flock with a shotgun and bowie-knife, less fearful of the wolf than of his own thieving countrymen.

We observe another Asian custom here, that of sleeping on the roofs in summer. The heavenly nights invite one out, and the flat housetop is a much pleasanter place to make one's bed than the cellar-like interior, with its earthly scents. The sluggard Mexican, who has killed the long hours of the common enemy by dozing in the sun, rouses toward sunset and spreads out the *colchon*, or wool mattress, if they are very poor, or a bed of skins. The stairway is a rickety ladder, leaning against the outer wall of the mud house, and the rapidity and ease with which the

natives go up and down is surprising. I have
seen women carry jars of water on their head,
not spilling a drop, as they ascend the ladder,
touching it only with their feet. The old people—
mummies of the time of Cheops—go to bed at
sunset; a little later the children and chickens
hop up the loose rounds; then the lord of the
estate, and his dusky spouse, with her cat; and
lastly the ratty dogs, moving nimbly, as the
trained ones of the circus. Haul up the ladder,
and the castle is secure. There is no fear of
rain. There is no dew, no fog or mist, to blur
the clear shining of the stars above. The low
wind is the very breath of heaven; the bright
night is filled with sleep.

So slept the Saviour of the world on the
housetop of Lazarus, at Bethany, whither he
had walked in the cool of the day. Looking
from that lowly bed toward the many mansions
of his Father's house, well might the homeless
guest utter the pathetic cry: " The foxes have
holes and the birds of the air have nests; but
the Son of Man hath not where to lay his head."

Near the City of the Pueblos, within sight of
the graceful spire of the Sisters' Chapel, was a
coyote tearing a stray lamb to pieces. We had
met the ninety-and-nine an hour before, returning to the fold from the river. The wild, tameless creature there was in perfect keeping with
the continued newness of a country where white
men have lived nearly three centuries. He
started, looked fearlessly out of the sage-bush,
and the clear moonlight outlined the true wolf's
head, with its fox-like muzzle and sharp, forward-
pointed ears. He glared at us a moment, and
then quietly and leisurely stalked away, amid a
general lament that we had neither gun nor pistol
at hand. The beast was of the " Æsop's Fable "
breed—a large, handsome fellow, whose pictorial
pelt would have made an elegant foot-rug.

Let me not close without telling what became
of the "regular bonanza." The day after our
return to Santa Fé, the many-named Mexican
called, bringing his fine *chalchuite*. He explained,
with impressive gesture and rhetorical flourish, he
was too poor to own so rich a jewel, fit for the
king's son, and would sell it, if *la Senora* would
pay him—naming the price. At first I was
appalled at the magnitude of the sum ; but the
stone of inimitable hue, lying in the lean, brown
hand, had a sort of magnetism. The familiar
tint was charming, matching as it did a tiny ring
long worn for remembrance, and with much
cracked Spanish and broken English, a bargain
was made, and we parted, with many a cordial
adios. No, not even in the close confidence of
print will I tell you, beloved, the price of the
princely jewel. The secret will go with me to
the grave. Enough that it was exhaustive. I
am blushing over it yet.

The following week I heard a low whisper that
Juan Fresco did not find the turquois at *Los
Cerillos ;* but got it in a trade with a wild savage,
ignorant of its worth. A Navajo, allowed to
leave the Reservation, under protection of a pass,
and pay a stealthy visit to his own hunting-
grounds, had let it go for four yards of red flannel. Cool John had slyly arranged the whole
affair, and whisked the stone out of his sleeve in
the very nick of time. Fortune turned his head,
as she has many a stronger one. He retired from
the box, and set up a saloon, the "San Francisco,"
under a bower of cedar boughs, in the near
mining camp. Being of a convivial turn, in
spite of mournful eyes and voice, at last accounts,
Juan Fresco was his own best customer at the
bar.

However, I had my costly prize, and in the
seclusion of my own room gloated over it, and fear-

ful of burglars, hid it at night under the edge of the
carpet behind the bureau. After much delibera-
tion regarding the shape in which it would best
appear, I sent the *chalchuite* to the leading jewel-
er of New York. Too precious for the mail, it
went express, and I carefully held a receipt
for its full value. In good time the little lavender-
box returned by mail. I untied the string with
nervous haste and lo! my pattern locket
lapped in red cotton, and the "regular bonanza."

A brief note explained Messrs. B. & B's " regret
to state the sample of turquois will not endure
polish or cutting. The color is a mere surface
stain on gneiss, and easily scales off, exposing
the brown stone, as you may readily discover by
trying it with your scissors-point. We have received several such specimens from New Mexico.
They have no commercial value. This has none
whatever, except to its owner."

Then I felt like the tender poet who sends off
a song that is his heart's delight, and receives
next week a very precious letter, in familiar
handwriting, accompanied by a printed circular,
bearing the awful words, " Declined, with thanks."

Yesterday I examined a collection of relics—
not exquisitely beautiful, but exquisitely old
—from various points along the valleys of the
San Pedro, the Gila, and the Rio Grande. They
were mainly broken potteries, a few sacred
whispering-stones from old *estufas*, rude arms of
iztli, and the familiar flint arrows, such as have
been discovered in every portion of the globe
where there are graves of men. Among many
trinkets offered, I chose a little looking-glass of
iztli, and an amulet of *chalchuite* from the ruins
of a prehistoric city near El Paso. It was close
to the Texas line, and within the limit of the
mound-builders' region. I selected these trifles

because they were feminine belongings, and brought me nearer than the pipes and hatchets could bring me to my dead and gone sisters. The mirror, about half the size of your hand, is made of *iztli*, or obsidian, an exceedingly hard, vitreous substance, plentiful in volcanic countries, of smoky tint, and capable of high polish. The art of working this intractable material is prac tically lost in our times, but when wrought by the Indigene was useful as iron or tempered steel.*

The amulet and twenty beads of *chalchuite* were hidden in a black glazed jar, of the shape made by natives to-day, buried in a cave many feet below the surface of the ground. It was accidentally opened, in 1878, by a party of miners digging for silver. Probably a treasure-house, abandoned at the last moment, when the besieged inhabitants fled before a victorious army. Stone hammers were found near the cave, arrow-heads, hatchets, serrated swords of *iztli*, like the Aztecan, and half a human skull, evidently broken by a blow of the hatchet or tomahawk.

The amulet is perhaps half an inch long, one-eighth of an inch thick—an irregular square, rudely carved and smoothed, probably by rub- bing with another stone. The veining on one side gives the semblance of a star. A hard tool and patient hand must have been required to drill a hole through this stubborn stone. The string which threaded it has gone to dust ; the hand which carved it and the race of which it is a faint trace are vanished into the voiceless past. Long lines of prostrate walls, miles of *acequias*, or irrigating ditches, broken potteries, profusely scattered, indicate a dense population once held the valley near El Paso, and lived in cities con-

* It is said by Pliny to have been discovered first in Ethiopia, by a man named Obsidius. Hence the name. Gems and whole statues were made of it. He also speaks of four elephants of obsidian dedicated by Augustus in the Temple of Concord.

taining twenty thousand or thirty thousand souls.
There is no reason to believe the modern inhabitants of this country belong to a proud line,
shorn of its ancient splendors. They have no
sort of history, and among a people without
written language, poetry, or music, tradition soon
becomes confused. All their remains and three
hundred years of continuous history show they
have steadily declined in power and numbers;
but they are and have always been miserably
poor. Their fabrics, arms, architecture are of the
coarsest, most primitive description.

The vessels of silver and of gold described by
early explorers to a waiting and expectant world
have not been found in this or any other spot in
New Mexico. They existed only in the fevered
fancies of adventurers, blinded by their own imaginings, drunk with their own conceits. If
metals we count valuable were concealed in the
ancient treasure-house, they are lost in the deep
grave with the dead centuries. Only these trifling
memorials have escaped the common doom.

My amulet is a sorry love-token; yet, for the
sake of the soft meaning it once bore, I touch
the trinket lightly. Rude in outline, utterly lacking in grace and luster, it represents a Western
idyl.

Young were the lovers, I know (for love is
ever young), and to eyes beloved each was beautiful and true. Perhaps she stood like Ruth
among the corn, as the warm blood flushed his
face, when he bound it with his love as a crown
unto her, fastening it with vows, and promises,
and never-ending kisses. Or did he set it as a
seal upon her arm, making its pulses beat fast to
a new music, under the secret magic of its circle?
Or was it hung on her neck, above the heart
which fluttered like a caught bird at its touch, in
the hour which comes but once in a lifetime?

Ah, well you know, gentle reader, how she cherished the keepsake, and pondered it over when his face was not there, little dreaming how one of a race unheard of should, centuries afterward, dream over it too, and call back her spirit from out the unrecorded past, her gracious presence and tender words.

All, all gone now. My young mound-builders—if mound-builders they were—sleep with the primeval giants. And, while a thousand wonderments hover about the poor keepsake, this only we do know: that they walked blindly along the path we call life ; slowly, and with many a failure, worked out their destiny. They loved, sinned and suffered, died, and were forgotten. The surface of the country is altered since that old love-making. Strong cities are leveled with the plains, tribes are scattered, languages lost, whole races are extinct; but humanity remains the same—the one thing that will outlast the world. These dead-and-gone tribes were not foreign to us. They were of our own blood, our elder brethren; and as their names and deeds are blotted out, leaving not a memory, so we are moving forward in the resistless march, holding in our hands messages appealing to futurity—messages addressed to darkness, dropped into oblivion.

The relics from the Rio Grande were buried down deep. Perhaps my young lovers whispered the sweet words which made Eden Paradise, before the witching eyes of Marie Stuart turned the hearts of men ; before Cleopatra shone ; before Lucretia spun. The *chalchuite* might lie in this rare, dry air till the crack of doom and suffer no change, as our old earth swings through the constellations, year by year. Possibly, its wearer was contemporary with the man of Natchez, whose bones were exhumed not long ago, under the Mississippi bluffs, in strata said to prove him not less than one hundred thousand years old.

If the story were told, we might not care to
know what manner of man the bygone mound-
builder was. His history must have been one of
wars, and the struggles of the chiefs were trivial
and petty to that of mighty Hector and Agamemnon, if we accept the testimony of the remains which still exist. Let us believe we lost
no grand epic in the Iliad of the lost race.

The great historian wisely says: " The annals
of mankind have never been written, can never
be written, nor would it be within the limits of
human capacity to read them, if they were written. We have a leaf or two torn from the great
book of human fate, as it flutters in the storm-
winds ever sweeping across the earth ; but we
have no other light to guide us across the track
which all must tread, save the long glimmering
of yesterdays, which grows so swiftly fainter and
fainter, as the present fades off into the past."

CHAPTER X.

AMONG THE ARCHIVES.—THINGS NEW AND OLD.

NORTH of El Palacio, is a waste spot of
earth, covering perhaps half an acre. It contains
neither grass, weeds, nor moss, not even a straggling sage-bush or forlorn cactus ; nothing but
bare desert sand and a solitary cotton-wood tree,
whose luxuriant leafage gives no sign of its
struggle for life in a region waterless ten months
of the year. High adobe walls bound the sterile
enclosure on two sides ; the third is occupied by
government buildings ; and the fourth is partly
wall and partly abandoned offices, always locked
and unused since the brave days when the Spaniards lorded it like princes in " The Palace."

Ever a lover of lonesome places, I had often wistfully eyed these mysterious apartments ; and one day, being sadly in want of entertainment, hunted up the keys and sallied across the back yard, determined to explore the secret places. The first door I tried to open was made of heavy double plank, studded with broad-headed nails. I fitted a key into the rough, old-fashioned lock, and, pushing with all my strength, it slowly swung on rusty hinges, into a room, perhaps seventeen by twenty feet in size, barely high enough for a man to stand upright in. As I stepped on the loose pine boards of the floor, a swarm of mice scampered to their burrows in the walls, and the deathlike smell of mildew and decay smote the afflicted sense. Well for the chronicles is it there are no rats in the territory. Involuntarily I paused at the entrance, to let the ghosts fly out ; and several minutes passed before my eyes, accustomed to the darkness of this treasure-house, could see the shame of its neglect.

I had entered the historic room of New Mex ico ! Tumbled into barrels and boxes, tossed on the floor in moist piles, lay the written records of events stretching over a period of more than three hundred years, the archives of a Province known as Nueva Espagña, large as France. In an atmosphere less dry than this they would have rotted ages ago. Nothing but the extreme purity of the air saved them from destruction.

It was mid-winter, and melted snow slowly trickled through the primitive roofing of mud and gravel. The sun shone brightly, and, though days had passed since the last white spot disappeared from the surface of the earth, still a hideous ooze filtered through the ashes and clay overhead, and dripped in inky streams down the pine rafters and walls. I am told the house was anciently used as a stable. If the first Spanish commandants and governor-generals kept their horses in this windowless cave, sorry am I for the gallant steeds they professed to love next to their knightly honor and the ladies.

The names of some of the *Conquestadores* have faded from history, and others live only in tradition. Nearly all the earlier important records have been destroyed. They accumulated rapidly in immense masses, and the heavy lumber was shifted from place to place by officials, to make room for things more valuable. Careless hands and the slow wear of time were not as effectual in blotting them out as a certain chief executive —a lineal descendant of Genseric, appointed by President of the United States—who made his administration memorable by building a bonfire of parchments and papers, filled with priceless material, never to be replaced. He also sold a quantity as waste paper. By happy accident, a portion of this merchandise was afterward recovered, though one might think it as well employed in wrapping tea and sugar as going to decay in this neglected den. We grow indignant over the spirit which could not spare one reader of the picture-writing of the Aztecs or the *quippus* of Peru. What shall we say of the man in authority who, in the best age of culture and research, abuses a trust like this, who deliberately fired whole wagon-loads of manuscripts of the deepest interest to the archæologist, the historian, and student.

He had not even the excuse of the first Archbishop of Mexico, who burnt a mountain of manuscripts in the market-place, stigmatizing them as magic scrolls ; and was more guilty than Cardinal Ximines, who in the trial by fire alone could exercise the sorcery concealed in the Arabic manuscripts of Granada.

The delusions of fifteen hundred years are not easily put to flight, and there might be a drop of charity for the bigotry and intolerance of the Spaniard; but the destroyer of history in New Mexico has no defense. I suppress his name. An archæologist from New England is now busy among a heap of the sold documents, piled away in the back room of an old shop by a citizen of Santa Fé, who forsaw that they might one day be of interest, possibly of value.

It was my pleasant work to help in overhauling the state papers, and the quiet hours of careful work were well rewarded. All sorts of papers were tossed together in the cavernous hole. I dug out quantities of printed matter of recent date, mixed with the old and weather-stained official documents, letters, copies of reports and dispatches, marking political changes from 1580, when Santa Fé was founded by Don Antonio de Espego, to the year 1879. The province at first was ruled by military governors, appointed by the viceroys of Mexico, and communication with them and with Spain was so rare they reigned as despots, in haughty pride of place, and bitterly abused their power to kill, enslave, plunder, and subdue the heathen claimed for an inheritance.

The first MS. opened bore the date 1620. It was illuminated with heavy seals and signed with strange, puzzling *rubricas;* but the signature was completely effaced. It was part of a frozen chunk, tied with hempen cord, and peeled off a block wet through and through. The excellence of the parchment-like paper kept it from dissolving into a lump of sticky pulp.

Some papers were soaked so it was necessary to spread them on boards, to be dried in the sun, before being deposited in a place of safety. Rich treasure for the mining of the future historian. The eternal west wind fluttered mockingly among

.crumpled leaves torn from the book of human fate, and a sudden gust whirled a yellow scrap high up in the branches of the cotton-wood tree. With the help of a Mexican boy, I rescued from ruin what proved a portion of the journal of Otervin, military commandant of Nueva Espagña, who undertook to reduce the Pueblos to subjection in 1681, and found them too many for him.

Mixed with high heaps of worthless trash were worn and water-stained fragments, precious as the last leaves of the Sybil. These, pieced together, were smoothed with care and laid by for after reference. Poor, perishing records of ambitions baffled and hopes unfulfilled; and, dreaming over the names of men who sought immortality on earth and now sleep forgotten, I deeply felt their teaching—the law that any lasting condition is impossible in the hurrying march we call life, where nothing is constant but change, nothing certain but death.

Through the lazy Mexican afternoons I groped along the musty annals with steady purpose, and in the shadowy history wandered back two centuries. Among the MSS. I lived in the days when William of Orange fought the grand battle which decided the fate of the Stuarts and established English dominion over the seas; when the sun of Poland was sinking in endless night with the dying Sobieski, our patriot hero of early romance, whose name, consecrated by poetry and heroism, dwells in memory with Emmet and Kossuth; when Madame de Maintenon, at the court of the king, who was worshipped as a demi-god, was writing long letters of the fatigues of court, and how she worried from morning till midnight, trying to reconcile the irreconcilable, and amuse the old tyrant, who was past being amused. Spain had been shaken by desperate wars, and out of armies nursed in victories came a host of adventurers to the New World, where glory and fortune were reported as waiting for every newcomer. They were not colonists, emigrants, as with us, who had everything to gain and nothing to lose; but men of the sword, used to command, who loved no music so well as trumpet and drum, the rattle and clang of arms. Reckless gamblers as Spaniards have been in all ages everywhere, they were ready to stake vast possessions on a venture in mines reported richer than ancient Ophir, and to risk assured fame for possible conquest, among nations whose walled cities were described as equal to the best strong- holds of Islam. The rich mediæval glow en- veloping some of the reports charms the literary forager, not overfond of statistics, who loves no figures so well as figures of speech. Men in their summer prime organized roving expeditions in quest of fortune, gallant freebooters, made ferocious by greed of gold, who started gayly, as to a regatta, for the unexplored province of Nueva Espagña.

They found the Promised Land one of which the greater part must forever remain an uninhab- itable magnificence. Yet everything reminded them of old Spain, especially of the Castiles. The chain of snowy peaks, accessible only to the untamable Apache, projected against the speck- less blue the blade of white teeth which suggested the name of Sierra Nevada. The dry, scorched table-lands, league after league, stretching away under the blazing sun a shadeless desert, were like the *mesas* in the dreariest portions of the kingdom of Philip—and the mud hovels of adobe, with open apertures for windows, were a perpet- ual reminder of the homeless habitations of the Castilian peasantry.

The few rich valleys (*pasturas*) capable of cul- tivation by irrigation were not unlike the *vegas*

8

of the East, and little streams of melted snow-water, filtered down from the "iced mountain-top," cold as snow, clear as glass, still bear the lovely names of the rills sparkling along the Alpujarras.

The old hidalgoes looked for better things than half-naked savages, mud huts, and stunted corn-fields. Sterile and forbidding as the country appeared, they believed an inheritance was reserved for them behind the gloomy mountain walls, beyond the awful cañon, where the black, rushing river is shut in by sheer precipices fifteen hundred feet high. Sustained by a faculty of self-persuasion equaled by no other people on the face of the earth, they pushed on and on through the very heart of the wilderness, nearly to the present site of Omaha. This was more than three hundred years ago; yet are the novel-writers complaining that we have no antiquity, no mystery, no dim lights and deep shadows, where the imagination of the story-teller may flower and bear fruit.

CHAPTER XI.

AMONG THE ARCHIVES.—A LOVE LETTER.

ONE day, while mousing or, as President Lincoln used to say, browsing among the manuscripts, and musing about the dead and-gone heroes, and how times have altered since they rode out like Paladins of romance to tempt Fortune in her high places, I came on a letter which differed from the commonplace documents littered about, and was not emblazoned with the splash of any great seal. It was very yellow and musty, stained in one corner by a blue book thrown on it in the time of President Johnson. It required the daintiest handling. Carefully I unfolded the sheet, almost thick as vellum and in danger of dropping to tatters, and marked a spot once sealed with wax, flaked off long ago. The address was Antonio Eusebio de Cubero, Secretary of Gen. Don Diego de Vargas, Governor of Nueva Mejico. I opened the quaint missive, and lo! a love-letter, dated Seville, November, 1692. It began with stately, sweet salute: " To my own true love and faithful knight, from his Rosita de Castile." Like the Dantean lovers,

> " I turned no further leaf."

Nearly two centuries the antique billet had lain entombed in this earthy sepulchre; now would I bring it to the light again, and, tenderly folding the sheet, I bore it to the quiet of my own room, for reading at leisure.

This is the way it runs, written in diminutive hand, indistinct at the beginning, now almost illegible. With tender words, not always in correctest spelling, the little Rose of Castile writes to Eusebio Antonio, that her father and big brother wage war in Algeria. She had just learned to sing, with her mandolin, a madrigal, which she quotes at length and will not bear translation. I cannot catch the subtle essence, the exquisite Spanish-Arab perfume and prison it in harsh English. I know nothing in our language so nearly approaching the dainty love-ditty as the song of Burns, which will live till the last lover dies :

> " Had we never loved so kindly,
> Had we never loved so blindly,
> Never met and never parted,
> We had ne'er been broken-hearted.'

She told how, when the young moon was shining, and the fat, cross duenna was fast asleep, she had crept from her side and out of reach of her snoring, to wander along the Guadalquiver, where the citron shade is deepest and the silver lilies shadow singing waters. She was tired of dances and of flattery, and that odious Manuelita, and, lighted only by the moon and the glow-worm, the maiden lingered by the fountain till the bell in the tower rang two. " There, by the bed of sweet basil—dost remember Eusebio caro ? "

And what for, lady fair ? *Ay de mi !* Is there a reader so dull as not to know, without telling, 'twas to dream, and to dream, and to dream ?

Easy to picture her in graceful youth and all beautiful. The delicate Murillo head ; the Andalusian eyes glancing this way and that from the arched window Moresque ; shyly she flitted out the barred gate among the myrtles, stepping so lightly she scarcely startled the dove who stirred in her nest ; the flower-like face draped by the veiling, envious *rebosa*, held close by the rose-leaf hand ; the one bright circlet shining on the taper finger—can you not see her stealing along through the golden orange orchard, the almond's snow-white glitter? There, with infinite love and longing, with lips waiting to be kissed, she listened to the nightingale's song to the rose, starting at the silken rustle of her dress ; and as the strokes of the bell shook the giant pillars of the cathedral, fleeing like a guilty thing back to the snoring, fat aunt. Only she lingered a moment to look up at the indigo sky and the slim Giralda tower, there by the bed of sweet basil—" dost remember, Eusebio caro ? "

Such was the soft Rosita de Castile, and she asks the old question : When dost thou dream of me, dearest ? It is a sort of treachery to publish the deep secret, and I beg pardon of the shade of the gentle lady, if it lingers round the hard clay of which these walls are made. O tender love! O fond young heart, that stopped beating nearly two hundred years ago! I fear Don Antonio Eusebio was hardly so true as thou wast. Knights-errant, tilting through the New World, had no such quest as the blameless Sir Galahad, though they pushed the *"pundonor"* to the very verge of nonsense. Cortez set an example which his successors were quick to follow. Under the garb of gallantry, they wedded *paramour*, and with high Castilian pride proclaimed their honor bright when they were ready to fight dragons and die in steel harness full knightly.

You remember, reader dear, Millais's "Huguenot Lovers"? Of course, you must, for you have often seen it, and even the poor prints retain some hint of the lovely original. In all her long galleries Art has no fairer creation. It is lovelier even than Ary Scheffer's "Marguerite," than the fallen "Francesca di Rimini." The loving arms clinging to the handsome youth; the wistful, upturned face, so anxious, pale and tearful, on the eve of parting, which her fears make sad as St. Bartholomew's—such charm was in the face of my Rosita de Castile; mine by right of adoption, though she died more than a century before I was born.

How he looked we know by the portraits of Velasquez. Tall and stately was he, lithe and sinewy as one skilled in arms, manly sports, and fond of hounds and hunting; a long lean hand, with blazing jewels—one a precious fire-opal, the Girasol of Zimapan; olive skin and heavy brows; eyes like sharp stilettos; peaked beard, curled mustachios, trimmed and perfumed; black dress-coat, silken hose, silver shoe-buckles, spotless neck-ruff; chains and ribbons of honor; golden cross richly broidered on his mantle; jingling spurs, the mark of knighthood—this was Don Antonio Eusebio de Cubero, who thought to swell his fortune and fill the measure of his fame under the royal banner upheld by Governor-General Vargas.

Nor must we forget to name the good long rapier, worn yet in old Spain, where the sword forever stays the scepter. Add to this pictorial dress the graces which wait on youth—refined courtesy and lofty presence, come of the habit of command—and you have the secretary of the hero who went, saw, and conquered Santa Fé for the crown of Spain.

The beloved Eusebio Antonio kept no copy of his vows and promises; but I warrant, when there were none but the angels to hear, they were given—made binding and strong. In fair Seville the young lovers stole from the lights and the dancing, down by the bed of sweet basil to seal their contract with solemn oaths.

> "Mixed with kisses, sweeter, sweeter
> Than anything on earth."

The dear Eusebio was lured away from Rosita's bower to that New World which is the old. Across the sea had floated, faint and far, like dying echoes coming near, stories of a land of wild men and beasts, strange birds, and hissing serpents; of mountains of rock inscribed with mystic hieroglyphs, and terraced pyramids, upholding undying fires—temples the incense of whose altars ascended forever into a sky of speckless sapphire. These were the regions of finest furs, of gold-dust and ivory, of silver, pearls, and precious stones, all to be had for the gathering. Such tales were as singing sirens, as airy hands beckoning in the shadowy distances of dim and unknown shores.

What wonder the young men were fired with the idea of enriching impoverished estates by the plunder of opulent cities, and old men approved their resolution to grasp some portion of this wealth, to march with triumphant banners through the length and breadth of the land, all the while striking stout blows for Holy Cross?

In that age of few books, when writing was a clerkly accomplishment, there had come down from the fathers many traditions of the hero who had wrested the scepter from the hand of Atahualpa on the heights of the Andes. The discoverer of the Mississippi was a century asleep under its rushing waters. They had heard the name and fame of the peerless Englishman—seaman, soldier, courtier, poet, historian—who sought a city of gold on the banks of the Oronoco. Nor could they believe that genius and valor died when the aged paralytic, beggared and heartbroken, laid his head on the block, saying : " It matters little how the head lieth, so that the heart be right," the noblest head that ever rolled in English dust.

The supernatural swayed men's minds in those days, and myriads of imaginary foes were to be fought, besides the beasts in their dens and the naked, painted savage. No doubt that Antonio Eusebio de Cubero felt equal to every danger he must face—the perilous voyage, and the many miseries which Rosita's fears magnified out of all bounds.

The parting for years so weary shook the heart of the little Rose. Better than I can tell, my reader knows it. The lingering clasp of hands, the yearning gaze, the tears, the vows, the prayers ; the slow ship (there was no steamer then), with gay pennons and fluttering signals, sailing straight into the sunset, into eternity, away, away out of the world ; a fading sail on the flushed water, a speck on the horizon's edge ; he is gone, taking with him her happiness, her smiles, her passionate young heart.

But they would return, those *Caballeros* on the

deck of the "Columella," heroes every one,
bringing the wealth of Pizarro and the glory of
Cortez. The thought was cheer and comfort to
Rosita in the long, slow waiting—one of the
hardest things to be learned in the lesson of loving. Men have a thousand objects to live for—
the whole world is theirs, and in their changeful,
many-colored life love is only one slender, shining thread; women have nothing but their hearts.
He went out to a field of limitless possibilities,
filled with the charm of novelty, variety, adventure; she to her maiden bower, her lute, her
embroidery, to dream over the love-words till his
very name would thrill and send the blood dancing through her veins; to wait through the dull
sameness of empty days, dropping one by one
into weary, silent nights; to watch the last light
against the towers, the last sparkles on the sea,
making it a sea of glass mingled with fire, and
entreat the Mother of Sorrows with piteous
prayers for the wanderer in the vague, far-off
country beyond them; to sicken for gracious
messages and letters that do not come, and yet
be loyal in the belief they have been written,
they are somewhere—this is the sweet patience
born of woman, the brave, persistent faith, almost
a religion.

It is the one who sails away who forgets; the
one who stays at home who remembers. He
was a false teacher who said Paradise is in the
shadow of the crossing of cimeters. You and I
know, dear reader, and our little Rose of Seville
knew, it is in the shadow of the one we love.

CHAPTER XII.

AMONG THE ARCHIVES.
(Continued.)

FROM the journal of Capitan-General Don Domingo Jeronso Petriz de Cruzate (what a Spanish ring there is in that name!), who was governor and military commandant of Nueva Mejico from 1684 to 1689, we can form some idea of the state of affairs in the province. But a few detached pages of this important document survive. They appear the clearest where all are confused

The Spaniards had been driven from the country as far south as the Texan line. Cruzate's little army failed in the reconquest of the liberty-loving Pueblos, and the service was finally entrusted to General Vargas, or, as it was anciently written, Bargas, to whom the faithful knight and true love was secretary.

The chronology of this period is some times in a hopeless tangle; but the march of Governor-General Don Diego de Vargas is pretty well connected. He lives in history as one of the most bigoted and brutal of the Conquistadores. As has been written of the Duke of Alva: " His vices were colossal, and he had no virtues." From shreds and patches of mouldy MSS. his march is traced with tolerable clearness, and the conduct of the foreigners was so nearly alike that their stories are much the same.

By and with consent of the royal audience, he left home and pleasures in the City of Mexico for El Paso del Norte, to organize one hundred friendly Indians and less than two hundred mounted men. Among the latter was the secretary, Antonio Eusebio de Cubero, who on fiesta

days wore a light glove on his casque, a love-knot
on his spear.

The country swarmed with a numerous and
enraged enemy, and every league of ground was
contested. Vargas seemed awake to the perils
of the situation, and to have a wholesome fear of
public opinion besides, for on the night before
marching he wrote to Count Galvas, Viceroy of
Mexico· "I have determined to risk life and all
in the attempt, and am prepared rather to be
considered rash to being looked upon as a man
of too much caution, thereby exposing my repu-
tation to remarks." He was successful from the
very outset. The reader will remember that the
Pueblos lived in community houses, built in a
hollow square. A whole tribe sometimes inhabited one house, and one after another they were
reduced to submission.

The invading army found game in abundance;
but the blessing of the early and the latter rain
is not for New Mexico, and the scarcity of water
made great suffering. "In roasting-ear time"
the bold land-robbers feasted in the cornfields;
" hares like those of the Castiles " furnished nourishing food; and in all their journeying simple
natives gave the fair visitants their choicest stores,
for paltry trinkets of glass pewter, and tinsel.
The blaze of their camp-fires attracted large numbers of rattlesnakes—" the serpent with tiger-col-
ored skin and castanets in its tail;" the mountain cat's green eyes glared at them from the
black rim of the illuminated circle; and lovely
gazelles shyly approached the springs, where they
had hitherto drank undisturbed, to sniff the tainted
air and gaze at the strangers.

There survives one description of a large torpid
lizard the explorers encountered, striped with red,
white and black bars—a hideous creature; and a
horned snake, kept in spirits, to be sent the

viceroy. Here, too, we hear first of the wonderful traveling stones, that within the distance of
a few feet of each other seek a common centre,
roll together, and lie close like eggs in a nest.
They were in the bottom of shallow basins in the
levels, and their magnetism was a source of wondering awe to the superstitious soldiery. The
reporter, a naturalist of some sort, whose name is
lost, begs a moderate subsidy, that he may em-
ploy natives to help capture the venomous beasts
and assist in making collections. The barbarians
refused to work, even with wages, and thus writes
Vargas : " I have been obliged to raze whole
villages to the ground, in order to punish their
obstinacy." Possibly here we have the secret of
the uninscribed ruins now slowly crumbling down
in the valleys by the narrowing waters of the
Pecos and the Rio Grande.

The chief burden is the Indian. The chronicles are heavily laden with details of grievances
the conquerors were obliged to bear from him.
How he refused to accept slavery as his best
estate; and, worse than that, how he rebelled
against the power which would force him to
worship the unknown, unseen God, whose sign
was the red cross, whose ambassadors' march was
tracked by the smoke of cities sacked and burnt,
lands made desolate, the widow's cry, the orphan's
wail.

The Spaniards were disciples of the school of
Narvaez, who on his death-bed, being urged by
his confessor to forgive his enemies : said "Bless
your heart, Father, I have none. I have killed
them all." In those good old times—for as the
poet sings,

" All times when old are good "—

the religion of the governor must be the religion of the governed. The Pueblos were and
still are sun worshipers; and every day their

deity—the peculiar friend of the red race—rose
with unveiled face, rejoicing the eyes and cheering the hearts of his children. Why should they
believe in One whose followers taught that sul-
phurous flames were in waiting for all who had
not money enough to pay for certain mystic rites
held over the dead body? Whenever there was
chance of escape, the Indians fled before the
mailed and mounted warriors fast as their own
mountain antelopes, and the Pueblos were rapidly
brought to submission. To perfect the surrender
of soul and body, after a city was taken, Father
Francisco Corvera baptized by thousands at a
time. He was attended by several Franciscan
priests, charged with the reconversion of those
fallen from the true faith. They were forced to
assemble before a large cross in the plaza. There
the red sinners were absolved from their sins, and,
on pain of death, forbidden their idolatrous dances,
especially the *cachina*, the delight of the aboriginal heart, and, as the old MS. words it, "were
to be obedient to the divine and human majesty."

Very devout was this Vargas. After the reduction of Jemez, he reported to the Viceroy of
Mexico, Count Galvas : " This action having been
fought the day before Santiago Day, I believe
that glorious apostle and patron saint interceded
in our behalf, and which was the cause of our
signal success."

Here are some of the mild requirements laid
on the baptized heathen by his order :

"They must keep crosses over their doors;
treat ministers with love and reverence ; and,
whenever they meet them, kiss the hem of their
habit, with submission and veneration. They
must have their bows in order and ten arrows, to
offend and defend; and none shall dare use the
arms of the Spaniards, for the reason they are
prohibited by the royal ordinances."

Fighting his way northward, near Zuni, he leveled a large pueblo, " the size of a long horse-race ; " but how long the horse-race was in that time your correspondent has no means of knowing. By his own autograph on the everlasting hills we know when and in what spirit the haughty hidalgo passed that point for the recapture of La Villa Real de Santa Fé, then in the hands of its rightful owners.

One hundred and ninety miles southwest of Santa Fé, ten miles from the Arizona line, fifty miles west of the dividing ridge of the continent —called, in consequence, Sierra Madre—is antique Zuni, a city of memory. It is one of the seven vanishing cities sought by Coronado in 1540, and by wandering knights from Spain and Portugal in the time of Philip Second. Capital of the fabled kingdom of Cibola, it is the most ancient and most interesting, because the least changed of all the pueblos of New Mexico.

When Governor-General Vargas and his gallant little army reached this pueblo, they halted for rest and recruiting, before pressing on to the City of Holy Faith. The General was accompanied by his secretary, the beloved Antonio Eusebio, and they must have looked with the deepest concern at the stout walls of the strange fortress. I have not been able to learn whether he attacked it or not. Even a successful and intrepid leader, with the help of the red allies, used to savage warfare, would deliberate well before besieging that city set on a hill, which must be carried by assault, in the face of arrows, slings, lances, huge stones rolled from above, and burning balls of cotton dipped in oil. The modern Zuni, a compact town of fifteen hundred souls, stands in the centre of the valley of the Colorado Chichito (Little Red River); but ancient Zuni, now in ruins, was several miles away, on the top of a

mesa, or precipice, one thousand feet high, almost
inaccessible from the valley.   It was built in five
stories, with thick walls of stone laid in mud
mortar, terraced from without and fortified by
towers.   A formidable citadel.

The camp of the victorious army was probably
in the present camping-ground, a choice spot,
where grass grows with tint of richest green,
lovely to the eye as fresh lilies—a garden beauty,
skirting the spring of cool, sweet water, about
fifteen miles from old Zuni.   To reach it from
Santa Fé, the traveler of to-day crosses a country
very beautiful and fertile, where rapid change of
geological structure makes varying change of
scenery.   Maize grows in the valley without irrigation—not an *acequia* in sight; and peaches,
planted by the Jesuit Fathers, are deliciously
sweet.   After straining over sand and rock, in the
hot, white sun-glare, with the fever-thirst which
comes from drinking alkali water, it must have
been a deep pleasure for the soldiery to leave the
trackless plain, and lie in the cool, rich grass,
restful alike to jaded steed and war-worn rider;
to feast their eyes on the delicate enamel of green
—the setting of this Diamond of the Desert;
and watch, as we have, the birds of strange note
and plumage coming and going, with merry
twitter, flirt and flutter, to bathe and drink in the
sparkling fountain.

Enchanting effects of light and color vary the
passing hours.   A rose-blush of exquisite haze
greets the rising sun; and the mirage—most
marvelous of Nature's mysteries—often swims in
mid-air in early morning, when the first warm
flush has faded.   The perfect blue, curtaining the
valley, is jeweled with opal and turquoise.   That
ethereal brilliance allows no " middle tones."
The sun sets as on the Nile, and when the flaring
disc sinks low suddenly the hidden splendor is

unveiled—"a vision sent from afar, that mortals may feebly learn how beautiful is Heaven."

CHAPTER XIII.

AMONG THE ARCHIVES.
(*Continued.*)

FROM Zuni dispatches were sent back to Count Galvas by a line of swift runners reaching to Mexico. Perhaps a letter to Seville from the faithful knight, who now had time for sweet thoughts of love, without which this were the wilderness without the manna. I hope the reader does not forget my young hero; for I love him dearly, and mean to stand up for him to the last, through evil as well as through good report. Skillful furbishers did what they could to restore the original luster to dulled and dinted armor, and in the idlesse of camp the secretary must often have looked up at two enormous pillars of sandstone towering high on the sides of the *mesa*, appearing chiseled into human figures of colossal size, fixed, immortal as the statues of Aboo Simbel. At evening, while my Rosita walked through the drowsy Spanish city,

> " Guarded by the old duenna,
> Fierce and sharp as a hyena,
> With her goggles and her fan
> Waving off each wicked man,"

and Antonia Eusebio was smoothing his draggled plumes, he probably heard from friendly Indians the wild legend still told there by the red light of the camp-fires. The tradition runs that Zuni is the only city on the earth which bore the weight of the Flood. Ages ago, an eternity before white men came, rain fell in streams from the sky; adobe houses melted away, and the whole world and everything in it was fast sinking from sight. The neighboring tribes escaped from the rushing waters to the top of this *mesa;* but the waves rose so fast nearly all perished before reaching the summit of the cliff. In the midst of their distress a black night (*noche triste*) fell on the land. Their God had forgotten them, the sun turned his face away from his children, and "darkness was the universe." Still the waters rose higher and higher, incessant, undiminished; still the people in blind panic pressed to the topmost foothold, threatened with the fast-rising overflow. Above the black abyss no light of sun or star, sign of promise, dove or olive. In desperate extremity, they sought to avert the curse by sacrifice. No time was there for song or prayer, altar-fire or incantation. They snatched the children of the *cacique* (a daughter lovely as light, a smile of the Great Spirit, and a son beautiful as morning), adorned them with a few gay feathers, and hurled them from the steep into the boiling abyss—an offering to an offended Deity. The waters were surging within a few feet of the top of the *mesa.* There the proud waves were stayed. The victims were changed to the stone columns, a sign from Heaven marking the mountain of refuge where the propitiatory offering was accepted, and everlastingly commemorating the Deluge.

The *mesa* is a mile across; an irregular figure, defined by abrupt bluffs, almost perpendicular. On it are the remains of two pueblos, whose outlines are clearly traceable—the dimensions of rooms and inner walls. Like all ancient towns, they were fortified with an outer wall in the shape

of the letter V, to resist invasions of warlike tribes,
and watch-towers were placed at regular intervals.
Crumbling walls, made of little blocks of stone
laid in mud-mortar, are scattered over the ground
in heaps from two to ten feet high. Here the
fox and coyote prowl by night, and the antiquarian haunts it by day. After careful investigation,
with Indian guides, they report the standing walls
rest on ruins of still greater age. The primitive
masonry must have been about six feet thick.
In the more recent buildings the walls are not
over eighteen inches thick. The small sandstone
blocks are laid with neatness and regularity.
Broken pottery is strewn about, and arrow-heads
of obsidian, flint, and jasper.

After the Deluge, when the waters abated off
the face of the earth, the tribes abandoned the hill
city, and lived in the pleasant valley till the Spanish invasion, when they again fled to the top of
the *mesa*. They turned at every place possible
and fortified strongly the two approaches by
which the outworks could be assaulted, and held
out against the foe a long time. At last the
hights were scaled. The mail-clad warriors, with
their swords of matchless temper, triumphed over
the rude arms of the feeble natives. From the
highest watch-tower the banner of the Cross was
unfurled against the brilliant sky, unflecked by
cloud or shadow ; and sun-lighted spears glittered
in the narrow streets of the devoted, the Holy
City.

Imprinted in the solid rock, as in clay, is shown
and may be seen this day the foot-print of the
first white man who reached the summit. When
you visit Zuni, the old guide, if you happen to
get the right one, will repeat this story, for a
slight consideration.

The Zunis are the Yankees of the Pueblos—
self-supporting, keen at a bargain, thrifty, orderly,

9

clean; that is, clean *for Indians.* I presume
every head in the Holy City could furnish numberless offerings such as Diogenes (oldest of
tramps) cracked on the pure altar of the chaste
Diana.

What Cholula was to the Aztec, Zuni is to the
Pueblos; sacred as the City of David to the sons
of Israel. Touching the religion of this people
opens a subject so broad and so charming I am
tempted to give it more than a passing glance,
but space forbids. They are pantheists in the
fullest sense of the word, and, though missions
have been established among them three hundred
years, they, like all aborigines, set their face as a
flint against change, and still keep to the ancient
beliefs and customs. They worship the Supreme
One, whose name it is death to utter; Montezuma, his brother and equal; and the Sun to
whom they pray and smoke, because his eye is
always open and his ear attends the prayers of
the red men. The Moon is the Sun's wife, and
eclipses are family quarrels, that will result in dis-
aster to the world if they are not soon reconciled.
The stars are their children; the largest is the
oldest.

Besides these superior deities, there is the
great snake, to which they look for life, by command of Montezuma.

Like our sea-serpent on the Atlantic Coast, he
glideth at his own sweet will, is seen at unexpected places, as suits his pleasure, is longer than
the tallest pine, and "thick as many men put
together."

It has been well said the barbarian is the most
religious of mortals. His dependence on the elements for food and comfort makes the primitive
man regard Nature with eager interest. Power-
less against her forces, if there be something mysterious, threatening, the untutored soul supplicates

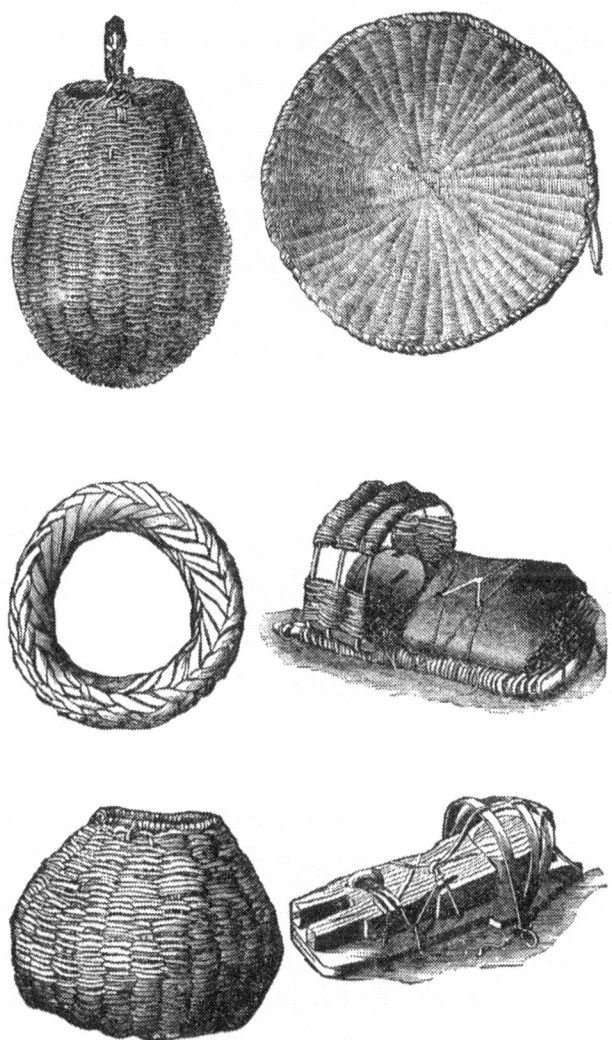

Zuñi Basketry, and Toy Cradles.

it in prayer, with the inborn faith down deep in every breast that behind the visible lies close the Invisible, the Creator, who rules the world he made.

They adore the rainbow, bright headband of the sky, rivers, mountains, stones, trees, bears, and other animals. Their fables appear meaningless to us; but we must not despise them, for many of our beliefs are equally so to them. The aboriginal brain can never comprehend why white men worship a sheet of bunting—white, red, spangled blue, with the eagle totem—suffer for it, fight for it in armies numberless as the sands of the desert, and die for it without murmur.

The myths of the furthest West are wonderfully like the myths of the furthest East. Studying them, one cannot fail in the conviction that humanity, in all the ages and races, is the same, formed on one model, unfolding under the influence of the same inspiration; that, left to their own will, men do like things under like conditions, and that certain religious ideas are born in every heart, sage or savage, making worship a human necessity. Here, as in ancient Thessaly, the powers of Heaven have haunts in the echoing mountain-sides, by pebbly springs, in the gloomy shades of the whispering pines, and under the rushing river and cataract.

In New Mexico, where the food supply depends so largely on the winds and the uncertain rainfall, the savage is most anxious to conciliate the gods who preside over these forces. There are altars for their worship, mystic stones among the gnarled cedars of the Zuni *mesa*, and a spring of sweet water, sacred to the rain god, rimmed with pebbles precious as the oracular jewels on the breast of the Jewish high priest. No animal is allowed to drink of the holy waters, and they are purified every year, with vessels dedicated to the

service—most ancient jars, handed down through
the generations since the evening and the morning were the first day.   No Zuni drinks from the
consecrated *ollas*, for the spirit of the spring is
always watching, and will avenge the indignity
with instant death.   Once a year, in August, the
cacique, with his chief counselors, visits the spring,
and washes its walls, with the elaborately-tinted
vases, which were hallowed by the first high priest.
The jars are ranged in order on the rim of the well.
The frog, the rattlesnake, the tortoise are painted
on them, animals sacred to the presiding deity.
Woe to the offender who shall profane them by
a touch!   A fate awaits him like that of Uzza,
when he put forth his hand to hold the ark in the
threshing-floor of Chidon.   The lightning of the
dread god of storms will strike the sinner dead.

Somewhere near is a mysterious divine bird,
kept in a secret shrine.   As Herodotus says of
the Phœnix : "I have never seen it myself, except
in a picture."

Like the old Greek, the Pueblo looks up and
sees the dead among the stars.   When the
Aurora flashes a strange, flickering light along
the northern sky, it is the mustering of the spirits
of the mighty warriors, whirling their spears and
marching with proud steps, as the shade of
Agamemnon strode across the fields of Asphodel.
The earthquake's rumble is the groaning and
turning in sleep of a big old giant, with voice of
thunder, eyes of fire, and breath of flame.   He
was so immense that he sprawled across the
whole plain, and so powerful the immortal gods,
finding they could not kill him, tore up a high
mountain and laid it on him, to keep him quiet.
What is this but Enceladus ?

> " Under Mount Etna he lies.
>   It is slumber, it is not death ;
> For he struggles at times to arise,
>   And above him the lurid skies
> Are hot with his fiery breath.

Zuñi Water Vases.

"The crags are piled on his breast,
    The earth is heaped on his head ;
But the groans of his wild unrest,
    Though smothered and half-suppressed,
Are heard, and he is not dead."

The best hope and strongest faith of the Pueblos are in the second coming of the great King, who is to raise the dead, judge the world, and reign in peace and righteousness.   Struggling with shadows and weird imaginings, working out their destiny with many a bitter failure, in anguish of heart they instinctively reach through the darkness for the almighty hand of the unseen helper.   The sons of Montezuma, as they love to call themselves, believe the fullness of time is come, and the return of their Messiah at hand.   He will leave his bright sun-house, to right the wrongs and heal the woes of the race so mercilessly stricken down by the Spaniards. Then there will be no more death, neither sorrow, nor crying ; neither shall there be any more pain. Their ideas are vague and dim.   Legends treacherous as memory, and growing fainter from generation to generation, for their wise men are without open vision, and their sagamores have neither written prophecy nor guiding stars.

The view from the top of the *mesa* is unspeakably beautiful.   Twined among multitudes of peaks, like tangled ribbons, are streakings of azure and purple, beneath which, as we know by experience, are out spread valleys, broad, treeless, scorched with a tropic heat, which at noonday seems like quivering flame.   The pre-historic ruins cover about thirty acres, and are scattered in confusion on the level plateau under the windwhipped cedars.   Here, until within a few years, was kept the consecrated fire burning for centuries—the Montezuma fire ; but time fails to tell it all.   Another day we will come again, and hear the fanciful traditions, the misty old superstitions which hover about the neglected shrines.

They are given with an opulence of fancy which
throws mists before your eyes. In the hush of
solitude, the effect of the place is mysterious,
and reflection drops easily into belief. Few
worshipers now sacrifice in the primeval temples,
where of old they must have flocked by hundreds,
cherishing the promise of the second coming of
Montezuma from the pleasant land where the sun
rises. The chiefs crouch with faces toward the
east as the morning star goes softly out, and the
gray dawn melts into the light of day, yearning
as human hearts have yearned in all ages, seeking
a sign from Heaven. The legend runs that he
who shall first behold the King in his beauty
shall receive some great favor at his hand. Sometimes they wait in silence ; again they chant a
hymn to their god, watching till he shakes his
"plumes of fire" above the mountain-tops and
shoots his radiant spears across the roseate sky.
But the oracles are dumb. Well are they keeping the mighty secret !

CHAPTER XIV.

AMONG THE ARCHIVES.
(*Continued.*)

A FEW miles from Zuni, as we move eastward,
there gradually comes to view a bold, high, sandstone rock, a quadrangular wall, white, veined
with yellow, named Inscription Rock. It is
nearly a mile in length and more than two hundred feet in hight. Approaching it, tower and
turret, architrave and pillar rise slowly into view.
We see a mighty structure Nature has wrought
in noble architecture, and that no extravagant
coloring gave it the old Spanish name *El Moro*
—The Castle. The surface of the mountain-wall

on the north and south faces is written over with names otherwise lost to history, records that light the dark way like shining torches. Some are deeply and beautifully cut into the plane surface and reach back more than three hundred years. The older inscriptions are Spanish, carefully graven upon the vertical faces, about the hight of a man's head from the ground. Usually a date, a brief memorandum of the purpose and line of march of the Castilian soldiery, the names of travellers exploring the country, or Franciscan friars going into the wilderness in search of the lost tribes of Israel.

At the foot of the towering steep is a gushing spring of sparkling water, and fresh grass, such as is not often seen except in narrow valleys among the arid plains of the territories. After rest, food, siesta, the traveler, looking up to the immense table of stone before him, naturally adds his own name to the constantly-increasing list on the written mountain, which has now grown into a confused mass of hieroglyphs—Indian signs, the favorite being the track of a moccasin, indicative of marching; decayed and decaying inscriptions, and names of old adventurers. Let us loiter awhile and read, for it is not often such a register is laid open to any tourist.

Close to the left corner, almost hidden by brushwood, is the oldest date, engraved in the rock nearly a century before the landing of the Pilgrim Fathers—Don José de Basconzales, 1526. This is the sole record of his expedition, at once his history and his cenotaph. He went with an exploring party from the City of Mexico, and never returned; nor were they heard of after leaving Zuni. Whether they perished in secret defiles, cut off by the skulking Apache, who dogged every step of the invader, or gave out through fatigue and thirst in the deep cañons and sterile *vegas*, belongs to the voiceless past. In some unnamed spot he sleeps with the silent majority—a mighty company.

In the moist air of England these letters would be mossed over and wholly illegible; but the dry, dewless air of New Mexico holds decay in check, and in this regard almost equals the atmosphere of Egypt. Among recent inscriptions appear the autographs of the United States explorers—Whipple, Simpson, and others; and still nearer our day the signs manual of the Smiths, Joneses, Browns, and the rest. The sixth name on the list is the one whose fortunes we are trying to trace out and follow, less for the sake of his king and country than because he was attended by the true love and faithful knight of the little Rose of Castile.

It runs: Here passed Don Diego de Bargas, to conquer Santa Fé for the royal crown, New Mexico, at his own cost, in the year 1692.

Many secrets we cannot guess are hidden in the silence there, with the sands of ages drifted above them; but it is plain to see Vargas was in high feather when he made his proud record on the wall of El Moro. Observe the pert little crow, "at his own cost."

Luckily, there is still extant a number of documents bearing on his administration among the state papers at Santa Fé, or we might think the princely fellow, going out conquering and to conquer, scattered commissions and victories with a free hand.

How La Villa Real de Santa Fé was lost and won is an old tale and often told, and details of battles, at least of Indian fighting, are not interesting. Enough that, after the summer camp at or near Old Zuni, Vargas with his army pressed on to the siege of the Capital. The slayers were a few hundreds of white men, with red allies; the slain were of a number that has never been reckoned.

Father Francisco Corvera administered absolution to the entire command before battle, and, as the foreign army was preparing for a general onslaught, the Pueblos stole out in the night, leaving the city in possession of the fair race which left nothing but desolation in its track.

The brutal instincts of this Vargas (whom I hate, and the judicious reader must hate too) hardened and intensified with increasing power and advancing years. One of the worst of his bad race, he labored unceasingly for the conversion of the aborigines. His position allowed immeasurable sweep for cruelty which we may be sure he enjoyed to the utmost, and the cross became the object of bitter hatred to the heathen he claimed for an inheritance. He it was who wrote to the viceroy of Mexico, applying for more troops to carry on the crusade: "You might as well try to convert Jews without the Inquisition as Indians without soldiers."

Notwithstanding his religious zeal and boast recorded on Inscription Rock at Zuni, Vargas missed the high place at which he aimed, not, like Columbus and Cortez, because he deserved too greatly, but because the regiment in garrison and the corporation of Santa Fé, in 1695, presented charges to the viceroy, Count Galvas, against him for peculation. He was accused of using public money for private purposes; of drawing on the public treasury for purchase of corn, mules, etc. for settlers, and of selling them and pocketing the proceeds. "Also of having drawn drafts and received moneys for expenses never incurred."

He was removed from office 1697, and with him, doubtless, the faithful knight and true love, Don Antonio Eusebio de Cubero, who we will believe had the soul of a true knight, and no part or lot in these ignoble transactions.

Whatever he was, Rosita saw him with eyes anointed; from the beginning a hero predestined to triumph on every field he might enter. I do believe that, in the rough campaigning through the land of sand and thorn, he kept her lovely face—the Millais face—in his heart of hearts. That he never vowed a vow nor kissed a kiss that was not hers, and, loyal to his own Rose of Castile, as he was to his king, he marched in the triumph through the streets of Seville. There ministrels and troubadours hymned high praises (*romances* they were called), and bright lady-loves waved silken scarfs to the *conquistadores*, home from the far New World. They were men in the bloom of youth, the very flower of the Peninsula, and Antonio Eusebio de Cubero was proudest and noblest where all were proud and many noble.

From the arched window, set in quaint fret-work and arabesques, Rosita looked out and the banner over her was love. Perhaps the Millais face—that eager, anxious, haunting face—flushed a little at sight of the grand parade in the pomp and circumstance the old Spaniard loved so well. The soft, dark eyes were not bewildered by the rich confusion of color, the far-floating flags, the dazzle of steel and of silver. Swift glances singled out one beneath the wavy folds of the royal standard, brave as he was beautiful, whose prancing steed, flashing arms, crest, and plume were familiar, whose sash her own soft hands embroidered.

Let us picture reunion after years of separation, joy after anguish, the rapture of rescue from peril, and so leave them, walking with happy feet by the bed of sweet basil, as the first lovers walked in the cool of the day under the palms of Paradise.

While I write, the letter of the dear, dead

woman lies on the table before me; the fading
sign from a rose-leaf hand that has been part of
the dust of old Spain so many and many a year.
Frail thing, most perishable, outlasting kings,
thrones, the wrecks of states, the decay of ages!
Closing day finds me dreaming over it in the
waning light. I look to the purpling hills. As
the sun sinks, they change to fairy tents, under
a line of exquisite color, pink, orange, pale sea
green, the changeful fringe on the banner of
night, ending far up the zenith in a field of spotless azure. In the farness of the distance the
cold, white peaks of the Stony mountains warm
for one supreme moment in the solemn beauty
of the after-glow, their summits clear-cut against
the rainless blue.

Rapidly the shadows deepen. Violet changes
to leaden hues, rose dims to pearl gray, the
flushed white foreheads pale, the fires of sunset
burn out, and the short twilight, ending in gloom,
is the day's burial.

Human phantoms flit across the dusky spaces.
King and priest, savage and Christian, knight
and lady, shadows all, passing within the mighty
shadow. Under the low window I hear the
tramp of feet pacing to and fro like the ebb and
flow of the tide. The hurrying feet are ghost-
like, too, chasing the flying specters' gold and
fame. History is but repeating itself. The restless, dissatisfied souls of the New World are the
same brotherhood as those of the Castiles; the
same as when Solomon sent ships from Tarshish
to bring back gold of Ophir; the same jealous
souls as when the king was wroth because the
people shouted, Saul has slain his thousands and
David his ten thousands. Now, as then, morning and evening bring their old beauty, the cool
ing balm of the breeze follows the burning day.
The west wind cools no fever of heart or brain;

still are men searching for signs of gold and
fighting the old battle against oblivion, and still
do loving women sit by solitary fires and wait for
them to come.   These things have not changed ;
they will never change.   Humanity remains the
same.

The foreign charm which was the dower of the
historic city is dying fast, but not quite dead.
The spell, long lingering, is slow to pass away,
though student and antiquary are blowing the
dust from the books of Chronicles and letting
the white light of day into obscured and darkened chambers.

In this dimness once glowed the poetic coloring
of romance and chivalry, in which the valorous
Espego and his knights founded the City of Holy
Faith.   If the ghosts of the venturesome heroes
revisit the field of their victories, they may yet
be reminded of soft Andalusia.   There is a hint
of Castilian grace in the vanishing *sombrero*, in
the folds of the ever-falling but never-fallen *rebosa*,
a touch of passing sweetness in the prolonged
adios.   Blent with the familiar benediction, now
in my ear, " *Vago usted con Dios que usted lo pase
bien*" (" May you depart with God and continue
well "), the hovering shades might hear the
dreamy plash of bright fountains and the light
love song under the barred windows of fair
Cordova.

CHAPTER XV.

THE JORNADA DEL MUERTO.

NEAR the southern boundary of New Mexico
the Spanish explorers were opposed by a barrier
of all on earth most to be dreaded—a shadeless,
waterless plateau, nearly one hundred miles long,

from five to thirty miles wide, resembling the steppes of Northern Asia. Geologists tell us this is the oldest country on the earth, except, perhaps, the backbone of Central Africa; at least the one which has longest exhibited its present conditions, the one longest exposed to the influence of agents now in action, and, hence, bearing the most deeply-marked records of their power.

The portion I speak of appears to have served its time, worn out, been dispeopled and forgotten. The grass is low and mossy, with a perishing look—the shrubs, soap-weed, and bony cactus writhing like some grisly skeleton; the very stones are like the scoria of a furnace. You vainly look for the flight of a bird, such as cheered the eyes of Thalaba in the desert; no bee nor fly hums the empty air; and, save the lizard (the genius of desolation) and horned frog, there is no breath of living thing.

Certain tribes of Arabia have no name for the sea, and, when they first came to its shore, they asked, with a sad wonder: "What is this strange desert of water, more beautiful than any land?" Standing on the edge of the measureless waste, which is trackless as water, the first explorers might ask: "What is this strange ocean of sand, with its stillness more awful than any sea?"

In places the dead level of the plain sweeps with the exactness of a sheet of water, encircling as with a shore-line mountain-walls which on the west shut off the Rio Grande, and frequently insulating whole peaks and ridges. Friendly showers fall there two months in the year, and, instead of storms of rain, in spring it is burned by those of dust and sand They are caused by winds coming mainly from the northwest, carrying before them, like mist, clouds of pulverized sand and dust, and piling them in drifts when checked in their course. You can watch their

progress as they approach, beginning in a thin
haze along the horizon, for hours beforehand;
and when they reach you the dust penetrates
everything.   You eat it, you drink it, you breathe
it, you wear it like a coating, and the last handkerchief at the bottom of the box in your trunk
is gritty and smells of alkali.   The sand-storms,
as they are called, usually last one, sometimes
three days.   Occasionally they appear a procession of whirlwind columns, such as are seen in
autumn leaves, slowly moving across the desert
in spectral dimness.   Rejoice and be thankful if
the tempest passes without striking.   It will beat
the mules without mercy and lash your face like
a whip, if it reaches you.

Stories are told how, after a day of intense heat
and lifeless silence, a dark cloud rapidly lowers
from the sky of molten brass, and a sudden wind
whirls the sand in mounds, and so shifts it from
place to place.   Horses and mules fall flat, with
their noses to the ground; men lie down under
blankets, from which the sand must be shaken
occasionally, to escape being literally buried
alive.   Storms of such violence are rare, but every
old frontiersman can tell you of more than one.
The early Spaniards called the desert hot wind
solana, in memory of Mancha and Andalusia.   It
heats the blood terribly, produces the utmost dis-
comfort and nervous irritation.   Hence the Castilian proverb: "Ask no favor while the solana
blows."

A variation of the simoom of the Orient, it
cracks the skin, creates consuming thirst, and has
been known to produce death.

The reader need hardly be reminded that the
destruction of Sennacherib's host is supposed to
have been caused by the simoom.   Undoubtedly,
Byron had it in mind when he wrote the Hebrew
melody, which has the majestic thunder-roll of
organ music,

" The Assyrian came down like the wolf on the fold."

Once feel the parching, torrid heat; once face
that suffocating desert-wind, and you readily
comprehend death was instantaneous. There
was no waste of miraculous force in the power
which destroyed all the mighty men of valor, and
the leaders and captains, in the camp of the king
of Assyria

" For the Angel of Death spread his wings on the blast,
And *breathed* in the face of the foe as he passed;
And the eyes of the sleepers waxed deadly and chill,
And their hearts but once heaved and forever grew still."

The spot I am trying to describe is the battle-
ground of the elements. In winter it is made
fearful by raging storms of wind and snow.
There men and animals have been frozen to
death, their bodies left the lawful prey of the
mountain wolf. From the primeval years the
Apache has harried the hungry waste, hunting
for scalps; and, besides the savagest of savages,
it is now the favorite skulking-place of outlaws,
an asylum for fugitives escaping justice in old
Mexico and Texas.

In our times many a party cut off and many a
traveler murdered makes good the name it bears,
given by the first white men who dared its perils:
Jornada del Muerto—" Journey of Death."

Reports of sun-scorch and lava beds, sand,
sirocco, maddening thirst, and cheating mirage
did not daunt the bold land-robbers from Spain.
They were pledged to wrest their secrets from
the mountains, and bring them to lay at the feet
of their imperial master. Disciplined in the
hardships of foreign wars, they lived for glory
and worshiped Fortune. They had seen service
in almost every clime. Some had tilted with the
Moor; some had fought the infidel on the blue
Danube, and hunted the Carib in Hispaniola;
and later came captains whose waving plumes
had been the colors to rally on when the royal

standards were fallen. The mysterious country, mountain-locked and guarded by savage sentinels, who seemed to require neither rest, food, nor sleep, and were so fleet of foot they could out-march the best cavalry horses, was a high stake, involving heavy risks and not to be lightly won. From accounts of Jesuit missionaries, who went with the cross, ready to die for their faith, the heroes of the seventeenth century learned that Nature in Nueva Espagña was not always in stormy mood. The fiery solana spent its strength in three days, and the lull following it was like clear shining after rain. If the snow of winter was deep, it was not lasting (only a Christmas storm) ; and friendly natives taught them that the stony Sierras could be brought to yield gold, silver, copper—all the precious metals.

Along their sides were sparkling springs, and at their feet green valleys, where Summer nestled long and lovingly—*pasturas* in which an abiding June encamped and ruled the year. They were tufted with the short, delicate buffalo grass, lovely with its strange clusters of pistillate flowers and bunches of rosy stamens, and so strongly and closely matted it could well bear the tread of the monstrous Cibola (buffalo). Over all, like the purple mountain veils, threaded with fire, hung a delicious mystery.

The old-time heroes were deeply superstitious and well versed in legendary lore. As they penetrated the *Jornada*, spectral illusions haunted them. Demons lurked in the tall soap-weed, and glared over their tops, grimacing threaten-ingly.

When, weakened by long fastings, the sky spun round, goblins, " with leathery wings like bats," filled the air, and foul fiends, which could be exorcised only by prayer, made every step a terror. Fearless leaders, who regarded enterprise honorable in proportion to its peril, and had looked death in the face as if they loved it, quailed before the undiscovered country, the pathless *Jornada.*

In bivouac at sunset, there was much crossing of forehead and breast, murmur of aves and amens ; not whispered, but outspoken, as became the " Swords of the Church."

They set up their swords in the sand, knelt before the blessed sign on their hilts, and fervently prayed the Holy Mother's protection. So comforted, they slept, perchance to dream of cool fountains in far *plazas ;* of glassy ponds, with white-breasted swans asleep among the reeds and rushes on the margin ; of rushing books, shaded by dripping willows ; and the low undertone of of the halcyon sea, whose soft-beating surf breaks on the shores of old Spain.

It is amusing to read of their superstitious dread of horned frogs, which hopped out of the way, then " turned and faced them with basilisk eyes." The sameness of the scenes was sickening ; the glare of the fierce sunshine blinded them ; and, with cracked lips and burning eyes they hailed the mirage with shouts, and, horse and rider seeing eye to eye, they dashed away for the mocking lake, to curse the cheat and thirst the more.

Traversing the desert is not now what it was in the age of fable. The delusions of the past vanished with the darkness to which they belonged. We are living in better times. Summer, winter, moonbeam or starbeam will never shine on goblins more. The " leathery wings " have floated away from cactus thicket and mezquit jungle ; ghost, fairy, demon, genii all have fled into the listening silence. They were phantoms following the century of credulity, whose foremost man, clear-eyed and conscien-

tious, aimed his inkstand at the Devil, and whose
veteran campaigner from the siege of Granada
went wandering up and down the everglades of
Florida, seeking an enchanted fountain—an ever-
flowing spring, of which one draught would
restore to his war-worn body the freshness of
youth, and add to his term of life years enough
to discover and conquer a third world.

The *Jornada* still has its alarms; but men of
the nineteenth century see no angry eyes in the
red glow of sunset; overhead hovers no evil
spirit of earth or air, under cover of night's blue
and starry banner.

The centre of the ninety-mile desert is now
broken by a watering-place, the cheering oasis
which relieves the long strain on body and soul.
In 1871 Major John Martin dug one hundred and
sixty feet, and struck a sweet, abundant fountain,
deliciously cool, soft, with a slight taste of
sulphur. Its depth is forty feet, and the heaviest
draughts have never lessened the supply. It is
pumped by a windmill, which the wind sometimes makes his own; and the gurgle and plash
as the stream falls into the huge tanks, is a sound
in the ear of the traveller sweet as his first hearing
of the nightingale. Before the well was made
water was hauled in barrels to the station from
the Rio Grande, fifteen miles away. The nearest
fuel at that point is eighteen miles distant.

At Fort Craig, the southern terminus of the
solitary place, the modern tourist fills his water-
kegs and canteens, tightens his cartridge-belt,
and looks carefully to the condition of his animals.
The loss of a breast-strap or horse-shoe would
be a hindrance not easily overcome, and supplies
of every kind must be carried. The road is
excellent, and, if there is no accident, the well
may be reached in one day's journey. Even in
its best aspect it is entered the first time with

forebodings, a vague dread, like pushing out into
an unknown sea. The sun-glare is so hard to
bear that night is often the accepted time for the
mournful crossing. As the sun declines, the
lonesome dark falls like a drop-curtain. The
stars flash out; the sky above, intensely clear, is
a steel-blue shield, set thick with diamonds. A
tropic brilliance fills it with a glow like the mild
twilight of other latitudes, and the moon's splendor
makes beautiful even the seared and jagged cliffs
of the Sierra de los Organos. Three thousand
feet above the level of the river are their shafts,
pale gray in the silvery light; masses of granite
up-heaved in some mighty convulsion, long
stilled, standing against the rainless blue like
tombstones over a buried world.

If there is talk in the ambulance, it is in
subdued tones. The assumption of cheerfulness
by humming snatches of old songs is a dreary
impertinence. Hour after hour we travel in
silence, unbroken but by the grind of wheels
plowing through the sandy soil. In answer to
your utmost listening, you may catch the yelp
of the red fox, or from the far-off mountain the
coyote's shrill cry. Sometimes the driver drops
to sleep, and the wagon stops. Lift the canvas
curtain, and look out. The soft wind blows in
even cadence and swell, but meets only the
hushed night and its burning lights. The Milky
Way is a solid white gleam, where the invisble
gods are walking. The missing stars are here.
How low they swing in their serene and silent
spaces. Beneath the solemn grandeur of the
heavens, the work of Him in whom is no haste,
no rest, no weariness, no failure, we bow in awe.
What a little speck is our wagon-train; what an
atom is self, the object round which our weak
thoughts revolve.

The mountain-rim is restful to the sight.

There are the gushing springs, cool as snow;
and the shady pines, whose never ceasing song
we cannot hear. How still it is! No ripple of
water, no stir of leaf or bough, grass or blossom,
or any green thing. Ominous crosses by the
wayside mark the graves of travellers, scalped,
tortured, and mangled. The weight of the
tragedy is on us. We feel a near kinship to the
sleepers below, and would not tremble to see
them rise and shake their gory locks at us. The
vacant space lies stark and unmoved, as it lay
centuries ago, when the first gold-hunters, in
fear and yet in triumph, braved its unknown
depths. The prostrate plain, the rigid outlines
of the naked landscape, the intolerable dumb
lifelessness are indeed *del Muerto.*

And here I pause to describe the weapons used
by wild tribes of Indians who infest the *Jornada.*
On my wall, beside a victorious banner furled
and bruised arms hung up for monuments, are
the full equipments of an Apache chief, killed
near Fort Stanton, New Mexico. The shield,
made of thick, tanned buffalo hide, is stiff and
hard, and resounds under your knuckles like a
drum. In being made it was stretched over a
light frame of basket-work and dried. It is
twenty inches across, and as round as the shield
of the elder Ossian.

An outer cover of dressed deer-skin envelops the
buffalo hide, drawn smooth and gathered round
the edge on the under side with a leather thread.
Traced in blue-black ink on it are round figures,
which may represent the sun or a spring, and
zigzags, which by straining one's fancy may be
imagined to represent mountains.

At the upper rim of the shield are the decora-
tions; three pea-fowl feathers, probably amulets,
and a medicine-bag of black muslin containing a
dry powder which the warrior rubs on his heart

before going into battle, " to make it big and brave."

A scrap of iridescent shell is fastened to the centre, and there on occasion, and around the edge, dangle bloody tufts, the reeking scalps of the enemy. It was carried on the left arm by two straps slipped over the hand, and was kept in motion while in action, by which means the hostile arrows glanced off.

But it was not proof against the mightier arms of the white race, and two bullet-holes through the shield show how the red chief came to his death.

The spear is an ugly weapon six feet long, about as thick as a broom-handle, and made of an extremely light wood, to me unknown, painted red in one band three inches wide near the head. The point is a piece of iron, probably an old Mexican bayonet, twenty-two inches long, socketed into the pole, and further strengthened in its place by a cord of deer-skin wrapped tightly round it many times.

Before Indians knew the use of iron, the spear, or lance, as it is usually called, was pointed with obsidian, or some other flinty substance, hammered and ground to a sharp edge. Sometimes the heel of the shaft is balanced with eagle feathers, while others are caught along the shaft, giving steadiness to the flight and gratifying the taste of the owner.

The quiver is twenty-seven inches long, is made of white cow-skin tanned with the hair on, sewed with a thread of deer-skin, and is large enough to contain a sheaf of two dozen arrows. A fringe of the same material dangles at each end of the quiver and adorns the waist-belt. When it was in use a band of cow-skin, four inches wide, held it across the shoulder.

The arrows are shafts two feet long, made of

a species of yucca, tipped with hoop-iron and old knife-blades, which are roughly ground on each side, sharply pointed and edged, probably by rubbing with stone. They are winged with three feathers of the wild turkey, stripped from the quill and tied round the shaft at equal distances with very fine tendons, like the E violin string. The iron points are all that betray intercourse with white men, and were probably stolen from the refuse of some camp.

An Apache boy, of ten or twelve years of age, will strike a cent three times out of five at a distance of fifteen yards. Practice of bow-shooting begins as soon as these boys are old enough to hold the weapon, and ends only with death.

At fifty yards the well-ponted iron arrow is dangerous and sure, and the strong-armed Indian easily drives it through a two-inch plank. He can fire it more rapidly than an ordinary revolver, and even though he possesses "a heap firing-gun," as he calls a repeating rifle, he is never without the silent, unerring and deadly iron-headed arrow.

It is far superior to the gun for night-surprises and taking off sentinels, and on the hunt half-a-dozen animals may be killed before the rest of the herd are alarmed. It is to be relied on when ammunition fails, and so light as to be worn without the least encumbrance.

The wary Indian is careful of his arrows, although he has many, wasting none in random shots, and keeping his quiver well filled. Sometimes a thousand arrows are buried in the grave of a chief, a sign that his death will be avenged by his tribe.

A narrow band of red on the feathered end of the shaft is the only attempt at ornamentation.

A fringed leather arm-guard, or bracelet, is worn round the left wrist, to defend it from the blow of the bow-string. Sometimes it is made of gray eagle feathers and the vari-colored tips of humming-birds' wings.

In shooting-matches the contest is carried on by men and boys; betting is high and exciting, and sometimes entire fortunes such as a pair of moccasins, a pink calico shirt and blanket, are staked upon the hazard. The whole tribe, men, women and children, turn out as spectators. A bad shot is received with yells of derision, though failures by experts are rare. If the slender white wand aimed at is not touched, the shaft generally lodges in the circle of loose earth thrown up about the target to catch the arrows and prevent their blunting.

Said an old frontiersman to me, "I have never yet seen the Indian bow I could not break across my knee." I doubt if he could crack the one now before me. Many a hand has tried to string it and failed, completely as the suitors in the classic story. It is of Osage orange forty-two inches long, bent in the graceful curvature poetry assigns to the bow of the god of love.

Formerly to this ornament the wild tribes added a mighty war-club of mezquit wood, flat and crescent-shaped, with a round ball at the end.

In all the Indian weapons there is no sense of grace in outline, except the curved bow, no elegance in the winging, no brilliance in the rough stains of poor color. They simply mean business; the effect of the group now before me is savage in the extreme.

Arm the warrior with them, mount him on a half-wild mustang which he guides with the

knee, and he is a king of men.   Place on his
neck as a crowning garniture the ornament
taken from the body of the fallen chief, and
round his neck put a piece of doubled horsehide, with two rattle-snakes' tails, each containing eleven rattles dangling from it.
Imagine the brutish face painted in hideous
stripes, vermilion and blue; the buffalo-robe
blanket, the wild hair flying, the long lance
whirling, brandished in air, and add, if you
can, the war-whoop, a yell—

> —"As if the fiends from heaven that fell
> Had pealed the banner cry of hell."

Then you will have a picture of an Apache
Indian.

CHAPTER XVI.

SOMETHING ABOUT THE APACHE.

THE chase is the natural outlet for much
savagery; but the wild tribes of North America
are more hardly driven now than ever before,
owing to the rapid disappearance of game, especially the buffalo.   Time was when the *cibola*, as
they called him, fed, warmed, and clothed the
nomads.   Indians are now moved about as far
west as they can go, and the buffalo goes with
them, but is disappearing much more rapidly
than the Red Man is.

The narrowing limits of his range make many a
chase barren as that of the English party in the
Catskills, gayly hunting the great American
bison in the Summer of 1876.

He once ranged as far east as the Atlantic

seaboard in Virginia and the Carolinas. From Catesby we learn that, about the year 1712, herds of buffalo were seen within thirty miles of Charleston, South Carolina. The decrease of their main reliance for food and clothing alarmed the tribes years ago; and in the last generation they brought forward the fact in their pow-wows with commissioners : "The *cibola* is dying, and the red brother must keep peace with the pale face, and eat his spotted buffalo." (Indian for domestic cattle.) Such was the peaceful and alluring speech of the war chief of the Apaches ; but the promise of peace was never kept. To steal and murder, and, under the show of friendship beat out the brains of unsuspecting men ; to carry off to captivity worse than death the women and larger children, was merely a question of *opportunity.*

The "spotted buffalo of the white brother" is hardier than the ancient and lawful game which ranged in such vast herds along the Arkansas, Republican and Platte Rivers, and the future geographers will not regale ingenuous American youth with that blood-curdling, hair-whitening picture of the shaggy and ferocious beasts rushing to suicide over an awful precipice overhanging a bottomless abyss. The bison will rather take his place in natural history with the extinct dodo and the out-going cassowary.

The tanned skin of the buffalo is the best material for the manufacture of " tepes," and the " *bois de bache* " is as good fuel as the Indian desires. It has been erroneously stated that only the white man kills and wastes buffalo. They are, or have been frequently killed by war parties, who take what may be needed as food ; but the rest of the carcass falls to the portion of wolves and ravens, never far off. Young buffaloes fall a prey to the hungry gray wolf and coyotes, and a sick or wounded buffalo has a long train attendant of wolves, thirsting for his blood.

Coronado, the old Spanish explorer who crossed the Gila in 1540, wrote a curious and accurate description of the *cibola*, of which I copy a portion : " These oxen are the bigness and color of our bulls; but their horns are not so great. They have a great bunch upon their fore shoulders, and more hair upon their fore part than on their hinder part; it is like wool. They have, as it were, a horse's mane upon their back-bone, and much hair and very long from the knee downward. They have great tufts of hair hanging down their foreheads, and it seemeth they have beards, because of the great store of hair hanging down at their chins and throats. The males have very long tails, and a great knob or flock at the end ; so that, in some respects, they resemble the lion, and, in some, the camel. Their masters have no other riches or substance; of them they eat, they drink, they apparel, they shoe themselves ; and of their hides make many things, as houses and ropes ; of their bones they make bodkins ; of their sinews and hair, thread; of their horns, maws and bladders, vessels ; and of their calf skins, buckets, wherein they draw and keep water."

The whole living of the roving tribes is thus cut off with the buffalo. The Apache love of meat is not fastidious, and they are fond of mule and horse flesh. Deer, antelope—whatever the game may be—every portion, except the bones, is consumed, the entrails being an especial delicacy. They partially cook it, generally eating it extremely rare ; that is, about half raw. Fertile valleys in the territories bear a small proportion to the extent of arid deserts, lava beds, and plains of sand. Isolated peaks contain wood and springs, thus affording protection for

Navajo Indian with Silver Ornaments.

the sure-footed savage, who can outmarch our
best cavalry horses. The scant grass is soon
exhausted, so he must move from place to place,
or starve, and thus necessity is added to inclina-
tion ; and they roam over immense tracts of
country, seeking what they may devour.

They have smoke signals by day and fire
beacons at night, and systems of telegraphy
understood only by themselves. The displace-
ment and overturning of a few stones on a trail,
or a bent or broken twig, is a note of warning
like the bugle call to disciplined troops. They
cross the *Jornada del Muerto*, "journey of
death," as the ninety mile desert was called by
the Spaniard, with an ease and fleetness no white
man can imitate, and, swooping down from
refuges in the natural fortresses of the mountains,
pounce upon the travelers. The many crosses
dotting the roadsides of Southern Arizona and
New Mexico mark the graves of murdered men ;
indeed, the country seems one vast graveyard, if
we may judge by the frequency of these rude
memorials. Trained by their mothers to theft
and murder from childhood, they are inured to
all extremes of heat and cold, hunger and thirst.
They are cunning as the red fox and insatiate
as tigers, so ingenious in preparing for surprises
that they will envelop themselves in a gray
blanket, sprinkle it carefully with earth, to
resemble a granite bowlder and be passed within
a few feet without suspicion. Again, they will
cover themselves with fresh grass, and, lying
motionless, seem a natural portion of the field,
or hid among the yuccas, they imitate the
appearance of the tree, so as to pass for one of
the plants.

Three-fourths of the Apache country consists
of barren volcanic rocks and sterile ridges,
where no plow can be driven and no water

found, and campaigning in their country is exposure to severe privations and dangers, aside from the attacks of the natives. There is no hope of glory to cheer the soldier who upholds our flag in that dreary field; there is no stimulus but duty. If he succeeds, the feeblest echo reaches the ears of friends in the states; scant mention is made in the papers; there is small honor in killing an Indian, still less in falling before one. And the work is endless, fruitless. It is to be recommenced every Spring, and as regularly stopped in the Fall by the snows of Autumn. A passing interest is roused; but it is brief, because the atrocities are so frequent and monotonous; always the same tale of insult, torture, death; and every year the same inquiry is made at Washington, and runs along the frontier, What can be done with the Apaches?

They should be exterminated, you say.

Yes, dear reader; but, unfortunately for our gallant army, extermination is a game two can play at.

Very few know, or care to know, that in the Apache War, ending October, 1880, more than four hundred white persons were scalped and tortured to death with devilish ingenuity. The war began on account of the removal of about four hundred Indians from their reservation at Ojo Caliente (warm springs), New Mexico. This is the ideal of a happy hunting ground. Standing on the parade ground at Fort Craig, you look toward the Black Range mountains, clad in pine groves, abounding in game and the precious stones so rare in New Mexico and Arizona. Morning and evening wrap them in aerial tints of surpassing loveliness; and one can well imagine such a spot would be very dear to any one calling it home, be his color what it may. When the news came, the Indians received the announcement with deep grief and bitter curses. The reason assigned by our Government for the removal from this spot to the arid, volcanic *mesa* of Arizona was that two agencies might be consolidated, and the expense of maintaining them lessened. They went unwillingly, because this beautiful country was the land of their fathers, and because they could not live peaceably with the Indians of the San Carlos reservation, and only at the bayonet's point would they march. Their war chief was Victorio, successor to the renowned Magnus Colorado, who was the most influential and successful statesman and warrior the Apaches have had for a century. They left Ojo Caliente, with its green fields and glorious mountains, in the Spring of 1877. In September, of the same year, Victorio and his people stole away from San Carlos, saying they would rather die than live there. They were pursued by our cavalry, overtaken, and several of them killed; many women and children were taken prisoners. The rest under Victorio, escaped, went to Fort Wingate, and surrendered. They were sent back to Ojo Caliente, and held as prisoners of war until the order came from Washington for them to return to Arizona. Then they stole the cavalry horses and started on the war-path.

The war was a series of ambuscades and retreats, lasting a year and a half. The details of Indian fighting are much the same everywhere; but Apaches surpass in cunning, stratagy, secrecy, all the sons of men. They are an enemy not to be despised, and as friends are *never* to be trusted. Their signal system is so perfect that by it they act in perfect concert, and bands of fives, tens, and twenties, separated from each other by twenty,

thirty, even forty miles, manage to maintain
a perfect police intelligence over the vast
region once their own territory.

Victorio had one son named for the man
who, beyond all men of the civilized and
even savage world, has had the confidence of
his kind, Washington; the one white man
Indians admit to a place in their land of happy
spirits. He was shot near Fort Cummings,
and his death was a heavy blow to the chief,
whose fame and blanket he was to inherit,
whose pride was centered in his son. In the
Fall of 1879, Washington's body lay unburied in the deep defile where he fell; the
long hair matted and dried with blood, the
flesh shrunken and skin tanned like old leather.
In the dry, dewless air of New Mexico, bodies are not subject to decay as in the East,
and will shrivel like a mummy by exposure
to sun and wind. Long before this time the
flesh of the chief's son has probably been
gnawed clean from the bones by the ravening
mountain wolf.

Washington had but one wife, contrary
to the usual custom of his tribe, and at twenty,
wooed and won the "Princess," as we used to
call her, because she was of the royal family
of the illustrious Magnus Colorado. She was a
comely damsel, very young, who assumed some
dignity and state because of her high blood, and
she never forgot the ancient splendors of her line.

Victorio and his band were surrounded and
killed in the Castillos Mountains of Mexico, by
troops under General Terassas (Mexican), and
the war ended with a grand parade in the city of
Chihuahua. Cathedral bells rang, bands played,
and the victorious column marched the street
amid rousing cheers. Following General
Terassas and his command came prisoners,

women and children on mules and ponies; they were to be given away and find homes among their conquerors. Behind them were seventy-eight Mexicans, carrying poles twenty feet high, on which were scalps dangling like waving plumes. The whole head of hair was torn off instead of one tuft, and the slayer of Victorio, a Farhumara Indian bore aloft with pride a pole on which hung the gray scalp of the dead chief. At sight of it the cheers of the Mexicans were redoubled, and I could but think so barbaric a procession is rarely seen in one of the oldest and wealthiest cities of the North American Continent. There was great cause for rejoicing; the bravest and wiliest of the Apaches was dead, and he had no son to succeed him, for with Victorio's death the cause was lost. His wife cut off her hair, as the old Greek wives used to, and buried it, an offering to the spirit of the fallen chief to whom she was devoted, yet said to be less slavish than most Indian wives.

Victorio's band were all stout fighters and *devilish* when under the influence of whiskey or *tiswin*, an intoxicating drink made from corn. One of them, Rafael, split his child's head open with an ax, when drunk; another time stabbed his wife so that she died. He was then overcome by penitence, sacrificed all of his beads and most of his clothes to the dear departed, cut his and children's hair short, and sheared the horses' manes and tails. These manifestations of anguish over, he went up into a high hill, and howled with uplifted hands. That shape, outlined against the intense azure of the sky, was a most ridiculous sight. The funeral dirge was a long, slow, horrible wail. There is no Apache law to touch such a criminal; and this case is less distressing than one other which came under my notice in New Mexico. An old Indian bought a

young girl of her mother, paying her price in
ponies and blankets—much against her will—
she, like a sensible girl, preferring a younger
man. She ran away, and hid in dark cañons and
pine woods, but the bridegroom tracked her and
beat her on her head with his gun for running
off; and, worst of all, her mother thought the
son-in-law was exactly right in the matter.
Finally, when her skull was nearly broken, her
spirit was entirely gone, and she yielded to the
inevitable, as so many women of the higher
grade have done, and silently took up the heavy
burden of life alotted the wife of the most barbarous of barbarians. Women are of so little
account with these people that few of their
daughters are given a name, and even their
mothers often mourn at their birth, regarding
them merely as an incumbrance on the tribe.
They are pretty as children, but the exposure
and hard work of their lot change them to
wrinkled, muscular hags at thirty, and when
they die the Apache chief merely says: "It was
only a woman; no loss."

CHAPTER XVII.

OLD MINERS.

OBLIVON scattereth her poppies even in
guarded chambers where the Muse of History
holds sleepless watch, and the broken, disconnected
annals of New Mexico in the seventeenth century are like dreamy legends or misty fables of
the heroic ages.

The avaricious and despotic governors of the
province made no secret of their odious laws,
and apalling atrocities are put on rec

ın business manner, without concealment or
attempt at palliation. Many details are trivial
and there are long catalogues readable by no man
but Dr. Dryasdust. Running through dispatches
is an appeal for money, petitions for appropriation
the keynote of official song, from the Empress of
India down to the lowest official of the youngest
republic. How could the commandants open
mines, develop the resources of Nueva Mejico,
even with slave labor, without money or its equi-
valent? Beside this familiar wail are found
meager and detached accounts of long marches
among the peace-loving Pueblos, who hailed the
fair strangers as gods, and their horses as beautiful, immortal animals, tamed for the service of
their celestial visitants. These

——"most Gothic gentlemen of Spain"

were no believers in the rolling-stone theory.
We think of them as filled with restless energy ;
but in a half sheet of ancient MS. I find this
item, made probably by a peevish Churchman,
soured because he missed promotion : " Our
captains were great enemies to all kinds of labor.
They taught that gold was good for sore eyes
and disease of the heart. Their desire for it
was such they would enter into the infernal
regions and cross the three rivers of hell to obtain
it." One Captain Salazar, in the Valley of the
Del Norte, caught a *cacique* [chief] and chained
him, to make him tell where certain treasure
was hidden. After holding the savage in
confinement several months, the Christian put
him to torture ; but without avail. "We then let
him go," said the historian, dryly ; "for the miserable heathen could not tell what he did not know."

The blood of the Christian of that age ran riot
with the lust of gold and power ; the two pas-
sions swaying men of mature years, tempered in

11

youth by the soft influence of love. It is easy to
understand that the Pueblo Indians, who were
making some approaches to civilization in the
midst of savagery, then wore a yoke to which
the iron collar of thrall worn by Gurth, the
swineherd, was light as a lady's necklace.

History holds no deeper tragedy than the
record of foreign invasion in North America. The
man on horseback assumed that slavery was necessary, therefore right, therefore just ; and by the
grace of God (which meant the iron hand in the
glove of steel) he rewarded captains and corpor-
als with lands wide as whole counties, as yet
unmapped and unsubdued. His first object was
to pile high and yet higher the riches which maintained the splendor of his house. The old Castilian had the psychic identities of the modern
one—pride, vanity, intolerance, egotism, hatred
of labor, and fondness for bloody sports. In the
irresponsible positions held by the local tyrants
in Nueva Espagna there was boundless sweep
for gratification of these traits. Whatever was
not Romish or Spanish they regarded with haughty scorn. Adventurers those colonists were, but
adventurers of no common order. The spirit
of Crusades was yet alive, and each man felt himself a champion of the Cross, and with his sword
of matchless temper vowed to strike a blow for
Holy Church. Conversion was ever a prime object with the *Conquistador*. The saintly Isabella
had it always at heart, and one of the latest acts
of her reign was to commend to the fathers the
souls of her unbelieving subjects across the sea.
The fanatic zeal of the *padres* reached through
every grade, and the *hidalgos* gloried in the title
" Swords of the Church." The temples of sin,
as the little mud *estufas*, or chapels, of the Indians
were called, must be leveled, false gods and alter-
fires overthrown, and the heathen brought to the

true faith, under their converting steel. The earliest revolt of the Pueblos, after the first conquest, grew out of the whipping of forty natives, because they refused to accept the new religion and bow to the hated cross of the unseen God of the stranger.

The early colonists were all miners ; but, owing to the care taken in concealments of them by the natives, little is left to indicate operations, except miles of earth cut into running galleries and driven tunnels. Slavery everywhere, when applied to field labor, is destructive to human life. What must it have been when directed to mining, under taskmasters who did not value one life at a pin's fee ?

Even with the aid of science, machinery, and the many humanities of the nineteenth century, it is still the most melancholy of trades. The task of him who "hangs in midway air" to gather samphire is not half so dreadful as work done in danger from every element.

The ruins of a large prison among the placers of the Miembres Mountains, abandoned mines reopened, and traditions of Indians clearly show that the conquered races were treated as though they did not belong to the human family. There is infinite pathos in the banishment of the untamed Indian from the free Sierras and the glad sunshine to gloomy caverns, where thousands were actually buried alive. They were driven to toil under the lash and at the bayonets' point; in peril from falling walls, deadly gas, sudden floods, and the work was done by manual labor alone. They broke the rocks with miserable tools and insufficient light, and mixed the ores slowly and painfully with naked feet. Quartz was ground in rude *arrastres*, or mills to which men and women were yoked like cattle. Every ounce of precious metal was literally the price of blood.

So changless are the Spaniard and the Indian
that the description of a miner near Chihuahua,
written last year, will do tolerably well for the
Pueblo of the seventeenth century. Then, as
now, the Spaniard was the overseer. The peon
is the slave of to-day. As a rule, Mexicans,
however intelligent and educated, have no genius
for machinery. They blow, crush, and drill as their
fathers did before them, and for transportation
of ore they prefer a train of mules to a train of
cars. The miner in the sepulchral shades of San
Domingo has never heard of crushing-mills or
cars. A yard-square piece of untanned hide,
stretched on two sticks, is his wheelbarrow.
The drill, the pick, the crowbar are his only tools.
Out of the black door of the mine he steps
quickly, lightly, though weighted by a sack containing a hundred and fifty pounds of ore. A
broad band of rawhide attaches the burden to
his forehead. He is naked, as when he came
into the world. His neck and limbs are like a
prize-fighter's. The perspiration streams from
his sooty face and body, and his breast heaves
spasmodically. There are no air-shafts, and for
two hours he has been down in the hydrogen of
the mine. The path he has travelled, in ascending,
winds hither and thither ; now up, then down ;
now in a chamber of whose extent he has no
conception ; now through a gallery narrow as
the cavity of a sugar hogshead—so narrow that,
to bear his cargo through, he must double and
crawl like a panther ; now along a slippery
ledge, where the slightest error in the placement
of a hand or foot is instant death, because on
one side is an abyss which for the matter of vision might as well be fathomless. Now it turns a
sharp corner ; now it traverses rough masses of
rocks, which are not all *débris* from blasting, for
some of them have tumbled from the roof, and

may be followed by "companion pieces" at any
moment. Woe to him whom they catch! Thus
for more than half an hour the poor wretch has
come. To such a feat, performed regularly six
times a day, what is crossing the rapids of Niagara on a wire? What wonder that the breast
heaves and the sweat pours? Have you not
heard a man escaped from drowning tell of the
agony thrilling him the instant the life-saving air
rushed into the cells of his collapsed lungs?
Something like that this poor miner and his comrades say they suffer every time they pass the
door of the mine, suddenly into the rarefied atmosphere of the upper world. Horrible life! And
how wretchedly rewarded! Between mining and
morals there is no connection, still the question
comes: Was it for this God gave him a soul?

The man's first act, on stepping into daylight,
is to snatch the little tallow-dip from its perch on
his head and blow it out. It cost him a *claco*
only; but it was such a friend down in Tartarus!
Without it, could he have ever risen to the light?
As its glimmer came dancing up the rugged
way, how the darkness parted before him and the
awaiting gulfs revealed themselves! He proceeds
next to the door of the roofless house. A man
meets him, helps him unload, takes the sack to
a rough contrivance and weighs it, giving a ticket
of credit. Not a word is spoken. They are like
gliding ghosts. Resuming the emptied sack, the
naked wretch turns, walks quickly to the entrance
of the mine, lights the friendly taper, looks once

> ———"to sun, and stream, and plain,
> As what he ne'er might see again,"

re-enters the rocky jaws, and wades back through
the inner darkness. Yet he is not alone. He is a
type. He has comrades whom he will meet on
the way; comrades in the extremest pit, wherein
the sounds of rueful labor are blended with
mournful talk.

The friction of the coming and going of miners has polished the slippery floor to glassy smoothness. With the help of guides, we descended the black pit, and deep in the heart of the mountain sought the men at work. The wretched candle each one carried served not so much to illuminate our way as it appeared to burn a little hole in the darkness. Perspiration fairly rained from us ; but we came to see, and pushed on in the black solitude, till strength and courage almost failed. At last we observed, far off to our right, a light dimly reddening the rocky wall. Miners at work! Good! Just what we came for. Slowly, carefully, painfully we drew near the beacon. There was no sound of voices, no ring of hammers, nor echo of blows. A solitary workman was playing the mystic art. He had not heard our approach, and we stopped to observe him before speaking. A little basket at his left contained a few tallow dips and some *tortillas* Close by, in position to illuminate brightly about two feet of the wall directly in front of him, was his lighted candle. A pile of fine crushed ore, the result of his labor, covered the floor to his right, and on it lay an iron bar and a pick. Above him extended a vault in the darkness without limit. He had come there about the break of day in the upper world. He came alone, and alone he had remained. Not a word had he heard, not one spoken. The candles not merely lightened his labor : but, since each one would burn about so long—a certain number exhausting by noon, another bringing the night —they also kept his time. The solitude was awful! In the uncertain light the naked, crouching body seemed that of an animal. We spoke to him. The voice was kindly, yet it sounded in his ears, so long attuned to silence, like a pistol-shot. He started up in attitude of defense.

He may be squatted at the base of the same wall to-day. Pity for him, wherever he is! Pity for all of his craft!"

CHAPTER XVIII.

THE NEW MINERS.

THE modern Mexican is true to the traditions of old Spain—jealous of foreigners, opposed to change, ever copying the past.

There is a legend across the waters that one morning, not a great while ago, the glorious angel who keeps the keys of the viewless gate gave Adam permission to come back and look after his farm. Watched by Gabriel, chief of the guard angelic, the spirit (oldest of all created, yet forever young) dropped through the silent starry spaces, among rushing planets and blazing suns, numbered only in Heaven, poised above the Alps, and looked over Germany. The men were smoking meerschaums, drinking beer, and talking metaphysics. Disgusted, he fled in swift flight toward France. There he saw nothing but polite frivolities. The soul of our common ancestor was saddened. France was even worse than Germany. He did not linger. Taking wing while morn still purpled the east, he crossed the mountains into Spain, and, resting incumbent on air, surveyed the kingdom. One glance across it sufficed. The spirit folded his radiant wings. "Ah!" he cried, enraptured. "Home again! Here all is just as I left it." This old story well illustrates the influence of Iberain aversion to change, which has been felt wherever Spain has had a lasting foothold in the New World. The antiquated mining implements of the by-gone generations of New Mexico are the queerest things in the world to the Leadviller, used to the ponderous quartz mills, driven by invisible power, moving like a free intelligence.

When the mines in the Placer Mountains, thirty miles southwest of the City of Holy Faith, were in operation, they were worked by the old-fashioned Spanish *arrastre*, the rudest, most wasteful of mining machines. It consists in nothing more than two large flat stones, attached to a horizontal beam and drawn around by a mule (in the days of slavery by men and women), upon a bed of flat stones. The process of grinding the ore was slow, the amalgamation imperfect, and not more than one-third of the gold could be separated from the quartz.

There is good reason for believing that mines near Santa Fè were worked in this way before Hudson entered the river which bears his name. They were probably *en bonanza* in the years when the great Queen, steering the English ship through stormy seas, paused amid the breakers to listen to the wooing of Robert Dudley.

The Spaniard in that day mined with stone hammers, and it is surprising to us they could sink deep shafts with such wretched appliances. They were ignorant of carbonates of silver, and took nothing but the argentiferous galena from the vein, throwing away nine-tenths of the best-paying mineral. There is little statistical knowledge of the working of any one mine in this territory, but old Church records are said to show that the ten per cent. in tithes collected for it amounted to about ten millions. This was realized from mines adjacent to Santa Fè. In each of the ravines running into the Cañada de las Minas (Glen of Mines) more or less of "float" is found. This is silver-bearing galena ore, washed from lodes crossing the ravines, and is certain indication of silver leads in close vicinity.

In 1846, when Gen. Kearney took possession of Santa Fè, nearly all the miners left the placers, never to return. Many reasons are given for their hasty flight, one of which is that, being Mexicans, they feared impressment into the American service, and escaped while they could. It is believed that mining operations in the hight of prosperity then suddenly stopped, as the abandoned and decaying town of Francisco near by shows; and but little has since been done to revive the business until within the last few years.

Los Cerillos Mines, now being rapidly opened up, are in a chain of low conical mountains north of the Galisteo, twenty miles from the capital city. In these ranges are found syenitic rocks, carboniferous limestone and sandstone formations, the latter containing coal. They are traversed for thirty or forty miles with valuable lodes, the veins running from the northeast to the southwest, and almost daily fresh "Spanish traces," old workings, come in sight, to cheer the heart of the prospector. After the rebellion of 1680 the Indians returned to their pueblos and submitted to the foreign yoke, on condition that mines should not be reopened. It would appear the treaty was kept in good faith, and that the very ancient mines remained untouched during the subsequent period of Spanish rule. Some of these old diggings in Los Cerillos have been so carefully concealed that it requires the keenest scrutiny to find them. The shaft of the Santa Rosa Mine, on reöpening, was found to have been sunk fifty-five feet. One shaft is one hundred and sixty-five feet to water. How much deeper no man can tell. The *débris* and precious mineral were carried up on the backs of *peones*, and the notched cedar trees which were their only ladders two hundred years ago are still the means of descent to the venturesome traveler, exploring the rediscovered galleries.

The early proprietaries followed no rules in prospecting. They were led by whim, or most frequently by dreams, the medium of communication preferable to the patron saints. The most prejudiced observer can not help admiring the boldness and energy of their movements. And the fields are just as rich to-day. If they paid under such feeble, unskilled management, they must be much more profitable now, with the help of science and delicate machinery. For three hundred years and more the sands have been washed out at the base of Los Cerillos; but not until very recently have those washing for precious grains of metal thought of looking to the *source*, the core of the mountains, for the best deposits. This was the process of experiment and experience in the great California Gulch at Leadville.

In these volcanic hills, still bearing marks of the fiery lava flow, are the Montezuma Turquoise Mines, which are marvels of deep excavation. In one instance half a mountain is cut away by Indians of the pre-historic period, in their search for the coveted, the priceless *chalchuite*, the Aztecan diamond.

The tradition runs that anciently the gold and silver-bearing ores were borne on the backs of *burros* to Chihuahua, Mexico (six hundred miles away), for reduction; that long trains of the patient creatures, lean, thirsty, and beaten with many stripes, were perpetually coming and going along the Valley del Norte, curtaining it with clouds of yellow dust.

It seems a baseless tradition. If the gold-hunters could reduce their ores in Chihuahua, why not in Santa Fè as well? In 1867 the larger portion of El Palacio, then standing, was cleared away, and, among many curious relics brought to light, after long burial, was a clumsy smelting furnace, thoroughly bricked up on every side and worn with long and hard usage. From its ashes were taken out bits of charcoal, showing clearly that ages ago, time out of mind, the Spaniards discovered and used it in smelting their ores.

The ancient method of washing for silver was a very simple process. The operator required nothing but a crowbar, a shovel, and a tanned skin. This last he fashioned into a water-tight basin by stretching it upon a square frame. Filling it with water, he stood over it, rocking in it a little tub holding sand and grit, from which, washed free of clay and earth, he separated the worthless pebbles, and selected the valuable particles.

In old ranches through the country we occasionally see an antique candlestick of beaten silver, or a salt-cellar of hammered *plata*—heirlooms proving that in long-gone generations silver was found and in quantities.

Ask how old they are, and the ever-ready " *Quien sabe* " is the answer.

From the beginning of the seventeenth till the eighteenth century there was a rapid succession of rebellions and civil wars, with Santa Fé as the field and the important strategic point. In 1680 the Pueblos allied with the Teguas— described as a nation of warriors—and routed the Spaniards, driving them from the land as far south as El Paso del Norte.

Another army was mustered and sent up from the City of Mexico, but feared to take the offensive, and for twelve years the land had rest, was quiet, as before the foreign invasion. It was in this interval of twelve years that the ancient mines were hidden. All the old mineral workings were covered and carefully concealed, and death was the penalty for any who should reveal to white

men where precious metals or stones were to be
found. After 1692 mining in the province was
abandoned, and to this day it is the rarest thing
for a Spaniard or an Indian to engage in mining.
They seem to have forsaken it forever.

It is said that in the whole compass of East
Indian literature there is not a single passage
showing a love of liberty. The millions appear
created for the gratification of one man. If the
West Indian be, indeed, his brother, then were
brothers never so unlike. To the North American, freedom is the very breath of his nostrils, and
the degradation of slavery worse than slow torture or sudden death.

In irrepressible yearning for liberty the Pueblos
escaped from mines, such as I have attempted to
describe, to inaccessible mountain fastnesses, the
steeps of distant cañons and hiding-places in
dens of animals. How many perished in these
realms of silence and despair none but the record-
ing angel can testify. The polished armor of the
invaders covered hearts hard as triple brass, and
silken banners floated over knights whose avarice
was equalled only by their cruelty. The fugitives
were tracked and hunted down with bloodhounds,
as though they were beasts of prey.

As has been written of the same tragedy then
being enacted in Peru : " It was one unspeakable
outrage, one unutterable ruin, without discrimina-
tion of age or sex. From hiding-places in the
clefts of rocks and the solitude of invisible caves,
where there was no witness but the all-seeing sun,
there went up to God a cry of human despair."
The Bishop of Chiapsa, himself a Spaniard, affirms
that more than fifteen millions were cut off in his
time, slaves of the mines. On the Northern Continent history is but an imperfect guide. That
the rich valleys of the Rio Grande and the Pecos
once held a dense population is plainly proved

by the ruins of cities slowly crumbling away. We
have only dim glances into long, dark spaces; but
there is light enough to see the conqueror's daily
walk was on the necks of the conquered natives,
who swiftly declined to an abject and heart-
broken race.

So great was the horror of the first conquest
that the memory of it has been kept alive through
ten generations. The Pueblo mother still shud-
ders as she tells the story of ancient wrong and
woe to her children; and the unwritten law yet
binds the red race to secrecy, and is a hindrance
in the opening of mines in the territories.

Princely fortunes were made, and, if tribes,
whole nations, were swept off the face of the earth;
they were but so many heathen less to cumber
the ground and drag the march of conquest. To
understand how valueless human life was then,
look down the steep sides of the old mines reopened. Rows of cedar pegs serve, you see, as ladders along the black walls, from the bottom to the
entrance. Imagine a man climbing up, weighted
with a sack containing a hundred pounds of ore,
fastened to his back by a broad band of raw-hide
across his forehead. The slightest error in the
placement of hand or foot must miss the hold, and
the burden-bearer be dashed to pieces; but it
could have been no loss, else better means would
have been provided. There must have been hundreds at hand to take his place.

When did Spain stretch forth her hand, except
to scatter curses? It is part of my faith, derived
from the study of history—in fact, it is the great
lesson of history—that nations are punishable,
like individuals, and that for every national sin
there is, soon or late, a national expiation. Does
not Spain place the doctrine beyond question?
No European power has had such opportunities
for noble achievement; yet what good has come

through her ?   What grand idea or benign principle, what wholesome impression upon mankind?
She was the Tarshish of Solomon ; her mines
were the subject of quarrel between the Roman
and Carthagenian ; in the day of Christ she still
supplied the world with the royal metals.   Such
were her resources in the beginning.   Afterwards,
when commerce reached out through the Pillars
of Hercules and drew the West in under its influences, a people of masterful genius, sitting where
Europe bends down so close to Africa, would
have stretched a gate from shore to shore and by
it ruled the earth.

Yet later she received the gift of the New
World.   Where is the trophy marking her
beneficent use of the gift?   She had already
ruined the civilization which had its seat in the
pillared shades of the Alhambra.   In her keeping
were placed the remains of the Aztec and the
relics of the Incas, only to be destroyed.   Drunk
with the blood of nations, she who ruthlessly
subjected everything to the battle-ax, the rack,
and the torch is now dying of slow decay.

Could the breath blow from the four winds and
breathe upon the Indians, reckoned by millions,
who perished under Spanish rule; if their dust
could but come together, and all those slain live
again and testify, alas ! for Castelar, wisest of
visionaries, awaiting the Republic of Europe to
bring about the resurrection of his country."

CHAPTER XIX.

THE man on the frontier who has no speculation in his eyes is dead as Banquo. The contagion of soul, says the ancient philosopher, is quicker than that of the body, and I have yet to see the one with soul so dead as to refuse a venture in mines, and wholly resist the fever which spares neither age nor sex, yet is not fatal or even unpleasant. While the craze lasts, it affects the brain, quickening the imagination and distorting the vision. Under its powerful alchemy discolored stones by the wayside become bowlders of ore, it seams bare cliffs with veins of gleaming metal, plants mines in impossible places, converts vertical strata into immense deposits. All the way it silvers the dreams of night and lengthens them unbroken into the day. Knowledge comes to the fever-smitten without study. One glance at a lofty mountain-range is sufficient to determine if it be metalliferous, and, balancing a lump of ore on his gritty forefinger, he can tell its exact per cent. of silver.

The victim of the epidemic carries scraps of grimy stuff in his pockets, wrapped in dirty cloths, and a small magnifying glass, into which he puckers his fevered eyes many times in the twenty-four hours, and surveys his uncoined treasure with doating glances. He unselfishly allows confidential friends to look through the lens, and expects enthusiastic admiration in return for the privilege. Unless the confidential friend is an enemy in disguise, he will gloat over the earthy specimens too. He talks little, if at all, apparently in a generous burst of feeling about

175

bonanzas. *En bonanza* means literally smooth
sailing, a fair breeze, etc., and is used by Mexican
miners, applied to exceedingly rich ores or
"shoots." Free translation, "booming." His
voice is pitched in a low key—a loud, impressive,
I may say distracting whisper. The delirium is
pleasurable, for the man's hopes are indomitable,
and a secret trust covers a dark stratum, so to
speak, of fear; but he is reticent, grave as though
his shafts had pierced to the very center of
gravity.

The arithmetic man, who loves figures, has
estimated that in the flush times of Colorado the
successful were one to every five hundred honest
miners. He has not brought in returns from the
territories, and there is, in consequence, broader
sweep for imagination in the undeveloped regions,
where mining is yet partly experiment.

The fortunes of two or three millionaires
balance the losses of thousands, like the many
deaths which go to make up a victory. Are you
the five hundredth or eight hundredth happy
child of Destiny, the victorious captain for whom
the unnamed heroes fell? You? Of the bonanza
king we daily hear by telegraph, photograph,
autograph. Of the vast army of the defeated—
nothing. Singly they tramp back home, steal in
darkly at dead of night, ravage the pantry, and,
having slept off fatigue, are ready to deny having
thought of Leadville and Golden.

One of the cheapest and easiest ways of reaching a mine is by a "grubstake." This euphonious
word means a certain sum (say one hundred and
eighty dollars) advanced to a man by another,
with more money and less time, and the prospector has an interest in whatever he may find.
You meet him on every road, every highway,
every by-way, and where there is no way in the
territories. The prospective millionaire gener-

ally wears an umbrageous hickory shirt, sleeves
usually rolled to the elbow, exposing arms not the
fairest, buckskin or brown duck pants, or a ready-
made suit, ready to be unmade at the seams, and
a hat of superlative slouch. His head is shaggy
as a buffalo's, with sun-scorched hair, and his face,
lined with fierce sunbeat and wrinkling wind, is
a glossy red, as though it had been veneered,
sand-papered, and varnished. He carries a striking hammer, weighing from five to eight pounds.
Does it look like an enchanter's rod? In his
hand it may prove a fairy wand, potent as the
double-headed hammer of Thor. His *burro*, or
donkey, is not much larger than a sheep, yet able
to bear three hundred pounds' weight. On the
patient, long-suffering brute is strapped a blanket.
Above it are piled rations of bacon, sugar, crackers, a pick and shovel, and a tin pot for boiling a
coarse brown powder, called in bitter (very bitter)
sarcasm coffee. In seeking claims, he is oftenest
attended by a partner, familiarly and affectionately called " my pard." In this land of sudden
death, where every man carries pistols and loves
to use them, one lone prospector may be picked
off almost anywhere, and his bones left in deep
cañon or lonesome gulch, and no questions asked.
It is best to hunt in couples. Like the intelligent and reliable contraband of other days, the
honest miner is forever bringing in good news.
" Lee is just where we want him!" " The latest
find is prodigious, the best thing yet, and lacks
nothing but capital for development to equal anything in the Comstock Lode or Santa Eulalia!"
This last is a mine worth having, where the early
diggers set no value on common ore, but sought
" pockets," rich with silver; a soft yellow clay,
scooped out rapidly and easily with horn spoons.
Sometimes they were of immense extent, require-
ing years to exhaust.

13

I have not been able to learn why the miner is always named the honest miner; but such is the fact. To this well-worn adjective are sometimes added reticent and successful, when the speaker wishes to be unusually impressive. It has been written that mining speculations, like transactions in horse-flesh, have a tendency to blunt moral perceptions, and soured politicians insinuate it was first phrased by ambitious patriots who were anxious to secure his suffrage. Be that as it may, the honest miner is our man now. Though he does not pretend to be a poet, his is the vision and faculty divine. He is attended by presences to other eyes unseen, like the inspired sculptor, who in a heavenly fervor of inspiration hewed the rough block of marble by the roadside and let the prisoned angel out. By break of day, while the warm valley still holds the night in its bosom, he is up and on the march. The shadow of a great rock or a sighing pine has been his shelter, the overarching blue canopy his tent, the world is his field. For his unfailing appetite there are crackers, bacon, and coffee. Like Macaulay's fellow-traveler, he breakfasts as if he had fasted the day before, and dines as though he had never breakfasted. His *burro* is happy as that melancholy beast can be on a little grama grass (*Ætheroma oligistarchon*) or twigs and leaves of scrub oak. He wanders from the borderline northward, among cold, sharp, icy crags, where desolation dwells in matchless state; where, among treeless, bald peaks, she holds and guards her Paradise, perfect even to the grim, painted savage, who, with scalping-knife, instead of flaming sword, does the duty of the sentinel-angel at the gate. Lava-beds do not stop him, nor chaparral, mezquit, or cactus jungle, or the pricking "Spanish bayonet." In withering wind, in blinding snow and drifting sand, the undaunted fellow pushes his search for rich leads.

Such persistent energy directed to any other business would command success; but will it in prospecting? That depends. If he fails in finding a good thing (say a lode worth a million or so) in a given district, it does not shake his steadfast confidence. He makes a new deal, and begins again, for he " is bound to spot the treasure."

The claim-stake is usually a pine board, marked with certain inscriptions in pencil, which ooze from within glazes over and makes indelible. Pleasant and consoling to him is it to know that no wise man from the East—no scientist, no geologist—has ever found a valuable mine. " Them literary fellows have to take a back seat " when it comes to locating a claim. Luck, chance, accident, and the prospector are the powers to be depended upon then. But when he does strike the big lead, and the crumbly ore, with its glittering white-and-yellow streakings, is reported inexhaustable, then these wholesome adages floor the honest miner. A man cannot see very far underground. It takes a mine to work a mine. Luck may find the lead, but science molds the silver brick ; and to these precious truths are added the proverb so dear to gentlemen of the profession of the renowned Oakhurst : " There's nothing certain about luck, except that it's bound to change."

The old Spaniards had the national love of gambling—the gambler's unreasoning hope and his blind belief in luck. If Fortune frowned to-day, she would brightly smile across the green cloth to-morrow. If gold is not in this glittering, cheating mica, it is hidden elsewhere, awaiting him who is bold enough to risk the chances of winning. The same trait is deeply marked in the American of our generation. Mining is a business to which all other occupations are dull and tame. The lumps of soft, blue-looking rock, not much harder than clay, streaked and spangled with shining threads, are dear to the American as they were to the Castilian heart and eye.

A man undertaking a scheme in which the odds are five hundred to one against success might be considered a simpleton elsewhere; but not so on the frontier. Thousands, armed with pretended stoicism, fevered with anxiety, rush West, "to look into mines a little," dig deep, and find at the bottom of the shaft what the gods of Olympus sent as underlying all the ills—Hope.

It is as certain as the sun rises and sets that the gambling and not the commercial instinct predominates in mining transactions. The fascination is in the hazard. The spell, so binding usually, is not of avarice, but lies in that delicious, feverish, intoxicating *charm of chance.* To borrow the words of one who has tried it: "There is a delight in its agony, a sweetness in its insanity, a drunken, glorious intensity of *sensation* in its limitless swing between a prince's treasures and a beggar's death, which lend life a sense never known before; rarely, indeed, once tasted, ever abandoned."

CHAPTER XX

THE ASSAYERS.

A CERTAIN room in El Palacio is devoted to assaying the precious ores. Its blackened, time-stained rafters look as though they might fall any moment; but believers in luck rest in calm assurance that the catastrophe will not occur in their time. Vainly is the tale told how the very day Governor Merriwether took possession of the Palace, to assume the executive duties of the territory, the roof of the room in which he

had once been a prisoner fell in. Nobody scares
at that old story now. The slanting beam overhead will not drop till we are out of the way;
the crumbling adobes will hold together awhile
yet. No use running till you are hurt. There
is too much actual danger about us to allow the
sensationalist a chance to waken fears.

The mud walls of the room I speak of were
once papered; but the hanging has flaked off, revealing the brown ground, making splotches here
and there, like a disease. Cobwebs of pre-historic
antiquity hang in lines, like ropes of dirty rags.
The one north window is obscured by dust and
fly-specks, the dull panes and deep walls letting
in a dim and not religious light. It was formerly
a bedroom, I believe. Of the living things which
still may burrow in the walls, as the French
women say, I beseech you to suppose them.
The bare floor is dusty and gritty with sand. In
one corner is a barrel of charcoal; beside it pine
kindling and old newspapers. A long pine table
holds the assayer's tools—the many contrivances
necessary to his vocation. Scales that weigh
with the delicate nicety of Portia's, blow-pipes,
bottles of acids, mortar and pestles, little hammers,
and sieves, beside waiting specimens, done up in
muslin, carefully separated and labeled. Such
stones come in every mail, every train, every
ambulance, every pocket. "Blossom rocks"
adorn window-sill and mantelpiece, street-corners
and counters, serve as paper-weights and door-
props, and are a stumbling-block and rock of
offense along the sidewalks.

I am not here to talk of chlorides, pyrites,
sulphurets, silica, and manganese; but only to
remark, *en passant*, that free gold and ruby silver
are pretty terms—very pretty, indeed—and easily
understood by any lady in the land.

At this table presides the refiner and purifier

of silver—the Man of Destiny. It may be a
Freiburg professor, with flowing beard and a
name in harsh discord with the mellifluous Spanish
titles, or a graduate of a New York school of
mines. No matter. He understands his business
and on his fiat hang hopes high as the sky, for to
him are submitted samples of raw ores believed
valuable, and now comes the question: Is the
deposit represented rich enough to justify deep
digging—in other words, to make a mine of?
The honest miner's flush of hope and sinking of
fear are comparable only to the tremor of the
quivering aspirant for literary fame, who, with
darling MS. in hand, respectfully addresses the
torturer, and withdraws to await his doom.

The small, square furnace glows with fervent
heat, and the room is suffocating. With, beaded
forehead and dripping chin, the assayer weighs,
pulverizes, sifts the fine dust in the cupels, to
undergo the only sure test, the trial by fire. His
hidden power revives the old romantic ideas of
scholars, to whom the ancient and secret science
of alchemy was a religion, part of the sublime,
cabalistic wisdom revealed unto Adam, to console
him for the loss of Paradise; for which study
philosophers shut themselves up to lifelong toil
in cells and caves. He is of the order of mystics,
who grew lean and pale pondering brass-bound
volumes of wicked-looking hieroglyphs; who
understood the charm of the burning belt and
the ciphered girdle. He deals with strange
crucibles and subtle compounds; by a wizard
spell masters the forces of the earth, the
transmutation of metals, and by magic numbers
discovers the golden secrets of Nature. While
the cabala combination is being applied, that
laboratory is the center of many hopes.

How often, ah! *how* often does it prove the
gold is dull lead, the silver is become dross. The

waiting miner is " not in harmonization with his
environments." He hovers about the Palace,
trying to cover his eager anxiety under the
studied stoicism of the frontiersman. Sometimes
the sun looks down upon him, as it rises, and
finds him a patient watcher, waiting for the cooling of the metal. He has silently outwatched the
stars, only to learn that specimens believed very
rich (his darling promises) are worthless—not a
speck, not a pinhead of precious mineral to be
seen in a dozen cupels. What he held was so
much fairy gold that turns to dust and dross.

The gold-seeker, in the first chill of disappointment, refuses to credit the report; but the refiner's furnace has spoken with tongues of fire.
There is the evidence of his own senses; he cannot doubt the testimony. He quickly recovers
his stolid composure, takes a square meal, possibly a square drink, and, led by the spirit of unrest, is ready to face the inevitable hardships of
another long search for rich leads.

He rises, after an adverse stroke of fate, buoy-
ant as ever with irrepressible hope—as Dr. Johnson says of second marriages, "the triumph of
hope over experience." In the morning the disappointment seems like something belonging to
the vanished night. Five, eight, ten years may
have brought nothing but anxiety, excitement,
ill-luck; but his superior sagacity and daring
must win at last.

Away he goes, with *burro* and "pard," off on
another prospecting tour, across unmeasured
wastes of sand, under a brassy sky, over alkali
plains, lava-beds, and waterless *pasturas*, which
lead to springs that may be poison.

A childish credulity weakens the judgment of
the honest miner. He accepts without reserve
the pleasing myths which form a sort of legendary history; the unwritten annals of gold and

silver-bearing mountains. Airy fables, poetic traditions are received as authentic records. There are delightful touches in these tales, with which I should love to embellish and enrich my page ; but not to-day. They belong to the mysteries and subtleties known only to the elect— the chosen few who see behind the cloud spanned with promise, iris-hued and glittering, the prize awaiting the venturesome Argonaut.

The pay-streak is possibly in a *vega* of sea-like vastness and level ; but more likely in the stony mountain heart, threaded by shining lines, as the crimson veins warm ours. Wherever it is, he is the man to strike it. And this conviction abides with him, a constant happiness, as he traverses the length and breadth of the mineral region.

Do you laugh at his fond delusions ?

The mania for precious metals is not a modern craze. It is older than the Pyramids.

Is he chasing a chimera ?

No, dear reader, he is feeling his way in the checkered path which all men at some period of their lives have sought ever since the first prospector groped along the strand down by the storied Euphrates, that dim and shadowy river, winding between myth and history, which waters the old, old land Havilah, where there is gold.

If a cold-blooded newcomer advises the honest miner to settle down to some good, steady, legitimate business, he rejects the idea with lofty scorn. That is well enough for the cautious idiot, who does not know a true fissure-vein when he sees it. The every-day trades, the tame, beaten paths are not in the prospector's line of march. He is for the short cut to fortune. Familiar with dangers, there is one foe he cannot fight. In lone hillsides and desolate cañons there is lying in wait for him an enemy more deadly than the skulking Apache—a peculiar form of intermittent fever, called mountain fever. It lurks in the air, ready to lift the dread cloud hiding the mystery which forever enshrouds the Unseen World.

The human race is nomadic, and the old Aryan blood is strong, and crops out on the *vegas* of the Rocky Mountains clearly as on the arid plains of Mesopotamia. To be sure, in Adam we are all one, and he was a quiet citizen of the world. In Noah we are all three, and after the Deluge— but this is getting into deep water.

Revenons. Occasionally it happens that a sample of ore, "the queer-looking stuff" on which moderate expectation is based, is brought out of the furnace, and the button in the cupel is not silver, but a lump of pure gold. O rapturous moment known to the few, the beloved children of Fate! O day to be remembered under the coffin-lid! The owner of such returns (not larger than a pea) treads on air. He tries to hide his exultation; but the secret will out. He plans; he builds. He is going to sail the seas; to start before many days to hear the syrens of the Mediterranean; to visit the abiding-places of poetry and history, the lands of undying summer; to see the kingdoms of the earth and the glory of them. And well may he dream dreams and see visions! Money is but another name for freedom. He who holds it has all the world before him where to choose his place of rest.

My reader, familiar with " The Last of the Barons," may remember the picture of Adam Warner endeavoring to turn copper into gold. In the solitude genius everywhere creates for itself, by night and by day, hanging over the burning Eureka, stinting himself and child to feed the devouring furnace, asking no sympathy in his lonely chamber, living apart with his works and

fancies, like a god amidst his creations, and coming very near the grand discovery concealed for
a later generation to penetrate. The fascination
of mining is what those elder sages experienced
in a lifelong witchery over minds bent to the
study of alchemy. What wonder men were devoted to a pursuit, in which even Bacon and
Newton wasted precious hours, which promised
results so august? Besides costly chemicals,
there were thrown into the crucibles youth,
health, hope, love, yes, life itself, to vanish as
vapor, slowly, slowly, surely, surely.

The worst thing about mining, as formerly
about alchemy, is that it allures on its victims to
destruction. One gets near and ever nearer
the object; so trifling a sum additional will complete the work and secure the promise. Time,
toil, expensive appliances are demanded; but the
glorious result justifies all these, and many
another risk more fearful.

Nature has done in the Rocky Mountains precisely what the ancient sages tried to do. Here
the last secret combination has produced the
medium; the striking hammer is smiting the
rocks; in the death-like stillness of remote solitudes the blow reverbates, and at its compelling
stroke the earth opens, and lo! the philosopher's
stone is discovered. Prospero's wand was not
mightier.

At night the clear, red glow of the furnace
reddens the walls of the assayer's room, coats
with bright gilding gloomy rafters overhead, and
lends a sick'y light to the flickering flame of the
coal-oil lan p. Then the place is suggestive of the
great centre of the earth, where doomed souls go
wandering up and down in a joyless, endless
wrestling with fire. The silent men are like dismal ghosts. If they speak, it is in repressed
tones. Their low voices, the obscurity of the

room, the intense heat, the air of secrecy and
mystery give the feeling that some agony is con-
ducting—a battle, a fire, a drama involving high
interests. The mighty cause is a tragedy ; possibly a crime.

Sometimes a woman, a girlish shape, looks in
with innocent eyes, as though she thought the
assayer in woeful peril. She flits away like a
spirit blest, wandering from the cool, sweet fields
Elysian, to pity for one moment the sad dwellers
in the near purgatory.

Souls in torment are here, in fact, when " specimens" on which star-high hopes were grounded
prove to be fire-clay and galena, and the long,
slow dream is as a vision of the night.

The conduct of some "miner men," after a
claim has been located, and the one hundred
dollars' worth of work which the law exacts is
done, is a study. In this age of doubt and question, their unwavering faith gives us fresh confidence in skeptical, sorely-tried human nature.
They gaze into narrow prospect-holes, about the
size of a seventy-five barrel cistern, with a depth
of trust, an immovable resting on the promise in
the future comparable with nothing I know,
except the serene complacency of the setting hen.
She feels the stir of life beneath her brooding
wings, and he has visions

> ———"impalpable and unperceived
> Of other's sight."

You see only a hole in the ground ; a shallow
cistern which holds no water. Nature has revealed her secrets to him, as she does not to the
unbeliever. Hence his robust faith.

From that prospect-hole riches will roll up by
the bucketful.

" How will they get up ?" asks the uninspired
tourist, heartlessly.

Honest miner, teetering a scrap of galena on

his forefinger, stares steadily at the faint mountain-line and murmurs: "Oh! I must bide my time. One of these days capital will come along—capital will come along—come along— along."

It must be admitted that capital is often a good while on the road. This hour, scores about us are prospecting, opening abandoned workings, following the ancient Tegua-Spanish traces, with hopeful hearts. They are enchanters. Hear them talk, and you behold the beauty of which they dream. They have neither crucibles nor carpet, nor do they pour ink in your palm, as Hassan did; yet are they prophets and seers, and their visions all foreshow another Leadville.

The Lodestone Rocks are not far off. Come not near, unless you are ready to be dashed against them.

Only fifty dollars laid out in work, and a mine possibly worth thousands. *Quien sabe?* "Who knows?" "Who knows?"

Taking a stern Methodist view of the business as now proceeding in the territories, I should call mining a game of chance—exciting, fascinating, bewildering—which defrauds no one but your- self.

CHAPTER XXI.

THE RUBY SILVER MINE.—A TRUE STORY.

MINING atmospheres are rife with stories, mar- velous, startling, that would be incredible, did we not know it is always the incredible which happens. Of the many tales floating about Santa Fé, I give one to you, beloved, which shows how strangely things come round in this round world of ours.

The patient reader who has graciously followed my rambling, scrambling steps through New Mexico may possibly remember that a large portion of the MSS. comprising the archives of the territory, was sold as waste paper and found way into the various shops of the city. Santa Fè being the largest town and commercial center of New Mexico, from it they were widely dispersed in every direction, and on this accidental scattering of leaves hangs my story and a fortune.

One night in the Autumn of 1879 I sat boring myself into inanity over the *Pharos of the Occident* (which is a misnomer, the newspaper being anything but light reading), when a visitor was announced.

" *Me parece un minero*," said Dolores Lucia Marina Feliciana Flores.

I was pleased at the thought of a visitor, even on business, and, in dread of being left alone with *The Pharos*, insisted *el minero* should not be interviewed in the Assay Office, but here. The ' Palace " halls are neither long nor lofty, being the length of two moderate rooms on the ground floor. and in a few minutes there stood in the deep doorway a figure, as revealed by the shaded student's lamp, unmistakably that of a miner. His face was sunburnt to a vermeil red and made prematurely old by exposure. Wrinkled by drying wind and pitiless sunbeat, his appearance was weather-worn, showing days of wanderings without shelter and lodgings on the cold, cold ground.

The contagion of good manners is a happy thing. In Spanish-speaking countries, though all else be lacking, there is ever the most exquisite politeness, and the man removed his slouch of a hat with a profound and sweeping bow. His uncovered head was thatched with a thick shock of carrot-colored locks, which are the inheritance of " the sandy complected," to speak after the manner of the poke-berry districts of our own Indiana. The strip of forehead shaded by his hat was dotted with large, assertive freckles, which in the exposed portion of his face were " in one red burial blent." He closed the door carefully and, with an air of secrecy, dropped his voice to a certain loud whisper, peculiar to sick-rooms and miners in confidence, and his whisper gradually sank to the ledger lines below, as he made his report; for, though rather untimely, his call was not unexpected.

I spread *The Pharos* on my table, and he slowly proceeded to unload his pockets and his red handkerchief, and empty on the paper various ores, kept separate, tied in rags and marked. To him they represented all precious things, besides gold and silver; to me they appeared formless, jagged lumps of dull-looking stone.

The story of the Argonaut was long—too long for any but a frontiersman, with plenty of leisure to speak and to hear—and was given in the style of oratory perfected by the Cousin of Sally Dillard.

He could not sit still, but started every few minutes, as at a calling voice, and strode hurriedly up and down the room, restless, eager, nervous, like one who, after long and exhaustive strain, suddenly slackens the tension. With the utmost minuteness he gave the history and described the locality of each particular sample, and tied them again, one by one, each in its own grimy cloth and label. This done, he hesitated, cleared his throat, rose from his chair, apologized for trespassing upon our valuable time (as though we had anything *but* time), opened the door, looked up and down the hall, as if he feared some ear was airing at the key-hole. Satisfied with the reconnaissance, he closed it again and

with stealthy step returned to the table. Evidently two hours of rigmarole had failed to free
his soul. There was something still unsaid. We
silently awaited the revelation. " There is one
specimen left," he began, doubtfully, and looked
at me much as to say : Can a woman keep or be
trusted with a secret ? Perhaps he read
assurance in my face, for he fumbled in his vest
(from the Semitic shop hard by, painfully new
and pathetically cheap), and out of its deepest
corner produced a little bag of buckskin, tied with
a leather string. He untied it with nervous
haste, and his wistful light blue eyes, burned in
deep hollows with miner's fever, brightened as he
spoke, scarcely above his breath, in an awe-inspir-
ing whisper : " Here we air. Here's the richest
thing yet." Shaking the bag, there dropped into
the palm of his left hand a reddish purple stone,
without streakings or glitter. " Ruby silver," he
said, softly. " Ruby silver, and plenty of it.
There's no end to the lead."

He reached it to me tenderly, as though it
could break at a touch. I did as was expected
of me—scraped the fragment of mineral with
a pen-knife, peered at it through the magnifying glass, hefted it on my forefinger, and made
the sagacious observation : " It looks well. I
should say a very rich specimen."

" It's from the Cañon de los Angelos," said the
miner.

I remembered it as a dismal gorge, torn up
and riddled by volcanic action, a blasted wilderness of gashed and riven stone peaks, bearing
aloft gnarled and twisted firs, their utmost summits a region of ice, lifted above the limit of
life. The silence unbroken but by the howl of
wild beasts and the war-whoop of the savage ;
where only fresh mountain-heaps of piled-up
lavas, marking the throes of the earthquake, vary

the forbidding gloom which baffles the traveler
entering it with a sense of approaching the Valley
of the Shadow of Death.   As soon expect water
in desert-sand as gold in that lava-flood, silver in
those melted rocks!

"How did you come to prospect in that dreadful cañon?" I asked.

"The strangest thing in the world," said the
miner, "how I first lighted on it.   I bought a
plug of tobacco (it was six years ago), and carried it home in a piece of an old letter, dated
sixteen hundred and something.   I disremember
the year.   It was writ on thick yellow paper, to
one of the Spanish governors, when Arizona and
New Mexico was one.   My wife was a-studyin'
Spanish (you can't git along here without some),
and she brought the dictionary to bear and spelt
the thing out.   It told about a rich lead in the
Cañon de los Angelos; but the paper was tore
off in the very place I most wanted, so I couldn't
exactly spot it.   For nigh onto five years I've
prospected.   I've hunted off and on, in hot and
cold, wet and dry.   I've been hungry and
thirsty.   I've scorched and I've froze.   Oncet I
was nearly drowned by a sudden rise at night,
when I camped in an *arroya*.   One winter I was
snow-blind.   Many and many's the week I've
heard no voice, nothing but the yelp of the coyote
and the wind among the pines.   Many and many
a time I've smelt the grizzlies; but, as luck
would have it, I never run onto one.   A lion or
a panther will run when he's hurt and roar; but
a grizzly doesn't, and, after bein' hit, shot
through the heart, instead of dyin', he lives long
enough to chaw up the hunter."

Dear reader, beware of starting the Rocky
Mountaineer on bear stories.   You will feel the
daisies growing over you before he slackens the
strain of his eloquence.

" Did you spend all these six years in the
Cañon ? " I inquired, by way of bringing the
prospector back to the subject in hand.

" Oh ! no. By spells I went at other bizness;
but the idee of a fortune a-waitin' for me in Los
Angelos, and that old Spanish letter made me
sour on everything. You know it is in Valencia
County."

I did not, but made an amiable effort to look
as though I did.

" There's curious old things down there in
them old lava-beds."

" What things ? " I asked, for the first time
rousing to any interest, for my antiquarian blood
began to stir.

" Heaps of ruins, cities, ragged walls, sixty
feet high and ten feet thick, scattered over miles
and miles. The rafters air charred with the
banked-up fire of the volcano; but I see one
beam as sound as the day it was laid up."

" And how did the timber appear ? "

" 'Twas piñon, squared with a stone hatchet or
hammer and covered with markings—Indian
signs, maybe—furrowed with a stone gouge.
Then there was a drawin' of the sun, and a sort
of a *neye ;* the lava had buried deep, and people
who like old potteries can get a wagon-load
there. About four feet down I struck a room,
about ten feet square, where there was a big fireplace ; and in it was a crane, with a clay hook,
and on the end of the hook was a bone. By the
side of the fire was a skeleton—the old man
a-watchin' his bone a-roastin' on the hook, when
here comes the lava and seals him up tight.
Over yonder, at the Fonda, I've got his skull;
and here " (he opened the revolver-pocket this
time)—" here's the old fellow's finger-bone. I've
lots of the same old arrowheads and a flint
tomahawk."

I was greatly interested in the still relics of remote generations ; but we had not reached the mine, and the evening was far spent. " These were near your ruby silver mine ? " I said, suggestively.

"Oh! no. As I was sayin', I found the bones of a dog close to a spring of sweet water, and I knowed then I was a-gettin' warm. My time was pretty nigh out. The snow was so deep I hid my tools, and give up for the winter and hired out to the freighters. As soon as winter broke I lit out one moonshiny night. Somehow the prospectors in Santa Fé got wind of my moves. I don't know how, unless I told in my sleep, for I kept dumb as the dead, and I was afeered they'd track me. I hunted round that Spring in a ring of five miles. First, I found the *acequia* which kept the buried city in water. I followed it in a blind lead for three-quarters of a mile, to a broken dam. The trail to the dam came next. When I tell you cedars thick as my body air growin' on that trail, you have an idee how long it's been since tracks has been made in it."

Just there I think the prospector drew on his imagination for his facts ; but his audience held their peace, and he continued :

"It was a mighty poor zigzag ; but it led to smelters."

"To smelters!" we both exclaimed, in a breath ; then followed a thrilling pause. The prospector had reached his climax, and he walked up and down the floor excitedly, tossing the ruby silver back and forth in his hands, like the hands of Esau.

"To old smelters!" he repeated, with emphasis. He struck the Colossus-of-Rhodes pose on the wolf-skin rug and continued :

"They was made of adobes, and was raised some twenty foot above the ground, and had saw hard service. I prowled around there a full month, hackin' and diggin' alone; for I dassent tell anybody but a Pueblo Indian, and threatened to kill him if he ever made sign to white man. It was my last throw. I was hard up. My old pard was dead, give out with rheumatism. My wife had went back to the States. My credit (never anything to brag on) went after my wife" (he smiled, for the first time), "and I see plain luck must come soon or never; but I never lost my grip. I knowed I was a-gittin' warm. There's no sign like the buried towns. It's certain indication of diggin's not far off. It's the rule all over the territories. I lived on venison, venison, till it was worse than old mutton. About three mile away was a lake, where I scooped up salt with my hands; but venison and salt gets monotonous week in and week out. There was plenty of charcoal (had been used by the miners, whoever they was), and I made out that the dam led the water of the Abo to the works. From the old furnaces I found another overgrown trail, that run to this mine."

"What sort of mine is it?"

"One of the covered-up ones. It's certain hundreds of years old, buried under felled timber. Some of it had rooted. I was a month gittin' through, and it took a sharp eye to sight it." The speaker modestly blinked the milky orbs under their pink lashes, and continued: "The shaft is eighty feet deep or more, walled up with pine, and drifts runnin' to the right and left a hundred feet or so. I've set my stakes and the papers is all made out. It's mine, and no divide, and not a soul on earth knows about it except you two and me."

I have seen so many ruined prospectors hunting mines that are nothing but myths, it was cheering to learn there could be no mistake about this discovery.

" You have fairly earned all you have found," I said, in sympathy.

" *Gracias, Señora*," said the rich man, dramatically waving the Esau hand, evidently enjoying his Spanish.

"You see this specimen will run twelve hundred to the ton, and there's no end to the lead." He teetered the stone on his trembling forefinger. " I've had a hard time! My wife never got done mournin' she ever spelt out the old letter. She'll feel better now. I've struck it, and I guess I've struck it rich."

And he had. With a farewell toss up of the ruby silver specimen, till it struck the muslin ceiling overhead, the fortunate man, haggard and shaken, yet hilarious, took his leave.

CHAPTER XXII.

THE RUBY SILVER MINE.—(*Continued.*)

SIX months later, in the shade of a light umbrella, I sauntered along the beach at Cape May. Down by the summer sea, where lovers walk with lingering step, rapt, heedless as the dead, of aught but tender glances and soft words whispered under the sound of the surf. After the desert silence and parching dryness of the territories, it was a deep pleasure to breathe once more the salt, moist air, to hear the mighty monotone, and watch the restless play of light and color on breakers rolling in from the far Bermudas, beating against the shore like the tireless heart of earth.

Thinking upon nothing but simple enjoyment

of earth, sea, and sky, I strolled in quiet sympathy with the unknown crowd, when suddenly
an open carriage, drawn by two horses, stopped
near us.   It was light as a wicker toy, the airiest,
fairiest thing manufactured since the night Cin-
derella rode to the ball.   So slight in construction
one might think it would scarcely bear the
weight of one person, had we not seen that every
portion was perfectly wrought.   The tempered
steel and light wheels would endure a severe
strain.   Ornate as burnish could make it, gilding
and varnish sparkled in the sunlight, gay rosette
and flying ribbon were not lacking.   Instead of
cloth, the lining was plaited violet satin, of exquisite tint.   I have never seen so elegant a turn-
out elsewhere.   The cushions were fit for an empress' laces and velvets to trail on, a seat where
a king might rest and keep the soil from the
ermine and velvet of his coronation robe.

The small horses seemed made for the fairy
carriage.   They were coal-black, perfectly match-
ed, without a white hair on them.   Your correspondent knows precious little about horses, except one ancient pony, which lost an eye in a
pre-historic raid on a corn-crib; but ignorance
itself could see these were of no common blood.
The broad faces and delicate ears, the luminous
eyes, soft as an antelope's, the arching necks,
veiled with silken manes like the fluffy hair of
young girls, come of no menial race, such as
haul drays and drop on pavements in the streets.
The mettlesome, high-bred beauties, pawing im-
patiently with hoofs like polished ebony, were
such steeds as dash through the Ouida novels or
come home at the masters' call under the black
tents, the Arab houses of hair.   We had started
for the light-house, three miles away, and in the
dazzle of all that luxury and ease the brightness
went out of the day.   My walk suddenly became

hard and long. It required the entire skill and
strength of the liveried driver to manage the
reins, while the occupant within leaped nimbly
out to adjust some portion of the harness. He
was dressed in garments of finest fabric and freshest cut, in which the tailor had missed the easy
fit so coveted by gentlemen. A Pactolian watch-
chain streamed across his breast, and lightisk.
gloves on massive hands gave the wearer the aspect of being pretty much all gloves. A host
of idlers gathered in a moment, and, with them,
I stopped to admire the equipage, perfect in
make and ornament, costly as money can buy,
and then and there broke the tenth command-
ment.

Evidently the envied man felt fussy and grew
fidgety under all those staring eyes. I rubbed
mine (not so young as they once were), to clear
a confused, bewildering recollection. Could it
be? No! impossible! To reassure myself, I
looked toward the sea, then back again to the sky,
the town. It was no spirit of earth or air, no cheat
of vision or brain. The territorial sunburn had
faded from his face, but lingered in the scorched
carrot hair, and Rocky Mountain wrinkles are
not easily ironed out. Well I knew those early
crow's feet at the corners of the milky blue orbs.
The owner of the princely establishment, with its
rare belongings, was none other than our frontier
friend, once sole proprietor of the Dives Mine, in
the Cañon de los Angelos, which sold for eighteen
hundred thousand dollars.

The golden key opens many doors ; but it takes
time and some skill to fit it into the lock. The
lavender kids split as the Dives miner hastily
jerked them off, to fasten a harness-buckle ; the
flash of a superb diamond ring followed the
movement. He threw the delicately tinted gloves
on the ground, with words more emphatic than

correct, muttered under a scant fringe of pink
moustache, then turned a deprecating, apologetic
glance toward the crowd.

An instant the ancient prospector held me
with his glittering eye. It said, plainly as
whisper in my ear: I beg you do not tell on me.

I did not. He hurried back to his place. The
Esau hand, with its blazing diamond, closed the
door with a heavy slam. It did not hold. He
banged it again, and yet once more, growing very
red in the face, before he could lean away from our
gaze back on the violet cushions. From that
soft recess he called loudly to the driver to " git."
There were a few significant nods as the night-
black steeds sped with swift grace over the wet
beach, but nothing was said except by a very
charming young lady, fresh from Ollendorf. She
released a loving arm to bend forward a moment
and wave her fine little handkerchief at the vanishing show, exclaiming: "*Adieu, monsieur
le nouveau riche.*"

The sweet girl graduate had taken the sense
of the meeting. When the purple and gold
passed from sight, the throng fell into line as
before the interruption, and in placid enjoyment
yielded to the dreamy spell of vesper sunlight
and lulling sound. All was refined, serene,
restful.

The mild ripples, changeful as the hues of
the dolphin, came and went, leaving their
slight tracery in the sand, secret messages from
hidden depths far away. The blue waters murmured mystic music to fair and gracious maidens
and youths of gentle, graceful mien; tender
cushats, cooing and wooing and sighing, but not
for the touch of vanished hands. The rhythmic
ebb and flow charmed the sense with hints of
warbling peris and dying cadences of mermaids'
songs. Earth and ocean in perfect tune, the

very air thrilled with a tremulous harmony,
while youth and beauty wove their low, sweet
idyl. Lapwings glided along the sands, where
the sick lady rested in her invalid chair, under a
gayly-striped awning.   White gulls screamed
and circled round a ship lying at anchor in the
shining bay, her flag a wavy line of brilliant
color against the pale horizon. Beyond it, in
dim perspective, a long procession of vessels
slowly sailing. An endless picture, suggestive
of famous places and unknown nations, gathered
treasure of pearl and amber, spicery and silks,
and happy home, coming from voyages through
halcyon seas, by distant fragrant shores. The
wind was warm, its breath was balm, the world
was lulled to rest.

A flush of pink fell from out the tranquil sky.
It dropped fresh roses on faded cheeks, and in
its blush I saw the young face beside me as it had
been the face of an angel. Then I thought the
beautiful is wealth, the world over. My darling
holds in her slender hand the keys of the palaces.

The walk to the light-house was not so bad,
after all.

My holiday ended, I returned to the City of
Holy Faith, and exactly a year from the date of
this story took my constitutional walk in the
splendor of sunlight such as never falls on land
or sea east of the Rocky Mountains. No fear
of rain to drive me indoors, no speculations about
clear or cloudy to-morrows, we know a radiant
shining will lighten the coming morning, just as
it filled the sky of yesterday. With the Pueblos,
I am a devout sun-worshipper and love at his rising to salute the lord of light and life, and again
" under the sad passion of the dying day " to
watch his departure. Returning from my invisible altar on old Fort Marcy, I threaded my way

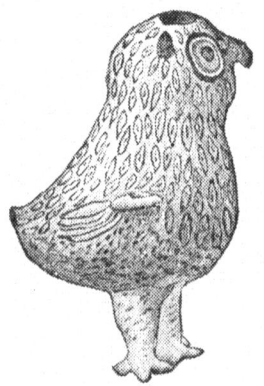

Zuñi Effigies.

through cramped and crooked streets, and, making the round of the Plaza, saw beside the gate a *burro* being loaded with a miner's outfit. He was not much larger than a dog; beyond compare the most wretched of his miserable race, a pitiable wreck. He was mangy and sore-eyed, his tail tapered to a stumpy point, the tuft at the end fallen beyond the reach of any "restorer." Patches of hair worn off in various portions of his body exposed wrinkled, leathery hide, and the dark cross over the shoulders was pitted with scars, like marks of small-pox. There was not enough flesh on those protrusive bones to make one meal for the ravening mountain wolf, or a respectable lunch for half a dozen carrion crows. Arid and dusty, the creature looked like the mummy of some antediluvian animal. Easy to see his portion had been kicks, scourge, goads, abuse; no champagne savannah, no green meadow or lush blue grass in his line of travel; but life-withering marches in snowy and sandy desert, where scant herbage and meagre shrub were enough for the starving slave.

Yet the sorry beast was not senseless nor altogether broken in spirit. A train of mules went by. Among them he recognized an old acquaintance, a fellow-sufferer. He lifted his head and plucked up heart for a passing salute, essaying a feeble bray. The unwonted sound was too great an effort for the gaunt throat. It died in a hoarse rattle and was buried in a succession of notes, the strangest mortal ear has heard since that old day Jubal first struck the gamut.

Pick, shovel, bags of crackers, blanket, and coffee-pot were piled high on the tough burden-bearer, and, watching the loading done by a Mexican boy, a tall man lazily leaned against the diminutive brute, apparently reckless of the danger of upsetting donkey and cargo, and sending them sprawling across the sidewalk. There was nothing to draw attention in his familiar uniform —high-top boots, cactus-proof buckskin pants, hickory shirt, red neck-handkerchief; but under the broad slouch hat were straggling locks that caught my eye—a peculiar tinge of reddish bronze, the *cabello del oro* of the Argonaut of '79.

The never-resting wheel of fortune had made the downward curve. The Dives miner had summered in Saratoga, betting on cards and horses, had staked tens of thousands on the hazard of a dicer's throw, lost everything, and now was back to the starting-place, ready to try again. I remembered the purple and gold, the dash and glitter of the rich man at Cape May. The apparition of prancing steeds of matchless beauty, with dainty limbs, too dainty for the sand they touched but to spurn, flitted before me.

Gambler though he was and deserved it, the forlornness of the change would touch a harder heart than yours or mine, dear reader. I stepped toward the gate. At that moment Dives—perhaps I had best say Lazarus—poked the poor *burro* with a sharp stick and, in a high, gay voice, struck up :

> "Of all the wives you e'er can know,
> There's none like Nancy Lee, I trow."

Then, as Bunyan hath it, he went on his way and I saw him no more.

This story sounds like a pure invention. Does it not? I confess to trifling attempts in decorative art, a tiny dash of color, the least bit of embroidery, just to round a corner and give a little life to dullness, you know, but not now. My hero is to-day a day-laborer, working in the great King Henry lead in the Shakespeare district of New Mexico—the man who for one

brief summer reckoned his money by hundreds
of thousands. You can see him when you go.

CHAPTER XXIII.

MINE EXPERIENCE.

THE reader who graciously follows me to the
end of this brief history will readily comprehend
why it must be somewhat obscure. " I could a
tale unfold " better worth the hearing, but like
the poor ghost I am forbid to tell the secrets of
my prison house. It need harrow up no soul to
hint that the scene was laid and drama played
not a thousand miles from Tucson, Arizona.

Imagine a *vega* of sea-like vastness, in a rock-
setting of ghostly Sierras whose rent crags pierce
through the rich blue air far above the snow line.
In the primeval years the Apaches possessed the
country, and with the poetic instinct which never
quite forsakes the savagest of savages they
called this range the Mist-Befringed Mountains.
To reach the valley from the west, we leave the
main road and cross rough masses of lava which
block the way. The seeming barrier ends in a
narrow pass, a mile or so from wall to wall,—a
mighty stone corridor stately as Karnak, and
gloomy with the all-pervading silence of death.
At the end is a high natural gateway of red
granite; passing under it we emerge into a smooth
expanse level as water, an amphitheatre whose
blank surface is relieved by scattered masses
of lava upheaved in some fiery earthquake long
stilled their rigid outlines jagged and bristling
There is no verdure to soften the foothills so
savagely hacked and split in yawning cracks.
No tender moss, no shrub, no sparkling water or

waving branches brighten the leaden hues of the
gray desert; treeless, windless, waterless. If
herbage ever grew there it is now overdrifted
with sand. The wonderful mirage—most marvelous of Nature's mysteries—swims over it in
the dreamy haze of early morning. A deep,
dark coolness follows the burning day, and the
jeweled sky, of opal and turquoise, is unspeakably beautiful. Other change there is none.

It would seem a place for the unclean condor
to lay her eggs on the bare rocks, and the eagle
to wheel and scream and stir up her nest with
wings which battle the storm; but there is no
trace of bird or insect life, no wolf or antelope,
coyote or lizard.

It is the one place in which I have stood
where the earth is as still as the sky. Suppose
we call the dreary region with its adamantine
rocks the Foothills of the Mountains of the
Moon. There in the beginning silence set her
seal, unbroken till eighteen hundred and——
some odd years. For reasons obvious, I cannot
be exact regarding dates.

In a memorable hour the death-like hush was
startled by the ring of a single hammer on the
torn mountain wall at the west end of the *vega*.
Blow on blow against the riven clefts resounded
through the warm blue silence.

Was it a Bostonian seeking the Infinite? Did
he see beyond the verge of sight, like the young
Aladdin led on by the Genii of the Cave?

All day the one man toiled, digging, hewing,
breaking, scraping pieces of stone with a pen-
knife. What he sought he evidently found, put
some of it in his pockets, other portions in his
haversack, and wound out of the cavernous
gloom at sunset through the narrow defile to the
world outside the lifeless plain. He is brave

beyond the bravest who would stay there till midnight,

"Alone in the terrible waste with God."

A week passed, and one crisp and clear morning—owing to very high altitude the nights here are always cool—three men passed under the rock gateway, each with tools and determination of iron. Steadily they worked in the long hot day, stopping for lunch and a short rest at noon. Only the all seeing eye was upon them, no human ear was there to hear, yet at intervals they looked around as though in an enemy's country, and their rare speech was in suppressed voices. They bent with faces to the ground as children hunt for nuts. They peered into cracks and crevices and pried up loose stones, scattered *débris*, broke them open, and gazed at their interior under a hand mirror. Occasionally the lightest man, a mere strippling, mounted the shoulders of the other two and seized something above their heads. Were they a trio of poets obeying the charge of the Bard of the Sierras, "Lean your ladder not against the clouds, but against the solid Rocky Mountains and climb there?" They saw something which thrilled their pulses, and bore off a load in sacks just as the snow crowned peaks blushed with the ineffable beauty of the afterglow. Then darkness leaped from the mountain walls and held the valley, in the starry silence, lone as the land Havillah before the first gold seekers crossed the river on their endless quest.

Another week brought a picnic party largely composed of ladies, two gentlemen in army blue, girls made of roses and dimples, curls and ribbons, young men with eager, handsome faces. Rocky Mountain ladies are always well mounted and are fearless horsewomen. Diana Vernon might envy their dash and daring, and in this

rarified atmosphere horses are mettlesome and
endure as they cannot in the low countries.
There was much prancing and spurring through
the rugged defile, and many a rider less bold
would have been unseated even on the sure-
footed ponies. They brought little twigs of
pinones from the *cañons* and made fires with
matches scraped on boot heels; they unpacked
hampers, opened cans, played games, shouted,
sung, wild with overflowing spirits; they ate,
drank and were merry, all the while hunting and
hunting. Lovers strayed in pairs to dusky
recesses in the mountain rim, not on purpose to
be lost nor to find the four-leaf clover, nor yet to
learn how to make love dials of daisies. They
sought something more than the hasty charm of
a stolen kiss. They looked for shining stones,
gleaming metal, precious clay, and every one
carried in a pocket handkerchief minute sec-
tions of the adamantine Foothills of the Mountains of the Moon. Even uninstructed eyes can
trace the rust colored, red-brown lines of "blossom rock," and it is following a captivating lead
to yield one's self to its beguiling ways.

One youth and maiden tracked it far up the
cañon to a gnarled and twisted pine which over-
hung the edge of a sheer crag to which it clung
by roots clutching like claws. In the dry, dewless air the needles of the pine lay in soft carpet-
ing undisturbed for ages. They sat and rested
beneath the skeleton tree, and listened to soft
æolian airs faintly stirring the bare branches overhead. Then she sang in the sweetest voice.

"Is this a dream? Then waking would be pain."

And in answer he tossed up his cap and it
lodged in the pine, and they clapped their hands
in an impromptu chorus, "No, no, no! a thousand times, no!" If there be elves in the Mist-
Befringed Mountains they must have laughed at

this frolicsome glee, for such sounds are a new
revelation there. The young couple were not
crazy, they had heaved up a rough brown stone,
and striking it with a heavy hammer they saw—
ay de mi! the electric flash of wedding rings.
The zigzag lines of "blossom rock" held wreaths
of orange flowers, hitherto unattainable, and now
they felt so near their sweetness they were filled
with delight. The poor young things had
thought best to bear their poverty apart (he was
a second lieutenant), but now they could hear
marriage bells in every stroke of the magic hammer, in every throb of their happy hearts.

A stray dove, bewildered and lost, lighted at
their feet, tame because ignorant of men, and
they hailed the gentle bird as an omen. Then he
called her his dove-eyed darling, talking the
sweet foolery my gray-haired reader laughs at,
but would give a year of peaceful life to hear
again for one half-hour.

O day of bridal brightness whose splendor
lives in the illuminated Book of Chronicles!—let
me linger a moment over its unfading beauty.
The lovers locked their happy arms together and
trod lightly over enchanted ground, in the silence
of perfect happiness,—all that is left us of the
lost language of Eden. Wherever their sparkling glances fell, myrtles sprung up. O never,
on land, or in sea, grew flowers like those which
bloomed in their foot-prints along the sandy beds
of "blossom rock."

The lieutenant was bare-headed, for he never
got his cap, though he stoned it valiantly and
even shot his revolver at the limb where it hung.
A frontier lady is full of expedients as Robinson
Crusoe, and the girl he loved, with deft and taste-
ful fingers devised a cap from her silken kerchief
and trimmed it with a drooping feather from her
own riding hat. Very proud was the face

beneath it, and he bowed in admiration of her ingenuity and murmured some soft nonsense you do not care to hear.

They joined the party in the plain with an assumption of indifference, transparent as mica, —a flimsy ruse, old as the oldest lovers,—and of course every one saw just how matters stood the instant they appeared. He went to look after the pony, tied by a *lariat* to a block of stone, patted her never so gently, stroked her mane, and called her " Pretty girl, pretty girl." The maiden sat on a striped Navayo blanket and in an arch bewitching way sang to an old Spanish air full of trills and graces this song:

"QUIEN SABE?" *

I.

" The breeze of the evening that cools the hot air,
That kisses the orange and shakes out thy hair,
Is its freshness less welcome, less sweet its perfume,
That you know not the region from whence it is come?
Whence the wind blows, where the wind goes,
Hither, and thither, and whither—who knows? Who knows?
Hither and thither—but whither—who knows?

II.

" The river forever glides singing along,
The rose on the bank bends adown to its song,
And the flower, as it listens, unconsciously dips
Till the rising wave glistens and kisses its lips.
But why the wave rises and kisses the rose,
And why the rose stops for those kisses—who knows? Who knows?
And away flows the river—but whither—who knows?

III.

" Let *me* be the breeze, love, that wanders along
The river that ever rejoices in song;
Be *thou* to my fancy the orange in bloom,
The rose by the river that gives its perfume.
Would the fruit be so golden, so fragrant the rose,
If no breeze and no wave were to kiss them? Who knows? Who
knows?
If no breeze and no wave were to kiss them? Who knows?"

Before the singer lay the desert grim and bare, girdled by scarred, seamed mountains—a boundry wall touched with purplish tints of

---

* I need hardly tell my reader the words " *Quien Sabe?* "··
" Who knows?"—are the unanswerable answer forever on the Spanish-speaking tongue.

supreme beauty. Behind her, a dim outline of
snow and granite in the far horizon, the Sierra
Nevada projected against the rainless blue, the
blade of snow-white teeth which suggested its
Castilian name. The valley had a fascination from
its absolute loneliness. Not a cloud flecked the
blue above, not a breath stirred the air while the
song was sung.

The elders gave it a divided attention, being
intent on lumps of treasure which they "hefted"
in their palms, balanced on their forefingers, and
gazed at affectionately through a glass into which
they puckered their eyelids, making gathers of
the crow's feet quite frightful to see. As each
one passed the glass to his neighbor he nodded
in dumb approval, with a look of mystery smiling
and smiling, and the more enthusiastic winked
and rubbed their hands as it went the rounds.

Such withcraft is there in one small hand
mirror!

After lunch at picnics there is usually a period
of "nooning" while gentlemen smoke and ladies
recline, or seek *siestas* in friendly shade ; but there
was no quiet here and to the last no flagging of
the high festivity.

A rose-blush of exquisite haze, a phantasm
"mystic, wonderful," floating through the vapory
architecture of the Sierras, seemed the very soul
of the halcyon day. The adorable girl who
turned more than one head by smoking cigarettes,
waved her hand at the shade and called loudly,
"Look, see, the day is dying, its spirit is passing.
Turn your faces to the west and be attentive."

Gaily they hastened to gather round the fair
speaker. With low mutterings and many tragic
gestures she drew a circle in the sand, stood in
the centre and blew a whiff of smoke, north,
south, east, west, as Moqui Indians invoke the
sun with their incantations.

" Now," said the self-elected priestess, with solemn accent, " now watch without speech or breath, and we will have a token and a sign from the god of the Pueblos."

Humoring her fancy, they waited in silence and lo! before their eyes the shape darkened, glowed, transmuted into a mass of glittering gold.

" The oracles have answered," she cried. "Good bye, O Sun, ruler of this hour, take thanks from thy white children for the golden promise of to-day. Believers, salute him."

All obeyed, and with bare head and uproarious cheers waved hats and handkerchiefs in good bye to the day and the friendly powers that be. The merry cavalcade, laughing and shouting, rode straight into the golden fire and flaming snow, each one carrying heavy weights of stone, every heart beating lightly.

Rapidly the voices died away. The metallic luster of the sky melted into opalescent pearl and purple. Day and night kissed and parted. Suddenly the stars looked out in serene eternal beauty on the smouldering fires, the vanishing trace of man, and the *vega* alone with the night,—the hushed desolation doubly drear for the apparition of loveliness which endured but for a day.

The next morning brought more men with picks and hammers, mules laden with kegs of water, shovels and various cooking utensils and traps. There was a stir and bustle, two tents were pitched; a conspicuous figure was a cook " come up from de Souf durin' de wah,"—sign of a permanent camp. Against stubborn clay and quartz rock work goes on slowly, but it did go on in the Mist-Befringed Mountains. It took many weeks to survey a certain district and make excavations, one deep as a well. They were made against obstacles which daunt men of

weak will; lack of fuel, **lack of water**, torrid sun-
heat, chill, benumbing **nights.** The plain was
dotted with holes very like graves, marked with
little pine head-boards bearing dates and figures.
They have sweet names: "Baby Mine," "Golden
Fleece," "Sleeping Beauty," "Maud Muller,"
"Highland Mary," "Daystar," "The Fair
Ophelia." This last is the deepest excavation.

Usually claim stakes, for such they are, in out-
of-the-way places mark the "Old Bourbon,"
"The Right Bower," "Dying Gasp," "Wake up,
Jake," "New Deal," "Chance Shot," "The Blue
Pup," and so on. The titles are indication of
the vein of tender sentiment which runs deep in
the heart of woman. Evidently gentle souls
fluttered about the head-boards when they were
set in the ground. They were standing there
to-day.

*   *   *   *   *   *   *

That row of stars, dear reader, means,

"Thoughts which do lie too deep for tears."

Sometimes in quiet Sunday afternoons a party
of lovely women, the charmed number not less
than the graces nor more than the muses, ride
out from Las Lunas, through the frowning
avenue and lonesome gorge, and haunt the silent
valley as mourners are wont to linger about new-
made graves. To avoid trouble in remembering
names I group them.

Allow me to present my charming friends the
Pleiads. Years, tears, or study, perhaps all com-
bined, have dimmed the brilliance of one face.
They tread softly and slowly, are very depressed,
and appear to find a mourner's consolation in
reading the head-boards. Under the funeral
shadow cast by the overhanging pine (the Lieutenant's cap is still there) they sit on newly
spaded earth and compare experience and

sorrows. A dove in the skeleton tree, listening, might hear subdued laments : "O why did I to··h the ʻSleeping Beauty?ʼ" "ʻOf all the sad words of tongue or pen,ʼ" "ʻAll that glitters is not gold,ʼ" and as they bend above the " Highland Mary," one hums an old song, beginning :·

" Thou lingering star with lessening ray.'

Sung with tenderness and pathos it floats through the deathlike stillness like a dirge. Can it be possible these sad-eyed mourners are the bright spirits of the picnic, who made that shining day

——"a beauteous dream,
If it had been no more ? "

'Twere vain to tell thee all.

Just when it matters not, these women pon-dered over maps, meaningless to them as the fif-teen puzzle which has proved the streak of id· iocy in the entire human family ; over Miner's Handbooks, over the "Prospector's Complete Guide to Wealth." They grew familiar with frightful engravings, flaming pictures of red hot underground machinery, lurid as the Insurance Chromo. Light literature and the newspapers were forsaken, and instead their tables were lit-tered with such pamphlets as " Treatises on the Patent Amalgamator," " The best method of reducing Argentiferous Ores," and " The Hy-draulic Ram,"—a horrible subject. The femi-nine mind does not readily adjust itself to this sort of lore, and though novel and highly instruc-tive they were forced to confess it was "trying." The owner of " The Fair Ophelia" almost lost her reason in a frantic and futile effort to master the workings of the diamond drill, and to com-prehend the advantages the double oscillating cylinder engine has over the steel or percussive system of drilling.

While these exhaustive studies went on, the students discoursed of fissure veins, of float, leads, developments, face rock, bed rock, pyrites, chlorides, sulphurets. Alternating anguish and ecstacy shook their slender frames; one day brought a dazzling promise, the next a blank contradiction which told on their nerves with the force of a blow. Everything was shifting and uncertain except the assessments. There was a sense of security in having one thing to be relied on, and they were brought in with exact regularity. The moon did not wax and wane with more unvarying certainty, and obligations of all sorts were met with unquestioning promptness, not to say alacrity.

How many months' pay went into these rich experiences your historian is unable to record. The Pleiads, though brilliant in the social circle, were not trained to strict business habits, and it is possible, indeed quite probable, no account of expense was kept. In that time the battered old pun about lying on your oars (not to be despised and able to bear a good deal of abuse yet) was dinned in ears to which the antique witticism was already familiar. The note of warning fell lightly as snow falls on snow, leaving no imprint; and the toilsome excavating went bravely on. A judicious friend — merely a looker-on—advised selling out. The old frontiersman was assailed with indignant scorn. Much learning had made him mad.

"What! sell out now, *now*, in the face of such a prospect."

"After all this outlay!"

"After holding on so long! Now!"

"Not if I know myself."

"Nor I."

"Nor I."

"Nor I."

Before the seven-fold chorus and harpings the dismayed counsellor hastily retreated to his adobe office, and the Pleiads looked forth as the morning, fair as the moon, clear as the sun, and terrible as an army with banners.

Patient investigation fails to show up (unconsciously one drops into mining phrase in mining countries) any offer to buy, but the very thought of selling out was rousing—a reflection on the fair owner of "The Fair Ophelia." Varying rapture and despair wore those lovely women to faded spectres, for the long, slow lesson of waiting is a fearful strain on tense nerves. Well for their balance is it that housekeeping is so difficult on the barren frontier.

Despite the wholesome restraint of domestic duty, the daily task of making something out of nothing, they wiled away long afternoons telling stories worthy the best days of Monte Christo, Captain Kidd and the gallant Sinbad. A childish credulity overtook them. Though highly intellectual and very superior, educated in modern "culture" (Boston accent), they showed a capacity for belief that was amazing.

How diligently they groped along the tangled lines on the agonizing maps! How glibly they talked of metalliferous foothills, of bonanza kings, of "extracting" and "separating processes," of running galleries and driven tunnels. You know it is the amateur who is most sanguine in every enterprise. The joint stock of enthusiasm owned by the Pleiads lightened the way but was not inexhaustible. Notwithstanding enlivening converse in learned phrase—a kind of foreign language—hope flickered, the fever burned their eyes into hollows, and the judicious friend shook his white head in secret, forecasting how long this sort of thing was going to last.

When the crisis came Electra fainted dead

away,—dropped as if shot through the heart. She was a good deal reduced with study of secrets hid in " The Smelter," and the book slipped from her nerveless hand as she reached out to receive the dispatch.

It came at the close of the short twilight of a day never to be forgotten. She was sitting in the *portal* to catch the last rays on the printed page, for her eyes are not so young as they once were, and in this land there is brief margin time of silver gray sky and drowsing earth. There trotted along the sheep paths and through the cramped and crooked streets a *burro* with all the speed a *burro* can make, goaded forward by a stick sharpened to that end. Mounted on him without bridle, saddle, whip or spur, was a boy recognized as a sort of messenger in the camp of the Mist-Befringed Mountains,—a boy beautiful as a princess' page, with real Murillo head and luminous oriental eyes beaming with steady light in the olive face. There was exceptional grace in the movement of his limbs as he dismounted ; his voice is always sad, and the soft *"Buenos dias Señora,"* conveyed no hint whether the bearer brought tidings good or ill. Bareheaded, he yet contrived to make the courtly Spanish bow, shook back his jetty locks, and bending low delivered the letter. The boy's lovely name is Rafael Antonina Molino, and the dispatch was a leaf torn from a scratch-book, scrawled in haste with a hand that evidently trembled in the writing. It ran :

Near Las Lunas.

At last! About noon yesterday the digger in " The Fair Ophelia" struck soft carbonates genuine Leadville carbonates, and are now down four feet. They show up better and better.

Your own Jason.

P. S.—Send me a white shirt. I am to speak at the ratification meeting to-night.

A thrilling pause—a scream, a bursting shower of tears, kisses, embraces, a confusion of tongues in which the word "carbonate" was the only one common to all. Such a sunshiny storm is possible only to nervous women intensely wrought. In the *Mêlée* a natty little jacket, brought by mail from Altman's and almost as good as new, was absolutely ripped to pieces. When mines are *en bonanza* (free translation "booming") who cares for New York jackets?

I shrink from the attempt to picture what Carlyle might call the resplendent weeks which followed, while a test ton of ore was sent to Silver City for reduction. Still less can I venture to touch the forlorn portrait of the judicious friend who advised selling out. He repented in sack cloth and alkali dust, and meekly apologized three times a day and again at bed time. So vanquished, he kept close in his earth works and hardly took courage to share the general joy. They are living yet who believe there was a dash of sarcasm in the withered smile with which he modestly used to inquire after the wealth of Denmark's daughter. Through the resplendent weeks (I love that exquisite word) the spectres scarcely lost sight of each other, and they were very pallid. They mooned about like young lovers in a trance, and like them saw with eyes anointed. A glory rested on our dull earth, tinging it with rose-bloom and amethyst, as the wintry moon, looking through pictured windows, warmed the snowy breast of Madeline, utterly *tê montée*, a riotous prodigality possessed them. Their bank account was a sight to see, and under the sweet influence of the Pleiads the poor rejoiced and beggars thrived.

In happy nights, too sweet for sleep, they gathered lilies of Damascus and drank from springs shaded by plumy palms of Judea. They painted birds, long legged birds on panels, and sets of china containing a thousand pieces each. Ever they whispered, murmured, dreamed. Soon as the delirium passed and the fever cooled they resolved to flee " the finest climate in the world," beloved of reporters, which every one rushes away from as soon as he has the money to go.

Take care! Take care! These are the shores of doom. Among other curious formations in the adamantine Foothills of the Mountains of the Moon are the Lodestone Rocks. Swiftly, swiftly, the ship was drawn to them. The gilded argosy with its precious freightage, swelling sail and triumphant banner went to pieces. Rosebloom and violet faded into the light of common day. The poor headboards beside the open graves are the last of the wreck, marking the spot where hopes rose so brightly they appeared sure prophesies unrolled.

[Dear reader, on whom I lean in tender confidence, forgive this secret tear over the lifeless clay of " The Fair Ophelia." I sat by its cradle, I followed its hearse.]

The judicious friend ventures abroad now. He smiles shrewdly and the mourners dream no more. They see with cleared vision, and will take one of the many roads which lead to the Golden Milestone, and their dreams will all come true when galena sells for a dollar an ounce.

CHAPTER XXIV.

THE RUINS OF MONTEZUMA'S PALACE.

No AMERICAN antiquities except, perhaps, the Old Mill at Newport, have figured so largely in imagination and in print as the pre-historic ruins along the Gila River, in Penal County, Arizona. More than thirty years ago antiquarian hearts were deeply stirred by accounts of travellers, then very rare, describing the Casas Grandes as great cities of hewn stone built in a rich and noble architecture like that of Egypt. Rhetorical flourishes and bold flights of fancy, colored the pictures drawn before the days of photography. Communication with this region was difficult, and travelling hundreds of miles the stories naturally grew along the way, taking wider outlines and warmer coloring. The gold seekers of California varied their explorations by ascending the Gila, almost as unknown to them as the White Nile. Rapturous reports came back, and for years the Caas Grandes ranked with Veii and Karnak. I greatly regret having no copy of those Pacific newspapers to compare the impressions of the last generation, groping in the misty twilight of half-seen wonders, with plain facts come to actual sight and touch in the light of to-day.

The walled cities, capable of holding many thousand souls, were supplied with water by acequias leading from the river. They were represented by enthusiastic Bohemians as aqueducts of solid masonry and fairly equal in durability and strength to the Maxima Cloaca of Rome. Charming traditions embellished the beguiling descriptions, lovely myths and airy fables floated in the warm, blue silence above the

218

House of Montezuma, whose lordly name is itself a stimulus to imagination. They were the work, so ran the tales, of lost races, mysterious, invincible, all-conquering, vanished into the voice-less past. They had reached a high civilization, as the magnificent remains attest, and had passed from the earth leaving no sign but colossal ruins, no records but strange hieroglyphs, which, en-graven on rocks in the neighborhood of the Casas, undoubtedly formed their history.

These mural records are heaps of weather-worn rocks and detached boulders covered with figures rudely scratched or painted, bearing signs of great age. They possibly served as boundary lines, the hieroglyphs being tribal signs of treaties. One flighty romancer who understood his own language imperfectly, testified that the " pictured rocks" were written over with deeply carved in-scriptions like the Hebrew, Chaldean and Gothic characters. They have been foundation stones for imaginary pyramids with sculptured facades, which were compared to the temples of Palenque and Tuloom, "made of hewn stone so admirably fitted they seem 'born so' and require neither mortar nor clamps." Pottery was found in pro-fusion, glazed and painted, always in fragments too small and scattered to be fitted together. Yet the visionaries likened the miserable scraps to ceramics of antique India and the inimitable vases of Etruria.

From the early times the Apache, savagest of savages—the red man incurably wild—has swept the plains and has held the mountain fastnesses, carrying terror and torture from the upper waters of the Pecos far into old Mexico. The shadowy region, mountain-locked like some vast strong-hold guarded by naked sentinels, was a resistless temptation to lovers of the marvellous. The deserted cities slowly crumbling down by the shallow waters of the Gila must have been the work of a people who maintained their supremacy in the face of savagery. There was much to stir the fancy, ever strongest of flight under skies most unknown, in the idea of walled and fortified cities in the centre of barbarian hordes, able to withstand their warfare and beat back their encroachments. Poet, sightseer, archæologist, reporter, padre, missionary, rovers of every sort came by turns to the Casas Grandes, and gave their impressions in poetic coloring ; and over all, like the dreamy mountain haze whose soft radiance purples hill and plain, hung a delicious mystery. Who should lift the secret veil and question the past till it gave back some answer ? It was an alluring borderland between civilization and barbarism ; on the North American Continent the last footing of phantoms peopling the unknown, till the whistle of the locomotive, which has broken so many illusions, put the pale shades to flight, and brushed away the cobweb and rose-bloom of the old Spanish poets.

The Maricopa is a dreary country, arid and inhospitable. Even the Mark Tapley of travellers observed, while there : " This is not a jolly place." The days are hot as the desert where the White Nile rises ; so hot the very lion's manes are burnt off. The nights are heavenly.

The rivers are tricksy streams—sometimes wet, sometimes dry—but give enough water to irrigate meagre cornfields. Occasionally they rise in the very centre of barrenness, flow a mile or so, and are lost in the sand ; then rise unexpectedly and run again.

The season, I remember, was unusually dry. Every one described by travellers and official papers for whole generations contain that report. From this concurrent testimony it is safe to conclude that every season is unusually dry. I testify that one party was made dry as mummies; but, being under bonds to see all that was to be seen, we were bound for the Casas Grandes.

To reach them, we must enter the fabled realm of the visionaries; where the Indian emperor, garlanded by beauty, reclining on crimson and gold, floated among opal mountains (the name still attaches to a snowy range) and far-reaching valleys, sown thick with jewels—a region fearful to land in, because of the one-horned rhinoceros and the monstrous Cibola (buffalo).

As we walked about while waiting for the ambulance, the Indian men tagged after us, eyeing the travellers with their intolerable fixed stare; but the women sat still in their places. There was no breeze to stir the air, no changing clouds enlivening the bare and brilliant sky, no sound of wheels, no tramp of men audible in the sandy soil. The isolation was perfect as that of a reef in mid-ocean.

The earth lay in stillness unbroken, and the mute and moveless Indian woman was the type of a deadness which rests on the land forever.

Wonderful are the works of an inspired imagination! This is the region where the West Indian king reveled as he sailed, and, like another Antony, kissed away kingdoms and provinces We had read the chronicles and saw that day the favorite of the harem, whose voice was like running water in the ear of the thirsty, her step like the bounding fawn, her grace like the swaying reed, her smile a glance of the Great Spirit. She is known in our times as the Pimo Squaw. She leaned against a crazy mud wall, which she appeared to prop, and was so nearly the same shade of clay that at first the statuesque shape seemed carved in it. A stumpy figure, nude to the waist draped in one buckskin skirt. The leathery skin, tanned by long exposure to the

fierce sun's beat and roughening wind, was
darkly veined and coarse. To eyes accustomed
to see in woman's form the fairest of all fairness—

"A thing to dream of, not to tell"—

the sight is not alluring. She was scarcely
twenty-five years of age; but the pitiless climate
(which we are constantly called upon to admire)
had worn wrinkles in her face deep enough to
bury her youth in. Her small, shapely feet were
cased in moccasins; the slim hands, idly resting
in her lap, were burnt to a mahogany color (the
cinnamon tint entirely lost) and knotted with the
hard work of corn-grinding. Her one ornament
was a sea-shell, tied round her throat by a deer-
skin string.

Nourmahal had a Mongol cast of features—
narrow button-hole eyes, almost no eye-brows,
high cheek-bones, thick lips, tattooed chin. As
the angelic portion of our party (delicately
referring to the writer) approached for nearer
view, she made no sign, except to turn the
dull Chinese eyes, which a short study of
inscriptions on tea-boxes would give the right
oblique, and fix them on us with a tireless,
unwinking gaze.

The ruins are twenty miles from the villages of
the Pimos, a branch of the Pueblo Indians, and
only twelve miles from the town of Florence on
the South Pacific Railroad. The wagon road
runs along the Gila Valley, a level bottom of
varying width with abrupt scarped banks of earth.
The plain is of a pale gray color, with a low mossy
grass, its monotony being relieved by groves of
mezquit, a species of acacia resembling our locust,
but with foliage more delicate and almost shadeless. The stunted trees grow branching from
the ground so low as to be nearly trunkless;

knotted, gnarled, dwarfed, black of bark, vaster of root than of top, yet with a certain grace derived from the small emerald green leaves delicately set on trembling fronds. Occasionally a val-de-verde appears, a peculiar and striking growth of green body, bark, leaf and limb, never very large and not over eight inches in diameter; and here and there is a prickly pear, twenty feet in height, loaded with red, pear-shaped fruit.

The shifting outlines of the Tucson Mountains, never five minutes the same, are drawn in perfect relief against a sky of unrivalled brilliance; the purest sapphire, free from every taint of mist, fog, or vapor. The exquisite fineness of the atmosphere shows clearly the high and rugged peaks of the Sierra Catarina, and one picture-like summit, called Pichaco, overlooks the chain of hills below through a veil of dying blue. Close to the river's brim the willow tosses its branches in the eternal west wind, lightly as a lady's plume, and bears a profusion of lilac flowers rarely beautiful. On the sterile mesa appears the suwarrow (Cereus Giganteus) of a peculiar and fantastic shape, and a wild verbena repeats the shade of the far-off hill purples.

Miles away from the dead cities we struck the bed of an ancient acquia, very large and perfectly defined, the main artery by which the river bottom, only a mile or so wide here, was irrigated in former times. Mezquit trees, apparently falling into decay from age, stand in the dry, abandoned ditches, whose various branches may be traced in every direction, a network of irrigating canals. Here and there elevations in the plain proclaim the existence of fallen walls; and depressions, from which the earth was used to make the adobe are close by. Nearer the city of silence, immense quantities of broken pottery

strew the ground, an arrowhead or stone axe
comes to light, and the least excitable visitor
must admit that the Gila Valley, where desolation reigns supreme, was once densely populated.
We have, in addition, the strong testimony of
adjacent artificial mounds, supposed to have been
burial places; but the mythical mines of silver
and gold laid down on the oldest maps, referred
to by the oldest missionaries, do not yet appear.
A popular theory has been held that the Casas
were habitations of companies of miners who
worked undiscovered placers hard by. Happily
this conceit has been exploded.

The ruins stand on a low, broad mesa, or
table-land, rising slightly from the main road,
and are covered by a thicket of mezquit trees
not exceeding twenty feet in height, but conceal-
ing the dun-colored walls till we were close on
them. Passing beyond the leafy screen we saw,
within the space of one hundred and fifty yards,
three buildings. Two are battered and decaying, so ruinous as to baffle the effort of the tourist to form an idea of their original size, the
shape being, as in all these remains, a parallelogram. Their walls were standing sufficiently
to trace the plan thirty five years ago.

We bent our steps to the main building, largest and best preserved, and with a keen sense of
disappointment beheld the structure so dear to
archæologists and known for three centuries as
the House of Montezuma. Though familiar by
picture and description, I had thought to find
some display of regal power in architectural
grace and finish; remnants of mouldings, broken
lines of cornices, and at least one lofty portal
through which the tawny courtiers might have
filed in barbaric pomp to salute the Rocky
Mountain King. It is merely a tremendous
mud house, on which the centuries have spent

their strength in vain, standing in the hush of
utter solitude, battling time and the elements.
There is nothing picturesque about it. No
friendly lichen, running creeper or trailing ivy
can live in this dry dewless air and with tender
verdure clothe the nakedness of the ragged structure. Against the sand blast no wreathing vine
can cling, and in its embrace soften the mass of
ugliness harshly outlined against the bare and
brilliant sky, unflecked by cloud or shadow.
Our spirits went down, down before the legendary Palace of Montezuma we had come so far
to see. For this we had strained over lava beds,
through the sunburnt ways of the wilderness,
across valleys of sand, sage desert, and greasewood plain, breathing, eating, drinking alkali,
and wearing its dust like a dingy travelling suit!
Instead of poetry here was certainty.

The mountain rim was a refreshment to the
vision. There the aerial hues, so like the stuff
which dreams are made of, gave the only ideal
touch to a scene forbiddingly real. No hint of
beauty or excellence of workmanship is found in
a near view of the Casa, which is entitled to
admiration only on account of its age, and to
a hold on fancy because its origin and uses are
unknown. Desolate and isolated now, time was
when it was encircled by similar buildings
grouped in villages scattered broadly over the
wide plateau. In every direction are broken
lines of fallen walls, oblong heaps crumbled
down to the dust whence they sprung; and the
extent of irrigation must have made the valley a
cultivated garden, or a field of corn large enough
to sustain a vast population.

But there was little time for sentiment. Our
surveys must be made in haste. The walls are
entirely adobe; in no portion is there any stone
used. Instead of the modern Spanish-American

15

adobes, moulded to about six times the size of our
ordinary bricks, this aboriginal "palace" is built
of large blocks of concrete (called by Mexicans
tapia), three feet or more in length, by two feet in
width and thickness. They are of irregular size,
indicating that a box or mould was used in the
manufacture into which the mortar was cast
where it was to remain in the walls; and as it
dried the cases were moved along. A recent
chemical analysis of the concrete shows the
secret of its durability under the wasting and
wearing of ages in a structure certainly a ruin
for three hundred years, and with a pre-Spanish
existence of a century and perhaps more. Seventeen per cent. of the mortar is carbonate of
lime. Probably lime was burned and mixed
with the sand and gravel of the country, which
contains a very adhesive clay, tough and lasting.

The walls are perpendicular within, slightly
tapering without, four feet thick, facing the cardinal points of the compass, almost the true
meridian. The building was fifty-eight feet long
and forty-three feet wide, the highest point of
the standing wall being thirty-five feet. It was
originally four or five stories high, being about
eight feet from floor to ceiling. In the
centre of each wall were narrow doors for
entrance into the main compartments, three feet
wide, five feet high, and growing narrower at the
top, except the one in the west front, which is
two feet by seven or eight. Over each door is a
port-hole whose dimensions I am unable to give.
The Indian's love of dark houses is apparent
here; the only light admitted into the small
numerous rooms was through these holes in the
deep walls. The central room, with only one
opening, must have been as dismal as a dungeon.
It has been surmised that this was a sort of
watch-tower, eight or ten feet higher than the

outer stories, probably one story above all the rest when the Casa was entire. Some of the port-holes have been filled in with mortar as though the window, if window it was, admitted too much light.

Father Font, who visited this ruin in 1776, writes: " It is perceptible the edifice had three stories. The Indians say it had four; the last being a kind of subterranean vault. For the purpose of giving light to the rooms nothing is seen but the doors, and some round holes in the middle of the walls which face to the east and west, and the Indians said that the Prince, whom they called the ' Bitter Man,' used to salute the sun through these holes (which are pretty large) at its rising and setting. All the roofs are burnt out except that of one low room, in an adjoining house, which had beams, apparently cedar, small and smooth, and over them reeds of equal size and a layer of hard mud and mortar, forming a very curious roof, or floor."

The different stories are easily identified by the ends of beams remaining in the walls, or by the holes into which the beams projected. They are round rafters of cedar, or sabino, supporting the floors, being perhaps six inches in diameter and half a foot apart. The nearest mountain bear-ing such trees is many a weary mile away. The charred ends of beams prove that the interior was destroyed by fire, but the massive four-foot wall suffered no change by flaming floor, rafter, or roof. The trees were hacked by a blunt tool, probably a stone hatchet ; evidently iron was unknown to the architect of Casas Grandes. The Indigene substituted for it tempered copper and tools of wrought obsidian. A few bone awls, or flakers, for making arrow heads, have been dug out of the gravel, and a metate, or corn grinder, broken jars and a tomahawk of flint, have been found, but there is no tracery made by iron.

Adobe walls are wonderfully durable in this dry, equable climate, and with slight repairs last a thousand years. Disintegration begins at the base, where moisture gathers, and the walls, seamed and furrowed near the earth by the action of heavy yearly rains, are held together merely by their great thickness. Their inner surface is smoothly plastered with lime cement, little wrinkled marks standing as they appeared when first dried after the finish was laid on. There is no sign of stairway, and ascent was probably made outside on scaling ladders, as the Pueblos go up their terraced domiciles throughout New Mexico and Arizona. The rough coating without is flaked off in some places by the continuous action of war- ring winds which carry sand. Even more than rain, this incessant agent is operating on the old dun-colored adobes, and unless repairs are made in the scarred and furrowed foundations, this most interesting of antiquities must before long become a shapeless wreck. There can have been no considerable shock of earthquake in the period during which it has been known to us; even a slight tremble would bring the time-worn fabric down to hopeless destruction.

Standing on the mesa, the traveller sees in every direction heaps of ruins, of which the Casas Gran- des was the centre and principal. About two hun- dred yards to the north-west is a circular inclos- ure, also a ruin. It is supposed to have been a corral for cattle, which, unless, as some assume, it was used as a menagerie, would make it of more recent date, as the Indians were without domestic animals before the conquest. Archi- tectural remains have been well called the bal- ance wheels of tradition. After actual sight and touch there is no room for dreams and visions.

Temples and towers proclaim worship, sculptures hint of refinement, wealth and elegant tastes. Coins tell of commerce, and frescoes like those of Pompeii and Rome are illuminated books of Chronicles.

This antique pile is expressive of a low condition of art. Its size is impressive when we consider that it was completed without the aid of domestic animals or iron, but by hand labor alone. The only idea left in the mind of the visitor is that it was designed to accommodate great numbers of persons; a cumbrous human hive. There is no forest growth above it by which to date the passage of years; and the ceaseless delving of the archæologist has failed to find a key, accepted by all as the true one, to the age and purpose of so remarkable a building. Excavations made on an appropriation by the Legislature of Arizona resulted in nothing. A citizen of Florence reports finding a piece of gold resembling coin in the debris, and it is said that a hollow sound has been heard by those jumping on the floor of the inner room. Part of the walls have fallen, which may account for the noise. That ghost is laid and no voice or breath of living thing disturbs the dreaming pilgrim and baffled antiquarian as in mournful procession they carry off their relics—bits of broken plaster and pottery.

The earliest reporters describe eleven buildings in close proximity to each other, and there can be no reason to doubt their record, judging by the high heaps of mud and gravel lying in every direction about the great Casa. Compassing it is a prostrate wall extending four hundred and twenty feet from north to south, and two hundred and sixty feet from east to west, which they believed was a part of the Casa itself—a natural

mistake which has given many a highly exagger-
ated idea of the structure inclosed by it.

The first recorded mention of Casas Grandes is
made in 1540, by Captains Diaz and Saldibar,
who with twelve intrepid men marched from the
city of Culiacan and ascended the Gila as far as
Chichiticale, or Red House, on the border of the
Colorado Desert. They had from friendly
Indians glowing descriptions of the seven cities
of Cibola, in which whole streets were said to be
occupied exclusively by workers in gold and
silver. "They had sculptured silver and spear
heads and drinking cups of precious metals."
Fired by these beguiling fables Coronado led a
little army of picked men, fifty soldiers, a few
infantry, his particular friends and the monks, in
search of fairy land, the vanishing seven cities of
Cibola. His secretary records that when the
general passed through all the inhabited region to
the place where the desert begins and saw there
was "nothing good," he could not repress his
sadness notwithstanding the marvels which were
promised further on.

The traveller of 1880 has much the same sensation as that which smote the soul of the dashing
Coronado of 1540. In the time of the latter the
whole of the North American Continent east of
the Rio Grande was called Florida. It is not
surprising that much inaccurate information prevailed regarding the geography of Nueva Espagna, but it is easy to identify Casas Grandes
with the "Red House" standing in a mezquit
jungle on the edge of the desert, the first ruin
seen on the Gila by one ascending from its
mouth. In certain lights the walls have a reddish
tint, and again appear white on account of pebbles contained in the plaster.

In 1694 Father Kino visited the Casas Grandes.
He heard traditions of the Pimos running back

four hundred years; it had been a ruin for ages,
and was destroyed by fire in the war with the
Apaches. "The principal room in the middle is
four stories, the adjoining rooms on its four sides
are of three stories, with walls so smooth and
shining that they appear like burnished tables.
At the distance of an arquebuss shot, twelve other
houses were to be seen, also half fallen, having
thick walls, and all the ceilings burnt except in
the lower room of one house." He mentions
also canals for irrigation, "which had capacity for
carrying half the water of the river." The good
priest took peaceable possession of the forsaken
spot, set up the cross within the dreary walls and
made the place a holy shrine with the celebration
of mass.

Of the old descriptions that of Father Font,
who visited the scene in 1779, is most valuable.
I regret not having space for a longer extract
from his journal: "The large house or Palace of
Montezuma," he says, "according to the histories
and meagre accounts of it which we have from
the Indians, may have been built some 500
years ago; for, as it appears, this building was
erected by the Mexicans when, during their
transmigration, the Devil led them through
various countries until they arrived at the
promised land of Mexico; and in their sojourns,
which were long ones, they formed towns and
built edifices." He further speaks of ruins in
every direction. "The land is partially covered
with pieces of pots, jars, plates, etc." He was
the first one who discovered that the outer wall
was a fortification, "a fence which surrounded this
house and other buildings." Within the last
thirty years the Casa de Montezuma has been
often described, and so much speculation has
been expended as to its origin and uses that I
hesitate to push out into that dark sea.

There is a succession of ruined cities, forming a continuous chain of evidence, from Utah to the City of Mexico.   I have examined many of these dead pueblos and can discover no essential in which they differ from each other, from the living pueblos now inhabited, or from the Casas Grandes. All are community houses, where a whole tribe may dwell, built of adobe in the shape of an ob- long square around an open court.   Inclosing this was an outer wall or fortification with towers at regular intervals for the posting of sentinels. The old pueblos were built on a table land so as to afford an outlook for sentries and an oppor- tunity for watching depredations on the corn lands in the valleys below ; and often at a distance are found the remains of a circular watch-tower, a signal station near the city.   Such are the pre- historic vestiges along the McElmo, Colorado, San Juan and the Rio Mancos, and the widely dispersed remains in the Ehaco and Mancho. Such is the solitary watch-tower in the Cañon of the Hovenweep, Utah.   The north ernmostbuild- ings discovered in Arizona and Colorado are exact copies of the Southern and Moqui pueblos, varying with situation and with the quality of material used.   Generally   the   earth   of   the country was mixed with ashes and clay.   The lack of individuality in the Indian race gives you the feeling that if you see one you have seen all ; so it is in regard to their habitations.   The same- ness of the remains, and their close likeness to the Casas Grandes and the modern buildings, must strike the most careless observer.   Yet they are not more alike than the builders themselves.

There are few, if any antiquities, that have not been searched through and through and reported on.   The hunter, miner, scout, surveyor, priest and sightseer have overlooked no hill or plain where there is a trace of human dwelling.   Undoubtedly

the adobe houses wherever found are the work
of a semi-civilized, agricultural people with whom
the Spaniards came in conflict, and who are
described by them as Pueblo, or Town Indians,
to distinguish them from the nomads or wandering tribes of the primitive race. An immense
amount of romance has been wasted on the old
mud houses, which makes them hardly less wonderful than the enchanted city Tiahuanco,
which was built in a single night by an invisible hand; but the time is come to put out
wavering lights and to banish shifting shadows.

I am convinced that the Palace of Montezuma
was designed as a fortress, a centre from which
many villages radiated and to which the inhabitants fled for refuge in a last extremity. The
lightness of the floor rafters in the lower story
precludes the possibility that the building was
used as a granary. Any one of the many rooms
full of grain must have crushed the floors, if not
the walls themselves. Again, it has been declared
to have been a temple for the sun worshippers;
but the smallness and multiplicity of the rooms
and the many doors and port holes oppose such
a surmise, though the dismal central room
and the circular passages between the rooms
might suggest priestcraft, and heathen rites and
sorceries.

It may have been, like the castle of the middle
ages, the nucleus around which the city gradually grew up, but more probably it rose from
the needs of the citizens, many of whom must
have toiled in its erection. For many, many
years the Apache has harried this land. It is the
Indian law to destroy all that he cannot carry
away, and the pottery is always broken, the
interiors are always fired. The builders of adobe
houses, wherever found, were open to incursions
of the same enemy which still infests the Mex-

ican border. To me these remains have no new meanings. They merely prove that the North American Continent has been inhabited from a remote period; something which I believe has never been disputed.

The undated tradition is that the spot which I am trying to describe is one of the stopping places of Montezuma on his southward march to Anahuac. All legends point to an emigration from north to south. Coming from the ends of the earth, or from fabled Azatlan, the first halt the Montezumas made was at old Zuni; this was the second station; the third was near Chihuahua, Mexico, where enormous ruins, exact reproductions of these are standing isolated in a luxuriant valley, the tottering monuments of a peculiar tribe or tribes of a bygone nationality. Nothing is to be learned from the natives there, who, like all Pueblos, love to call themselves sons of Montezuma, or from the Mexicans round about. Whatever requires a moment's thought is dismissed by the ever-ready, meaningless, *Quien sabe ?* "Who knows ?"

CHAPTER XXV.

TO THE CASAS GRANDES.

THE Casas Grandes on the Laguna de Guzman in Northwestern Chihuahua are similar in every respect to the ruined fortresses of New Mexico and Arizona. The points of resemblance are so close and so numerous as to be decisive, proving them to be the work of the same people under similar, though somewhat superior, institutions. On my table is an unbroken vase unearthed from this most venerable

Tesuke Water Vases.

ruin of North America: a veritable antique, rare and valuable. It is of a light clay color, glazed without and within. The shape, the peculiar markings in geometrical lines, white, black and maroon red, prove the hand of its manufacturer. I should recognize it instantly in any collection as a Pueblo water jar of ancient workmanship, better made than any which we have from the Pueblos now. It contains the following memorandum : " This *olla* or *tanaja* was excavated from the ruins of the Montezuma Casas Grandes in the State of Chihuahua in the year 1864, and according to Indian tradition is 800 years old. These Casas Grandes (great houses) were reduced to ruin, by siege, in 1070." This is signed, "William Pierson, American Consul in 1873."

It is the only whole jar and much the finest specimen I have ever seen. Still it is greatly inferior to the coarsest Wedgwood china in our shops. There has never appeared a monument or relic proving the existence of a people of more advanced culture than the red race with which the European came in contact. How the peculiar civilization which this vase represents came from the North, as every tradition declares it did, is a question that has been argued many times in many ways. Among a vanquished, declining people, without even the lowest forms of picture-writing, language rapidly alters; and philologists tell us that American languages are the most changeful forms of human speech. Legends soon become confused; the links of connection are easily lost; and even in its best estate tradition is treacherous as memory. Scholars have held that the adobe houses are traces of the Toltecs, the polished predecessors of the fierce and bloody Aztecs, under whose dominion the former broke and scattered. Plausible theories, more or less conclusive, have perplexed the student of indigenous races. One solution, as soon as it was suggested, touched me with the force of absolute conviction, because it was so direct and simple an answer to the puzzling questions following an examination of the antiquities of North America.

The Pueblo or town-building Indians were the skirmish line of the Aztec nation when the Mexican Empire was in the height of its greatness. The Aztecs were restless, aggressive, greedy of power and insatiate in their lust for dominion. To rove and to conquer was the national pastime. The green banners of Anahuac floated defiantly in the tropic airs of the remotest provinces on the Gulf of Mexico, and dauntless warriors upheld their colors in pristine splendor along the extreme coasts of Honduras and Nicaragua. They formed the unshackled, sovereign nation, possessing the highest civilization in North America, speaking a language by far the most finished and elegant of the native tongues, said to be of exceeding richness.

The Pueblos, whom we believe to be a rough off-shoot of that stock, degraded descendants of haughty princes, are yet a self-sustaining people, independent of the Government, the only aborigines among us not a curse to the soil. In some old time whereof history is silent and about which there are no traditions, nor even the airy hand of a misty legend to beckon us back and point the way, the half-civilized tribes of Mexico must have sought fresh fields for conquest and occupation. They probably marched in detached clans speaking different dialects, but more or less united under one central government, and with the arts and means of instruction brought from Anahuac they set forth to colonize outlying countries to the north. A glance at the map shows only one route by which they could advance. West of the Sierra Madre and up the Gila and its tributaries, toward the great cañon of the Colorado, colonies were planted along the river banks, and possibly the emigrant fraternized with the native. Captain Fernando Alarcon discovered the Rio Colorado in 1540, and passed various tribes without being able to communicate with them, except by signs, until he reached a people who understood the language of an Indian whom he had brought from Mexico. From this tribe he learned of a similar people, far to the eastward, who lived in great houses built of stone. From Mexico the Southerners brought the art of building with adobe and with stones laid in mud mortar, which alone distinguishes them from the tribes ·dwelling in wigwams, shifting tents and lodges of buffalo skins and boughs. There was a system of communication between their fortified towns, worn footpaths betraying a constant coming and going, and deep trails furrowed by the tread of busy feet through centuries.

The ancient builders invariably chose commanding positions overlooking their cultivated fields for their pueblos, and added story after story to the houses, usually terraced from without, where a few defenders could defy almost any number of assailants with savage arms. Apaches were treated as barbarian hordes. There is no mention of these Bedouins until a century after Coronado's day, from which fact we may infer that they were kept at bay.

Gradually the tide of emigration pressed up to the Aztec Mountains and San Francisco Peaks, but there the march of the victorious invader was suddenly stopped by a barrier utterly impassable—the cañons of the Colorado

and Chiquito Rivers, which, united, form a gulf
at least 300 miles long, and which in places are
a mile in depth. It lay directly across their
course, a stupendous chasm which wings only
would have enabled them to cross. No sea or
desert could so effectually have hindered their
progress northward. They turned toward the
East, took possesion of the rich valleys of the
Colorado and Chiquito, where streets of towns
and irrigating canals are still traceable for miles,
and followed its branches to their sources. All
the towns are along the river. The bottom
lands are fertile with alluvial deposits. There
are large cotton-wood trees and impenetrable
thickets of arrow and greasewood among the
numberless lagoons and sloughs which, at the
annual rise of the river, are filled to overflowing
and irrigate the soil. But no vegetation can
live beyond the limit of these overflows. A
white efflorescence covers the ground, where it
is useless to plant, where nothing edible for man
or beast will grow.

On the neighboring streams the chiefs founded
the kingdom of Cibola, where now we see extensive ruins attesting the size of the old towns, all
of which were fortified and built on the same
general plan. Old Tuni was the capital city, set
on a hill of rock and reached only by one zigzag
path, where a handful of soldiers could defy the
cavalry of the world. In a similar condition the
ruins of the seven Moqui villages are found, and
North of them is the site of an adjacent colony.
To the north-east they moved from the head of
Flax River to the southern tributaries of the San
Juan, the Cañon de Chaco and the Valle de
Chelly, "where," says Lieutenant McCormick,
"half a million might have lived," being strewn
with the ruins of dead cities.

At last, by following up the headwaters of the

ABANDONED PUEBLO.

Rio de San Juan to the Colorado Mountains,
they penetrated the Rio Grande Valley, a fertile
and widely·extended region destined to be subdued and colonized.   From this point their
imperious course was down the valley from the
north, as all traditions point; and, naturally, the
conquerors built a vast stronghold at Taos to
protect that beautiful valley from attacks of the
wild tribes, mainly Utes—a gloomy, forbidding
citadel of savage aspect, set on a hill overlooking
the Rio Grande.   So strong a retreat is it that
in 1847, when the Mexicans of the modern village of Taos could no longer defend themselves
against the armies of the United States, they fled
to this abandoned pueblo, a few miles distant, and
there sustained a protracted siege, yielding finally when provisions utterly failed.   The grim
and threatening fortress was never captured by
the Spaniards, though many times attacked.
The terraces bristled with spears and battle-axes,
through the little windows arrows were show-
ered, and stones and burning balls of cotton
dipped in oil were hurled from slings.   The
lower story, a well-filled granary—and the cisterns within the court, enabled the red men " to
laugh a siege to scorn."

The route which we have rapidly sketched
was discovered and maintained by the armies of
many generations; the changes described in a
paragraph were brought about by wars lasting
through ages.   Well did those migratory tribes
know the fierce delight of battle which thrills
alike the blood of the white man and the red, when
once within the heat and fury of its deadly
charm.

In the course of time the entire valley of the
Rio Grande from latitude 37° to latitude 32°, a
distance of over 400 miles, was thickly settled.
It must have been a scene of constant activity,

with its clusters of towns, whose streets are yet plainly visible and may be followed for miles; and becoming the dominant nation, in the main valley where the villages are nearest to each other, the Aztecs found it unnecessary to fortify their dwelling places. Out-lying settlements, such as Pecos and Grand Quivira, in the country swept by Comanches and Arapahoes, and Laguna and Acoma, near the Navajos, were defended by outworks like those in the Colorado basin.

Near El Paso are widespread ruins of the prehistoric epoch, and it is so short a march from that crossing to the lovely and productive valley of Rio Corralites and its lake, the Laguna de Guzman, that it is most reasonable to suppose the casès on this stream were built by a colony from that region. The Indians and Mexicans of our day are exactly right in asserting that the "great houses" are the work of Montezumas who came from the North, and at various stations fortified themselves against the roving tribes. So it comes that the Town Builders of New Mexico and Arizona, who are without history or hieroglyphic writing, have no record or even legend of the dim and distant starting point when the exodus from Mexico began. They brought a species of civilization quite foreign to the nomads who confronted them, battled for supremacy, and disputed their sway. The civilization was necessarily inferior to that of the source whence it sprung. This is the condition in all migratory movements. The wealthy, cultured classes are conservative, slow to change; the dissatisfied spirits, adventurers with little to leave or to take, strike out of the beaten paths in hope of bettering their fortunes.

The colonial beginnings were a poor representation of the splendors of Tezcuco where North

American civilization, under the commanding genius of the second Montezuma, reached its height. But the pilgrims brought with them glorious memories. They must have seen the sacred city Cholula, with its 400 temples, its huge pyramid, wrought by the giant Haloc, nearly 200 feet high, the sides measuring 450 yards at its base. It was a terraced tower, a landmark, a beacon and a shrine to all Anahuac, where the smoke from the undying altar-fires went up as incense to the gods, new every morning and fresh every evening. There were no writhing victims on that hill of sacrifice; the gentle Quetzelcoatt delighted not in blood; his offerings were bread and roses and all sweet perfumes. The townsmen in their new homes built council-houses, meagre and poverty-stricken compared with the Southern temples, and kindled the sacred fires. Each village had one or more of these estufas, where holy rites were conducted in the utmost secrecy. A priesthood of chosen warriors, consecrated to the ministry, watched the altar-fire, and it was never suffered to die out.

In all probability the later emigrants brought with them the Montezuma idol. Possibly some had been in the kneeling ranks of those who kissed the earth at the sound of conch and atabal which heralded the approach of the great king, the child of the sun. Hardly had they dared to lift their eyes, before the splendor of the canopy of green featherwork fringed with sparkling pendants, which shaded his jewelled plumes. They could not fail to remember the floating robes of gorgeous dyes, the blazing arms making the glance dizzy with the shining of precious stones; and, best of all, that princely presence in the midst of worshipping subjects, who held themselves but as dust beneath the golden soles of the royal sandals. They could not forget the

wall of orbed shields about his sacred person,
the keen sparkle of burnished spear tips, the flying flags of various colors which the Indian
loves so well, and the shouts of thousands on
thousands of loyal subjects who counted not
their lives dear unto themselves but for their
service to their emperor. The all-conquering
Montezuma was at first only a proud memory.
By degrees a halo and a light appeared round the
name of the king of kings. Men love to trace
their descent back to some storied greatness, and
all barbarous nations delight to associate their
origin with the deities. The yearning to be as
gods, is one of the instinctive impulses of the
human heart. It began in Eden and is as old as
the first man.

From reverence of the compelling spirit which
left its imprint on vast regions, various tribes and
long periods of time, it is easy to pass to adoration. The valley of the Rio Grande was once a
valley of gods; they breathed in the winds,
frowned in the storms; their wrath was the
earthquake and their smile was fair weather.
The central idea ceaselessly recurring in the
pantheistic religion of the Pueblos of the nineteenth century is the shining figure of Montezuma, and their belief in his return is the dearest
of all their faiths. As in the Greek legends, we
cannot define the line between myth and history,
but we are forced to believe so widespread a
religion must have had a beginning remote from
the degraded, broken-hearted creatures who pray
to him daily. The dim memories of a great past
never quite fade away from among any people.
The dreamy, mythical, departed grandeur of
their ancestors has led the Pueblos to the hope
of a restoration; for with them the vague past
and the indefinite future are both better than the
dull, tame present. The hope in every breast,

slow to die, if indeed it ever dies, looks to a regen-
eration, a lifting up of the bowed race so mercilessly stricken down by the Spaniards.   The
caciques who guard the sacred fires watch at
the daybreak for the second coming of the law-
giver, prophet and priest, and pray with faces
toward the sun-house where he takes his kingly
rest in the abode of his fathers.   In the golden
dawn of some morning, fairest where all are fair,
he shall push back the curtains of his tabernacle
intolerably bright, and with roll of drums, music
of reeds and beauty of banners shall return to his
own again.

It is the tendency, even in carefully recorded
annals, to make one man the doer of all heroic
deeds.   The unnamed dead live in the life of one
king of men.   The lesser lights wane and pale
before its splendor, and finally all mingle in a
resplendent focus, and one immortal stands forever the representative of the epoch, a sceptred
deity.   Such are the demigods of Southern Europe: such is the fair-haired Odin of the mead-
drinking warriors in sheepskin and horsehide;
such is King Arthur, gone away under promise
to return from

> The island valley of Avilion,
> Where falls not hail, or rain, or any snow,
> Nor ever wind blows loudly.

And such is the Messiah of the Town Builders,
brother of the sun, equal of the one Omnipotent
God, uncreated and eternal, whose name it is
death to utter.

Tried by the delicate test of language, there is
no analogy between the modern Town Builder
and the Mexican of the South; but this is not
conclusive.   Centuries of changing environment
work miraculous changes in any people.   How
much is the modern Briton like his ancestor, the
cave dweller, clad in skins of the beasts which

almost shared his den, living on roots and bow-
ing down at strange altars ? Even in the same
generation, in the best age of the most enlightened of kingdoms, how much does the Irish
gentleman resemble his degraded tenant, the
peat-digger? Nay, they can scarcely comprehend each other's speech. Of the heroes, numbered by hundreds of thousands, who upheld our
victorious banner during the great Rebellion, how
many names will remain at end of the year 2880?
Possibly one. The least observant traveller
through the country of the Pueblos must notice
that it has changed for the worse since the "great
houses" were built. They stand on the rim of
the Colorado Desert, and if we accept the theory
of the geologists that this is the dry bed of an
inland sea, the climate must once have been very
unlike what it is now—waterless ten months of
the year, and at summer noon as hot and as stifling as the air of a limekiln. Scientists unite in
testifying that the rainfall west of the Rio Grande
is much less than formerly. The present streams
are shrunken threads of those which once flowed
in their channels when forests were more abundant. Northern Arizona has hills whose bases
are covered with dead cedar trees, immense belts
untouched by fire, proving that the conditions
friendly to the growth of vegetation are restricted
to narrowing limits. Spots that have been productive are barren; springs gushed from the
ground which at present is dry and parched, and
an agricultural people has lived where now no
living being could maintain existence. Everything indicates that this region was formerly
better watered. Many rivers of years ago are
now rivers of sand, and the Gila at its best, after
gathering the confluent streams, San Pedro and
Salado, is not so large in volume as an Indiana
creek. Ethnologists try to prove that the

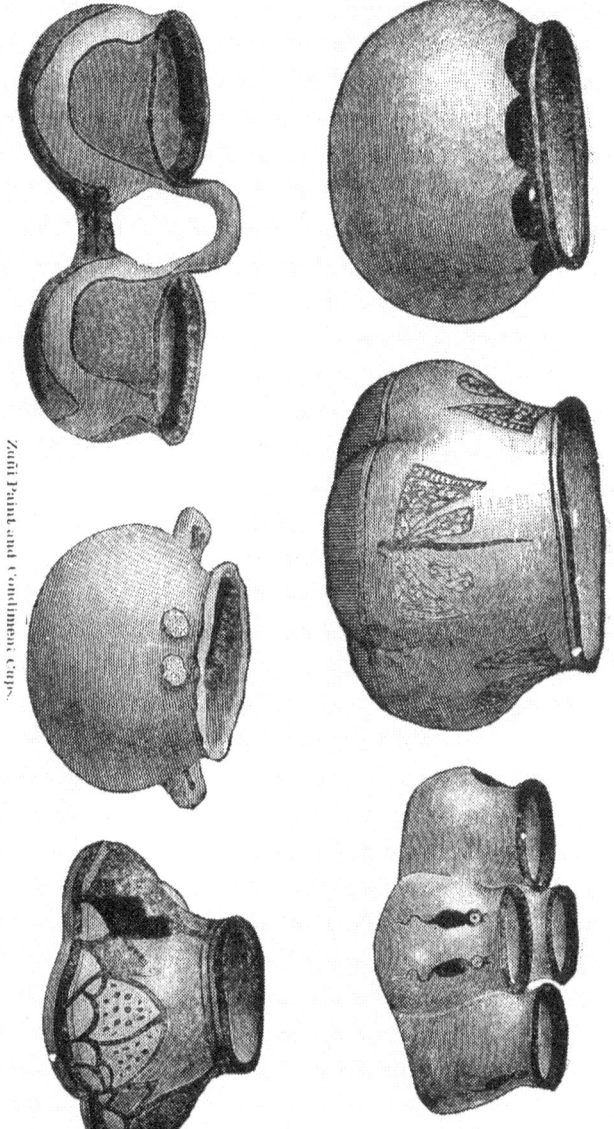

Zuñi Paint and Condiment Cups.

Town Builders came from the extreme North, perhaps originally from Kamtchatka, and that the adobe houses and Montezuma worship were of indigenous growth, founded by the monarch who bears the proudest name in Indian history. There are no Pueblos North of the thirty-seventh parallel, and the decline of the race began long before the Spanish invasion. It will be remembered that the Casas Grandes was a roofless, crumbling ruin, without a history more than 300 years ago. The Pueblos must have been a mighty nation in the prime of their strength, and legends of their ancient glory before they passed under the hated Spanish yoke are cherished among the different tribes. Reduced as they were in numbers and power, their battle for freedom was a long and gallant struggle. They were finally brought into subjection, even to the Moquis who lived perched in tiny houses on scarred, seamed cliffs of volcanic rock, where nature's fires are burnt out, in a barren country, arid and inhospitable, absolutely worthless to white men.

Never was life so lonely and cheerless as in the desolate hovels of the Moquis. Their land is not a tender solitude, but a forbidding desolation of escarped cliffs, overlooking wastes of sand where the winds wage war on the small shrubs and venturesome grasses, leaving to the drouth such as they cannot uproot. A few scrubby trees, spotting the edge of the plain as if they had looked across the waterless waste and crouched in fear, furnish a little brushwood for the fires of the Moquis, who are fighting out the battle for existence that is hardly worth the struggle. Fixed habitation anywhere implies some sort of civilization. The flinty hills are terraced, and by careful irrigation they manage to raise corn enough to keep body and soul

together. The seven villages within a circuit of
ten miles have been isolated from the rest of the
world through centuries, yet they have so little
intercourse with each other that their tribal languages, everywhere subject to swift mutations,
are entirely unlike. Diminutive, low-set men
wrapped in blankets passively sitting on the bare,
seared rocks in the sun, are the ghastly proprie-
tors of a reservation once the scene of busy
activities. They number only 1,600 souls;
shreds of tribes almost exhausted, surrounded
by dilapidated cities unquestionably of great
antiquity. The sad heirship of fallen greatness
is written in the emptiness of their barren estates.
Fragments of pottery are profusely scattered
about; and deeply-worn foot-paths leading from
village to village, down the river bank and winding up to the plain, mark the ancient thorough-
fares which are now slightly trodden or utterly
deserted.

How the Indians were enslaved and driven to
the mines, and how they perished there by thousands, is a matter of familiar history. They
were an abject and heart-broken people after the
Conquest, and their decline still goes steadily on.
Whole tribes are extinct. Others have united
with each other for safety, and within the memory of citizens of Santa Fe the feeble remnant
of the tribe at Pecos joined that at Jemez, which
speaks the same language.

After all, the question is not so much whence
they come as whither they go. The human family
is never at rest; its condition is one of change.
From the beginning nations and peoples have
come and gone—vanished, where? Who knows?
Who cares? They moved forward in the resistless march, served the end for which they were
created, died and were forgotten. They come
like shadows, so depart. Across these desolate

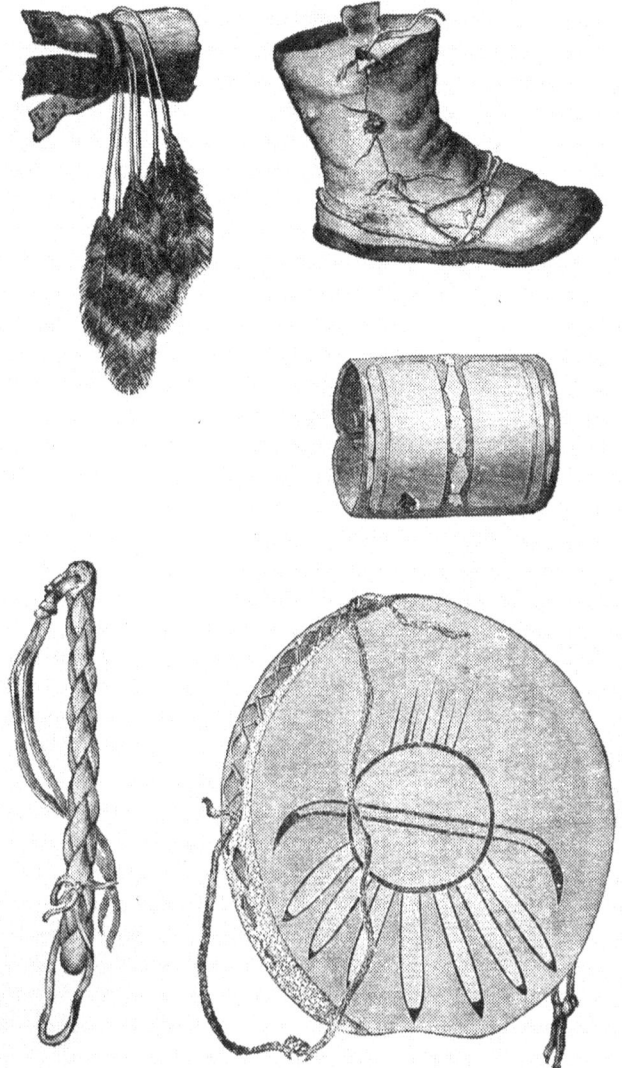

Pueblo Wristlets, Moccasins, etc.

Rocky Mountain ranges a turbulent stream of humanity once ebbed and flowed in perpetual unrest. Then there were tribes chasing, tribes fleeing, nation rising up against nation, scattering, absorbing, driving each other into annihilation; and the hills echoed the triumphant music of the scalp dances over the graves of slain thousands. The history of those mighty turmoils and revolutions must remain forever unwritten. The present aborigines are but a forlorn wreck of what they were in the long ago, when mountain princes from the South were supreme rulers in a realm of confederacies, whose boundaries cannot be measured.

The civilization of the Town Builders is not so much overthrown as it is worn out. Their bows are broken, their fires burn low; and the sluggish, stolid sons of Montezuma creep at a petty pace " along the way to dusty death." The inroads of warring bands are not fatal as their own system of communism. A closely-kept people must become effete ; and marriage within the forbidden degrees, for ages on ages, produces a diminutive, emasculate growth. In the tribes most isolated, where race distinctions are sharply drawn, this blood degeneration is most apparent. Very many are scrofulous, and albinos with pink eyes and wiry, white hair (strange sights!) are frequent among the Zunis and Moquis. Physicians tell us that it is a species of American leprosy, consequent on the poverty of blood through lack of alien infusion.

The weakening of this most interesting nationality resembles the quiet decline of one stricken in years. As in the empire, so in the individual ; according to the predetermined doom it cannot last, another must have its place. A peculiar people, utterly lacking in self assertion, through whole decades living in servitude under an enforced religion, they have run their race, worked out their destiny, and in the decrepitude of extreme old age, ruins and tribes, the dead and the dying, are crumbling away together.

CHAPTER XXVI.

A FRONTIER IDYL.

OUR picnic was in the month of May and we started from Santa Fè in the early morning. On three sides the drowsy old town is guarded by mountains royal with purple and glittering with gold. Thirty miles away one snowy peak seemed an airy tent let down out of heaven, and across it the breeze blows as freshly as airs across Eden when the world was young.

The road wound beside the little river Santa Fè, whose waters go softly, after rippling down in icy cascades from a lake pure as Tahoe, formed by melting snows from the mountain top. Along its margin the red willow tosses its branches lightly as a lady's plume, and back in the hill country the pine-trees sigh to each other their never ceasing song. Over the rocks clambering goats look down and shake their beards at the traveller, and the tinkle of a bell falls pleasantly on the ear as Mexican boys drive their flocks to the river; and where the sheep are drinking an Indian woman carrying a black jar on her head, erect and stately, comes to wash her poor rags in the stream.

It is all like the old Bible pictures. The somber landscape though sadly lacking color is serene and pastoral,—so filled with the beauty of peace and restful silence we thought of the ancient pilgrims journeying in the shining white light of the Delectable Mountains, and their talk with loving shepherds by the wayside. No fear of rain to spoil our pleasure ; there will not be one drop, nor is there even dew. Yesterday we breathed balm and incense ; to-morrow we know will be just like to-day. The south wind has "quieted the earth," and the blue overhead is without spot of cloud, vapory mist or fog.

Our party was quite large. In advance a well mounted Lieutenant, in the glory of his first shoulder straps, rode close to the bridle rein of a young girl whose flying veil gave short glimpses of a beautiful face lighted with eyes of radiant hazel and the brightest smiles. They were a pair of lovers, loved by us at first sight. In an ambulance came a stout lady with color rather high than delicate, whose unhappy bonnet would not stick to her head but kept slipping down her back. Beside her sat a weak woman from Illinois, born tired and unable to find time to rest since that wearisome date, having barely life enough to be proud of her ten-year-old Rosa as though children were the rarest things in the world. On a little *burro*, or donkey, was a school teacher without special escort, but looked after by a dry old bachelor who had one romance in his life and still wore the miniature of a face, dearly loved and early lost, which has been only dust thirty years. For the old love's sake he treated all women with delicate reserve, seeing in them kinship to the lost ideal they in some sort represent. A dream unbroken, for where death sets his seal the imprint is eternal and endureth forever. Then there rode along a blonde and pensive artist, the author of many rejected manuscripts, who carried sketching paper and a neat box of pencils. He wore his hair long and boots small, smoked cigarettes incessantly, and eyed the gay Lieutenant in bitterness of soul. Several light carriages whirled past us; and Brown, the photographer, dashed by on his own buckboard drawn by gallant gray mules. I had only time to notice the stranger beside him had the blackest eyes and wore a diamond ring of unusual size and brilliance which blazed in the sunlight as he courteously lifted his hat. Among the last to appear was an alumnus from Colorado College, who had electrified the whole board of trustees with his graduating speech entitled, "The Centennial State—a Nation's Benediction." This callow youth had made the eastern tour, had a nodding acquaintance with the crowned heads of Boston, and in conscious superiority overshadowed his companion, the Baptist minister, one of the meekest spirits that ever starved its way to heaven.

The army ambulance moved slowly through the sandy red soil but we did not care; the mountains—how grand they are!—were a perpetual delight. The fineness of the atmosphere gave exquisite tints to the near foothills and the vast horizon. Clusters of wild verbenas purpled the plain—a deeper shade of the far away hill purples—and strange flowers, yellow and pink, nestled in the short, moss-like grass. They never felt dew or rain, yet they did not appear stunted or starved, but looked up brightly in the sterile sand as from a garden bed.

Now and then a Pueblo Indian strode silently across our way, and a Mexican in picturesque striped blanket saluted us in Spanish fashion with a "*Buenos dias señoras,*" as he drove his cruelly loaded donkey toward the city. Lazy Mexicans squatted in rows sunned themselves against the low walls of their houses; and on a chimney a flock of pigeons tamely perched, and watched the movements of a mower cutting the grass which grew scantily on the flat mud roof of his miserable hut.

When we reached the chosen ground a fire was already kindled from the resinous boughs of the *piñon*, and lovers were straying off in shady places to find out what words the daisies are saying to youth and beauty.

Brown, the photographer, introduced his guest, a fine old Spaniard named Oreto. He wore the easy air of a man familiar with good society, and the lofty courtesy which marks the true Castilian, I may say the true gentleman, anywhere. He claimed to be hidalgo—literally, son of a Goth—by which is meant pure Catholic Spanish blood, without a taint of Jew or Moor; was educated at Salamanca, and by training conservative was quick to denounce Castelar and his politics as highly pernicious. In a quiet way he was a great talker; the flashing eyes alone betrayed the intensity of his feeling, and as no one entered into debate with him, he fell to extolling the glory of old Castile. Gradually the whole party was attracted to him, and he became the centre of a circle of interested listeners.

The fair rider with fluffy curls blown by the mountain breeze against the arm she leaned on, bent forward and asked, " Why leave your own country for this wild New World ? "

" It is long to tell the state troubles which drove me from home and made me a wanderer, for out of Spain every land is exile ; too long for even a summer day."

" But not too long for our interest," she answered with a charming animation; "you are alone in life," she added with a glance at the band of mourning crape on his *sombrero*.

" Catalina and my niñita are with the saints," —he crossed his breast reverently. " When I

laid them in the vault at Valladolid my heart
felt heavy and cold.   I thought the long voyage
and sight of new places might warm it, and I
might find some diversion, or as our neighbors
over the Pyrenees say 'distraction,' by imitating
my ancient countryman in a chase after 'the
fountain of youth.' "

"That is in our own hearts." said Romeo,
with an arch glance at Juliet.

"Yes, so experience teaches.   I am last of my
name and house, and"—his voice sunk mourn-
fully—" I had buried the wife of my youth, whom
I loved with a great love, after we had lived
together twenty years."

He sighed and turned his eyes toward the
mountain-top shining like silver in the keen,
clear light, and the artist fell to sketching Oreto's
profile.

"Time is the great consoler," said the languid
Illinoisian, trying to adapt her harsh English to
the spoken music of the stranger.   A southern
sky makes a gentle voice, and the Spanish tongue
has a matchless trick of melting all it touches
into a melody.

"*La Señora* is most kind, but it is too late;
the heart has no second spring.   Do you see the
white line down the mountain-side?" he asked,
abruptly changing the subject evidently painful
to dwell upon.

"Yes, it is a brook rising in a spring, cold as
ice, clear as glass."

"Then, instead of my dull, sad story let me tell
you the tradition of the Blue Fountain, the name
of the spring,—*Fontaine-bleu*, as the French
Fathers used to call it."

"By all means; a story, a story!" the ladies
cried in chorus.

"You do me proud," said Oreto with a sweeping bow, "and since you honor me with your attention I promise not to weary it."

We disposed ourselves in various attitudes about the speaker. The rising generation gathered in graceful groups under the stunted pines, and the setting generation sat on buffalo robes and cushions against the gnarled and twisted trunks of the *piñones*. Little Rosa was coaxed to her mother's lap, and the stout lady reclined on the back seat of the ambulance, loosened her bonnet strings and made herself extremely comfortable while we listened to the

LEGEND OF THE BLUE FOUNTAIN.

"Once upon a time," the Spaniard began, with his grave smile, "away to the North in the country you call Montana lived a young Indian hunter, tall and straight and very handsome. From boyhood he had heard stories of happy hunting-grounds where the *pasturas* were always fresh and game was always in sight. So one bitter cold morning he put on his snow-shoes and fur mittens, wrapped himself in his warmest bearskin, and struck southward, following the stony mountain ranges till he reached this lonesome region."

"Did he travel all alone?" asked little Rosa.

"Only the travelling winds went with him. But he did not know what fear is, though at night he heard the coyote's cry, the bellowing of the bison and the howl of the prairie wolf. The sun, which he worshipped, shone friendly all the way; gradually the breeze blew softer, the earth grew warmer and greener. After one long day's march he drank deep of the spring in yon hillside, laid his bent bow and quiver of arrows on the rock, and went to sleep in the soft warm sand by the Blue Fountain.

"An Indian warrior sleeps lightly, and in his slumber appeared a form—a woman's, such a shape as is seen nowhere but in dreams and Andalusia." The stranger paused and looked dreamily on the ground like one busy with memory, and in sympathy I thought of the lost Catalina and the little one lying in the gloomy vault of Valladolid. We respected his silence, and after a moment he continued:

"The spirit spoke to the dreamer in words of infinite tenderness, and appeared to watch and guard him. On waking he took a long draught of the cool snow water, and gazed searchingly into its blue depths."

"Was it really blue?" broke in Rosa.

"Sky blue and silver," said the Castilian, adding one of the endearing diminutives in which his language is so rich and which I did not quite comprehend. "Many times he tried to catch a glance of the fairy face which came into his sleep, making it better than any waking. Long he gazed into the watery mirror; it reflected only his own tawny face and the spotless sky above it. The white sand boiled from unknown depths below, bubbles came to the top and broke on the stony brim, but the ceaseless gush and flow of the waters was a chime in his ears without meaning.

"He lingered about this spot, so runs the tale, many weeks, praying for the appearance of the water maiden. She came into his sleep but never blest his waking eyes, and when the rainy season, which is so very dreary, set in, the disappointed youth went back to his tribe. The vision haunted him; in vain he tried to shake it off; the *vega*, so lone, so dim, so untrodden, was filled with strange enchantment. The brook went flowing through his memory, glancing now in sun, now in shadow, as it gushed

from the mountain side, vanishing at last like
fairy gold in the sand   The laughing girls of
the tribe tried to rouse him from indifference,
but could not stir him to join in their songs and
games.   In the time of the corn harvest the
present of a blood-red ear, the Indian's *rose
d'amour*, did not move him to any feeling, and
he turned with glance averted from the flying
feet in the bewitching *cachina* dance.

"'He is moonstruck,' said the girls; 'give him
the crooked ear, for the fool is fit for nothing
but to sit in the sun with the very old men.'"   He
heeded neither jest nor laugh, and determined
to come back to the Blue Fountain.   When he
set out an airy figure seemed to go before and
beckon him on, as the swan maidens of the
German lakes beckon young knights into their
little boats drawn by snowy swans harnessed
with silver chains.

"Southward, southward he strode, following
the ancient march of Azatlan, and, in sight of
the beloved spring, he climbed the steep, fleet
and untired as the red deer, to find the same
sparkling fountain, and the shining brook below
it running into the valley as it will run on forever.

"Again he lay down on the soft, warm sand,
and once more the delicate phantom appeared to
his closed eyes, whispered gently in his ear, and
bent above his head as if to kiss him."

Here the lovers "changed eyes," leaned a
trifle closer together, and I saw Romeo pick up
a blue ribbon dropped from Juliet's sleeve and
slip it into his watch pocket.

"Then a frantic love took possession of the
hunter.   Day after day, night after night, his
wasting form was laid beside the singing cas-
cade; ever he sighed, murmured, dreamed.   The
strength left his limbs, his blood beat hotly:

summer waned and cold winds blew, but never
cooled the fever of his brow.   Sometimes after a
day's hunt, returning at evening he fancied he saw
a misty outline against the dark steep, but it melted
away as he neared it and instead of a living woman
he reached out to clasp the empty air.   Then the
warrior began to understand this water spirit
was of the race of Souls, and as such could not
wed a mortal; to possess her, therefore, he must
be like her—must die.   So one day when the
world was all bright and his soul all dark, while
she sung a song of wonderful music he stretched
his arms to reach the shadowy siren and plunged
from the black ledge you see yonder into the
unknown depths below."

"And was he never heard of afterward?"
asked Juliet, while the roses on her cheek deepened in betrayal of her thoughts.

"Never, *hermosura*," said the Spaniard with
an admiring gesture, "but old Pueblos about
here say two shapes rise out of the spring where
there used to be but one, float in the air and
hover above it.   They are oftenest seen about
dusk in the rainy season.   I have never seen
them myself."

"I wonder if they do show that way," said
Rosa with a puzzled face.

"*Quien sabe*," said Oreto mysteriously, at the
same time handing her the kernel of a *piñon* nut
which he cracked in his white front teeth.

And here let me record that the words "*Quien
sabe*," "who knows," are the end of controversy,
the finish of debate, the limit of human understanding, having a very different meaning according to the persons speaking.   With Oreto it was
as much as to say, there is room for argument
on both sides.

All this time our stew had been simmering,
gypsy fashion, over the fire, keeping a friendly

and impatient knocking at the pot lid, and was
now pronounced done. The stout lady roused
up from her nap, set her bonnet bias across her
eyebrows, said she was glad the young Comanche
came to his senses at last, and then addressed
herself to the making of coffee.

I met Oreto frequently, and never saw him
unbend from the Hamlet air—"Man delights
not me, no, nor woman either,"—except on this
one holiday. So to speak, he flavored the whole
picnic. He gayly insisted on seasoning every
dish. "I will not ruin the *olla* for Americans,
with too much red pepper," he said; "the
merest *soupçon*, as the French put it." Then he
contrived a nice, cool-looking salad from some
crisp leaves, to me unknown, and served it with
a deftness and tact that would have graced a
courtier. To tell the whole truth, the elegant
Castilian had so much manner it was rather
fatiguing to keep up with him.

Dinner over, he took a large silk handkerchief
and showed how two prisoners of the Inquisition were once knotted together with ropes, and
allowed their freedom if they could untie them,
trying the puzzle on the lovers, who, of course,
struggled violently to be free,—I need hardly
add without success. Had he experimented on
some of the married couples possibly the result
might have been different. Following this was
a gay barcarole about strolling on the Prado,
glancing eyes, winged feet and envious veils.
"It should have castanets in the chorus; if Señor
Brown will lend me his hat it will answer."

Thus appealed to, the photographer could not
choose but offer his brand new stovepipe to his
guest, who thumped it vigorously, greatly to
Señor Brown's annoyance, who stood looking
foolish, bareheaded in the sunshine. And again

17

I marked the size and lustre of the diamond ring.

The singer's voice was a trifle cracked, but we were not fastidious, the ladies hung on every word, and when the song ended, the applause was hearty and genuine. The blonde artist produced a flute which luckily for us had a missing joint, and insinuated he could be prevailed upon to sing; but we knew " The Raven " would be his doleful strain and upon the hint no one spoke.

" Now a thousand pardons," said Oreto, " for consuming your time and courtesy. I must have a *siesta*, without which you know a Spaniard is lost forever and a day." From under the seat of the buckboard he unrolled a short cloak and threw it in Moorish style across his shoulders, lifted his *sombrero*, revealing a nobly turned head with dashes of gray in the blue-black hair, and his face resumed its expression of habitual melancholy. As he walked off to the shadow of a great rock the alumnus from Colorado college, who knows it all, said in a loud whisper, "There goes Don Pomposo. He feels like the Corliss engine at the Centennial."

The old bachelor shot the fledgling a glance that should have killed him, but the youth, though poor by nature and exhausted by cultivation, was wiry and did not fall asunder. In fact he never flinched. My thoughts wandered from the gay company and the man who had no respect for " the stranger within the gates," to the lone exile and the varied fortunes at which he had hinted, and I said aloud, " The Señor Oreto looks like a man who has a history."

And he has.

I dismiss the picnic in the brilliant periods of the Pharos of the Occident. The editor-in-chief, being also an insurance agent, naturally dealt in large figures, and gave free rein to his warm, not to say fiery imagination: "The picnic of last week was an event long to be remembered. The day was beautiful, nature enchanting, woman divine. Old Baldy lifted his rugged front and snowy crown before us, and the river sung its sweetest cadence. Among distinguished guests present we name the fascinating Gonzalez Felipe Oreto, a cosmopolitan born in old Castile, the friend of our artist, James Brown. For æsthetic culture, refinement of manner and general elegance the versatile Castilian has few equals and no superiors. Rumor has it he will soon lead to the altar a fair widow well known to our city, and we learn with extreme pleasure that he has been prevailed on to cast in his lot with us and become a citizen of the most desirable of all the territories."

From this time the popularity of the delightful Gonzalez Felipe Oreto steadly increased. The young ladies gazed at him with undisguised admiration, the mothers smiled on him, but his attentions were too evenly distributed to indicate the least preference. One day he dashed all hopes by publishing in the *Pharos of the Occident* the poem given below. He told his landlady, in the deepest confidence, it was addressed to a noble lady of Valencia, who had deigned to give him a sweet souvenir in return for his verses and present.

My reader need hardly be told it was all over town before night—that pretty secret of Oreto's.

TO ISABELLA RASCON—WITH A SHELL.

The years have brought you many gifts
  Since first you heard them tell
How the voice of the sea is hid
  In the windings of a shell.
And where'er it may be exiled,
  From its own warm Eastern main,
Bend your ear to the crystal cell,
  And you hear the sea again.

I list to the murmurous sound
  But it never shapes one word.
I cannot guess what it would tell,
  That echo always heard.
Does it speak of the strange, rich life
  Far down in the surging waves,
Where purple mullet and gold fish rove
  The depths of coral caves?

Where Ocean's throbbing heart is stilled,
  And wandering Peri's rest,
'Mid the pearl and amber jewels
  He loves to wear in his breast?
Perchance the mellow strain was caught
  From the song of mermaid fair,
Dreamily chanting, as she smoothed
  The rings of her long, wet hair.

Or, lingering yet, the echo faint
  Of a life once held within.
Some hidden shape that breathed and died
  Afar from the breakers din.
Never had Sultan roof like this,
  Never king such castle wall,
What was it wrought this wondrous dome
  And filled this crystal hall?

Deserted now, but whispering low
  The secret hid in the sea.
Ask what the mystic music means,
  And it answers, ceaselessly,
With that weird song,—tender and low
  As the voice of brooding dove
Who murmurs but a single note,
  Keynote of life—it is Love.

Ah, when you hear that pleading sound,
  Dream not of siren or sea.
Believe it the spirit of Love,
  Forever singing—of me.

Some weeks after the picnic I sat working a highly useless lamp mat in my parlor, which in pleasant Mexican fashion is divided from the office by a curtained doorway. There passed the barred window a dapper little man, whipping his boot with a short riding whip as he went along, whom I recognized as a government agent from Los Indios. I heeded not the conversation, easily overheard, or rather the monologue which languished, till a sudden animation of voice betrayed the true purpose of the visitor as he asked, "Was there a fellow hangin' 'round here not long ago, calling himself Oreto; a sort of literary and sentimental adventurer, pretending to be in heavy mourning?"

"Yes, he had quite a turn for story telling and amusing children. The *caballero* appears to have fallen on evil times—a sad face, wouldn't be a bad model for the Master of Ravenswood."

"Exactly; his face is mighty sad about this time. Interested friends have taken secure boarding for him and relieved him of his wig and big diamond ring—the property of a lady in Zuloago. His real name is Gomez, a gambler and murderer from the city of Mexico. He ran off to Chihuahua, which soon got too hot to hold him and his little games, moved on to Los Indios, where he played three card montè once too often for even territorial morality, and the noble *hidalgo* is now smiling his melancholy smile behind the grated windows of the county jail."

"He had rather an agreeable manner," said the listener with a long yawn, "but I never took much stock in the man."

CHAPTER XXVII.

THE PIMOS.

THE minds of men untrained are strangely alike. There is such sameness of arts, customs, inventions, such likeness in their religious beliefs under like stages of development, we must reach the conclusions that on subjects of deep human interest certain ideas are inherent in human hearts, despite alien blood and long epochs of separation. All barbarians have their priests or medicine men and prophets, are firm believers in necromancy, incantations, the power of witch-craft, and have deep faith in the great Spirit as the peculiar guardian of their race. Some tribes have a fear of the devil who must be worshipped

in order to be propitiated.   With them old times
are best, and all traditions run back to a golden
age of innocency in a Region of Delight where
the rivers sparkled with sweet water, the maize
was always ripe, and high born warriors revelled
and feasted on the game ever in sight.   There
was no work, no disease, no old age.   This
Elysium was lost by crime, and the Arcadian
days ended forever.   The sinful world was destroyed by a Flood from which only one prophet
and his family escaped.   Every Rocky Mountain
tribe has its legend of the deluge and belief in
the second coming of the Divine Man who is to
right all wrongs, correct all miseries and mis-
takes; returning some bright morning to renew
the dull world to youth, and then Paradise will
be regained.   For this revelation they wait, as
the prophetic souls were found waiting to be
guided by the star which led to the divine child
of Mary.

The Pueblos jealously guard their wretched
little chapels (*estufas*) from the prying eyes of
strangers, and the gentlest of visitors is rebuffed
by their dumb secrecy.   In different ways I have
gathered many traditions.   Some are childish
and witless to my understanding; others wearing symbolic veils are graceful as the Greek
myths, and hold a significance as rich.   Fables
of the nomads will do for another day.   The
Pueblos take our attention first.   The great variety of climate in North America produces
various habits of life which temper and color the
fables; and I believe there is no myth without
some meaning.   The vapory conceits we treat so
lightly were not empty phantasms to the brain
that shaped them in the beginning, and some
heart has thrilled to each airy, insubstantial
legend.

Certain old instincts run in all bloods.   The

inborn desire of the soul to account for its origin,
to ask whence come I, what am I, perplexes the
bewildered savage burrowing in his cave as it
did the learned questioners, a mixed multitude
crowding the Academy, reverently listening to
the wondrous maid of Alexandria—Hypatia the
Beautiful.

What is truth? asked the Governor of Judea
as truth Incarnate stood before him in the Judgment Hall; and men are yet demanding of
science, nature, philosophy, the origin of being,
the destinies, the soul and its limitations. Turning from the seen to the unseen, from the outer
to the inner life, from the tangible to the unreal,
longing to know the beginning and the end of
all. It is the old yearning to be as God; old as
the first man. To comprehend the stirring of
the divinity within, which neither feeds nor
sleeps but lives on separate from the body, opens
endless questioning. This is the study of sages;
about it the wisest debate and ponder, and of it
the savage, blanketless and naked, where the soft
seasons allow him to roam, asks with a blind
ignorance infinitely pathetic.

To him the hidden forces which rule the uni·
verse are divinities to be entreated by prayer,
propitiated by sacrifice and offerings. The savage's whole life is penetrated by religion, from
the hard little cradle to which he is swathed, to
the shallow pit where he lies uncoffined when
life's struggle is over.

The tribes near Santa Fè and the larger American towns of New Mexico have mixed the religion of Christ with the old superstitions in a
curious, almost painful manner. I once visited
Tesuque with a view to gaining some knowledge
of their primitive ceremonials. The usual protracted smoking was indulged in; there followed
a stupid meaningless silence, considered the

heignt of politeness ; then we partook of cold
refreshments consisting of little apples carefully
wiped on the sheepskin which covered baby's
cradle as a blanket. We climbed the rickety
ladders, admired the excellence of the bearskins,
counted the bags of shelled corn and rough potteries baked in their mud furnaces, surveyed a
chromo in feverish colors named the Queen of
Heaven, and when the time was ripe I modestly
inquired if we might be permitted to visit the
estufa. The head man of the tribe (cacique)
whom we named Hiawatha, smiled blandly,
showing ivory white teeth without a flaw, and
said "Si, Signora," with a cheerful alacrity quite
foreign to the usual aboriginal stoicism. We followed him into the courtyard and Minnehaha
followed us and stonily stared. The dusky
maiden in the march of progress is escaping
from buckskin draperies. She wears the garment called by the French *intimate*, skirt of
Navajo blanket, black ground with tracings of
red embroidery, not unlike the familiar Greek
pattern, calico shawl gay as the scarf of Iris.
She is without beauty of any sort ; is raw boned
and high shouldered, inclining to fat ; of an
ashy sunburnt skin, flat face, high cheek bones,
thick lips, mannish gait, harsh voice. She is
nearly akin (if there's anything in likeness) to
the Mongolian Ah Sin, and to ward off the sun
that day carried a yellow parasol over her heavy
head. They all stared unmoved as we climbed a
ladder leaning against the side of a high pen
made of pine logs and mud plaster,—a roofless
enclosure perhaps eighteen feet square. As we
looked down, a number of birds like swallows
flew out, and save their mud-built nests against
the logs the ancient *estufa* was empty. The old
arrow-maker was joking when he conducted us
to the altar place ; the shrine was abandoned, the

sacred fire was dead, the secret temple with all
its holy and guarded mysteries was laid open to
women even! It was plain the Queen of
Heaven had usurped the place of the lord of life
and light. The chief smiled broadly and Minnehaha wrapped the pink calico rebosa round her
head and laughed as if she would die. I hate to
be beaten in this way, and while the gentlemen
went off to look at a bear skin, I approached
the youthful princess in the attitude of inter-
viewer. "Gentle maiden," I said, mustering my
small stock of Spanish, "do you remember when
the Montezuma fire burned in this deserted
estufa ?"

"Si, Signora."

"Was it many years ago?"

"Si, signora."

"Perhaps fifteen years?" (insinuatingly).

"Si, signora."

"Ah, can you remember so long? What sort
of wood was consecrated to the shrine?"

"Si, signora."

"Did it flame up to the roof, or was it merely
a bank of coals; your mother" (tenderly) "has
told you of it I know."

"Si, signora."

"Then tell me all you know, if it will not
trouble you too much, and I promise you a beautiful string of blue beads."

"Si, signora."

This intellectual feast was broken up by an
untimely giggle from a gentle maiden not of
aboriginal blood, and we made our adieux. I
afterward learned the sweet girl was only sham-
ming; she understood Spanish well enough, but
chose this pretense to outwit strangers. A distinguished success.

We were completely floored and made haste
to cover our retreat by leaving the mud-walled

village for a nooning and lunch under a clump
of gnarled cedars hard by. The Indian is not
disappearing at a satisfactory rate before the
march of civilization. A swarm of children, the
dirtiest and raggedest imaginable, followed us
and held out their hands for the remains of our
lunch. The biscuits were snatched by a youthful Indigene like the greedy boy of the First
Reader who refused to give his dear playmates a
crumb of his cake, and I had to fairly slap his
hands to make him divide. He then swallowed
the lemon rinds and would have devoured the
sardine boxes if he could. So much alike are
the sons of men !

To reach the old superstitions in their purity
we must push away from the track of the locomotive ; far as possible from censer and cross,
parish priest and Protestant missionary. So we
set out with the determination of the mythic
Roton, who resolved to go till he arrived
at the roof of heaven ; away to the Moquis
of the North and the Papagos of the South.
Below the Gila dwell in close neighborhood
the Maricopas and the Pimos, or as the old
Spaniards wrote it Pimas, whom they found three
hundred years ago irrigating the lands and rais-
ing two crops of corn a year, just as they do
now. The Coco-Maricopas are a branch of the
Pueblos, and these tribes inhabit a large region,
mostly perfect desert, between the head of the
Gulf of California and that extensive cordillera
of which the Sierra Catalina forms the most
westerly range. A volcanic country in which
since the introduction of man, the surface of the
the earth as well as the climate has undergone
great changes.

After straining over scorching deserts, alkali
plains, sage bush and greasewood wastes, it was
a deep pleasure to rest our tired eyes on the

bright corn lands on both sides of the river Gila, which runs through the Pimo reservation about twenty-five miles. The three great *acequias* with their various branches comprise nearly five hundred miles, and extend over a tract of land eighteen miles in length. The fields are fenced with crooked sticks, wattled with brush, mainly of the thorny cactus and mezquit. The Salic or rather Slavic law prevails among the aborigines. Instead of studying graceful culture and decorative art, the farming is done by the women. When harvest time comes, the men turn into the fields and help, besides lightening the labor by standing around in the shade and looking on, or sprawling on the floor swinging the baby as it hangs suspended in a box, hanging by a cord from the ceiling. Sometimes the mother carries a large basket on her head and the papoose sitting on a sort of side-bustle astride her hip. A civilized baby would tumble off instantly, but the native infant holds on to her smooth, shining sides in an attitude wonderfully like the missing link, our Simian ancestor, riding the calico pony in gay circus ring. This baby does not cut monkey-shines, but stares at the stranger as stolidly as his father and mother. The Pimo customs are like the Coco-Maricopas in everything but burial rites. They bury their dead but their neighbors burn them. The Maricopa bodies are placed on a funeral pyre of resinous wood and utterly consumed, in classic fashion.

Reporters say the mourners go into a profound mourning of tar. On inquiry I learned the "tar" is a portion of the ashes of the dear deceased mixed with the dissolved gum of the mezquit, (a species of acacia which yields a concrete juice like gum arabic). They smear their faces with the hideous plaster, and let it remain as a mark of deep grief till it wears away.

A widow, the next day after her bereavement, is offered in market by the town crier to any one who wants a wife. If an able-bodied squaw, good at hoeing, and stout enough to balance the baby on top of the basket of corn overhead, she is usually courted, " wooed, won, married and all " within a few days, though custom allows her to continue the periodic howling and tar deep-mourning several days after the new honey-moon begins to shine.

I was charmed at thought of being among Pagans assisting at such heathen obsequies, and felt it the spot to find the ancient lore I sought, through many a weary mile of lava bed and tropic scorch. I was among the changeless, unimpressible American Indians, living among demons and goblins, spirits of earth, air, fire, water, whose beliefs are untainted by mixture of Christian ideas. Here I discovered the flickering, mythic lights which produce such lovely effects, changing gods to men, and making demigods of heroes. Among these untutored children of nature, every misty outline and vapory mountain haze might be an aboriginal soul floated out into the unknown dark on its wanderings toward the bright sun house. In the shadows of vast cañons the block elves have their haunts, and lie in wait for bewildered spirits, and hurl spectral missiles along the pathless space surrounding " the dance house of the ghosts." The Pueblos are all sun-worshippers, and the Pimos tell us the road to the sun house is beset with perils. In the darkness of the dread mystery of death, deep waters are to be crossed, many-headed monsters bellow and roar, fire flames before the eyes, and whirl-winds lift the affrighted spirit from his feet and toss him in mid air. Four is a sacred number with them, derived from adoration of the four cardinal points; the soul flutters about the body

four days, and sometimes stones are thrown across
the warrior's grave to scare away the evil spirits.
In the unlighted valley the brave must be provided with a pipe for his solace, with weapons
suited to his rank, choice armor approved to fit
him as he enters the kingdom of souls. Lifeless,
he may yet grope through the cold clay, and
touching with icy fingers the trusted arms, will
not tremble in defenceless march through the
horror of the awful shades.

Is this not the instinct of the antique Scythian
buried on the field with the blade in which victory still lingers? The pathos of the singer
breaking his heart and harp together.

> " Lay his sword by his side, it hath served him too well
> Not to rest near his pillow below ;
> To the last moment true, from his hand ere it fell
> Its point was still turned to a flying foe.
> Fellow-lab'rers in life, let them slumber in death,
> Side by side, as becomes the reposing brave,—
> That sword which he loved still unbroke in its sheath,
> And himself unsubdued in his grave."

Four days the howlers howl, and further to
cheer the dread passage four nights a fire is kindled on the warrior's grave to open a path for
the blinded footsteps in the fearful " dead man's
journey," and lead them to the sun, the safe,
final resting place. There the chief will take up
his weapons again and spend a blissful eternity
fighting his old enemies, the Yumas, and we may
be sure slaying his thousands and revelling in
blood, like the Viking in the halls of the Val-
halla, with his comrades hacked to pieces in
many a morning fight, but always ready with
whole limbs and flashing, undinted armor, to
appear at dinner. Food is placed on the fresh
earth, the best corn bread, flesh of antelope and
jars of water, that the lone one may be comforted by gifts from the world he has left. These
tender offerings bestowed, the property of the
hero is portioned out to the tribe, fields divided

among those who need land, his grain, chickens,
dogs, bows, etc., fairly distributed. No wrang-
ling among heirs, no lawyers to absorb estates,
all is done fairly and equitably, in a submission
to precedent worthy our imitation.

Nor do the Pimos refuse to be comforted.
Cattle are driven up and slaughtered, and deeply
burdened with sorrow, every man loads down his
squaw with beef, and feasts whole days on funeral
baked meats. Dare I disgust my dear friend,
the classic reader, by saying these barbarian feasts
are reminders of the tremendous banquet in the
pavilion of Agamennon, where the "steer of
full five years" was killed, skinned, and cooked
before the eyes of the Grecians.

Homeric champions—Trojan peers and scep-
tered kings of Greece—were not made wretched
by indigestion, and I suspect (low be it spoken!)
they took pepsin in the natural state. With their
enviable appetites they were ready to eat off-
hand; the squarest of meals never came amiss,
and their capacity for tough beef, rare done, was
prodigious and unfailing. So far very like our
Rocky mountaineers, but unhappily the red warriors are not embalmed in verse by the imperish-
able poets.

When the Indian woman dies no high sepulchral feasts, no games and honors, such as Ilion
to her hero paid. With scant ceremony she is
wrapped in her poor shroud, the moccasins of
her own make fastened to her shapely feet; the
carrying-strap worn across the forehead, and the
paddle go with the cold hands. Sad emblem of
woman's destiny in the wilderness; pathetic
tokens that even in the mystic land of shades she
must be the silent, uncomplaining slave of her
brutish, savage lord.

This is the Pimo legend of the Creation: The
world was made by an earth prophet. In the begin-

ning it stretched fair and frail as a line of light
across the darkness of empty space. A wise
Sagamore lived in the Gila valley, and one night
a royal eagle came to the door and warned him
of a deluge close at hand. The prophet wrapped
his mantle of fur around him, for it was winter,
and laughed the gray messenger to scorn. The
kingly bird shook his white head, spread wide his
wings and soared away to heaven. Again the
eagle came with his warning cry, the waters were
near and would soon burst overhead; but the
sachem drowsily groaned at the wakening voice
and turned on his bed of buffalo skins and slept.
Three times the broad wings shadowed the
sleeper, and the friendly voice entreated him to
flee the wrath of the gods, but the prophet gave
no heed. Then quick as the eagle disappeared
in the blue and starry silence, there came thunder, lightning, and a mountain of water like an
earthquake overspread the valley of Gila, and the
morning sun shone on only one man saved from
destruction by floating on a ball of resin—Szeukha,
the son of the Creator. He was enraged at the
royal bird, thinking him the mover of the flood,
and made a rope ladder of tough bark like the
woodbine, climbed the naked, riven cliff where
the eagle lived, and slew him. He then raised
to life the mangled bodies of the slain on which
the eagle had preyed, and sent them out to
re-people the world. In the centre of the vast
eyrie he found a woman, the eagle's wife, and
their child. These he helped down the rope ladder and sent on their way, and from them are
descended that race of wise men called Hoho-
cam, ancients or grandfathers, who were guided
in all their wanderings by an eagle. Southward
they marched past forests of oak, sycamore,
cedar and flowering trees, past mountains of
crystal and gold, and rivers murmurous with song

flowing over beds of stars, till they reached a
deep blue lake kissed by soft winds, sparkling in
the sunlight.   On its borders they planted a city
with streets of water—old Tenochtitlan, which
white men call Mexico.   Through the uncounted
centuries since the deluge, Szeukha has not
dropped out of Indian memory.

Because he killed the bird of prophecy he had
to do a sort of penance, which was never to
scratch himself with his nails but always with a
little stick.   The custom is still adhered to by
the unchanging Pimos, and a splinter of wood,
renewed every fourth day, is carried for this purpose, stuck in their long coarse hair and plied
with extreme energy and enjoyment.   Stern are
the duties of the historian, and truth obliges me
to record the Pimos do not scratch their heads
for nothing.

They are good fighters, and have been a wall
of defence against the incursions of Apaches, at
one time the only protection for travellers
between Fort Yuma and Tucson.   They appear
comfortable in their huts,—which are snug dens
of oval shape made of mud and reeds thatched
with *tule* or wheat straw,—quietly contented with
their industrious wives and their own lazy selves.
They make a kind of wine like sour cider, not
nearly so good though, and quaff the vinegar
bowl with sombre hilarity after the corn bread
and mutton are disposed at dinner.

The tributaries of the Gila bear sweet, soft,
meandering Spanish names which I forget.   They
are rivers of the leaky sort, disappearing by
fitful   turns   and   capriciously   starting   up
again in the deeply worn channels.   Even in its
best strength the Gila (river of swift water) is not
so large as an Indiana creek which we would
blush to call river.   It contains three kinds of
fish ; trout, buffalo, and humpback, all equally

mean, of slippery, muddy, flavor and most inferior quality.

Not far from the Pimo villages, eleven in number, are the written rocks, mentioned in the oldest histories and described at length by the early explorers and the modern traveller. At the base of an immense bluff are heaps of boulders covered with figures of men and animals, rudely carved with some coarse instruments. Uncouth shapes of birds, footprints, snakes, and the ever recurring print of a moccasin, indicative of marching. Many writers attach a value to these ancient inscriptions; one old Spanish adventurer discerned in them letters like the Gothic, Hebrew and Chaldean characters. They are not there to-day; among hundreds of piled-up boulders and detached stones there is no tracery like the letters of any known language. Some of the markings are centuries old and partly effaced, others written over and over again. The under sides of the rocks, also, are sculptured where it would be impossible to cut them as they lie, and some weigh many tons. These last must have fallen from the mountain after the hieroglyphs were made. There can be no doubt of their great antiquity and the large numbers of carved stones prove it to have been a resort ages on ages ago, but I doubt the importance of the lines, to me meaningless zigzags. Indians are the laziest of mortals, and in their childish way love to scribble worthless signs, rude pictography on their skins and the hides of animals, their walls and potteries. The "Pedros Pintados" which took such hold on Spanish imagination were probably boundery lines between tribes, and the tortoise, snake and so on are the ancient tribal symbols, treaties possibly. If they had the deep significance claimed by easily excited chroniclers the story would run like this: The sons of the

18

North have waded a lake of blood, have swept
like the whirlwind across the Sierras ; the bow
has rattled, the arrow flew.   We have broken
the bones of the Apaches, scooped out their eyes
and warmed our hands in their smoking blood.
We have scalped the proud warriors and beaten
out the brains of their children.   Whoop la !
Now let the earth tremble, for the wolves are let
loose on the slain !

There are widely scattered ruins in the Gila
valleys showing it was once densely populated,
but the remains are so monotonous they command little interest.   The visitor who has seen
one has the type of all.   A certain melancholy
pathos invests every ruin ; houses where men
have lived and died are more or less haunted, but
the relics of New Mexico and Arizona are desti-
tute of anything like grace or comeliness.   The
makers and builders never got beyond the rough
adobe, the stone hatchet and flint arrow-head,
and nothing is proved by them except that this
country has been inhabited from a remote period
by a people not differing greatly from the
Pueblos of to-day.

As we journeyed up the valley we saw herds
of antelopes, always too distant for a shot.   The
Rocky mountain antelope is a most beautiful and
graceful animal, of compact form and exceeding
strength.   The lithe limbs are delicate and fleet,
feet small and elegant, tail short and tufted.   It
is light fawn color, under parts white ; its
luminous dark eyes are like those of the gazelle
of the Orient.   Shy and not easily approached
the Indians domesticate them by trapping when
very young.   They have the gentlest, most
confiding way of laying their heads in your lap,
and looking up with the lustrous eyes which have
furnished poets with lovely imagery from the
days of Solomon to the nights of Byron.   I

know no creature with such an appealing manner
and such swift grace of movement; they speed
across the still, wide plain, in the farness of the
distance appearing like low flying birds.

Though we are not in the Navajo country we
see now and then their famous blanket, striped in
gayest blue, yellow and red, this last color so
dear to the Indian eye, made from ravelling out
flannel which they buy of the white traders.
The dyes are vegetable and absolutely fadeless.
The blanket is coarse, hard and heavy ; a good
one will shed water like rubber, and wear a great
while as a horse or saddle blanket. The Indian
women spin wool in a slow, simple way by rolling
in their hands, and they spend all their spare
time for months in making one blanket which
may sell for thirty-five dollars, or if very brilliant
in color and close in texture, for fifty or a hundred
dollars. When on the march even, the Navajo
woman has her little contrivance for weaving, on
the mule with her, or across her shoulder if on
foot, and in five minutes after the halt is
sounded she sits under a tree weaving away as
composedly as though she had been at it for
hours. The loom is nothing but sticks placed
horizontally, one at top, two at bottom, far
enough apart to accommodate warp of the
blanket's length or breadth. Between these the
warp is stretched, and to one straps are attached
to throw over the limb of a tree. At the bottom
are other straps, for the feet to operate in beating
up the filling. In her silent, joyless, persevering
fashion the work goes steadily on, and the weaver
is satisfied to see it grow at a rate incalculably
slow.

A sufficient measure of civilization is the
treatment of women, and among Apaches we
find the deepest degradation. The Pueblo wives
are incomparably better off than those of the

nomads. The contrast between them and their
sisters of the fairer race is more painful than that
between men of the two races. I have seen
young hunters with stately forms, erect, lithe and
sinewy, and one warrior who might have been a
model for Uncas, the favorite hero of our early
friend Cooper.

We all remember the anecdote Galt tells of
Benjamin West. When in Rome his friends
agreed that the Apollo of Vatican should be the
first statue shown to the young Philadelphia
Quaker. It was enclosed in a case, and to try
the effect on him suddenly the keeper threw open
the doors. "A young Mohawk warrior," exclaimed West.

But the likeness is only in the body. The
ideal head of the Apollo with its clustering locks,
the exquisite sensitive face with its delicate
molding of lip and chin, the Phidian forehead and
nose, are in highest contrast with the sensual,
sluggish lineaments of the red man.

Among the various tribes there is a dire mono-
tory, and in nothing are they more alike than in a
lofty scorn of work. The man glories in his lazi-
ness, the woman exults in her slavery. I have seen
an Indian try a heavy lift and set the bag of corn
down again with a "Ugh! squaw's work." If
we insinuate he should do the little hoeing for
their scant supply of beans the woman resents
the idea. "Would you have a warrior work like
a squaw?" is her indignant response to the suggestion.

I once saw a married couple trudging home,
if their cold, smoky, dirty den may be called by
that dear name. The husband, perhaps twenty
steps in advance of the woman who bore on her
back a bag of corn. The noble red man (see J.
F. Cooper), waited for her to come up to him,
she hastening her pace as she saw it. Then he

slung nis rifle on her pack, folded his arms across his noble breast, and strode forward with easy gliding step, in untrammeled dignity. How I longed to hand that noble red man over to the mercies of a woman's rights convention.

The husband may disfigure or insult the wife at pleasure, divorce her without form or ceremony by a mere separation, and she has no protection or appeal; sometimes his conduct drives her to suicide. In divorce it is the unwritten law of the wilderness that children go with their mother. Among the wandering tribes mother and baby are not divided even in death. A merciful barbarity gives one blow with the hatchet, and the little one rests with the best love it can know on earth. They have few children; four are a large family, twins are unknown, nearly all reach maturity. Among the wild tribes where polygamy is the rule it is not a cause of complaint among the women, from the fact that it implies a division of labor, and the latest wife lords it over her predecessors. Even among savages there is no love like the last love.

The Pimo Indians are not made of "rose-red clay," they are dark brown, differing in complexion from the Appalachians east of the Rocky mountains and the olive hues of the California tribes. Historians say they have ever been the the most active and industrious of the Pueblos; still that does not imply the energy and activity of the white race. They sit for hours in front of their huts, motionless as a group of petrifactions. In a mild climate their wants are few and simple, and a little of this world's goods obtained without much work and less worry is sufficient for the calm philosophers who despise the arts of the white race and steadily march in the paths of the forefathers.

I must not leave their country without men-

tion of the wooing of the young Pimo warrior.
All Pueblos have but one wife, and no girl is
obliged to marry against her will, however eligi-
ble the parents may consider any offer. If his
bent of love be honorable, his purpose marriage,
Romeo first wins over the parents by making
them presents, such delicacies as pumpkins,
beans, coyote skins, or if he is very wealthy a
pony. Then, in banged locks and straggling
braids of hair, he sits at the door of the lady of
his choice serenading her for hours, day after
day, tooting with all his might on a flute of cane,
an instrument of torture with four holes in it.
He hides himself in a bush and like the nightingale "sings darkling." Sometimes Juliet is a
coquette and takes no notice of the tender
demonstration, leaving him to keep up the plain-
tive, shrill noise till

> "Night's candles are burnt out, and jocund day
> Stands tiptoe on the misty mountain tops."

If no notice is taken of the appeal there is no
further sign ; he may hang up his flute, with its
bright pencillings and gayly tufted fringes, and
there is no mortification in the rejection. Should
she smile on his suit she comes out of the coop-
like den and the ceremony is ended. Romeo
takes her to his house and the bride is at home.
If he is a man of moderate means the house is
built of four upright stakes, forked at one end,
driven into the ground ; across these other sticks
are laid to support the roof, which may be of
corn shucks, or straw or rushes. If he is ambitious to have a lasting, palatial mansion it will
be walled round with stakes, plastered and roofed
with mud. An opening for a door is left about
three feet high to creep in at. These residences
are from five to seven feet high, so one cannot
stand upright in every one. Adjoining the wigwam is a bower of boughs open on all sides ; in

this shady lodge are the few potteries in which Juliet does the cooking, and here the happy pair sit on their heels when at rest, and Romeo smokes while she grinds the corn in the *metate* of stone.

It is expected that the bridegroom will pay the parents all his means admit to compensate them for the loss of a hand in the cornfield. The Indian wife never hears of protoplasm, equal suffrage, social science and the like. She often builds the wigwam after Romeo has cut the poles, always bears them on her shoulders in the march, plows the fields with a crooked stick, raises the beans, hoes the corn, bakes the cakes, without a complaint. If her beady, black eyes mark his coming and look brighter when he comes I cannot tell why. He is sullen and still, a dusky shape, the very perfection of gloomy indifference. Perhaps if he eats the *tortillas* with an appetite her soul is glad and she has her reward. If she is content, why sow the seeds or dissatisfaction by telling her she is a beast of burden and he is a beast of prey?

The trip through the Pimo country was made memorable by my first bivouac. 'Twere vain to tell thee all; how a mule drank alkali water, swelled up and died in an hour, how part of the party had to push forward with a disabled team, leaving a broken wagon and luggage to wait the relief, and how a long, hot day brought us to a government station. This was a mud shanty thatched with cedar boughs and plastered with clay. The edifice was divided into three rooms, the first was a stable where a gay little pony was pacing round and round without a halter. The next was the guest chamber. As I approached, there issued from it a fragrance, the triple extract of raw hide, burnt bacon and old pipe. The appartment, perhaps sixteen feet square, was

without door or window. The "accommodations" were a mud fireplace in the corner where
one might make coffee and fry eggs, and a pile
of sheepskins on which the visitor might spread
his blanket and sleep,—if he could. The cedar
and mud roof slanted as though it would tumble
down any minute. The clay floor was unswept,
the walls fringed with cobwebs and adorned with
strings of red pepper, saddles and bridles. In
one corner lay bags of shelled corn ; on a swinging shelf were newspapers, an odd volume of
Oliver Twist and sporting magazines. The third
room was sacred to herdsmen and *rancheros*.
The keeper of this lodge in a vast wilderness
was a retired minstrel, and his photograph as
jolly endman broadly smiled upon us, dangling
from enormous deer's antlers which upheld decorative art in lieu of a mantel piece. I took
peaceable possession of the only chair and my
fellow traveller through life's journey lolled in
luxurious ease on the end of a candlebox, while
we surveyed the "accommodations." There
were three chromos of Evangeline on the walls :
presumably the peddler closed out his stock
there. One picture of that melancholy maiden
sitting on a nameless grave is depressing ; two
are hardly endurable ; three are heart-breaking.
I gave way before them and said, "We will try
an Indian lodge under the open sky." My resolution made the idea at once become a pleasant
thought. In a barren country the householder,
a pilgrim and a stranger, develops a versatile
genius second only to that of Bernini the Florentine sculptor, artist, poet, musician, who gave an
opera in Rome where he built the theater, in-
vented the engines, cut the statues, painted the
scenes, wrote the comedy and composed the
music. In the spirit of communism which per-
vades the Territories I rummaged the abandoned

baggage and found blankets, buffalo robes, a
mattress, one attenuated pillow stuffed with
feathers pretty much all quill, made "riant" by
a pink calico case ruffled all round. No sham
about that pillow.

A clump of stunted pines was the chamber,
carpeted with the soft needles undisturbed for
ages. A Navajo blanket made a striped roof,
its weight a security against puffs of wind even
if we had not fastened it with strings and tent
pins driven into the warm, gravelly sand. The
pretty recess, so like a play-house, had a fine
charm; spicy with the fresh scent of the pines,
shadowed by a great rock, the pink pillow
looked rather lumpy but restful and inviting. I
felt sure there were pleasant dreams, or better
yet, dreamless sleep in the unexpected luxury.

While I smoothed its tumbled ruffles the gay
troubadour came from high pastures with his
herds to let them drink at the precious spring,
and then fold them in a corral made of stakes of
mezquit wattled with cactus.

The grama grass on which they feed is
described in the books as incomparably the most
nutritive in the world, which may account for the
grand development of bone in the animals
throughout the region. All the wild grasses of
the country are peculiar in curing themselves
in the stalk. The grama bears no flower, shows
no seed, but seems to reproduce itself from the
roots by the shooting up of young, green and
vigorous spires, which are at first inclosed within
the sheaths of their old and dried-up predecessors, which by their growth they split and cast
to earth, themselves filling their places. The
vast region swept from immemorial ages by the
Apaches is covered with this sort of low, mossy
grass, and it enables those most savage of savages to make their wonderful marches with

their wiry little ponies, which endure extra-
ordinary fatigue so long as they have this feed in
abundance, and are allowed to crop it from
native *pasturas.*

The troubadour who kept the wayside inn was
a handsome scamp, a captivating runaway from
civilization, calling himself John Smith, which I
am sure is not his name. He apologized for the
absence of his cook (who had no existence on
earth), and in festal mood, with many flourishes, insisted on displaying his own skill in the
culinary science. He graduated under the celebrated Micawber many years ago, and would like
nothing better than a "hot supper of his own
getting up."

With the help of a Mexican *peon*, he deftly
and rapidly concocted and served in the Evangeline apartment various poisons, liquid and solid,
spreading them on a pine table covered with
newspapers. Conspicuous among the dishes
were hot death-balls, with lightning zigzags of
deadly drugs, known on the frontier as "soddy
biscuit." Under the beguiling name of spring
lamb we had paid an exhaustive price for a section of ancient ram which might have battered
the walls of Babylon. Fire made no impression
on it, and the chops rebounded under the teeth
like India-rubber. However we had the usual
reserve of crackers, ham, canned fruit, and I
drank to the general joy of the whole table in a
glass of withered lemonade. The gentlemen ate
with cannibal appetite, and so far from dropping
dead, as I feared, seemed refreshed by the reflection. The banquet ended, we insisted on music
from the obscured, let me not say fallen, star, and
the banjo was brought forth from its case under
the festive board. Brudder Bones had a rich
and delightful voice, and we listened to him with
unaffected enjoyment. One by one the herds-

men came by leading their lean and thirsty sheep, making a picturesque spectacle as they passed to the spring.

Back of the miserable hut stretched a plain, level as water, three miles to the foot-hills; far beyond were the Sierras, purple to the snow line, then a shining silver chain. Their unspeakable beauty haunts me still like some enchanting vision in which I beheld a new heaven and a new earth. Beyond the bower rose a heap of boulders, bare except for the tall yucca's cream-white blossoms which decked them in bridal brightness, and a species of night-blooming cereus that with the declining day unfolded every petal and filled the air with a fragrance like white lilies. On a bench in front of the hut sat a prospector and the belated travellers; lounging on blankets and skins were half a dozen soldiers, a Pueblo Indian, a negro and a Mexican *peon*. The banjo did its best for the musician occupying the candle box; I was enthroned in the only chair. A mixed company, representative of the border races.

What should we sing but "Tenting to-night boys," and "Oft in the stilly night," the twilight song with its tender memories of the lost loves buried many a year ago? Lastly, in the solemn beauty of the afterglow, we gave "John Brown's Body" with a rousing chorus in honor of the graves forever green and glorious.

A line of crimson lights flamed along the mountain peaks, then the drop curtain of violet and pearl gray fell softly through the speckless sapphire and over the darkening hills. 'Twas time to say good-night; most of the herdsmen wrapped themselves in blankets and rolled like logs on the ground; the passive ragged *peon* bowed in courteous grace with gently spoken *adios*, and lay against the side of the hut, his delicate face

upturned to the sky. Old uncle Ned made a
tiny fire of pine cones "to toas my feet, missis,"
as he muffled head and ears in an army coat on
which a shred of shoulder strap hinted of better
days. We, too, said "good-night." Besides the
old songs my ear was haunted with dim æolian
soundings mingling an evening strain from the
Koran:

> "Have we not given you the earth for a bed,
> And made you husband and wife?
> And given you sleep for rest,
> And made you a mantle of night?"

But I could not sleep thus mantled in that
Eden bower. The air was so electric that five
lines of fire followed my fingers as I drew them
across the buffalo robe. I was in that state known
to most women and a few men when my eyelids
would *not* close. I felt as if the seven doors of
the enchanted lantern were opened and I could
see all over the world. There was nothing to
fear, but a sense of strangeness and awe held me.
The spangled arch which upholds the throne of
God,—its splendor robbed me of my rest;
my spirit was not fitted to the magnificent
infinite palace. Of the exquisite beauty of that
balmy semi-tropic night I hardly trust myself to
speak. Through the soft perfumed dusk through
the leafy tent, the stars glowed resplendent.
None missing there; the lost Pleiad found her
sisters; Aldebaran shone in the East; Arcturus
and his sons; Orion belted and spurred with jewels. The blanket slipped from its fastenings and
there was no curtaining to veil the far-off mystery of my boundless bed-room. The cool night
breeze fanned my face as I watched the lofty
spaces so solemn, so wondrous fair. I had often
slept in the ambulance with curtains close-but-
toned; that was a room. The walls of this apartment were limitless.

Restlessly turning on the pink pillow I thought
of eyes that are looking down, not up at the
starry hosts, and the voice now beyond them
which used to sing to the air of " Bonnie Doon,"

'Forever and forevermore,
The star, the star of Bethlehem."

The goats and sheep were at rest, the hurt
lamb had ceased its bleat, the light in the ranche
went out.   In the stilly night silence all, save the
low wind soughing in the pines making midnight
hush the deeper.   The long howl of a dog in the
distance.   Was he barking at the silver boat in
the blue bay overhead ?   What sailors manned
that fairy craft ?   Did they understand the mysteries and could they answer my weary question-
ings ? What saw they in the unfathomable depths?
and what meant that signal shot from the slendeı
bow across the trackless blue,. dropping spark·
les of fire through the dusk ?

Good night, Good night!

THE END.

www.ingramcontent.com/pod-product-compliance
Lightning Source LLC
Chambersburg PA
CBHW060424030726
47495CB00003B/729